LADY ROSE'S DAUGHTER
BY
Mrs. Humphry Ward

LADY ROSE'S DAUGHTER

Published by Yurita Press

New York City, NY

First published circa 1920

Copyright © Yurita Press, 2015

All rights reserved

ABOUT YURITA PRESS

Yurita Press is a boutique publishing company run by people who are passionate about history's greatest works. We strive to republish the best books ever written across every conceivable genre and making them easily and cheaply available to readers across the world.

I

"Hullo! No!--Yes!--upon my soul, it is Jacob! Why, Delafield, my dear fellow, how are you?"

So saying--on a February evening a good many years ago--an elderly gentleman in evening dress flung himself out of his cab, which had just stopped before a house in Bruton Street, and hastily went to meet a young man who was at the same moment stepping out of another hansom a little farther down the pavement.

The pleasure in the older man's voice rang clear, and the younger met him with an equal cordiality, expressed perhaps through a manner more leisurely and restrained.

"So you are home, Sir Wilfrid? You were announced, I saw. But I thought Paris would have detained you a bit."

"Paris? Not I! Half the people I ever knew there are dead, and the rest are uncivil. Well, and how are you getting on? Making your fortune, eh?"

And, slipping his arm inside the young man's, the speaker walked back with him, along a line of carriages, towards a house which showed a group of footmen at its open door. Jacob Delafield smiled.

"The business of a land agent seems to be to spend some one else's--as far as I've yet gone."

"Land agent! I thought you were at the bar?"

"I was, but the briefs didn't come in. My cousin offered me the care of his Essex estates. I like the country--always have. So I thought I'd better accept."

"What--the Duke? Lucky fellow! A regular income, and no anxieties. I expect you're pretty well paid?"

"Oh, I'm not badly paid," replied the young man, tranquilly. "Of course you're going to Lady Henry's?"

"Of course. Here we are."

The older man paused outside the line of servants waiting at the door, and spoke in a lower tone. "How is she? Failing at all?"

Jacob Delafield hesitated. "She's grown very blind--and perhaps rather more infirm, generally. But she is at home, as usual--every evening for a few people, and for a good many on Wednesdays."

"Is she still alone--or is there any relation who looks after her?"

"Relation? No. She detests them all."

"Except you?"

Delafield raised his shoulders, without an answering smile. "Yes, she is good enough to except me. You're one of her trustees, aren't you?"

"At present, the only one. But while I have been in Persia the lawyers have done all that was necessary. Lady Henry herself never writes a letter she can help. I really have heard next to nothing about her for more than a year. This morning I arrived from Paris--sent round to ask if she would be at home--and here I am."

"Ah!" said Delafield, looking down. "Well, there is a lady who has been with her, now, for more than two years--"

"Ah, yes, yes, I remember. Old Lady Seathwaite told me--last year. Mademoiselle Le Breton--isn't that her name? What--she reads to her, and writes letters for her--that kind of thing?"

"Yes--that kind of thing," said the other, after a moment's hesitation. "Wasn't that a spot of rain? Shall I charge these gentry?"

And he led the way through the line of footmen, which, however, was not of the usual Mayfair density. For the party within was not a "crush." The hostess who had collected it was of opinion that the chief object of your house is not to entice the mob, but to keep it out. The two men mounted the stairs together.

"What a charming house!" said the elder, looking round him. "I remember when your uncle rebuilt it. And before that, I remember his mother, the old Duchess here, with her swarm of parsons. Upon my word, London tastes good--after Teheran!"

And the speaker threw back his fair, grizzled head, regarding the lights, the house, the guests, with the air of a sensitive dog on a familiar scent.

"Ah, you're fresh home," said Delafield, laughing. "But let's just try to keep you here--"

"My dear fellow, who is that at the top of the stairs?"

The old diplomat paused. In front of the pair some half a dozen guests were ascending, and as many coming down. At the top stood a tall lady in black, receiving and dismissing.

Delafield looked up.

"That is Mademoiselle Le Breton," he said, quietly.

"She receives?"

"She distributes the guests. Lady Henry generally establishes herself in the back drawing-room. It doesn't do for her to see too many people at once. Mademoiselle arranges it."

"Lady Henry must indeed be a good deal more helpless that I remember her," murmured Sir Wilfrid, in some astonishment.

"She is, physically. Oh, no doubt of it! Otherwise you won't find much change. Shall I introduce you?"

They were approaching a woman whose tall slenderness, combined with a remarkable physiognomy, arrested the old man's attention. She was not handsome--that, surely, was his first impression? The cheek-bones were too evident, the chin and mouth too strong. And yet the fine pallor of the skin, the subtle black-and-white, in which, so to speak, the head and face were drawn, the life, the animation of the whole--were these not beauty, or more than beauty? As for the eyes, the carriage of the head, the rich magnificence of hair, arranged with an artful eighteenth-century freedom, as Madame Vigée Le Brun might have worn it--with the second glance the effect of them was such that Sir Wilfrid could not cease from looking at the lady they adorned. It was an effect as of something over-living, over-brilliant--an animation, an intensity, so strong that, at first beholding, a by-stander could scarcely tell whether it pleased him or no.

"Mademoiselle Le Breton--Sir Wilfrid Bury," said Jacob Delafield, introducing them.

"Is she French?" thought the old diplomat, puzzled. "And--have I ever seen her before?"

"Lady Henry will be so glad!" said a low, agreeable voice. "You are one of the old friends, aren't you? I have often heard her talk of you."

"You are very good. Certainly, I am an old friend--a connection also." There was the slightest touch of stiffness in Sir Wilfrid's tone, of which the next moment he was ashamed. "I am very sorry to hear that Lady Henry has grown so much more helpless since I left England."

"She has to be careful of fatigue. Two or three people go in to see her at a time. She enjoys them more so."

"In my opinion," said Delafield, "one more device of milady's for getting precisely what she wants."

The young man's gay undertone, together with the look which passed between him and Mademoiselle Le Breton, added to Sir Wilfrid's stifled feeling of surprise.

"You'll tell her, Jacob, that I'm here?" He turned abruptly to the young man.

"Certainly--when mademoiselle allows me. Ah, here comes the Duchess!" said Delafield, in another voice.

Mademoiselle Le Breton, who had moved a few steps away from the stair-head with Sir Wilfrid Bury, turned hastily. A slight, small woman, delicately fair and sparkling with diamonds, was coming up the stairs alone.

"My dear," said the new-comer, holding out her hands eagerly to Mademoiselle Le Breton, "I felt I must just run in and have a look at you. But Freddie says that I've got to meet him at that tiresome Foreign Office! So I can only stay ten minutes. How are you?"--then, in a lower voice, almost a whisper, which, however, reached Sir Wilfrid Bury's ears--"worried to death?"

Mademoiselle Le Breton raised eyes and shoulders for a moment, then, smiling, put her finger to her lip.

"You're coming to me to-morrow afternoon?" said the Duchess, in the same half-whisper.

"I don't think I can get away."

"Nonsense! My dear, you must have some air and exercise! Jacob, will you see she comes?"

"Oh, I'm no good," said that young man, turning away. "Duchess, you remember Sir Wilfrid Bury?"

"She would be an unnatural goddaughter if she didn't," said that gentleman, smiling. "She may be your cousin, but I knew her before you did."

The young Duchess turned with a start.

"Sir Wilfrid! A sight for sair een. When did you get back?"

She put her slim hands into both of his, and showered upon him all proper surprise and the greetings due to her father's oldest friend. Voice, gesture, words--all were equally amiable, well trained, and perfunctory--Sir Wilfrid was well aware of it. He was possessed of a fine, straw-colored mustache, and long eyelashes of the same color. Both eyelashes and mustache made a screen behind which, as was well known, their owner observed the world to remarkably good purpose. He perceived the difference at once when the Duchess, having done her social and family duty, left him to return to Mademoiselle Le Breton.

"It was such a bore you couldn't come this afternoon! I wanted you to see the babe dance--she's too great a duck! And that Canadian girl came to sing. The voice is magnificent--but she has some tiresome tricks!--and I didn't know what to say to her. As to the other music on the 16th--I say, can't we find a corner somewhere?" And the Duchess looked round the beautiful drawing-room, which she and her companions had just entered, with a dissatisfied air.

"Lady Henry, you'll remember, doesn't like corners," said Mademoiselle Le Breton, smiling. Her tone, delicately free and allusive, once more drew Sir Wilfrid's curious eyes to her, and he caught also the impatient gesture with which the Duchess received the remark.

"Ah, that's all right!" said Mademoiselle Le Breton, suddenly, turning round to himself. "Here is Mr. Montresor--going on, too, I suppose, to the Foreign Office. Now there'll be some chance of getting at Lady Henry."

Sir Wilfrid looked down the drawing-room, to see the famous War Minister coming slowly through the well-filled but not crowded room, stopping now and then to exchange a greeting or a farewell, and much hampered, as it seemed, in so doing, by a pronounced and disfiguring short-sight. He was a strongly built man of more than middle height. His iron-gray hair, deeply carved features, and cavernous black eyes gave him the air of power that his reputation demanded. On the other hand, his difficulty of eyesight, combined with the marked stoop of overwork, produced a qualifying impression--as of power teased and fettered, a Samson among the Philistines.

"My dear lady, good-night. I must go and fight with wild beasts in Whitehall--worse luck! Ah, Duchess! All very well--but you can't shirk either!"

So saying, Mr. Montresor shook hands with Mademoiselle Le Breton and smiled upon the Duchess--both actions betraying precisely the same degree of playful intimacy.

"How did you find Lady Henry?" said Mademoiselle Le Breton, in a lowered voice.

"Very well, but very cross. She scolds me perpetually--I haven't got a skin left. Ah, Sir Wilfrid!--very glad to see you! When did you arrive? I thought I might perhaps find you at the Foreign Office."

"I'm going on there presently," said Sir Wilfrid.

"Ah, but that's no good. Dine with me to-morrow night?--if you are free? Excellent!--that's arranged. Meanwhile--send him in, mademoiselle--send him in! He's fresh--let him take his turn." And the Minister, grinning, pointed backward over his shoulder towards an inner drawing-room, where the form of an old lady, seated in a wheeled invalid-chair between two other persons, could be just dimly seen.

"When the Bishop goes," said Mademoiselle Le Breton, with a laughing shake of the head. "But I told him not to stay long."

"He won't want to. Lady Henry pays no more attention to his cloth than to my gray hairs. The rating she has just given me for my speech of last night! Well, good-night, dear lady--good-night. You are better, I think?"

Mr. Montresor threw a look of scrutiny no less friendly than earnest at the lady to whom he was speaking; and immediately afterwards Sir Wilfrid, who was wedged in by an entering group of people, caught the murmured words:

"Consult me when you want me--at any time."

Mademoiselle Le Breton raised her beautiful eyes to the speaker in a mute gratitude.

"And five minutes ago I thought her plain!" said Sir Wilfrid to himself as he moved away. "Upon my word, for a dame de compagnie that young woman is at her ease! But where the deuce have I seen her, or her double, before?"

He paused to look round the room a moment, before yielding himself to one of the many possible conversations which, as he saw, it contained for him. It was a stately panelled room of the last century, furnished with that sure instinct both for comfort and beauty which a small minority of English rich people have always possessed. Two glorious Gainsboroughs, clad in the subtlest brilliance of pearly white and shimmering blue, hung on either side of the square opening leading to the inner room. The fair, clouded head of a girl, by Romney, looked down from the panelling above the hearth. A gowned abbé, by Vandyck, made the centre of another wall, facing the Gainsboroughs. The pictures were all famous, and had been associated for generations with the Delafield name. Beneath them the carpets were covered by fine eighteenth-century furniture, much of it of a florid Italian type subdued to a delicate and faded beauty by time and use. The room was cleverly broken into various circles and centres for conversation; the chairs were many and comfortable; flowers sheltered tête-à-têtes or made a setting for beautiful faces; the lamps were soft, the air warm and light. A cheerful hum of voices rose, as of talk enjoyed for talking's sake; and a general effect of intimacy, or gayety, of an unfeigned social pleasure, seemed to issue from the charming scene and communicate itself to the onlooker.

And for a few moments, before he was discovered and tumultuously annexed by a neighboring group, Sir Wilfrid watched the progress of Mademoiselle Le Breton through the room, with the young Duchess in her wake. Wherever she moved she was met with smiles, deference, and eager attention. Here and there she made an introduction, she redistributed a group, she moved a chair. It was evident that her eye was everywhere, that she knew every one; her rule appeared to be at once absolute and welcome. Presently, when she herself accepted a seat, she became, as Sir Wilfrid perceived in the intervals of his own conversation, the leader of the most animated circle in the room. The Duchess, with one delicate arm stretched along the back of Mademoiselle Le Breton's chair, laughed and chattered; two young girls in virginal white placed themselves on big gilt footstools at her feet; man after man joined the group that stood or sat around her; and in the centre of it, the brilliance of her black head, sharply seen against a background of rose brocade, the grace of her tall form, which was thin almost to emaciation, the expressiveness of her strange features, the animation of her gestures, the sweetness of her voice, drew the eyes and ears of half the room to Lady Henry's "companion."

Presently there was a movement in the distance. A man in knee-breeches and silver-buckled shoes emerged from the back drawing-room. Mademoiselle Le Breton rose at once and went to meet him.

"The Bishop has had a long innings," said an old general to Sir Wilfrid Bury. "And here is Mademoiselle Julie coming for you."

Sir Wilfrid rose, in obedience to a smiling sign from the lady thus described, and followed her floating black draperies towards the farther room.

"Who are those two persons with Lady Henry?" he asked of his guide, as they approached the penetralia where reigned the mistress of the house. "Ah, I see!--one is Dr. Meredith--but the other?"

"The other is Captain Warkworth," said Mademoiselle Le Breton. "Do you know him?"

"Warkworth--Warkworth? Ah--of course--the man who distinguished himself in the Mahsud expedition. But why is he home again so soon?"

Mademoiselle Le Breton smiled uncertainly.

"I think he was invalided home," she said, with that manner, at once restrained and gracious, that Sir Wilfrid had already observed in her. It was the manner of some one who counted; and--through all outward modesty--knew it.

"He wants something out of the ministry. I remember the man," was Sir Wilfrid's unspoken comment.

But they had entered the inner room. Lady Henry looked round. Over her wrinkled face, now parchment-white, there shone a ray of pleasure--sudden, vehement, and unfeigned.

"Sir Wilfrid!"

She made a movement as though to rise from her chair, which was checked by his gesture and her helplessness.

"Well, this is good fortune," she said, as she put both her hands into both of his. "This morning, as I was dressing, I had a feeling that something agreeable was going to happen at last--and then your note came. Sit down there. You know Dr. Meredith. He's as quarrelsome as ever. Captain Warkworth--Sir Wilfrid Bury."

The square-headed, spectacled journalist addressed as Dr. Meredith greeted the new-comer with the quiet cordiality of one for whom the day holds normally so many events that it is impossible to make much of any one of them. And the man on the farther side of Lady Henry rose and bowed. He was handsome, and slenderly built. The touch of impetuosity in his movement, and the careless ease with which he carried his curly head, somehow surprised Sir Wilfrid. He had expected another sort of person.

"I will give you my chair," said the Captain, pleasantly. "I have had more than my turn."

"Shall I bring in the Duchess?" said Mademoiselle Le Breton, in a low tone, as she stooped over the back of Lady Henry's chair.

That lady turned abruptly to the speaker.

"Let her do precisely as she pleases," said a voice, sharp, lowered also, but imperious, like the drawing of a sword. "If she wants me, she knows where I am."

"She would be so sorry--"

"Ne jouez pas la comédie, ma chère! Where is Jacob?"

"In the other room. Shall I tell him you want him?"

"I will send for him when it suits me. Meanwhile, as I particularly desired you to let me know when he arrived--"

"He has only been here twenty minutes," murmured Mademoiselle Le Breton. "I thought while the Bishop was here you would not like to be disturbed--"

"You thought!" The speaker raised her shoulders fiercely. "Comme toujours, vous vous êtes trop bien amusée pour vous souvenir de mes instructions--voilà la vérité! Dr. Meredith," the whole imperious form swung round again towards the journalist, "unless you forbid me, I shall tell Sir Wilfrid who it was reviewed his book for you."

"Oh, good Heavens! I forbid you with all the energy of which I am capable," said the startled journalist, raising appealing hands, while Lady Henry, delighted with the effect produced by her sudden shaft, sank back in her chair and grimly smiled.

Meanwhile Sir Wilfrid Bury's attention was still held by Mademoiselle Le Breton. In the conversation between her and Lady Henry he had noticed an extraordinary change of manner on the part of the younger lady. Her ease, her grace had disappeared. Her tone was humble, her manner quivering with nervous anxiety. And now, as she stood a moment behind Lady Henry's chair, one trembling hand steadying the other, Sir Wilfrid was suddenly aware of yet another impression. Lady Henry had treated her companion with a contemptuous and haughty ill-humor. Face to face with her mistress, Mademoiselle Le Breton had borne it with submission, almost with servility. But now, as she stood silent behind the blind old lady who had flouted her, her wonderfully expressive face, her delicate frame, spoke for her with an energy not to be mistaken. Her dark eyes blazed. She stood for anger; she breathed humiliation.

"A dangerous woman, and an extraordinary situation," so ran his thought, while aloud he was talking Central Asian politics and the latest Simla gossip to his two companions.

Meanwhile, Captain Warkworth and Mademoiselle Le Breton returned together to the larger drawing-room, and before long Dr. Meredith took his leave. Lady Henry and her old friend were left alone.

"I am sorry to hear that your sight troubles you more than of old," said Sir Wilfrid, drawing his chair a little nearer to her.

Lady Henry gave an impatient sigh. "Everything troubles me more than of old. There is one disease from which no one recovers, my dear Wilfrid, and it has long since fastened upon me."

"You mean old age? Oh, you are not so much to be pitied for that," said Sir Wilfrid, smiling. "Many people would exchange their youth for your old age."

"Then the world contains more fools than even I give it credit for!" said Lady Henry, with energy. "Why should any one exchange with me--a poor, blind, gouty old creature, with no chick or child to care whether she lives or dies?"

"Ah, well, that's a misfortune--I won't deny that," said Sir Wilfrid, kindly. "But I come home after three years. I find your house as thronged as ever, in the old way. I see half the most distinguished people in London in your drawing-room. It is sad that you can no longer receive them as you used to do: but here you sit like a queen, and people fight for their turn with you."

Lady Henry did not smile. She laid one of her wrinkled hands upon his arm.

"Is there any one else within hearing?" she said, in a quick undertone. Sir Wilfrid was touched by the vague helplessness of her gesture, as she looked round her.

"No one--we are quite alone."

"They are not here for me--those people," she said, quivering, with a motion of her hand towards the large drawing-room.

"My dear friend, what do you mean?"

"They are here--come closer, I don't want to be overheard--for a woman--whom I took in, in a moment of lunacy--who is now robbing me of my best friends and supplanting me in my own house."

The pallor of the old face had lost all its waxen dignity. The lowered voice hissed in his ear. Sir Wilfrid, startled and repelled, hesitated for his reply. Meanwhile, Lady Henry, who could not see it, seemed at once to divine the change in his expression.

"Oh, I suppose you think I'm mad," she said, impatiently, "or ridiculous. Well, see for yourself, judge for yourself. In fact, I have been looking, hungering, for your return. You have helped me through emergencies before now. And I am in that state at present that I trust no one, talk to no one, except of banalités. But I should be greatly obliged if you would come and listen to me, and, what is more, advise me some day."

"Most gladly," said Sir Wilfrid, embarrassed; then, after a pause, "Who is this lady I find installed here?"

Lady Henry hesitated, then shut her strong mouth on the temptation to speak.

"It is not a story for to-night," she said; "and it would upset me. But, when you first saw her, how did she strike you?"

"I saw at once," said her companion after a pause, "that you had caught a personality."

"A personality!" Lady Henry gave an angry laugh. "That's one way of putting it. But physically--did she remind you of no one?"

Sir Wilfrid pondered a moment.

"Yes. Her face haunted me, when I first saw it. But--no; no, I can't put any names."

Lady Henry gave a little snort of disappointment.

"Well, think. You knew her mother quite well. You have known her grandfather all your life. If you're going on to the Foreign Office, as I suppose you are, you'll probably see him to-night. She is uncannily like him. As to her father, I don't know--but he was a rolling-stone of a creature; you very likely came across him."

"I knew her mother and her father?" said Sir Wilfrid, astonished and pondering.

"They had no right to be her mother and her father," said Lady Henry, with grimness.

"Ah! So if one does guess--"

"You'll please hold your tongue."

"But at present I'm completely mystified," said Sir Wilfrid.

"Perhaps it'll come to you later. You've a good memory generally for such things. Anyway, I can't tell you anything now. But when'll you come again? To-morrow--luncheon? I really want you."

"Would you be alone?"

"Certainly. That, at least, I can still do--lunch as I please, and with whom I please. Who is this coming in? Ah, you needn't tell me."

The old lady turned herself towards the entrance, with a stiffening of the whole frame, an instinctive and passionate dignity in her whole aspect, which struck a thrill through her companion.

The little Duchess approached, amid a flutter of satin and lace, heralded by the scent of the Parma violets she wore in profusion at her breast and waist. Her eye glanced uncertainly, and she approached with daintiness, like one stepping on mined ground.

"Aunt Flora, I must have just a minute."

"I know no reason against your having ten, if you want them," said Lady Henry, as she held-out three fingers to the new-comer. "You promised yesterday to come and give me a full account of the Devonshire House ball. But it doesn't matter--and you have forgotten."

"No, indeed, I haven't," said the Duchess, embarrassed. "But you seemed so well employed to-night, with other people. And now--"

"Now you are going on," said Lady Henry, with a most unfriendly suavity.

"Freddie says I must," said the other, in the attitude of a protesting child.

"Alors!" said Lady Henry, lifting her hand. "We all know how obedient you are. Good-night!"

The Duchess flushed. She just touched her aunt's hand, and then, turning an indignant face on Sir Wilfrid, she bade him farewell with an air which seemed to him intended to avenge upon his neutral person the treatment which, from Lady Henry, even so spoiled a child of fortune as herself could not resent.

Twenty minutes later, Sir Wilfrid entered the first big room of the Foreign Office party. He looked round him with a revival of the exhilaration he had felt on Lady Henry's staircase, enjoying, after his five years in Teheran, after his long homeward journey by desert and sea, even the common trivialities of the scene--the lights, the gilding, the sparkle of jewels, the scarlet of the uniforms, the noise and movement of the well-dressed crowd. Then, after this first physical thrill, began the second stage of pleasure--the recognitions and the greetings, after long absence, which show a man where he stands in the great world, which sum up his past and forecast his future. Sir Wilfrid had no reason to complain. Cabinet ministers and great ladies, members of Parliament and the permanent officials who govern but do not rule, soldiers, journalists, barristers--were all glad, it seemed, to grasp him by the hand. He had returned with a record of difficult service brilliantly done, and the English world rewarded him in its accustomed ways.

It was towards one o'clock that he found himself in a crowd pressing towards the staircase in the wake of some departing royalties. A tall man in front turned round to look for some ladies behind him from whom he had been separated in the crush. Sir Wilfrid recognized old Lord Lackington, the veteran of marvellous youth, painter, poet, and sailor, who as a gay naval lieutenant had entertained Byron in the Ægean; whose fame as one of the raciest of naval reformers was in all the newspapers; whose personality was still, at seventy-five, charming to most women and challenging to most men.

As the old man turned, he was still smiling, as though in unison with something which had just been said to him; and his black eyes under his singularly white hair searched the crowd with the animation of a lad of twenty. Through the energy of his aspect the flame of life still burned, as the evening sun through a fine sky. The face had a faulty yet most arresting brilliance. The mouth was disagreeable, the chin common. But the general effect was still magnificent.

Sir Wilfrid started. He recalled the drawing-room in Bruton Street; the form and face of Mademoiselle Le Breton; the sentences by which Lady Henry had tried to put him on the track. His mind ran over past years, and pieced together the recollections of a long-past scandal. "Of course! Of course!" he said to himself, not without excitement. "She is not like her mother, but she has all the typical points of her mother's race."

II

It was a cold, clear morning in February, with a little pale sunshine playing on the bare trees of the Park. Sir Wilfrid, walking southward from the Marble Arch to his luncheon with Lady Henry, was gladly conscious of the warmth of his fur-collared coat, though none the less ready to envy careless youth as it crossed his path now and then, great-coatless and ruddy, courting the keen air.

Just as he was about to make his exit towards Mount Street he became aware of two persons walking southward like himself, but on the other side of the roadway. He soon identified Captain Warkworth in the slim, soldierly figure of the man. And the lady? There also, with the help of his glasses, he was soon informed. Her trim, black hat and her black cloth costume seemed to him to have a becoming and fashionable simplicity; and she moved in morning dress, with the same ease and freedom that had distinguished her in Lady Henry's drawing-room the night before.

He asked himself whether he should interrupt Mademoiselle Le Breton with a view to escorting her to Bruton Street. He understood, indeed, that he and Lady Henry were to be alone at luncheon; Mademoiselle Julie had, no doubt, her own quarters and attendants. But she seemed to be on her way home. An opportunity for some perhaps exploratory conversation with her before he found himself face to face with Lady Henry seemed to him not undesirable.

But he quickly decided to walk on. Mademoiselle Le Breton and Captain Warkworth paused in their walk, about no doubt to say good-bye, but, very clearly, loath to say it. They were, indeed, in earnest conversation. The Captain spoke with eagerness; Mademoiselle Julie, with downcast eyes, smiled and listened.

"Is the fellow making love to her?" thought the old man, in some astonishment, as he turned away. "Hardly the place for it either, one would suppose."

He vaguely thought that he would both sound and warn Lady Henry. Warn her of what? He happened on the way home to have been thrown with a couple of Indian officers whose personal opinion of Harry Warkworth was not a very high one, in spite of the brilliant distinction which the young man had earned for himself in the Afridi campaign just closed. But how was he to hand that sort of thing on to Lady Henry?--and because he happened to have seen her lady companion and Harry Warkworth together? No doubt Mademoiselle Julie was on her employer's business.

Yet the little encounter added somehow to his already lively curiosity on the subject of Lady Henry's companion. Thanks to a remarkable physical resemblance, he was practically certain that he had guessed the secret of Mademoiselle Le Breton's parentage. At any rate, on the supposition that he had, his thoughts began to occupy themselves with the story to which his guess pointed.

Some thirty years before, he had known, both in London and in Italy, a certain Colonel Delaney and his wife, once Lady Rose Chantrey, the favorite daughter of Lord Lackington. They were not a happy couple. She was a woman of great intelligence, but endowed with one of those natures--sensitive, plastic, eager to search out and to challenge life--which bring their possessors some great joys, hardly to be balanced against a final sum of pain. Her husband, absorbed in his military life, silent, narrowly able, and governed by a strict Anglicanism that seemed to carry with it innumerable "shalts" and "shalt nots," disagreeable to the natural man or woman, soon found her a tiring and trying companion. She asked him for what he could not give; she coquetted with questions he thought it impious to raise; the persons she made friends with were distasteful to him; and, without complaining, he soon grew to think it intolerable that a woman married to a soldier should care so little for his professional interests and ambitions. Though when she pretended to care for them she annoyed him, if possible, still more.

As for Lady Rose, she went through all the familiar emotions of the femme incomprise. And with the familiar result. There presently appeared in the house a man of good family, thirty-five or so, traveller, painter, and dreamer, with fine, long-drawn features bronzed by the sun of the East, and bringing with him the reputation of having plotted and fought for most of the "lost causes" of our generation, including several which had led him into conflict with British authorities and British officials. To Colonel Delaney he was an "agitator," if not a rebel; and the careless pungency of his talk soon classed him as an atheist besides. In the case of Lady Rose, this man's free and generous nature, his independence of money and convention, his passion for the things of the mind, his contempt for the mode, whether in dress or politics, his light evasions of the red tape of life as of something that no one could reasonably expect of a vagabond like himself--these things presently transformed a woman in despair to a woman in revolt. She fell in love with an intensity befitting her true temperament, and with a stubbornness that bore witness to the dreary failure of her marriage. Marriott Dalrymple returned her love, and nothing in his view of life predisposed him to put what probably appeared to him a mere legality before the happiness of two people meant for each other. There were no children of the Delaney marriage; and in his belief the husband had enjoyed too long a companionship he had never truly deserved.

So Lady Rose faced her husband, told him the truth, and left him. She and Dalrymple went to live in Belgium, in a small country-house some twenty or thirty miles from Brussels. They severed themselves from England; they asked nothing more of English life. Lady Rose suffered from the breach with her father, for Lord Lackington never saw her again. And there was a young sister whom she had brought up, whose image could often rouse in her a sense of loss that showed itself in occasional spells of silence and tears. But substantially she never repented what she had done, although Colonel Delaney made the penalties of it as heavy as he could. Like Karennine in Tolstoy's great novel, he refused to sue for a divorce, and for something of the same reasons. Divorce was in itself impious, and sin should not be made easy. He was at any time ready to take back his wife, so far as the protection of his name and roof were concerned, should she penitently return to him.

So the child that was presently born to Lady Rose could not be legitimized.

Sir Wilfrid stopped short at the Park end of Bruton Street, with a start of memory.

"I saw it once! I remember now--perfectly."

And he went on to recall a bygone moment in the Brussels Gallery, when, as he was standing before the great Quintin Matsys, he was accosted with sudden careless familiarity by a thin, shabbily dressed man, in whose dark distinction, made still more fantastic and conspicuous by the fever and the emaciation of consumption, he recognized at once Marriott Dalrymple.

He remembered certain fragments of their talk about the pictures--the easy mastery, now brusque, now poetic, with which Dalrymple had shown him the treasures of the gallery, in the manner of one whose learning was merely the food of fancy, the stuff on which imagination and reverie grew rich.

Then, suddenly, his own question--"And Lady Rose?"

And Dalrymple's quiet, "Very well. She'd see you, I think, if you want to come. She has scarcely seen an English person in the last three years."

And as when a gleam searches out some blurred corner of a landscape, there returned upon him his visit to the pair in their country home. He recalled the small eighteenth-century house, the "château" of the village, built on the French model, with its high mansarde roof; the shabby stateliness of its architecture matching plaintively with the field of beet-root that grew up to its very walls; around it the flat, rich fields, with their thin lines of poplars; the slow, canalized streams; the unlovely farms and cottages; the mire of the lanes; and, shrouding all, a hot autumn mist sweeping slowly through the damp meadows and blotting all cheerfulness from the sun. And in the midst of this pale landscape, so full of ragged edges to an English eye, the English couple, with their books, their child, and a pair of Flemish servants.

It had been evident to him at once that their circumstances were those of poverty. Lady Rose's small fortune, indeed, had been already mostly spent on "causes" of many kinds, in many countries. She and Dalrymple were almost vegetarians, and wine never entered the house save for the servants, who seemed to regard their employers with a real but half-contemptuous affection. He remembered the scanty, ill-cooked luncheon; the difficulty in providing a few extra knives and forks; the wrangling with the old bonne-housekeeper, which was necessary before serviettes could be produced.

And afterwards the library, with its deal shelves from floor to ceiling put up by Dalrymple himself, its bare, polished floor, Dalrymple's table and chair on one side of the open hearth, Lady Rose's on the other; on his table the sheets of verse translation from Æschylus and Euripides, which represented his favorite hobby; on hers the socialist and economical books they both studied and the English or French poets they both loved. The walls, hung with the faded damask of a past generation, were decorated with a strange crop of pictures pinned carelessly into the silk--photographs or newspaper portraits of modern men and women representing all possible revolt against authority, political, religious, even scientific, the Everlasting No of an untiring and ubiquitous dissent.

Finally, in the centre of the polished floor, the strange child, whom Lady Rose had gone to fetch after lunch, with its high crest of black hair, its large, jealous eyes, its elfin hands, and the sudden smile with which, after half an hour of silence and apparent scorn, it had rewarded Sir Wilfrid's advances. He saw himself sitting bewitched beside it.

Poor Lady Rose! He remembered her as he and she parted at the gate of the neglected garden, the anguish in her eyes as they turned to look after the bent and shrunken figure of Dalrymple carrying the child back to the house.

"If you meet any of his old friends, don't--don't say anything! We've just saved enough money to go to Sicily for the winter--that'll set him right."

And then, barely a year later, the line in a London newspaper which had reached him at Madrid, chronicling the death of Marriott Dalrymple, as of a man once on the threshold of fame, but long since exiled from the thoughts of practical men. Lady Rose, too, was dead--many years since; so much he knew. But how, and where? And the child?

She was now "Mademoiselle Le Breton "?--the centre and apparently the chief attraction of Lady Henry's once famous salon?

"And, by Jove! several of her kinsfolk there, relations of the mother or the father, if what I suppose is true!" thought Sir Wilfrid, remembering one or two of the guests. "Were they--was she--aware of it?"

The old man strode on, full of a growing eagerness, and was soon on Lady Henry's doorstep.

"Her ladyship is in the dining-room," said the butler, and Sir Wilfrid was ushered there straight.

"Good-morning, Wilfrid," said the old lady, raising herself on her silver--headed sticks as he entered. "I prefer to come down-stairs by myself. The more infirm I am, the less I like it--and to be helped enrages me. Sit down. Lunch is ready, and I give you leave to eat some."

"And you?" said Sir Wilfrid, as they seated themselves almost side by side at the large, round table in the large, dingy room.

The old lady shook her head.

"All the world eats too much. I was brought up with people who lunched on a biscuit and a glass of sherry."

"Lord Russell?--Lord Palmerston?" suggested Sir Wilfrid, attacking his own lunch meanwhile with unabashed vigor.

"That sort. I wish we had their like now."

"Their successors don't please you?"

Lady Henry shook her head.

"The Tories have gone to the deuce, and there are no longer enough Whigs even to do that. I wouldn't read the newspapers at all if I could help it. But I do."

"So I understand," said Sir Wilfrid; "you let Montresor know it last night."

"Montresor!" said Lady Henry, with a contemptuous movement. "What a poseur! He lets the army go to ruin, I understand, while he joins Dante societies."

Sir Wilfrid raised his eyebrows.

"I think, if I were you, I should have some lunch," he said, gently pushing the admirable salmi which the butler had left in front of him towards his old friend.

Lady Henry laughed.

"Oh, my temper will be better presently, when those men are gone"--she nodded towards the butler and footman in the distance--"and I can have my say."

Sir Wilfrid hurried his meal as much as Lady Henry--who, as it turned out, was not at all minded to starve him--would allow. She meanwhile talked politics and gossip to him, with her old, caustic force, nibbling a dry biscuit at intervals and sipping a cup of coffee. She was a wilful, characteristic figure as she sat there, beneath her own portrait as a bride, which hung on the wall behind her. The portrait represented a very young woman, with plentiful brown hair gathered into a knot on the top of her head, a high waist, a blue waist-ribbon, and inflated sleeves. Handsome, imperious, the corners of the mouth well down, the look straight and daring--the Lady Henry of the picture, a bride of nineteen, was already formidable. And the old woman sitting beneath it, with the strong, white hair, which the ample cap found some difficulty even now in taming and confining, the droop of the mouth accentuated, the nose more masterful, the double chin grown evident, the light of the eyes gone out, breathed pride and will from every feature of her still handsome face, pride of race and pride of intellect, combined with a hundred other subtler and smaller prides that only an intimate knowledge of her could detect. The brow and eyes, so beautiful in the picture, were, however, still agreeable in the living woman; if generosity lingered anywhere, it was in them.

The door was hardly closed upon the servants when she bent forward.

"Well, have you guessed?"

Sir Wilfrid looked at her thoughtfully as he stirred the sugar in his coffee.

"I think so," he said. "She is Lady Rose Delaney's daughter."

Lady Henry gave a sudden laugh.

"I hardly expected you to guess! What helped you?"

"First your own hints. Then the strange feeling I had that I had seen the face, or some face just like it, before. And, lastly, at the Foreign Office I caught sight, for a moment, of Lord Lackington. That finished it."

"Ah!" said Lady Henry, with a nod. "Yes, that likeness is extraordinary. Isn't it amazing that that foolish old man has never perceived it?"

"He knows nothing?"

"Oh, nothing! Nobody does. However, that'll do presently. But Lord Lackington comes here, mumbles about his music and his water-colors, and his flirtations--seventy-four, if you please, last birthday!--talks about himself endlessly to Julie or to me--whoever comes handy--and never has an inkling, an idea."

"And she?"

"Oh, she knows. I should rather think she does." And Lady Henry pushed away her coffee-cup with the ill-suppressed vehemence which any mention of her companion seemed to produce in her. "Well, now, I suppose you'd like to hear the story."

"Wait a minute. It'll surprise you to hear that I not only knew this lady's mother and father, but that I've seen her, herself, before."

"You?" Lady Henry looked incredulous.

"I never told you of my visit to that ménage, four-and-twenty years ago?"

"Never, that I remember. But if you had I should have forgotten. What did they matter to me then? I myself only saw Lady Rose once, so far as I remember, before she misconducted herself. And afterwards--well, one doesn't trouble one's self about the women that have gone under."

Something lightened behind Sir Wilfrid's straw-colored lashes. He bent over his coffee-cup and daintily knocked off the end of his cigarette with a beringed little finger.

"The women who have--not been able to pull up?"

Lady Henry paused.

"If you like to put it so," she said, at last. Sir Wilfrid did not raise his eyes. Lady Henry took up her strongest glasses from the table and put them on. But it was pitifully evident that even so equipped she saw but little, and that her strong nature fretted perpetually against the physical infirmity that teased it. Nevertheless, some unspoken communication passed between them, and Sir Wilfrid knew that he had effectually held up a protecting hand for Lady Rose.

"Well, let me tell you my tale first," he said; and gave the little reminiscence in full. When he described the child, Lady Henry listened eagerly.

"Hm," she said, when he came to an end; "she was jealous, you say, of her mother's attentions to you? She watched you, and in the end she took possession of you? Much the same creature, apparently, then as now."

"No moral, please, till the tale is done," said Sir Wilfrid, smiling. "It's your turn."

Lady Henry's face grew sombre.

"LADY HENRY LISTENED EAGERLY"

"All very well," she said. "What did your tale matter to you? As for mine--"

The substance of hers was as follows, put into chronological order:

Lady Rose had lived some ten years after Dalrymple's death. That time she passed in great poverty in some chambres garnies at Bruges, with her little girl and an old Madame Le Breton, the maid, housekeeper, and general factotum who had served them in the country. This woman, though of a peevish, grumbling temper, was faithful, affectionate, and not without education. She was certainly attached to little Julie, whose nurse she had been during a short period of her infancy. It was natural that Lady Rose should leave the child to her care. Indeed, she had no choice. An old Ursuline nun, and a kind priest who at the nun's instigation occasionally came to see her, in the hopes of converting her, were her only other friends in the world. She wrote, however, to her father, shortly before her death, bidding him good-bye, and asking him to do something for the child. "She is wonderfully like you," so ran part of the letter. "You won't ever acknowledge her, I know. That is your strange code. But at least give her what will keep her from want, till she can earn her living. Her old nurse will take care of her, I have taught her, so far. She is already very clever. When I am gone she will attend one of the convent schools here. And I have found an honest lawyer who will receive and pay out money."

To this letter Lord Lackington replied, promising to come over and see his daughter. But an attack of gout delayed him, and, before he was out of his room, Lady Rose was dead. Then he no longer talked of coming over, and his solicitors arranged matters. An allowance of a hundred pounds a year was made to Madame Le Breton, through the "honest lawyer" whom Lady Rose had found, for the benefit of "Julie Dalrymple," the capital value to be handed over to that young lady herself on the attainment of her eighteenth birthday--always provided that neither she nor anybody on her behalf made any further claim on the Lackington family, that her relationship to them was dropped, and her mother's history buried in oblivion.

Accordingly the girl grew to maturity in Bruges. By the lawyer's advice, after her mother's death, she took the name of her old gouvernante, and was known thenceforward as Julie Le Breton. The Ursuline nuns, to whose school she was sent, took the precaution, after her mother's death, of having her baptized straightway into the Catholic faith, and she made her première communion in their church. In the course of a few years she became a remarkable girl, the source of many anxieties to the nuns. For she was not only too clever for their teaching, and an inborn sceptic, but wherever she appeared she produced parties and the passions of parties. And though, as she grew older, she showed much adroitness in managing those who were hostile to her, she was never without enemies, and intrigues followed her.

"I might have been warned in time," said Lady Henry, in whose wrinkled cheeks a sharp and feverish color had sprung up as her story approached the moment of her own personal acquaintance with Mademoiselle Le Breton. "For one or two of the nuns when I saw them in Bruges, before the bargain was finally struck, were candid enough. However, now I come to the moment when I first set eyes on her. You know my little place in Surrey? About a mile from me is a manor-house belonging to an old Catholic family, terribly devout and as poor as church-mice. They sent their daughters to school in Bruges. One summer holiday these girls brought home with them Julie Dalrymple as their quasi-holiday governess. It was three years ago. I had just seen Liebreich. He told me that I should soon be blind, and, naturally, it was a blow to me."

Sir Wilfrid made a murmur of sympathy.

"Oh, don't pity me! I don't pity other people. This odious body of ours has got to wear out sometime--it's in the bargain. Still, just then I was low. There are two things I care about--one is talk, with the people that amuse me, and the other is the reading of French books. I didn't see how I was going to keep my circle here together, and my own mind in decent repair, unless I could find somebody to be eyes for me, and to read to me. And as I'm a bundle of nerves, and I never was agreeable to illiterate people, nor they to me, I was rather put to it. Well, one day these girls and their mother came over to tea, and, as you guess, of course, they brought Mademoiselle Le Breton with them. I had asked them to come, but when they arrived I was bored and cross, and like a sick dog in a hole. And then, as you have seen her, I suppose you can guess what happened."

"You discovered an exceptional person?"

Lady Henry laughed.

"I was limed, there and then, old bird as I am. I was first struck with the girl's appearance--une belle laide--with every movement just as it ought to be; infinitely more attractive to me than any pink-and-white beauty. It turned out that she had just been for a month in Paris with another school-fellow. Something she said about a new play--suddenly--made me look at her. 'Venez vous asseoir ici, mademoiselle, s'il vous plaît--près de moi,' I said to her--I can hear my own voice now, poor fool, and see her flush up. Ah!" Lady Henry's interjection dropped to a note of rage that almost upset Sir Wilfrid's gravity; but he restrained himself, and she resumed: "We talked for two hours; it seemed to me ten minutes. I sent the others out to the gardens. She stayed with me. The new French books, the theatre, poems, plays, novels, memoirs, even politics, she could talk of them all; or, rather--for, mark you, that's her gift--she made me talk. It seemed to me I had not been so brilliant for months. I was as good, in fact, as I had ever been. The difficulty in England is to find any one to keep up the ball. She does it to perfection. She never throws to win--never!--but so as to leave you all the chances. You make a brilliant stroke; she applauds, and in a moment she has arranged you another. Oh, it is the most extraordinary gift of conversation--and she never says a thing that you want to remember."

There was a silence. Lady Henry's old fingers drummed restlessly on the table. Her memory seemed to be wandering angrily among her first experiences of the lady they were discussing.

"Well," said Sir Wilfrid, at last, "so you engaged her as lectrice, and thought yourself very lucky?"

"Oh, don't suppose that I was quite an idiot. I made some inquiries--I bored myself to death with civilities to the stupid family she was staying with, and presently I made her stay with me. And of course I soon saw there was a history. She possessed jewels, laces, little personal belongings of various kinds, that wanted explaining. So I laid traps for her; I let her also perceive whither my own plans were drifting. She did not wait to let me force her hand. She made up her mind. One day I found, left carelessly on the drawing-room table, a volume of Saint-Simon, beautifully bound in old French morocco, with something thrust between the leaves. I opened it. On the fly-leaf was written the name Marriott Dalrymple, and the leaves opened, a little farther, on a miniature of Lady Rose Delaney. So--"

"Apparently it was her traps that worked," said Sir Wilfrid, smiling. Lady Henry returned the smile unwillingly, as one loath to acknowledge her own folly.

"I don't know that I was trapped. We both desired to come to close quarters. Anyway, she soon showed me books, letters--from Lady Rose, from Dalrymple, Lord Lackington--the evidence was complete....

"'Very well,' I said; 'it isn't your fault. All the better if you are well born--I am not a person of prejudices. But understand, if you come to me, there must be no question of worrying your relations. There are scores of them in London. I know them all, or nearly all, and of course you'll come across them. But unless you can hold your tongue, don't come to me. Julie Dalrymple has disappeared, and I'll be no party to her resurrection. If Julie Le Breton becomes an inmate of my house, there shall be no raking up of scandals much better left in their graves. If you haven't got a proper parentage, consistently thought out, we must invent one--'"

"I hope I may some day be favored with it," said Sir Wilfrid.

Lady Henry laughed uncomfortably.

"Oh, I've had to tell lies," she said, "plenty of them."

"What! It was you that told the lies?"

Lady Henry's look flashed.

"The open and honest ones," she said, defiantly.

"Well," said Sir Wilfrid, regretfully, "some sort were indispensable. So she came. How long ago?"

"Three years. For the first half of that time I did nothing but plume myself on my good fortune. I said to myself that if I had searched Europe through I could not have fared better. My household, my friends, my daily ways, she fitted into them all to perfection. I told people that I had discovered her through a Belgian acquaintance. Every one was amazed at her manners, her intelligence. She was perfectly modest, perfectly well behaved. The old Duke--he died six months after she came to me--was charmed with her. Montresor, Meredith, Lord Robert, all my habitués congratulated me. 'Such cultivation, such charm, such savoir-faire! Where on earth did you pick up such a treasure? What are her antecedents?' etc., etc. So then, of course--"

"I hope no more than were absolutely necessary!" said Sir Wilfrid, hastily.

"I had to do it well," said Lady Henry, with decision; "I can't say I didn't. That state of things lasted, more or less, about a year and a half. And by now, where do you think it has all worked out?"

"You gave me a few hints last night," said Sir Wilfrid, hesitating.

Lady Henry pushed her chair back from the table. Her hands trembled on her stick.

"Hints!" she said, scornfully. "I'm long past hints. I told you last night--and I repeat--that woman has stripped me of all my friends! She has intrigued with them all in turn against me. She has done the same even with my servants. I can trust none of them where she is concerned. I am alone in my own house. My blindness makes me her tool, her plaything. As for my salon, as you call it, it has become hers. I am a mere courtesy-figurehead--her chaperon, in fact. I provide the house, the footmen, the champagne; the guests are hers. And she has done this by constant intrigue and deception--by flattery--by lying!"

The old face had become purple. Lady Henry breathed hard.

"My dear friend," said Sir Wilfrid, quickly, laying a calming hand on her arm, "don't let this trouble you so. Dismiss her."

"And accept solitary confinement for the rest of my days? I haven't the courage--yet," said Lady Henry, bitterly. "You don't know how I have been isolated and betrayed! And I haven't told you the worst of all. Listen! Do you know whom she has got into her toils?"

She paused, drawing herself rigidly erect. Sir Wilfrid, looking up sharply, remembered the little scene in the Park, and waited.

"Did you have any opportunity last night," said Lady Henry, slowly, "of observing her and Jacob Delafield?"

She spoke with passionate intensity, her frowning brows meeting above a pair of eyes that struggled to see and could not. But the effect she listened for was not produced. Sir Wilfrid drew back uncertainly.

"Jacob Delafield?" he said. "Jacob Delafield? Are you sure?"

"Sure?" cried Lady Henry, angrily. Then, disdaining to support her statement, she went on: "He hesitates. But she'll soon make an end of that. And do you realize what that means--what Jacob's possibilities are? Kindly recollect that Chudleigh has one boy--one sickly, tuberculous boy--who might die any day. And Chudleigh himself is a poor life. Jacob has more than a good chance-- ninety chances out of a hundred"--she ground the words out with emphasis--"of inheriting the dukedom."

"Good gracious!" said Sir Wilfrid, throwing away his cigarette.

"There!" said Lady Henry, in sombre triumph. "Now you can understand what I have brought on poor Henry's family."

A low knock was heard at the door.

"Come in," said Lady Henry, impatiently.

The door opened, and Mademoiselle Le Breton appeared on the threshold, carrying a small gray terrier under each arm.

"I thought I had better tell you," she said, humbly, "that I am taking the dogs out. Shall I get some fresh wool for your knitting?"

III

It was nearly four o'clock. Sir Wilfrid had just closed Lady Henry's door behind him, and was again walking along Bruton Street.

He was thinking of the little scene of Mademoiselle Le Breton's appearance on the threshold of Lady Henry's dining-room; of the insolent sharpness with which Lady Henry had given her order upon order--as to the dogs, the books for the circulating library, a message for her dressmaker, certain directions for the tradesmen, etc., etc.--as though for the mere purpose of putting the woman who had dared to be her rival in her right place before Sir Wilfrid Bury. And at the end, as she was departing, Mademoiselle Le Breton, trusting no doubt to Lady Henry's blindness, had turned towards himself, raising her downcast eyes upon him suddenly, with a proud, passionate look. Her lips had moved; Sir Wilfrid had half risen from his chair. Then, quickly, the door had closed upon her.

Sir Wilfrid could not think of it without a touch of excitement.

"Was she reminding me of Gherardtsloo?" he said to himself. "Upon my word, I must find some means of conversation with her, in spite of Lady Henry."

He walked towards Bond Street, pondering the situation of the two women--the impotent jealousy and rancor with which Lady Henry was devoured, the domestic slavery contrasted with the social power of Mademoiselle Le Breton. Through the obscurity and difficulty of circumstance, how marked was the conscience of race in her, and, as he also thought, of high intelligence! The old man was deeply interested. He felt a certain indulgent pity for his lifelong friend Lady Henry; but he could not get Mademoiselle Julie out of his head.

"Why on earth does she stay where she is?"

He had asked the same question of Lady Henry, who had contemptuously replied:

"Because she likes the flesh-pots, and won't give them up. No doubt she doesn't find my manners agreeable; but she knows very well that she wouldn't get the chances she gets in my house anywhere else. I give her a foothold. She'll not risk it for a few sour speeches on my part. I may say what I like to her--and I intend to say what I like! Besides, you watch her, and see whether she's made for poverty. She takes to luxury as a fish to water. What would she be if she left me? A little visiting teacher, perhaps, in a Bloomsbury lodging. That's not her line at all."

"But somebody else might employ her as you do?" Sir Wilfrid had suggested.

"You forget I should be asked for a character," said Lady Henry. "Oh, I admit there are possibilities--on her side. That silly goose, Evelyn Crowborough, would have taken her in, but I had a few words with Crowborough, and he put his foot down. He told his wife he didn't want an intriguing foreigner to live with them. No; for the present we are chained to each other. I can't get rid of her, and she doesn't want to get rid of me. Of course, things might become intolerable for either of us. But at present self-interest on both sides keeps us going. Oh, don't tell me the thing is odious! I know it. Every day she stays in the house I become a more abominable old woman."

A more exacting one, certainly. Sir Wilfrid thought with pity and amusement of the commissions with which Mademoiselle Julie had been loaded. "She earns her money, any way," he thought. "Those things will take her a hard afternoon's work. But, bless my soul!"--he paused in his walk--"what about that engagement to Duchess Evelyn that I heard her make? Not a word, by-the-way, to Lady Henry about it! Oh, this is amusing!"

He went meditatively on his way, and presently turned into his club to write some letters. But at five o'clock he emerged, and told a hansom to drive him to Grosvenor Square. He alighted at the great red-brick mansion of the Crowboroughs, and asked for the Duchess. The magnificent person presiding over the hall, an old family retainer, remembered him, and made no difficulty about admitting him.

"Anybody with her grace?" he inquired, as the man handed him over to the footman who was to usher him up-stairs.

"Only Miss Le Breton and Mr. Delafield, Sir Wilfrid. Her grace told me to say 'not at home' this afternoon, but I am sure, sir, she will see you."

Sir Wilfrid smiled.

As he entered the outer drawing-room, the Duchess and the group surrounding her did not immediately perceive the footman nor himself, and he had a few moments in which to take in a charming scene.

A baby girl in a white satin gown down to her heels, and a white satin cap, lace-edged and tied under her chin, was holding out her tiny skirt with one hand and dancing before the Duchess and Miss Le Breton, who was at the piano. The child's other hand held up a morsel of biscuit wherewith she directed the movements of her partner, a small black spitz, of a slim and silky elegance, who, straining on his hind legs, his eager attention fixed upon the biscuit, followed every movement of his small mistress; while she, her large blue eyes now solemn, now triumphant, her fair hair escaping from her cap in fluttering curls, her dainty feet pointed, her dimpled arm upraised, repeated in living grace the picture of her great-great-grandmother which hung on the wall in front of her, a masterpiece from Reynolds's happiest hours.

Behind Mademoiselle Le Breton stood Jacob Delafield; while the Duchess, in a low chair beside them, beat time gayly to the gavotte that Mademoiselle Julie was playing and laughed encouragement and applause to the child in front of her. She herself, with her cloud of fair hair, the delicate pink and white of her skin, the laughing lips and small white hands that rose and fell with the baby steps, seemed little more than a child. Her pale blue dress, for which she had just exchanged her winter walking-costume, fell round her in sweeping folds of lace and silk--a French fairy dressed by Wörth, she was possessed by a wild gayety, and her silvery laugh held the room.

Beside her, Julie Le Breton, very thin, very tall, very dark, was laughing too. The eyes which Sir Wilfrid had lately seen so full of pride were now alive with pleasure. Jacob Delafield, also, from behind, grinned applause or shouted to the babe, "Brava, Tottie; well done!" Three people, a baby, and a dog more intimately pleased with one another's society it would have been difficult to discover.

"Sir Wilfrid!"

The Duchess sprang up astonished, and in a moment, to Sir Wilfrid's chagrin, the little scene fell to pieces. The child dropped on the floor, defending herself and the biscuit as best she could against the wild snatches of the dog. Delafield composed his face in a moment to its usual taciturnity. Mademoiselle Le Breton rose from the piano.

"No, no!" said Sir Wilfrid, stopping short and holding up a deprecating hand. "Too bad! Go on."

"Oh, we were only fooling with baby!" said the Duchess. "It is high time she went to her nurse. Sit here, Sir Wilfrid. Julie, will you take the babe, or shall I ring for Mrs. Robson?"

"I'll take her," said Mademoiselle Le Breton.

She knelt down by the child, who rose with alacrity. Catching her skirts round her, with one eye half laughing, half timorous, turned over her shoulder towards the dog, the baby made a wild spring into Mademoiselle Julie's arms, tucking up her feet instantly, with a shriek of delight, out of the dog's way. Then she nestled her fair head down upon her bearer's shoulder, and, throbbing with joy and mischief, was carried away.

Sir Wilfrid, hat in hand, stood for a moment watching the pair. A bygone marriage uniting the Lackington family with that of the Duchess had just occurred to him in some bewilderment. He sat down beside his hostess, while she made him some tea. But no sooner had the door of the farther drawing-room closed behind Mademoiselle Le Breton, than with a dart of all her lively person she pounced upon him.

"Well, so Aunt Flora has been complaining to you?"

Sir Wilfrid's cup remained suspended in his hand. He glanced first at the speaker and then at Jacob Delafield.

"Oh, Jacob knows all about it!" said the Duchess, eagerly. "This is Julie's headquarters; we are on her staff. You come from the enemy!"

Sir Wilfrid took out his white silk handkerchief and waved it.

"Here is my flag of truce," he said. "Treat me well."

"We are only too anxious to parley with you," said the Duchess, laughing. "Aren't we, Jacob?" Then she drew closer.

"What has Aunt Flora been saying to you?"

Sir Wilfrid paused. As he sat there, apparently studying his boots, his blond hair, now nearly gray, carefully parted in the middle above his benevolent brow, he might have been reckoned a tame and manageable person. Jacob Delafield, however, knew him of old.

"I don't think that's fair," said Sir Wilfrid, at last, looking up. "I'm the new-comer; I ought to be allowed the questions."

"Go on," said the Duchess, her chin on her hand. "Jacob and I will answer all we know."

Delafield nodded. Sir Wilfrid, looking from one to the other, quickly reminded himself that they had been playmates from the cradle--or might have been.

"Well, in the first place," he said, slowly, "I am lost in admiration at the rapidity with which Mademoiselle Le Breton does business. An hour and a half ago"--he looked at his watch--"I stood by while Lady Henry enumerated commissions it would have taken any ordinary man-mortal half a day to execute."

The Duchess clapped her hands.

"My maid is now executing them," she said, with glee. "In an hour she will be back. Julie will go home with everything done, and I shall have had nearly two hours of her delightful society. What harm is there in that?"

"Where are the dogs?" said Sir Wilfrid, looking round.

"Aunt Flora's dogs? In the housekeeper's room, eating sweet biscuit. They adore the groom of the chambers."

"Is Lady Henry aware of this--this division of labor?" said Sir Wilfrid, smiling.

"Of course not," said the Duchess, flushing. "She makes Julie's life such a burden to her that something has to be done. Now what has Aunt Flora been telling you? We were certain she would take you into council--she has dropped various hints of it. I suppose she has been telling you that Julie has been intriguing against her--taking liberties, separating her from her friends, and so on?"

Sir Wilfrid smilingly presented his cup for some more tea.

"I beg to point out," he said, "that I have only been allowed two questions so far. But if things are to be at all fair and equal, I am owed at least six."

The Duchess drew back, checked, and rather annoyed. Jacob Delafield, on the other hand, bent forward.

"We are anxious, Sir Wilfrid, to tell you all we know," he replied, with quiet emphasis.

Sir Wilfrid looked at him. The flame in the young man's eyes burned clear and steady--but flame it was. Sir Wilfrid remembered him as a lazy, rather somnolent youth; the man's advance in expression, in significant power, of itself, told much.

"In the first place, can you give me the history of this lady's antecedents?"

He glanced from one to the other.

The Duchess and Jacob Delafield exchanged glances. Then the Duchess spoke--uncertainly.

"Yes, we know. She has confided in us. There is nothing whatever to her discredit."

Sir Wilfrid's expression changed.

"Ah!" cried the Duchess, bending forward. "You know, too?"

"I knew her father and mother," said Sir Wilfrid, simply.

The Duchess gave a little cry of relief. Jacob Delafield rose, took a turn across the room, and came back to Sir Wilfrid.

"Now we can really speak frankly," he said. "The situation has grown very difficult, and we did not know--Evelyn and I--whether we had a right to explain it. But now that Lady Henry--"

"Oh yes," said Sir Wilfrid, "that's all right. The fact of Mademoiselle Le Breton's parentage--"

"Is really what makes Lady Henry so jealous!" cried the Duchess, indignantly. "Oh, she's a tyrant, is Aunt Flora! It is because Julie is of her own world--of our world, by blood, whatever the law may say--that she can't help making a rival out of her, and tormenting her morning, noon, and night. I tell you, Sir Wilfrid, what that poor girl has gone through no one can imagine but we who have watched it. Lady Henry owes her everything this last three years. Where would she have been without Julie? She talks of Julie's separating her from her friends, cutting her out, imposing upon her, and nonsense of that kind! How would she have kept up that salon alone, I should like to know--a blind old woman who can't write a note for herself or recognize a face? First of all she throws everything upon Julie, is proud of her cleverness, puts her forward in every way, tells most unnecessary falsehoods about her--Julie has felt that very much--and then when Julie has a great success, when people begin to come to Bruton Street, for her sake as well as Lady Henry's, then Lady Henry turns against her, complains of her to everybody, talks about treachery and disloyalty and Heaven knows what, and begins to treat her like the dirt under her feet! How can Julie help being clever and agreeable--she is clever and agreeable! As Mr. Montresor said to me yesterday, 'As soon as that woman comes into a room, my spirits go up!' And why? Because she never thinks of herself, she always makes other people show at their best. And then Lady Henry behaves like this!" The Duchess threw out her hands in scornful reprobation. "And the question is, of course, Can it go on?"

"I don't gather," said Sir Wilfrid, hesitating, "that Lady Henry wants immediately to put an end to it."

Delafield gave an angry laugh.

"The point is whether Mademoiselle Julie and Mademoiselle Julie's friends can put up with it much longer."

"You see," said the Duchess, eagerly, "Julie is such a loyal, affectionate creature. She knows Lady Henry was kind to her, to begin with, that she gave her great chances, and that she's getting old and infirm. Julie's awfully sorry for her. She doesn't want to leave her all alone--to the mercy of her servants--"

"I understand the servants, too, are devoted to Mademoiselle Julie?" said Sir Wilfrid.

"Yes, that's another grievance," said Delafield, contemptuously. "Why shouldn't they be? When the butler had a child very ill, it was Mademoiselle Julie who went to see it in the mews, who took it flowers and grapes--"

"Lady Henry's grapes?" threw in Sir Wilfrid.

"What does it matter!" said Delafield, impatiently. "Lady Henry has more of everything than she knows what to do with. But it wasn't grapes only! It was time and thought and consideration. Then when the younger footman wanted to emigrate to the States, it was Mademoiselle Julie who found a situation for him, who got Mr. Montresor to write to some American friends, and finally sent the lad off, devoted to her, of course, for life. I should like to know when Lady Henry would have done that kind of thing! Naturally the servants like her--she deserves it."

"I see--I see," said Sir Wilfrid, nodding gently, his eyes on the carpet. "A very competent young lady."

Delafield looked at the older man, half in annoyance, half in perplexity.

"Is there anything to complain of in that?" he said, rather shortly.

"Oh, nothing, nothing!" said Sir Wilfrid, hastily. "And this word intrigue that Lady Henry uses? Has mademoiselle always steered a straightforward course with her employer?"

"Oh, well," said the Duchess, shrugging her shoulders, "how can you always be perfectly straightforward with such a tyrannical old person! She has to be managed. Lately, in order to be sure of every minute of Julie's time, she has taken to heaping work upon her to such a ridiculous extent that unless I come to the rescue the poor thing gets no rest and no amusement. And last summer there was an explosion, because Julie, who was supposed to be in Paris for her holiday with a school-friend, really spent a week of it with the Buncombes, Lady Henry's married niece, who has a place in Kent. The Buncombes knew her at Lady Henry's parties, of course. Then they met her in the Louvre, took her about a little, were delighted with her, and begged her to come and stay with them--they have a place near Canterbury--on the way home. They and Julie agreed that it would be best to say nothing to Lady Henry about it--she is too absurdly jealous--but then it leaked out, unluckily, and Lady Henry was furious."

"I must say," said Delafield, hurriedly, "I always thought frankness would have been best there."

"Well, perhaps," said the Duchess, unwillingly, with another shrug. "But now what is to be done? Lady Henry really must behave better, or Julie can't and sha'n't stay with her. Julie has a great following--hasn't she, Jacob? They won't see her harassed to death."

"Certainly not," said Delafield. "At the same time we all see"--he turned to Sir Wilfrid--"what the advantages of the present combination are. Where would Lady Henry find another lady of Mademoiselle Le Breton's sort to help her with her house and her salon? For the last two years the Wednesday evenings have been the most brilliant and successful things of their kind in London. And, of course, for Mademoiselle Le Breton it is a great thing to have the protection of Lady Henry's name--"

"A great thing?" cried Sir Wilfrid. "Everything, my dear Jacob!"

"I don't know," said Delafield, slowly. "It may be bought too dear."

Sir Wilfrid looked at the speaker with curiosity. It had been at all times possible to rouse Jacob Delafield--as child, as school-boy, as undergraduate--from an habitual carelessness and idleness by an act or a tale of injustice or oppression. Had the Duchess pressed him into her service, and was he merely taking sides for the weaker out of a natural bent towards that way of looking at things? Or--

"Well, certainly we must do our best to patch it up," said Sir Wilfrid, after a pause. "Perhaps Mademoiselle Le Breton will allow me a word with her by-and-by. I think I have still some influence with Lady Henry. But, dear goddaughter"--he bent forward and laid his hand on that of the Duchess--"don't let the maid do the commissions."

"But I must!" cried the Duchess. "Just think, there is my big bazaar on the 16th. You don't know how clever Julie is at such things. I want to make her recite--her French is too beautiful! And then she has such inventiveness, such a head! Everything goes if she takes it in hand. But if I say anything to Aunt Flora, she'll put a spoke in all our wheels. She'll hate the thought of anything in which Julie is successful and conspicuous. Of course she will!"

"All the same, Evelyn," said Delafield, uncomfortable apparently for the second time, "I really think it would be best to let Lady Henry know."

"Well, then, we may as well give it up," said the Duchess, pettishly, turning aside.

Delafield, who was still pacing the carpet, suddenly raised his hand in a gesture of warning.

Mademoiselle Le Breton was crossing the outer drawing-room.

"Julie, come here!" cried the Duchess, springing up and running towards her. "Jacob is making himself so disagreeable. He thinks we ought to tell Lady Henry about the 16th."

The speaker put her arm through Julie Le Breton's, looking up at her with a frowning brow. The contrast between her restless prettiness, the profusion of her dress and hair, and Julie's dark, lissome strength, gowned and gloved in neat, close black, was marked enough.

As the Duchess spoke, Julie looked smiling at Jacob Delafield.

"I am in your hands," she said, gently. "Of course I don't want to keep anything from Lady Henry. Please decide for me."

Sir Wilfrid's mouth showed a satirical line. He turned aside and began to play with a copy of the Spectator.

"Julie," said the Duchess, hesitating, "I hope you won't mind, but we have been discussing things a little with Sir Wilfrid. I felt sure Aunt Flora had been talking to him."

"Of course," said Julie, "I knew she would." She looked towards Sir Wilfrid, slightly drawing herself up. Her manner was quiet, but all her movements were somehow charged with a peculiar and interesting significance. The force of the character made itself felt through all disguises.

In spite of himself, Sir Wilfrid began to murmur apologetic things.

"It was natural, mademoiselle, that Lady Henry should confide in me. She has perhaps told you that for many years I have been one of the trustees of her property. That has led to her consulting me on a good many matters. And evidently, from what she says and what the Duchess says, nothing could be of more importance to her happiness, now, in her helpless state, than her relations to you."

He spoke with a serious kindness in which the tinge of mocking habitual to his sleek and well-groomed visage was wholly lost. Julie Le Breton met him with dignity.

"Yes, they are important. But, I fear they cannot go on as they are."

There was a pause. Then Sir Wilfrid approached her:

"I hear you are returning to Bruton Street immediately. Might I be your escort?"

"Certainly."

The Duchess, a little sobered by the turn events had taken and the darkened prospects of her bazaar, protested in vain against this sudden departure. Julie resumed her furs, which, as Sir Wilfrid, who was curious in such things; happened to notice, were of great beauty, and made her farewells. Did her hand linger in Jacob Delafield's? Did the look with which that young man received it express more than the steadfast support which justice offers to the oppressed? Sir Wilfrid could not be sure.

"'INDEED I WILL!' CRIED SIR WILFRID, AND THEY WALKED ON"

As they stepped out into the frosty, lamp-lit dark of Grosvenor Square, Julie Le Breton turned to her companion.

"You knew my mother and father," she said, abruptly. "I remember your coming,"

What was in her voice, her rich, beautiful voice? Sir Wilfrid only knew that while perfectly steady, it seemed to bring emotion near, to make all the aspects of things dramatic.

"Yes, yes," he replied, in some confusion. "I knew her well, from the time when she was a girl in the school-room. Poor Lady Rose!"

The figure beside him stood still.

"Then if you were my mother's friend," she said, huskily, "you will hear patiently what I have to say, even though you are Lady Henry's trustee."

"Indeed I will!" cried Sir Wilfrid, and they walked on.

IV

"But, first of all," said Mademoiselle Le Breton, looking in some annoyance at the brace of terriers circling and barking round them, "we must take the dogs home, otherwise no talk will be possible."

"You have no more business to do?"

His companion smiled.

"Everything Lady Henry wants is here," she said, pointing to the bag upon her arm which had been handed to her, as Sir Wilfrid remembered, after some whispered conversation, in the hall of Crowborough House by an elegantly dressed woman, who was no doubt the Duchess's maid.

"Allow me to carry it for you."

"Many thanks," said Mademoiselle Le Breton, firmly retaining it, "but those are not the things I mind."

They walked on quickly to Bruton Street. The dogs made conversation impossible. If they were on the chain it was one long battle between them and their leader. If they were let loose, it seemed to Sir Wilfrid that they ranged every area on the march, and attacked all elderly gentlemen and most errand-boys.

"Do you always take them out?" he asked, when both he and his companion were crimson and out of breath.

"Always."

"Do you like dogs?"

"I used to. Perhaps some day I shall again."

"As for me, I wish they had but one neck!" said Sir Wilfrid, who had but just succeeded in dragging Max, the bigger of the two, out of the interior of a pastry-cook's hand-cart which had been rashly left with doors open for a few minutes in the street, while its responsible guardian was gossiping in an adjacent kitchen. Mademoiselle Julie meanwhile was wrestling with Nero, the younger, who had dived to the very heart of a peculiarly unsavory dust-box, standing near the entrance of a mews.

"So you commonly go through the streets of London in this whirlwind?" asked Sir Wilfrid, again, incredulous, when at last they had landed their charges safe at the Bruton Street door.

"Morning and evening," said Mademoiselle Julie, smiling. Then she addressed the butler: "Tell Lady Henry, please, that I shall be at home in half an hour."

As they turned westward, the winter streets were gay with lights and full of people. Sir Wilfrid was presently conscious that among all the handsome and well-dressed women who brushed past them, Mademoiselle Le Breton more than held her own. She reminded him now not so much of her mother as of Marriott Dalrymple. Sir Wilfrid had first seen this woman's father at Damascus, when Dalrymple, at twenty-six, was beginning the series of Eastern journeys which had made him famous. He remembered the brillance of the youth; the power, physical and mental, which radiated from him, making all things easy; the scorn of mediocrity, the incapacity for subordination.

"I should like you to understand," said the lady beside him, "that I came to Lady Henry prepared to do my very best."

"I am sure of that," said Sir Wilfrid, hastily recalling his thoughts from Damascus. "And you must have had a very difficult task."

Mademoiselle Le Breton shrugged her shoulders.

"I knew, of course, it must be difficult. And as to the drudgery of it--the dogs, and that kind of thing--nothing of that sort matters to me in the least. But I cannot be humiliated before those who have become my friends, entirely because Lady Henry wished it to be so."

"Lady Henry at first showed you every confidence?"

"After the first month or two she put everything into my hands--her household, her receptions, her letters, you may almost say her whole social existence. She trusted me with all her secrets." ("No, no, my dear lady," thought Sir Wilfrid.) "She let me help her with all her affairs. And, honestly, I did all I could to make her life easy."

"That I understand from herself."

"Then why," cried Mademoiselle Le Breton, turning round to him with sudden passion--"why couldn't Lady Henry leave things alone? Are devotion, and--and the kind of qualities she wanted, so common? I said to myself that, blind and helpless as she was, she should lose nothing. Not only should her household be well kept, her affairs well managed, but her salon should be as attractive, her Wednesday evenings as brilliant, as ever. The world was deserting her; I helped her to bring it back. She cannot live without social success; yet now she hates me for what I have done. Is it sane--is it reasonable?"

"She feels, I suppose," said Sir Wilfrid, gravely, "that the success is no longer hers."

"So she says. But will you please examine that remark? When her guests assemble, can I go to bed and leave her to grapple with them? I have proposed it often, but of course it is impossible. And if I am to be there I must behave, I suppose, like a lady, not like the housemaid. Really, Lady Henry asks too much. In my mother's little flat in Bruges, with the two or three friends who frequented it, I was brought up in as good society and as good talk as Lady Henry has ever known."

They were passing an electric lamp, and Sir Wilfrid, looking up, was half thrilled, half repelled by the flashing energy of the face beside him. Was ever such language on the lips of a paid companion before? His sympathy for Lady Henry revived.

"Can you really give me no clew to the--to the sources of Lady Henry's dissatisfaction?" he said, at last, rather coldly.

Mademoiselle Le Breton hesitated.

"I don't want to make myself out a saint," she said, at last, in another voice and with a humility which was, in truth, hardly less proud than her self-assertion. "I--I was brought up in poverty, and my mother died when I was fifteen. I had to defend myself as the poor defend themselves-- by silence. I learned not to talk about my own affairs. I couldn't afford to be frank, like a rich English girl. I dare say, sometimes I have concealed things which had been better made plain. They were never of any real importance, and if Lady Henry had shown any consideration--"

Her voice failed her a little, evidently to her annoyance. They walked on without speaking for a few paces. "Never of any real importance?" Sir Wilfrid wondered.

Their minds apparently continued the conversation though their lips were silent, for presently Julie Le Breton said, abruptly:

"Of course I am speaking of matters where Lady Henry might have some claim to information. With regard to many of my thoughts and feelings, Lady Henry has no right whatever to my confidence."

"She gives us fair warning," thought Sir Wilfrid.

Aloud he said:

"It is not a question of thoughts and feelings, I understand, but of actions."

"Like the visit to the Duncombes'?" said Mademoiselle Le Breton, impatiently. "Oh, I quite admit it--that's only one of several instances Lady Henry might have brought forward. You see, she led me to make these friendships; and now, because they annoy her, I am to break them. But she forgets. Friends are too--too new in my life, too precious--"

Again the voice wavered. How it thrilled and penetrated! Sir Wilfrid found himself listening for every word.

"No," she resumed. "If it is a question of renouncing the friends I have made in her house, or going--it will be going. That may as well be quite clear."

Sir Wilfrid looked up.

"Let me ask you one question, mademoiselle."

"Certainly. Whatever you like."

"Have you ever had, have you now, any affection for Lady Henry?"

"Affection? I could have had plenty. Lady Henry is most interesting to watch. It is magnificent, the struggles she makes with her infirmities."

Nothing could have been more agreeable than the modulation of these words, the passage of the tone from a first note of surprise to its grave and womanly close. Again, the same suggestions of veiled and vibrating feeling. Sir Wilfrid's nascent dislike softened a little.

"After all," he said, with gentleness, "one must make allowance for old age and weakness, mustn't one?"

"Oh, as to that, you can't say anything to me that I am not perpetually saying to myself," was her somewhat impetuous reply. "Only there is a point when ill-temper becomes not only tormenting to me but degrading to herself.... Oh, if you only knew!"--the speaker drew an indignant breath. "I can hardly bring myself to speak of such misères. But everything excites her, everything makes her jealous. It is a grievance that I should have a new dress, that Mr. Montresor should send me an order for the House of Commons, that Evelyn Crowborough should give me a Christmas present. Last Christmas, Evelyn gave me these furs--she is the only creature in London from whom I would accept a farthing or the value of a farthing."

She paused, then rapidly threw him a question:

"Why, do you suppose, did I take it from her?"

"She is your kinswoman," said Wilfrid, quietly.

"Ah, you knew that! Well, then, mayn't Evelyn be kind to me, though I am what I am? I reminded Lady Henry, but she only thought me a mean parasite, sponging on a duchess for presents above my station. She said things hardly to be forgiven. I was silent. But I have never ceased to wear the furs."

With what imperious will did the thin shoulders straighten themselves under the folds of chinchilla! The cloak became symbolic, a flag not to be struck.

"I never answer back, please understand--never," she went on, hurriedly. "You saw to-day how Lady Henry gave me her orders. There is not a servant in the house with whom she would dare such a manner. Did I resent it?"

"You behaved with great forbearance. I watched you with admiration."

"Ah, forbearance! I fear you don't understand one of the strangest elements in the whole case. I am afraid of Lady Henry, mortally afraid! When she speaks to me I feel like a child who puts up its hands to ward off a blow. My instinct is not merely to submit, but to grovel. When you have had the youth that I had, when you have existed, learned, amused yourself on sufferance, when you have had somehow to maintain yourself among girls who had family, friends, money, name, while you--"

Her voice stopped, resolutely silenced before it broke. Sir Wilfrid uncomfortably felt that he had no sympathy to produce worthy of the claim that her whole personality seemed to make upon it. But she recovered herself immediately.

"Now I think I had better give you an outline of the last six months," she said, turning to him. "Of course it is my side of the matter. But you have heard Lady Henry's."

And with great composure she laid before him an outline of the chief quarrels and grievances which had embittered the life of the Bruton Street house during the period she had named. It was a wretched story, and she clearly told it with repugnance and disgust. There was in her tone a note of offended personal delicacy, as of one bemired against her will.

Evidently, Lady Henry was hardly to be defended. The thing had been "odious," indeed. Two women of great ability and different ages, shut up together and jarring at every point, the elder furiously jealous and exasperated by what seemed to her the affront offered to her high rank and her past ascendency by the social success of her dependant, the other defending herself, first by the arts of flattery and submission, and then, when these proved hopeless, by a social skill that at least wore many of the aspects of intrigue--these were the essential elements of the situation; and, as her narrative proceeded, Sir Wilfrid admitted to himself that it was hard to see any way out of it. As to his own sympathies, he did not know what to make of them.

"No. I have been only too yielding," said Mademoiselle Le Breton, sorely, when her tale was done. "I am ashamed when I look back on what I have borne. But now it has gone too far, and something must be done. If I go, frankly, Lady Henry will suffer."

Sir Wilfrid looked at his companion.

"Lady Henry is well aware of it."

"Yes," was the calm reply, "she knows it, but she does not realize it. You see, if it comes to a rupture she will allow no half-measures. Those who stick to me will have to quarrel with her.

And there will be a great many who will stick to me."

Sir Wilfrid's little smile was not friendly.

"It is indeed evident," he said, "that you have thought it all out."

Mademoiselle Le Breton did not reply. They walked on a few minutes in silence, till she said, with a suddenness and in a low tone that startled her companion:

"If Lady Henry could ever have felt that she humbled me, that I acknowledged myself at her mercy! But she never could. She knows that I feel myself as well born as she, that I am not ashamed of my parents, that my principles give me a free mind about such things."

"Your principles?" murmured Sir Wilfrid.

"You were right," she turned upon him with a perfectly quiet but most concentrated passion. "I have had to think things out. I know, of course, that the world goes with Lady Henry. Therefore I must be nameless and kinless and hold my tongue. If the world knew, it would expect me to hang my head. I don't! I am as proud of my mother as of my father. I adore both their memories. Conventionalities of that kind mean nothing to me."

"My dear lady--"

"Oh, I don't expect you or any one else to feel with me," said the voice which for all its low pitch was beginning to make him feel as though he were in the centre of a hail-storm. "You are a man of the world, you knew my parents, and yet I understand perfectly that for you, too, I am disgraced. So be it! So be it! I don't quarrel with what any one may choose to think, but--"

She recaptured herself with difficulty, and there was silence. They were walking through the purple February dusk towards the Marble Arch. It was too dark to see her face under its delicate veil, and Sir Wilfrid did not wish to see it. But before he had collected his thoughts sufficiently his companion was speaking again, in a wholly different manner.

"I don't know what made me talk in this way. It was the contact with some one, I suppose, who had seen us at Gherardtsloo." She raised her veil, and he thought that she dashed away some tears. "That never happened to me before in London. Well, now, to return. If there is a breach--"

"Why should there be a breach?" said Sir Wilfrid. "My dear Miss Le Breton, listen to me for a few minutes. I see perfectly that you have a great deal to complain of, but I also see that Lady Henry has something of a case."

And with a courteous authority and tact worthy of his trade, the old diplomat began to discuss the situation.

Presently he found himself talking with an animation, a friendliness, an intimacy that surprised himself. What was there in the personality beside him that seemed to win a way inside a man's defences in spite of him? Much of what she had said had seemed to him arrogant or morbid. And yet as she listened to him, with an evident dying down of passion, an evident forlornness, he felt in her that woman's weakness and timidity of which she had accused herself in relation to Lady Henry, and was somehow, manlike, softened and disarmed. She had been talking wildly, because no doubt she felt herself in great difficulties. But when it was his turn to talk she neither resented nor resisted what he had to say. The kinder he was, the more she yielded, almost eagerly at times, as though the thorniness of her own speech had hurt herself most, and there were behind it all a sad life, and a sad heart that only asked in truth for a little sympathy and understanding.

"I shall soon be calling her 'my dear' and patting her hand," thought the old man, at last, astonished at himself. For the dejection in her attitude and gait began to weigh upon him; he felt a warm desire to sustain and comfort her. More and more thought, more and more contrivance did he throw into the straightening out of this tangle between two excitable women, not, it seemed, for Lady Henry's sake, not, surely, for Miss Le Breton's sake. But--ah! those two poor, dead folk, who had touched his heart long ago, did he feel the hovering of their ghosts beside him in the wintry wind?

At any rate, he abounded in shrewd and fatherly advice, and Mademoiselle Le Breton listened with a most flattering meekness.

"Well, now I think we have come to an understanding," he urged, hopefully, as they turned down Bruton Street again.

Mademoiselle Le Breton sighed.

"It is very kind of you. Oh, I will do my best. But--"

She shook her head uncertainly.

"No--no 'buts,'" cried Sir Wilfrid, cheerfully. "Suppose, as a first step," he smiled at his companion, "you tell Lady Henry about the bazaar?"

"By all means. She won't let me go. But Evelyn will find some one else."

"Oh, we'll see about that," said the old man, almost crossly. "If you'll allow me I'll try my hand."

Julie Le Breton did not reply, but her face glimmered upon him with a wistful friendliness that did not escape him, even in the darkness. In this yielding mood her voice and movements had so much subdued sweetness, so much distinction, that he felt himself more than melting towards her.

Then, of a sudden, a thought--a couple of thoughts--sped across him. He drew himself rather sharply together.

"Mr. Delafield, I gather, has been a good deal concerned in the whole matter?"

Mademoiselle Le Breton laughed and hesitated.

"He has been very kind. He heard Lady Henry's language once when she was excited. It seemed to shock him. He has tried once or twice to smooth her down. Oh, he has been most kind!"

"Has he any influence with her?"

"Not much."

"Do you think well of him?"

He turned to her with a calculated abruptness. She showed a little surprise.

"I? But everybody thinks well of him. They say the Duke trusts everything to him."

"When I left England he was still a rather lazy and unsatisfactory undergraduate. I was curious to know how he had developed. Do you know what his chief interests are now?"

Mademoiselle Le Breton hesitated.

"I'm really afraid I don't know," she said, at last, smiling, and, as it were, regretful. "But Evelyn

Crowborough, of course, could tell you all about him. She and he are very old friends."

"No birds out of that cover," was Sir Wilfrid's inward comment.

The lamp over Lady Henry's door was already in sight when Sir Wilfrid, after some talk of the Montresors, with whom he was going to dine that night, carelessly said:

"That's a very good-looking fellow, that Captain Warkworth, whom I saw with Lady Henry last night."

"Ah, yes. Lady Henry has made great friends with him," said Mademoiselle Julie, readily. "She consults him about her memoir of her husband."

"Memoir of her husband!" Sir Wilfrid stopped short. "Heavens above! Memoir of Lord Henry?"

"She is half-way through it. I thought you knew."

"Well, upon my word! Whom shall we have a memoir of next? Henry Delafield! Henry Delafield! Good gracious!"

And Sir Wilfrid walked along, slashing at the railings with his stick, as though the action relieved him. Julie Le Breton quietly resumed:

"I understand that Lord Henry and Captain Warkworth's father went through the Indian Mutiny together, and Captain Warkworth has some letters--"

"Oh, I dare say--I dare say," muttered Sir Wilfrid. "What's this man home for just now?"

"Well, I think Lady Henry knows," said Mademoiselle Julie, turning to him an open look, like one who, once more, would gladly satisfy a questioner if they could. "He talks to her a great deal. But why shouldn't he come home?"

"Because he ought to be doing disagreeable duty with his regiment instead of always racing about the world in search of something to get his name up," said Sir Wilfrid, rather sharply. "At least, that's the view his brother officers mostly take of him."

"Oh," said Mademoiselle Julie, with amiable vagueness, "is there anything particular that you suppose he wants?"

"I am not at all in the secret of his ambitions," said Sir Wilfrid, lifting his shoulders. "But you and Lady Henry seemed well acquainted with him."

The straw-colored lashes veered her way.

"I had some talk with him in the Park this morning," said Julie Le Breton, reflectively. "He wants me to copy his father's letters for Lady Henry, and to get her to return the originals as soon as possible. He feels nervous when they are out of his hands."

"Hm!" said Sir Wilfrid.

At that moment Lady Henry's door-bell presented itself. The vigor with which Sir Wilfrid rang it may, perhaps, have expressed the liveliness of his unspoken scepticism. He did not for one moment believe that General Warkworth's letters had been the subject of the conversation he had witnessed that morning in the Park, nor that filial veneration had had anything whatever to say to it.

Julie Le Breton gave him her hand.

"Thank you very much," she said, gravely and softly.

Sir Wilfrid at the moment before had not meant to press it at all. But he did press it, aware the while of the most mingled feelings.

"On the contrary, you were very good to allow me this conversation. Command me at any time if I can be useful to you and Lady Henry."

Julie Le Breton smiled upon him and was gone.

Sir Wilfrid ran down the steps, chafing at himself.

"She somehow gets round one," he thought, with a touch of annoyance. "I wonder whether I made any real impression upon her. Hm! Let's see whether Montresor can throw any more light upon her. He seemed to be pretty intimate. Her 'principles,' eh? A dangerous view to take, for a woman of that provenance."

An hour or two later Sir Wilfrid Bury presented himself in the Montresors' drawing-room in Eaton Place. He had come home feeling it essential to impress upon the cabinet a certain line of action with regard to the policy of Russia on the Persian Gulf. But the first person he perceived on the hearth-rug, basking before the Minister's ample fire, was Lord Lackington. The sight of that vivacious countenance, that shock of white hair, that tall form still boasting the spareness and almost the straightness of youth, that unsuspecting complacency, confused his ideas and made him somehow feel the whole world a little topsy-turvy.

Nevertheless, after dinner he got his fifteen minutes of private talk with his host, and conscientiously made use of them. Then, after an appointment had been settled for a longer conversation on another day, both men felt that they had done their duty, and, as it appeared, the same subject stirred in both their minds.

"Well, and what did you think of Lady Henry?" said Montresor, with a smile, as he lighted another cigarette.

"She's very blind," said Sir Wilfrid, "and more rheumatic. But else there's not much change. On the whole she wears wonderfully well."

"Except as to her temper, poor lady!" laughed the Minister. "She has really tried all our nerves of late. And the worst of it is that most of it falls upon that poor woman who lives with her"--the Minister lowered his voice--"one of the most interesting and agreeable creatures in the world."

Sir Wilfrid glanced across the table. Lord Lackington was telling scandalous tales of his youth to a couple of Foreign Office clerks, who sat on either side of him, laughing and spurring him on. The old man's careless fluency and fun were evidently contagious; animation reigned around him; he was the spoiled child of the dinner, and knew it.

"I gather that you have taken a friendly interest in Miss Le Breton," said Bury, turning to his host.

"Oh, the Duchess and Delafield and I have done our best to protect her, and to keep the peace. I am quite sure Lady Henry has poured out her grievances to you, hasn't she?"

"Alack, she has!"

"I knew she couldn't hold her tongue to you, even for a day. She has really been losing her head over it. And it is a thousand pities."

"So you think all the fault's on Lady Henry's side?"

The Minister gave a shrug.

"At any rate, I have never myself seen anything to justify Lady Henry's state of feeling. On the famous Wednesdays, Mademoiselle Julie always appears to make Lady Henry her first thought. And in other ways she has really worn herself to death for the old lady. It makes one rather savage sometimes to see it."

"So in your eyes she is a perfect companion?"

Montresor laughed.

"Oh, as to perfection--"

"Lady Henry accuses her of intrigue. You have seen no traces of it?"

The Minister smiled a little oddly.

"Not as regards Lady Henry. Oh, Mademoiselle Julie is a very astute lady."

A ripple from some source of secret amusement spread over the dark-lined face.

"What do you mean by that?"

"She knows how to help her friends better than most people. I have known three men, at least, made by Mademoiselle Le Breton within the last two or three years. She has just got a fresh one in tow."

Sir Wilfrid moved a little closer to his host. They turned slightly from the table and seemed to talk into their cigars.

"Young Warkworth?" said Bury.

The Minister smiled again and hesitated.

"Oh, she doesn't bother me, she is much too clever. But she gets at me in the most amusing, indirect ways. I know perfectly well when she has been at work. There are two or three men-- high up, you understand--who frequent Lady Henry's evenings, and who are her very good friends.... Oh, I dare say she'll get what she wants," he added, with nonchalance.

"Between you and me, do you suspect any direct interest in the young man?"

Montresor shrugged his shoulders.

"I don't know. Not necessarily. She loves to feel herself a power--all the more, I think, because of her anomalous position. It is very curious--at bottom very feminine and amusing--and quite harmless."

"You and others don't resent it?"

"No, not from her," said the Minister, after a pause. "But she is rather going it, just now. Three or four batteries have opened upon me at once. She must be thinking of little else."

Sir Wilfrid grew a trifle red. He remembered the comedy of the door-step. "Is there anything that he particularly wants?" His tone assumed a certain asperity.

"Well, as for me, I cannot help feeling that Lady Henry has something to say for herself. It is very strange--mysterious even--the kind of ascendency this lady has obtained for herself in so short a time."

"Oh, I dare say it's hard for Lady Henry to put up with," mused Montresor. "Without family, without connections--"

He raised his head quietly and put on his eye-glasses. Then his look swept the face of his companion.

Sir Wilfrid, with a scarcely perceptible yet significant gesture, motioned towards Lord Lackington. Mr. Montresor started. The eyes of both men travelled across the table, then met again.

"You know?" said Montresor, under his breath.

Sir Wilfrid nodded. Then some instinct told him that he had now exhausted the number of the initiated.

When the men reached the drawing-room, which was rather emptily waiting for the "reception" Mrs. Montresor was about to hold in it, Sir Wilfrid fell into conversation with Lord Lackington. The old man talked well, though flightily, with a constant reference of all topics to his own standards, recollections, and friendships, which was characteristic, but in him not unattractive. Sir Wilfrid noticed certain new and pitiful signs of age. The old man was still a rattle. But every now and then the rattle ceased abruptly and a breath of melancholy made itself felt--like a chill and sudden gust from some unknown sea.

They were joined presently, as the room filled up, by a young journalist--an art critic, who seemed to know Lord Lackington and his ways. The two fell eagerly into talk about pictures, especially of an exhibition at Antwerp, from which the young man had just returned.

"I looked in at Bruges on the way back for a few hours," said the new-comer, presently. "The pictures there are much better seen than they used to be. When were you there last?" He turned to Lord Lackington.

"Bruges?" said Lord Lackington, with a start. "Oh, I haven't been there for twenty years."

And he suddenly sat down, dangling a paper-knife between his hands, and staring at the carpet. His jaw dropped a little. A cloud seemed to interpose between him and his companions.

Sir Wilfrid, with Lady Henry's story fresh in his memory, was somehow poignantly conscious of the old man. Did their two minds hold the same image--of Lady Rose drawing her last breath in some dingy room beside one of the canals that wind through Bruges, laying down there the last relics of that life, beauty, and intelligence that had once made her the darling of the father, who, for some reason still hard to understand, had let her suffer and die alone?

V

On leaving the Montresors, Sir Wilfrid, seeing that it was a fine night with mild breezes abroad, refused a hansom, and set out to walk home to his rooms in Duke Street, St. James's. He was so much in love with the mere streets, the mere clatter of the omnibuses and shimmer of the lamps, after his long absence, that every step was pleasure. At the top of Grosvenor Place he stood still awhile only to snuff up the soft, rainy air, or to delight his eye now with the shining pools which some showers of the afternoon had left behind them on the pavement, and now with the light veil of fog which closed in the distance of Piccadilly.

"And there are silly persons who grumble about the fogs!" he thought, contemptuously, while he was thus yielding himself heart and sense to his beloved London.

As for him, dried and wilted by long years of cloudless heat, he drank up the moisture and the mist with a kind of physical passion--the noises and the lights no less. And when he had resumed his walk along the crowded street, the question buzzed within him, whether he must indeed go back to his exile, either at Teheran, or nearer home, in some more exalted post? "I've got plenty of money; why the deuce don't I give it up, and come home and enjoy myself? Only a few more years, after all; why not spend them here, in one's own world, among one's own kind?"

It was the weariness of the governing Englishman, and it was answered immediately by that other instinct, partly physical, partly moral, which keeps the elderly man of affairs to his task. Idleness? No! That way lies the end. To slacken the rush of life, for men of his sort, is to call on death--death, the secret pursuer, who is not far from each one of us. No, no! Fight on! It was only the long drudgery behind, under alien suns, together with the iron certainty of fresh drudgery ahead, that gave value, after all, to this rainy, this enchanting Piccadilly--that kept the string of feeling taut and all its notes clear.

"Going to bed, Sir Wilfrid?" said a voice behind him, as he turned down St. James's Street.

"Delafield!" The old man faced round with alacrity. "Where have you sprung from?"

Delafield explained that he had been dining with the Crowboroughs, and was now going to his club to look for news of a friend's success or failure in a north-country election.

"Oh, that'll keep!" said Sir Wilfrid. "Turn in with me for half an hour. I'm at my old rooms, you know, in Duke Street."

"All right," said the young man, after what seemed to Sir Wilfrid a moment of hesitation.

"Are you often up in town this way?" asked Bury, as they walked on. "Land agency seems to be a profession with mitigations."

"There is some London business thrown in. We have some large milk depots in town that I look after."

There was just a trace of hurry in the young man's voice, and Bury surveyed him with a smile. "No other attractions, eh?"

"Not that I know of. By-the-way, Sir Wilfrid, I never asked you how Dick Mason was getting on?"

"Dick Mason? Is he a friend of yours?"

"Well, we were at Eton and Oxford together."

"Were you? I never heard him mention your name."

The young man laughed.

"I don't mean to suggest he couldn't live without me. You've left him in charge, haven't you, at Teheran?"

"Yes, I have--worse luck. So you're deeply interested in Dick Mason?"

"Oh, come--I liked him pretty well."

"Hm--I don't much care about him. And I don't somehow believe you do."

And Bury, with a smile, slipped a friendly hand within the arm of his companion. Delafield reddened.

"It's decent, I suppose, to inquire after an old school-fellow?"

"Exemplary. But--there are things more amusing to talk about."

Delafield was silent. Sir Wilfrid's fair mustaches approached his ear.

"I had my interview with Mademoiselle Julie."

"So I suppose. I hope you did some good."

"I doubt it. Jacob, between ourselves, the little Duchess hasn't been a miracle of wisdom."

"No--perhaps not," said the other, unwillingly.

"She realizes, I suppose, that they are connected?"

"Of course. It isn't very close. Lady Rose's brother married Evelyn's aunt, her mother's sister."

"Yes, that's it. She and Mademoiselle Julie ought to have called the same person uncle; but, for lack of certain ceremonies, they don't. By-the-way, what became of Lady Rose's younger sister?"

"Lady Blanche? Oh, she married Sir John Moffatt, and has been a widow for years. He left her a place in Westmoreland, and she lives there generally with her girl."

"Has Mademoiselle Julie ever come across them?"

"No."

"She speaks of them?"

"Yes. We can't tell her much about them, except that the girl was presented last year, and went to a few balls in town. But neither she nor her mother cares for London."

"Lady Blanche Moffatt--Lady Blanche Moffatt?" said Sir Wilfrid, pausing. "Wasn't she in India this winter?"

"Yes. I believe they went out in November and are to be home by April."

"Somebody told me they had met her and the girl at Peshawar and then at Simla," said Sir Wilfrid, ruminating. "Now I remember! She's a great heiress, isn't she, and pretty to boot? I know! Somebody told me that fellow Warkworth had been making up to her."

"Warkworth?" Jacob Delafield stood still a moment, and Sir Wilfrid caught a sudden contraction of the brow. "That, of course, was just a bit of Indian gossip."

"I don't think so," said Sir Wilfrid, dryly. "My informants were two frontier officers--I came from Egypt with them--who had recently been at Peshawar; good fellows both of them, not at all given to take young ladies' names in vain."

Jacob made no reply. They had let themselves into the Duke Street house and were groping their way up the dim staircase to Sir Wilfrid's rooms.

There all was light and comfort. Sir Wilfrid's valet, much the same age as himself, hovered round his master, brought him his smoking-coat, offered Delafield cigars, and provided Sir Wilfrid, strange to say, with a large cup of tea.

"I follow Mr. Gladstone," said Sir Wilfrid, with a sigh of luxury, as he sank into an easy-chair and extended a very neatly made pair of legs and feet to the blaze. "He seems to have slept the sleep of the just--on a cup of tea at midnight--through the rise and fall of cabinets. So I'm trying the receipt."

"Does that mean that you are hankering after politics?"

"Heavens! When you come to doddering, Jacob, it's better to dodder in the paths you know. I salute Mr. G.'s physique, that's all. Well, now, Jacob, do you know anything about this Warkworth?"

"Warkworth?" Delafield withdrew his cigar, and seemed to choose his words a little. "Well, I know what all the world knows."

"Hm--you seemed very sure just now that he wasn't going to marry Miss Moffatt."

"Sure? I'm not sure of anything," said the young man, slowly.

"Well, what I should like to know," said Sir Wilfrid, cradling his teacup in both hands, "is, what particular interest has Mademoiselle Julie in that young soldier?"

Delafield looked into the fire.

"Has she any?"

"She seems to be moving heaven and earth to get him what he wants. By-the-way, what does he want?"

"He wants the special mission to Mokembe, as I understand," said Delafield, after a moment. "But several other people want it too."

"Indeed!" Sir Wilfrid nodded reflectively. "So there is to be one! Well, it's about time. The travellers of the other European firms have been going it lately in that quarter. Jacob, your mademoiselle also is a bit of an intriguer!"

Delafield made a restless movement. "Why do you say that?"

"Well, to say the least of it, frankness is not one of her characteristics. I tried to question her about this man. I had seen them together in the Park, talking as intimates. So, when our conversation had reached a friendly stage, I threw out a feeler or two, just to satisfy myself about her. But--"

He pulled his fair mustaches and smiled.

"Well?" said the young man, with a kind of reluctant interrogation.

"She played with me, Jacob. But really she overdid it. For such a clever woman, I assure you, she overdid it!"

"I don't see why she shouldn't keep her friendships to herself," said Delafield, with sudden heat.

"Oh, so you admit it is a friendship?"

Delafield did not reply. He had laid down his cigar, and with his hands on his knees was looking steadily into the fire. His attitude, however, was not one of reverie, but rather of a strained listening.

"What is the meaning, Jacob, of a young woman taking so keen an interest in the fortunes of a dashing soldier--for, between you and me, I hear she is moving heaven and earth to get him this post--and then concealing it?"

"Why should she want her kindnesses talked of?" said the young man, impetuously. "She was perfectly right, I think, to fence with your questions, Sir Wilfrid. It's one of the secrets of her influence that she can render a service--and keep it dark."

Sir Wilfrid shook his head.

"She overdid it," he repeated. "However, what do you think of the man yourself, Jacob?"

"Well, I don't take to him," said the other, unwillingly. "He isn't my sort of man."

"And Mademoiselle Julie--you think nothing but well of her? I don't like discussing a lady; but, you see, with Lady Henry to manage, one must feel the ground as one can."

Sir Wilfrid looked at his companion, and then stretched his legs a little farther towards the fire. The lamp-light shone full on his silky eyelashes and beard, on his neatly parted hair, and the diamond on his fine left hand. The young man beside him could not emulate his easy composure. He fidgeted nervously as he replied, with warmth:

"I think she has had an uncommonly hard time, that she wants nothing but what is reasonable, and that if she threw you off the scent, Sir Wilfrid, with regard to Warkworth, she was quite within her rights. You probably deserved it."

He threw up his head with a quick gesture of challenge. Sir Wilfrid shrugged his shoulders.

"I vow I didn't," he murmured. "However, that's all right. What do you do with yourself down in Essex, Jacob?"

The lines of the young man's attitude showed a sudden unconscious relief from tension. He threw himself back in his chair.

"Well, it's a big estate. There's plenty to do."

"You live by yourself?"

"Yes. There's an agent's house--a small one--in one of the villages."

"How do you amuse yourself? Plenty of shooting, I suppose?"

"Too much. I can't do with more than a certain amount."

"Golfing?"

"Oh yes," said the young man, indifferently. "There's a fair links."

"Do you do any philanthropy, Jacob?"

"I like 'bossing' the village," said Delafield, with a laugh. "It pleases one's vanity. That's about all there is to it."

"What, clubs and temperance, that kind of thing? Can you take any real interest in the people?"

Delafield hesitated.

"Well, yes," he said, at last, as though he grudged the admission. "There's nothing else to take an interest in, is there? By-the-way"--he jumped up--"I think I'll bid you good-night, for I've got to go down to-morrow in a hurry. I must be off by the first train in the morning."

"What's the matter?"

"Oh, it's only a wretched old man--that two beasts of women have put into the workhouse infirmary against his will. I only heard it to-night. I must go and get him out."

He looked round for his gloves and stick.

"Why shouldn't he be there?"

"Because it's an infernal shame!" said the other, shortly. "He's an old laborer who'd saved quite a lot of money. He kept it in his cottage, and the other day it was all stolen by a tramp. He has lived with these two women--his sister-in-law and her daughter--for years and years. As long as he had money to leave, nothing was too good for him. The shock half killed him, and now that he's a pauper these two harpies will have nothing to say to nursing him and looking after him. He told me the other day he thought they'd force him into the infirmary. I didn't believe it. But while I've been away they've gone and done it."

"Well, what'll you do now?"

"Get him out."

"And then?"

Delafield hesitated. "Well, then, I suppose, he can come to my place till I can find some decent woman to put him with."

Sir Wilfrid rose.

"I think I'll run down and see you some day. Will there be paupers in all the bedrooms?"

Delafield grinned.

"You'll find a rattling good cook and a jolly snug little place, I can tell you. Do come. But I shall see you again soon. I must be up next week, and very likely I shall be at Lady Henry's on Wednesday."

"All right. I shall see her on Sunday, so I can report."

"Not before Sunday?" Delafield paused. His clear blue eyes looked down, dissatisfied, upon Sir Wilfrid.

"Impossible before. I have all sorts of official people to see to-morrow and Saturday. And, Jacob, keep the Duchess quiet. She may have to give up Mademoiselle Julie for her bazaar."

"I'll tell her."

"By-the-way, is that little person happy?" said Sir Wilfrid, as he opened the door to his departing guest. "When I left England she was only just married."

"Oh yes, she's happy enough, though Crowborough's rather an ass."

"How--particularly?"

Delafield smiled.

"Well, he's rather a sticky sort of person. He thinks there's something particularly interesting in dukes, which makes him a bore."

"Take care, Jacob! Who knows that you won't be a duke yourself some day?"

"What do you mean?" The young man glowered almost fiercely upon his old friend.

"I hear Chudleigh's boy is but a poor creature," said Sir Wilfrid, gravely. "Lady Henry doesn't expect him to live."

"Why, that's the kind that always does live!" cried Delafield, with angry emphasis. "And as for Lady Henry, her imagination is a perfect charnel-house. She likes to think that everybody's dead or dying but herself. The fact is that Mervyn is a good deal stronger this year than he was last. Really, Lady Henry--" The tone lost itself in a growl of wrath.

"Well, well," said Sir Wilfrid, smiling, "'A man beduked against his will,' etcetera. Good-night, my dear Jacob, and good luck to your old pauper."

But Delafield turned back a moment on the stairs.

"I say"--he hesitated--"you won't shirk talking to Lady Henry?"

"No, no. Sunday, certainly--honor bright. Oh, I think we shall straighten it out."

Delafield ran down the stairs, and Sir Wilfrid returned to his warm room and the dregs of his tea.

"Now--is he in love with her, and hesitating for social reasons? Or--is he jealous of this fellow Warkworth? Or--has she snubbed him, and both are keeping it dark? Not very likely, that, in view of his prospects. She must want to regularize her position. Or--is he not in love with her at all?"

On which cogitations there fell presently the strokes of many bells tolling midnight, and left them still unresolved. Only one positive impression remained--that Jacob Delafield had somehow grown, vaguely but enormously, in mental and moral bulk during the years since he had left Oxford--the years of Bury's Persian exile. Sir Wilfrid had been an intimate friend of his dead father, Lord Hubert, and on very friendly terms with his lethargic, good-natured mother. She, by-the-way, was still alive, and living in London with a daughter. He must go and see them.

As for Jacob, Sir Wilfrid had cherished a particular weakness for him in the Eton-jacket stage, and later on, indeed, when the lad enjoyed a brief moment of glory in the Eton eleven. But at Oxford, to Sir Wilfrid's thinking, he had suffered eclipse--had become a somewhat heavy, apathetic, pseudo-cynical youth, displaying his mother's inertia without her good temper, too slack to keep up his cricket, too slack to work for the honor schools, at no time without friends, but an enigma to most of them, and, apparently, something of a burden to himself.

And now, out of that ugly slough, a man had somehow emerged, in whom Sir Wilfrid, who was well acquainted with the race, discerned the stirring of all sorts of strong inherited things, formless still, but struggling to expression.

"He looked at me just now, when I talked of his being duke, as his father would sometimes look."

His father? Hubert Delafield had been an obstinate, dare-devil, heroic sort of fellow, who had lost his life in the Chudleigh salmon river trying to save a gillie who had missed his footing. A man much hated--and much beloved; capable of the most contradictory actions. He had married his wife for money, would often boast of it, and would, none the less, give away his last farthing recklessly, passionately, if he were asked for it, in some way that touched his feelings. Able, too; though not so able as the great Duke, his father.

"Hubert Delafield was never happy, that I can remember," thought Wilfrid Bury, as he sat over his fire, "and this chap has the same expression. That woman in Bruton Street would never do for him--apart from all the other unsuitability. He ought to find something sweet and restful. And yet I don't know. The Delafields are a discontented lot. If you plague them, they are inclined to love you. They want something hard to get their teeth in. How the old Duke adored his termagant of a wife!"

It was late on Sunday afternoon before Sir Wilfrid was able to present himself in Lady Henry's drawing-room; and when he arrived there, he found plenty of other people in possession, and had to wait for his chance.

Lady Henry received him with a brusque "At last," which, however, he took with equanimity. He was in no sense behind his time. On Thursday, when parting with her, he had pleaded for deliberation. "Let me study the situation a little; and don't, for Heaven's sake, let's be too tragic about the whole thing."

Whether Lady Henry was now in the tragic mood or no, he could not at first determine. She was no longer confined to the inner shrine of the back drawing-room. Her chair was placed in the large room, and she was the centre of a lively group of callers who were discussing the events of the week in Parliament, with the light and mordant zest of people well acquainted with the personalities they were talking of. She was apparently better in health, he noticed; at any rate, she was more at ease, and enjoying herself more than on the previous Wednesday. All her social characteristics were in full play; the blunt and careless freedom which made her the good comrade of the men she talked with--as good a brain and as hard a hitter as they--mingled with the occasional sally or caprice which showed her very much a woman.

Very few other women were there. Lady Henry did not want women on Sundays, and was at no pains whatever to hide the fact. But Mademoiselle Julie was at the tea-table, supported by an old white-haired general, in whom Sir Wilfrid recognized a man recently promoted to one of the higher posts in the War Office. Tea, however, had been served, and Mademoiselle Le Breton was now showing her companion a portfolio of photographs, on which the old man was holding forth.

"Am I too late for a cup?" said Sir Wilfrid, after she had greeted him with cordiality. "And what are those pictures?"

"They are some photos of the Khaibar and Tirah," said Mademoiselle Le Breton. "Captain Warkworth brought them to show Lady Henry."

"Ah, the scene of his exploits," said Sir Wilfrid, after a glance at them. "The young man distinguished himself, I understand?"

"Oh, very much so," said General M'Gill, with emphasis. "He showed brains, and he had luck."

"A great deal of luck, I hear," said Sir Wilfrid, accepting a piece of cake. "He'll get his step up, I suppose. Anything else?"

"Difficult to say. But the good men are always in request," said General M'Gill, smiling.

"By-the-way, I heard somebody mention his name last night for this Mokembe mission," said Sir Wilfrid, helping himself to tea-cake.

"Oh, that's quite undecided," said the General, sharply. "There is no immediate hurry for a week or two, and the government must send the best man possible."

"No doubt," said Sir Wilfrid.

It interested him to observe that Mademoiselle Le Breton was no longer pale. As the General spoke, a bright color had rushed into her cheeks. It seemed to Sir Wilfrid that she turned away and busied herself with the photographs in order to hide it.

The General rose, a thin, soldierly figure, with gray hair that drooped forward, and two bright spots of red on the cheek-bones. In contrast with the expansiveness of his previous manner to Mademoiselle Le Breton, he was now a trifle frowning and stiff--the high official once more, and great man.

"Good-night, Sir Wilfrid. I must be off."

"How are your sons?" said Sir Wilfrid, as he rose.

"The eldest is in Canada with his regiment."

"And the second?"

"The second is in orders."

"Overworking himself in the East End, as all the young parsons seem to be doing?"

"That is precisely what he has been doing. But now, I am thankful to say, a country living has been offered him, and his mother and I have persuaded him to take it."

"A country living? Where?"

"One of the Duke of Crowborough's Shropshire livings," said the General, after what seemed to be an instant's hesitation. Mademoiselle Le Breton had moved away, and was replacing the photographs in the drawer of a distant bureau.

"Ah, one of Crowborough's? Well, I hope it is a living with something to live on."

"Not so bad, as times go," said the General, smiling. "It has been a great relief to our minds. There were some chest symptoms; his mother was alarmed. The Duchess has been most kind; she took quite a fancy to the lad, and--"

"What a woman wants she gets. Well, I hope he'll like it. Good-night, General. Shall I look you up at the War Office some morning?"

"By all means."

The old soldier, whose tanned face had shown a singular softness while he was speaking of his son, took his leave.

Sir Wilfrid was left meditating, his eyes absently fixed on the graceful figure of Mademoiselle Le Breton, who shut the drawer she had been arranging and returned to him.

"Do you know the General's sons?" he asked her, while she was preparing him a second cup of tea.

"I have seen the younger."

She turned her beautiful eyes upon him. It seemed to Sir Wilfrid that he perceived in them a passing tremor of nervous defiance, as though she were in some way bracing herself against him. But her self-possession was complete.

"Lady Henry seems in better spirits," he said, bending towards her.

She did not reply for a moment. Her eyes dropped. Then she raised them again, and gently shook her head without a word. The melancholy energy of her expression gave him a moment's thrill.

"Is it as bad as ever?" he asked her, in a whisper.

"It's pretty bad. I've tried to appease her. I told her about the bazaar. She said she couldn't spare me, and, of course, I acquiesced. Then, yesterday, the Duchess--hush!"

"Mademoiselle!"

Lady Henry's voice rang imperiously through the room.

"Yes, Lady Henry."

Mademoiselle Le Breton stood up expectant.

"Find me, please, that number of the Revue des Deux Mondes which came in yesterday. I can prove it to you in two minutes," she said, turning triumphantly to Montresor on her right.

"What's the matter?" said Sir Wilfrid, joining Lady Henry's circle, while Mademoiselle Le Breton disappeared into the back drawing-room.

"Oh, nothing," said Montresor, tranquilly. "Lady Henry thinks she has caught me out in a blunder--about Favre, and the negotiations at Versailles. I dare say she has. I am the most ignorant person alive."

"Then are the rest of us spooks?" said Sir Wilfrid, smiling, as he seated himself beside his hostess. Montresor, whose information on most subjects was prodigious, laughed and adjusted his eye-glass. These battles royal on a date or a point of fact between him and Lady Henry were not uncommon. Lady Henry was rarely victorious. This time, however, she was confident, and she sat frowning and impatient for the book that didn't come.

Mademoiselle Le Breton, indeed, returned from the back drawing-room empty-handed; left the room apparently to look elsewhere, and came back still without the book.

"Everything in this house is always in confusion!" said Lady Henry, angrily. "No order, no method anywhere!"

Mademoiselle Julie said nothing. She retreated behind the circle that surrounded Lady Henry. But Montresor jumped up and offered her his chair.

"I wish I had you for a secretary, mademoiselle," he said, gallantly. "I never before heard Lady Henry ask you for anything you couldn't find."

Lady Henry flushed, and, turning abruptly to Bury, began a new topic. Julie quietly refused the seat offered to her, and was retiring to an ottoman in the background when the door was thrown open and the footman announced:

"Captain Warkworth."

VI

The new-comer drew all eyes as he approached the group surrounding Lady Henry. Montresor put up his glasses and bestowed on him a few moments of scrutiny, during which the Minister's heavily marked face took on the wary, fighting aspect which his department and the House of Commons knew. The statesman slipped in for an instant between the trifler coming and the trifler gone.

As for Wilfrid Bury, he was dazzled by the young man's good looks. "'Young Harry with his beaver up!'" he thought, admiring against his will, as the tall, slim soldier paid his respects to Lady Henry, and, with a smiling word or two to the rest of those present, took his place beside her in the circle.

"Well, have you come for your letters?" said Lady Henry, eying him with a grim favor.

"I think I came--for conversation," was Warkworth's laughing reply, as he looked first at his hostess and then at the circle.

"Then I fear you won't get it," said Lady Henry, throwing herself back in her chair. "Mr. Montresor can do nothing but quarrel and contradict."

Montresor lifted his hands in wonder.

"Had I been Æsop," he said, slyly, "I would have added another touch to a certain tale. Observe, please!--even after the Lamb has been devoured he is still the object of calumny on the part of the Wolf! Well, well! Mademoiselle, come and console me. Tell me what new follies the Duchess has on foot."

And, pushing his chair back till he found himself on a level with Julie Le Breton, the great man plunged into a lively conversation with her. Sir Wilfrid, Warkworth, and a few other habitués endeavored meanwhile to amuse Lady Henry. But it was not easy. Her brow was lowering, her talk forced. Throughout, Sir Wilfrid perceived in her a strained attention directed towards the conversation on the other side of the room. She could neither see it nor hear it, but she was jealously conscious of it. As for Montresor, there was no doubt an element of malice in the court he was now paying to Mademoiselle Julie. Lady Henry had been thorny over much during the afternoon; even for her oldest friend she had passed bounds; he desired perhaps to bring it home to her.

Meanwhile, Julie Le Breton, after a first moment of reserve and depression, had been beguiled, carried away. She yielded to her own instincts, her own gifts, till Montresor, drawn on and drawn out, found himself floating on a stream of talk, which Julie led first into one channel and then into another, as she pleased; and all to the flattery and glorification of the talker. The famous Minister had come to visit Lady Henry, as he had done for many Sundays in many years; but it was not Lady Henry, but her companion, to whom his homage of the afternoon was paid, who gave him his moment of enjoyment--the moment that would bring him there again. Lady Henry's fault, no doubt; but Wilfrid Bury, uneasily aware every now and then of the dumb tumult that was raging in the breast of the haughty being beside him, felt the pathos of this slow discrowning, and was inclined, once more, rather to be sorry for the older woman than to admire the younger.

At last Lady Henry could bear it no longer.

"Mademoiselle, be so good as to return his father's letters to Captain Warkworth," she said, abruptly, in her coldest voice, just as Montresor, dropping his--head thrown back and knees crossed--was about to pour into the ears of his companion the whole confidential history of his appointment to office three years before.

Julie Le Breton rose at once. She went towards a table at the farther end of the large room, and Captain Warkworth followed her. Montresor, perhaps repenting himself a little, returned to Lady Henry; and though she received him with great coolness, the circle round her, now augmented by Dr. Meredith, and another politician or two, was reconstituted; and presently, with a conscious effort, visible at least to Bury, she exerted herself to hold it, and succeeded.

Suddenly--just as Bury had finished a very neat analysis of the Shah's public and private character, and while the applauding laughter of the group of intimates amid which he sat told him that his epigrams had been good--he happened to raise his eyes towards the distant settee where Julie Le Breton was sitting.

His smile stiffened on his lips. Like an icy wave, a swift and tragic impression swept through him. He turned away, ashamed of having seen, and hid himself, as it were, with relief, in the clamor of amusement awakened by his own remarks.

What had he seen? Merely, or mainly, a woman's face. Young Warkworth stood beside the sofa, on which sat Lady Henry's companion, his hands in his pockets, his handsome head bent towards her. They had been talking earnestly, wholly forgetting and apparently forgotten by the rest of the room. On his side there was an air of embarrassment. He seemed to be choosing his words with difficulty, his eyes on the floor. Julie Le Breton, on the contrary, was looking at him--looking with all her soul, her ardent, unhappy soul--unconscious of aught else in the wide world.

"Good God! she is in love with him!" was the thought that rushed through Sir Wilfrid's mind. "Poor thing! Poor thing!"

Sir Wilfrid outstayed his fellow-guests. By seven o'clock all were gone. Mademoiselle Le Breton had retired. He and Lady Henry were left alone.

"Shut the doors!" she said, peremptorily, looking round her as the last guest disappeared. "I must have some private talk with you. Well, I understand you walked home from the Crowboroughs' the other night with--that woman."

She turned sharply upon him. The accent was indescribable. And with a fierce hand she arranged the folds of her own thick silk dress, as though, for some relief to the stormy feeling within, she would rather have torn than smoothed it.

Sir Wilfrid seated himself beside her, knees crossed, finger-tips lightly touching, the fair eyelashes somewhat lowered--Calm beside Tempest.

"I am sorry to hear you speak so," he said, gravely, after a pause. "Yes, I talked with her. She met me very fairly, on the whole. It seemed to me she was quite conscious that her behavior had not been always what it should be, and that she was sincerely anxious to change it. I did my best as a peacemaker. Has she made no signs since--no advances?"

Lady Henry threw out her hand in disdain.

"She confessed to me that she had pledged a great deal of the time for which I pay her to Evelyn Crowborough's bazaar, and asked what she was to do. I told her, of course, that I would put up with nothing of the kind."

"And were more annoyed, alack! than propitiated by her confession?" said Sir Wilfrid, with a shrug.

"I dare say," said Lady Henry. "You see, I guessed that it was not spontaneous; that you had wrung it out of her."

"What else did you expect me to do?" cried Sir Wilfrid. "I seem, indeed, to have jolly well wasted my time."

"Oh no. You were very kind. And I dare say you might have done some good. I was beginning to--to have some returns on myself, when the Duchess appeared on the scene."

"Oh, the little fool!" ejaculated Sir Wilfrid, under his breath.

"She came, of course, to beg and protest. She offered me her valuable services for all sorts of superfluous things that I didn't want--if only I would spare her Julie for this ridiculous bazaar. So then my back was put up again, and I told her a few home truths about the way in which she had made mischief and forced Julie into a totally false position. On which she flew into a passion, and said a lot of silly nonsense about Julie, that showed me, among other things, that Mademoiselle Le Breton had broken her solemn compact with me, and had told her family history both to Evelyn and to Jacob Delafield. That alone would be sufficient to justify me in dismissing her. N'est-ce pas?"

"Oh yes," murmured Sir Wilfrid, "if you want to dismiss her."

"We shall come to that presently," said Lady Henry, shortly. "Imagine, please, the kind of difficulties in which these confidences, if they have gone any further--and who knows?--may land me. I shall have old Lord Lackington--who behaved like a brute to his daughter while she was alive, and is, all the same, a poseur from top to toe--walking in here one night and demanding his granddaughter--spreading lies, perhaps, that I have been ill-treating her. Who can say what absurdities may happen if it once gets out that she is Lady Rose's child? I could name half a dozen people, who come here habitually, who would consider themselves insulted if they knew--what you and I know."

"Insulted? Because her mother--"

"Because her mother broke the seventh commandment? Oh, dear, no! That, in my opinion, doesn't touch people much nowadays. Insulted because they had been kept in the dark--that's all. Vanity, not morals."

"As far as I can ascertain," said Sir Wilfrid, meditatively, "only the Duchess, Delafield, Montresor, and myself are in the secret."

"Montresor!" cried Lady Henry, beside herself. "Montresor! That's new to me. Oh, she shall go at once--at once!" She breathed hard.

"Wait a little. Have you had any talk with Jacob?"

"I should think not! Evelyn, of course, brings him in perpetually--Jacob this and Jacob that. He seems to have been living in her pocket, and the three have been intriguing against me, morning, noon, and night. Where Julie has found the time I can't imagine; I thought I had kept her pretty well occupied."

Sir Wilfrid surveyed his angry companion and held his peace.

"So you don't know what Jacob thinks?"

"Why should I want to know?" said Lady Henry, disdainfully. "A lad whom I sent to Eton and Oxford, when his father couldn't pay his bills--what does it matter to me what he thinks?"

"Women are strange folk," thought Sir Wilfrid. "A man wouldn't have said that."

Then, aloud:

"I thought you were afraid lest he should want to marry her?"

"Oh, let him cut his throat if he likes!" said Lady Henry, with the inconsistency of fury. "What does it matter to me?"

"By-the-way, as to that"--he spoke as though feeling his way--"have you never had suspicions in quite another direction?"

"What do you mean?"

"Well, I hear a good deal in various quarters of the trouble Mademoiselle Le Breton is taking-- on behalf of that young soldier who was here just now--Harry Warkworth."

Lady Henry laughed impatiently.

"I dare say. She is always wanting to patronize or influence somebody. It's in her nature. She's a born intrigante. If you knew her as well as I do, you wouldn't think much of that. Oh no--make your mind easy. It's Jacob she wants--it's Jacob she'll get, very likely. What can an old, blind creature like me do to stop it?"

"And as Jacob's wife--the wife perhaps of the head of the family--you still mean to quarrel with her?"

"Yes, I do mean to quarrel with her!" and Lady Henry lifted herself in her chair, a pale and quivering image of war--"Duchess or no Duchess! Did you see the audacious way in which she behaved this afternoon?--how she absorbs my guests?--how she allows and encourages a man like Montresor to forget himself?--eggs him on to put slights on me in my own drawing-room!"

"No, no! You are really unjust," said Sir Wilfrid, laying a kind hand upon her arm. "That was not her fault."

"It is her fault that she is what she is!--that her character is such that she forces comparisons between us--between her and me!--that she pushes herself into a prominence that is intolerable, considering who and what she is--that she makes me appear in an odious light to my old friends. No, no, Wilfrid, your first instinct was the true one. I shall have to bring myself to it, whatever it costs. She must take her departure, or I shall go to pieces, morally and physically. To be in a temper like this, at my age, shortens one's life--you know that."

"And you can't subdue the temper?" he asked, with a queer smile.

"No, I can't! That's flat. She gets on my nerves, and I'm not responsible. C'est fini."

"Well," he said, slowly, "I hope you understand what it means?"

"Oh, I know she has plenty of friends!" she said, defiantly. But her old hands trembled on her knee.

"Unfortunately they were and are yours. At least," he entreated, "don't quarrel with everybody who may sympathize with her. Let them take what view they please. Ignore it--be as magnanimous as you can."

"On the contrary!" She was now white to the lips. "Whoever goes with her gives me up. They must choose--once for all."

"My dear friend, listen to reason."

And, drawing his chair close to her, he argued with her for half an hour. At the end of that time her gust of passion had more or less passed away; she was, to some extent, ashamed of herself, and, as he believed, not far from tears.

"When I am gone she will think of what I have been saying," he assured himself, and he rose to take his leave. Her look of exhaustion distressed him, and, for all her unreason, he felt himself astonishingly in sympathy with her. The age in him held out secret hands to the age in her--as against encroaching and rebellious youth.

Perhaps it was the consciousness of this mood in him which at last partly appeased her.

"Well, I'll try again. I'll try to hold my tongue," she granted him, sullenly. "But, understand, she, sha'n't go to that bazaar!"

"That's a great pity," was his naïve reply. "Nothing would put you in a better position than to give her leave."

"I shall do nothing of the kind," she vowed. "And now good-night, Wilfrid--good-night. You're a very good fellow, and if I can take your advice, I will."

Lady Henry sat alone in her brightly lighted drawing-room for some time. She could neither read nor write nor sew, owing to her blindness, and in the reaction from her passion of the afternoon she felt herself very old and weary.

But at last the door opened and Julie Le Breton's light step approached.

"May I read to you?" she said, gently.

Lady Henry coldly commanded the Observer and her knitting.

She had no sooner, however, begun to knit than her very acute sense of touch noticed something wrong with the wool she was using.

"This is not the wool I ordered," she said, fingering it carefully. "You remember, I gave you a message about it on Thursday? What did they say about it at Winton's?"

Julie laid down the newspaper and looked in perplexity at the ball of wool.

"I remember you gave me a message," she faltered.

"Well, what did they say?"

"I suppose that was all they had."

Something in the tone struck Lady Henry's quick ears. She raised a suspicious face.

"Did you ever go to Winton's at all?" she said, quickly.

"LADY HENRY GASPED. SHE FELL BACK INTO HER CHAIR"

"I am so sorry. The Duchess's maid was going there," said Julie, hurriedly, "and she went for me. I thought I had given her your message most carefully."

"Hm," said Lady Henry, slowly. "So you didn't go to Winton's. May I ask whether you went to Shaw's, or to Beatson's, or the Stores, or any of the other places for which I gave you commissions?" Her voice cut like a knife.

Julie hesitated. She had grown very white. Suddenly her face settled and steadied.

"No," she said, calmly. "I meant to have done all your commissions. But I was persuaded by Evelyn to spend a couple of hours with her, and her maid undertook them."

Lady Henry flushed deeply.

"So, mademoiselle, unknown to me, you spent two hours of my time amusing yourself at Crowborough House. May I ask what you were doing there?"

"I was trying to help the Duchess in her plans for the bazaar."

"Indeed? Was any one else there? Answer me, mademoiselle."

Julie hesitated again, and again spoke with a kind of passionate composure.

"Yes. Mr. Delafield was there."

"So I supposed. Allow me to assure you, mademoiselle"--Lady Henry rose from her seat, leaning on her stick; surely no old face was ever more formidable, more withering--"that whatever ambitions you may cherish, Jacob Delafield is not altogether the simpleton you imagine. I know him better than you. He will take some time before he really makes up his mind to marry a woman of your disposition--and your history."

Julie Le Breton also rose.

"I am afraid, Lady Henry, that here, too, you are in the dark," she said, quietly, though her thin arm shook against her dress. "I shall not marry Mr. Delafield. But it is because--I have refused him twice."

Lady Henry gasped. She fell back into her chair, staring at her companion.

"You have--refused him?"

"A month ago, and last year. It is horrid of me to say a word. But you forced me."

Julie was now leaning, to support herself, on the back of an old French chair. Feeling and excitement had blanched her no less than Lady Henry, but her fine head and delicate form breathed a will so proud, a dignity so passionate, that Lady Henry shrank before her.

"Why did you refuse him?"

Julie shrugged her shoulders.

"That, I think, is my affair. But if--I had loved him--I should not have consulted your scruples, Lady Henry."

"That's frank," said Lady Henry. "I like that better than anything you've said yet. You are aware that he may inherit the dukedom of Chudleigh?"

"I have several times heard you say so," said the other, coldly.

Lady Henry looked at her long and keenly. Various things that Wilfrid Bury had said recurred to her. She thought of Captain Warkworth. She wondered.

Suddenly she held out her hand.

"I dare say you won't take it, mademoiselle. I suppose I've been insulting you. But--you have been playing tricks with me. In a good many ways, we're quits. Still, I confess, I admire you a good deal. Anyway, I offer you my hand. I apologize for my recent remarks. Shall we bury the hatchet, and try and go on as before?"

Julie Le Breton turned slowly and took the hand--without unction.

"I make you angry," she said, and her voice trembled, "without knowing how or why."

Lady Henry gulped.

"Oh, it mayn't answer," she said, as their hands dropped. "But we may as well have one more trial. And, mademoiselle, I shall be delighted that you should assist the Duchess with her bazaar."

Julie shook her head.

"I don't think I have any heart for it," she said, sadly; and then, as Lady Henry sat silent, she approached.

"You look very tired. Shall I send your maid?"

That melancholy and beautiful voice laid a strange spell on Lady Henry. Her companion appeared to her, for a moment, in a new light--as a personage of drama or romance. But she shook off the spell.

"At once, please. Another day like this would put an end to me."

VII

Julie le Breton was sitting alone in her own small sitting-room. It was the morning of the Tuesday following her Sunday scene with Lady Henry, and she was busy with various household affairs. A small hamper of flowers, newly arrived from Lady Henry's Surrey garden, and not yet unpacked, was standing open on the table, with various empty flower-glasses beside it. Julie was, at the moment, occupied with the "Stores order" for the month, and Lady Henry's cook-housekeeper had but just left the room after delivering an urgent statement on the need for "relining" a large number of Lady Henry's copper saucepans.

The room was plain and threadbare. It had been the school-room of various generations of Delafields in the past. But for an observant eye it contained a good many objects which threw light upon its present occupant's character and history. In a small bookcase beside the fire were a number of volumes in French bindings. They represented either the French classics--Racine, Bossuet, Châteaubriand, Lamartine--which had formed the study of Julie's convent days, or those other books--George Sand, Victor Hugo, Alfred de Musset, Mazzini, Leopardi, together with the poets and novelists of revolutionary Russia or Polish nationalism or Irish rebellion--which had been the favorite reading of both Lady Rose and her lover. They were but a hundred in all; but for Julie Le Breton they stood for the bridge by which, at will, memory and dreamful pity might carry her back into that vanished life she had once shared with her parents--those strange beings, so calm and yet so passionate in their beliefs, so wilful and yet so patient in their deeds, by whose acts her own experience was still wholly conditioned. In her little room there were no portraits of them visible. But on a side-table stood a small carved triptych. The oblong wings, which were open, contained photographs of figures from one of the great Bruges Memlings. The centre was covered by two wooden leaves delicately carved, and the leaves were locked. The inquisitive housemaid who dusted the room had once tried to open them.--in vain.

On a stand near the fire lay two or three yellow volumes--some recent French essays, a volume of memoirs, a tale of Bourget's, and so forth. These were flanked by Sir Henry Maine's Popular Government, and a recent brilliant study of English policy in Egypt--both of them with the name "Richard J. Montresor" on the title-page. The last number of Dr. Meredith's paper, The New Rambler, was there also; and, with the paper-knife still in its leaves, the journal of the latest French traveller in Mokembe, a small "H.W." inscribed in the top right-hand corner of its gray cover.

Julie finished her Stores order with a sigh of relief. Then she wrote half a dozen business notes, and prepared a few checks for Lady Henry's signature. When this was done the two dachshunds, who had been lying on the rug spying out her every movement, began to jump upon her.

But Julie laughed in their faces. "It's raining," she said, pointing to the window--"raining! So there! Either you won't go out at all, or you'll go with John."

John was the second footman, whom the dogs hated. They returned crestfallen to the rug and to a hungry waiting on Providence. Julie took up a letter on foreign paper which had reached her that morning, glanced at the door, and began to reread its closely written sheets. It was from an

English diplomat on a visit to Egypt, a man on whom the eyes of Europe were at that moment fixed. That he should write to a woman at all, on the subjects of the letter, involved a compliment hors ligne; that he should write with this ease, this abandonment, was indeed remarkable. Julie flushed a little as she read. But when she came to the end she put it aside with a look of worry. "I wish he'd write to Lady Henry," was her thought. "She hasn't had a line from him for weeks. I shouldn't wonder if she suspects already. When any one talks of Egypt, I daren't open my lips."

For fear of betraying the very minute and first-hand information that was possessed by Lady Henry's companion? With a smile and a shrug she locked the letter away in one of the drawers of her writing-table, and took up an envelope which had lain beneath it. From this--again with a look round her--she half drew out a photograph. The grizzled head and spectacled eyes of Dr. Meredith emerged. Julie's expression softened; her eyebrows went up a little; then she slightly shook her head, like one who protests that if something has gone wrong, it isn't--isn't--their fault. Unwillingly she looked at the last words of the letter:

/# "So, remember, I can give you work if you want it, and paying work. I would rather give you my life and my all. But these, it seems, are commodities for which you have no use. So be it. But if you refuse to let me serve you, when the time comes, in such ways as I have suggested in this letter, then, indeed, you would be unkind--I would almost dare to say ungrateful! Yours always   "F. M."
    #/

This letter also she locked away. But her hand lingered on the last of all. She had read it three times already, and knew it practically by heart. So she left the sheets undisturbed in their envelope. But she raised the whole to her lips, and pressed it there, while her eyes, as they slowly filled with tears, travelled--unseeing--to the wintry street beyond the window. Eyes and face wore the same expression as Wilfrid Bury had surprised there--the dumb utterance of a woman hard pressed, not so much by the world without as by some wild force within.

In that still moment the postman's knock was heard in the street outside. Julie Le Breton started, for no one whose life is dependent on a daily letter can hear that common sound without a thrill. Then she smiled sadly at herself. "My joy is over for to-day!" And she turned away with the letter in her hand.

But she did not place it in the same drawer with the others. She moved across to the little carved triptych, and, after listening a moment to the sounds in the house, she opened its closed doors with a gold key that hung on her watch-chain and had been hidden in the bosom of her dress.

The doors fell open. Inside, on a background of dark velvet, hung two miniatures, lightly framed in gold and linked together by a graceful scroll-work in gold. They were of fine French work, and they represented a man and woman, both handsome, young, and of a remarkable distinction of aspect. The faces, nevertheless, hardly gave pleasure. There was in each of them a look at once absent and eager--the look of those who have cared much and ardently for "man," and very little, comparatively, for men.

The miniatures had not been meant for the triptych, nor the triptych for them. It had been adapted to them by loving hands; but there was room for other things in the velvet-lined hollow, and a packet of letters was already reposing there. Julie slipped the letter of the morning inside the elastic band which held the packet; then she closed and locked the doors, returning the key to its place in her dress. Both the lock and hinges of this little hiding-place were well and strongly made, and when the wings also were shut and locked one saw nothing but a massively framed photograph of the Bruges belfry resting on a wooden support.

She had hardly completed her little task when there was a sudden noise of footsteps in the passage outside.

"Julie!" said a light voice, subdued to a laughing whisper. "May I come in?"

The Duchess stood on the threshold, her small, shell-pink face emerging from a masterly study in gray, presented by a most engaging costume.

Julie, in surprise, advanced to meet her visitor, and the old butler, who was Miss Le Breton's very good friend, quickly and discreetly shut the door upon the two ladies.

"Oh, my dear!" said the Duchess, throwing herself into Julie's arms. "I came up so quietly! I told Hutton not to disturb Lady Henry, and I just crept up-stairs, holding my skirts. Wasn't it heroic of me to put my poor little head into the lion's den like this? But when I got your letter this morning saying you couldn't come to me, I vowed I would just see for myself how you were, and whether there was anything left of you. Oh, you poor, pale thing!"

And drawing Julie to a chair, the little Duchess sat down beside her, holding her friend's hands and studying her face.

"Tell me what's been happening--I believe you've been crying! Oh, the old wretch!"

"You're quite mistaken," said Julie, smiling. "Lady Henry says I may help you with the bazaar."

"No!" The Duchess threw up her hands in amazement. "How have you managed that?"

"By giving in. But, Evelyn, I'm not coming."

"Oh, Julie!" The Duchess threw herself back in her chair and fixed a pair of very blue and very reproachful eyes on Miss Le Breton.

"No, I'm not coming. If I'm to stay here, even for a time, I mustn't provoke her any more. She says I may come, but she doesn't mean it."

"She couldn't mean anything civil or agreeable. How has she been behaving--since Sunday?" Julie looked uncertain.

"Oh, there is an armed truce. I was made to have a fire in my bedroom last night. And Hutton took the dogs out yesterday."

The Duchess laughed.

"And there was quite a scene on Sunday? You don't tell me much about it in your letter. But, Julie"--her voice dropped to a whisper--"was anything said about Jacob?"

Julie looked down. A bitterness crept into her face.

"Yes. I can't forgive myself. I was provoked into telling the truth."

"You did! Well? I suppose Aunt Flora thought it was all your fault that he proposed, and an impertinence that you refused?"

"She was complimentary at the time," said Julie, half smiling. "But since--No, I don't feel that she is appeased."

"Of course not. Affronted, more likely."

There was a silence. The Duchess was looking at Julie, but her thoughts were far away. And presently she broke out, with the étourderie that became her:

"I wish I understood it myself, Julie. I know you like him."

"Immensely. But--we should fight!"

Miss Le Breton looked up with animation.

"Oh, that's not a reason," said the Duchess, rather annoyed.

"It's the reason. I don't know--there is something of iron in Mr. Delafield;" and Julie emphasized the words with a shrug which was almost a shiver. "And as I'm not in love with him, I'm afraid of him."

"That's the best way of being in love," cried the Duchess. "And then, Julie"--she paused, and at last added, naïvely, as she laid her little hands on her friend's knee--"haven't you got any ambitions?"

"Plenty. Oh, I should like very well to play the duchess, with you to instruct me," said Julie, caressing the hands. "But I must choose my duke. And till the right one appears, I prefer my own wild ways."

"Afraid of Jacob Delafield? How odd!" said the Duchess, with her chin on her hands.

"It may be odd to you," said Julie, with vivacity. "In reality, it's not in the least odd. There's the same quality in him that there is in Lady Henry--something that beats you down," she added, under her breath. "There, that's enough about Mr. Delafield--quite enough."

And, rising, Julie threw up her arms and clasped her hands above her head. The gesture was all strength and will, like the stretching of a sea-bird's wings.

The Duchess looked at her with eyes that had begun to waver.

"Julie, I heard such an odd piece of news last night."

Julie turned.

"You remember the questions you asked me about Aileen Moffatt?"

"Perfectly."

"Well, I saw a man last night who had just come home from Simla. He saw a great deal of her, and he says that she and her mother were adored in India. They were thought so quaint and sweet--unlike other people--and the girl so lovely, in a sort of gossamer way. And who do you think was always about with them--at Peshawar first, and then at Simla--so that everybody talked? Captain Warkworth! My man believed there was an understanding between them."

Julie had begun to fill the flower-glasses with water and unpack the flower-basket. Her back was towards the Duchess. After a moment she replied, her hands full of forced narcissuses:

"Well, that would be a coup for him."

"I should think so. She is supposed to have half a million in coal-mines alone, besides land. Has Captain Warkworth ever said anything to you about them?"

"No. He has never mentioned them."

The Duchess reflected, her eyes still on Julie's back.

"Everybody wants money nowadays. And the soldiers are just as bad as anybody else. They don't look money, as the City men do--that's why we women fall in love with them--but they think it, all the same."

Julie made no reply. The Duchess could see nothing of her. But the little lady's face showed the flutter of one determined to venture yet a little farther on thin ice.

"Julie, I've done everything you've asked me. I sent a card for the 20th to that rather dreadful woman, Lady Froswick. I was very clever with Freddie about that living; and I've talked to Mr. Montresor. But, Julie, if you don't mind, I really should like to know why you're so keen about it?"

The Duchess's cheeks were by now one flush. She had a romantic affection for Julie, and would not have offended her for the world.

Julie turned round. She was always pale, and the Duchess saw nothing unusual.

"Am I so keen?"

"Julie, you have done everything in the world for this man since he came home."

"Well, he interested me," said Julie, stepping back to look at the effect of one of the vases. "The first evening he was here, he saved me from Lady Henry--twice. He's alone in the world, too, which attracts me. You see, I happen to know what it's like. An only son, and an orphan, and no family interest to push him--"

"So you thought you'd push him? Oh, Julie, you're a darling--but you're rather a wire-puller, aren't you?"

Julie smiled faintly.

"Well, perhaps I like to feel, sometimes, that I have a little power. I haven't much else."

The Duchess seized one of her hands and pressed it to her cheek.

"You have power, because every one loves and admires you. As for me, I would cut myself in little bits to please you.... Well, I only hope, when he's married his heiress, if he does marry her, they'll remember what they owe to you."

Did she feel the hand lying in her own shake? At any rate, it was brusquely withdrawn, and Julie walked to the end of the table to fetch some more flowers.

"I don't want any gratitude," she said, abruptly, "from any one. Well, now, Evelyn, you understand about the bazaar? I wish I could, but I can't."

"Yes, I understand. Julie!" The Duchess rose impulsively, and threw herself into a chair beside the table where she could watch the face and movements of Mademoiselle Le Breton. "Julie, I want so much to talk to you--about business. You're not to be offended. Julie, if you leave Lady Henry, how will you manage?"

"How shall I live, you mean?" said Julie, smiling at the euphemism in which this little person, for whom existence had rained gold and flowers since her cradle, had enwrapped the hard facts of bread-and-butter--facts with which she was so little acquainted that she approached them with a certain delicate mystery.

"You must have some money, you know, Julie," said the Duchess, timidly, her upraised face and Paris hat well matched by the gay poinsettias, the delicate eucharis and arums with which the table was now covered.

"I shall earn some," said Julie, quietly.

"Oh, but, Julie, you can't be bothered with any other tiresome old lady!"

"No. I should keep my freedom. But Dr. Meredith has offered me work, and got me a promise of more."

The Duchess opened her eyes.

"Writing! Well, of course, we all know you can do anything you want to do. And you won't let anybody help you at all?"

"I won't let anybody give me money, if that's what you mean," said Julie, smiling. But it was a smile without accent, without gayety.

The Duchess, watching her, said to herself, "Since I came in she is changed--quite changed."

"Julie, you're horribly proud!"

Julie's face contracted a little.

"How much 'power' should I have left, do you think--how much self-respect--if I took money from my friends?"

"Well, not money, perhaps. But, Julie, you know all about Freddie's London property. It's abominable how much he has. There are always a few houses he keeps in his own hands. If Lady Henry does quarrel with you, and we could lend you a little house--for a time--wouldn't you take it, Julie?"

Her voice had the coaxing inflections of a child. Julie hesitated.

"Only if the Duke himself offered it," she said, finally, with a brusque stiffening of her whole attitude.

The Duchess flushed and stood up.

"Oh, well, that's all right," she said, but no longer in the same voice. "Remember, I have your promise. Good-bye, Julie, you darling!... Oh, by-the-way, what an idiot I am! Here am I forgetting the chief thing I came about. Will you come with me to Lady Hubert to-night? Do! Freddie's away, and I hate going by myself."

"To Lady Hubert's?" said Julie, starting a little. "I wonder what Lady Henry would say?"

"Tell her Jacob won't be there," said the Duchess, laughing. "Then she won't make any difficulties."

"Shall I go and ask her?"

"Gracious! let me get out of the house first. Give her a message from me that I will come and see her to-morrow morning. We've got to make it up, Freddie says; so the sooner it's over, the better. Say all the civil things you can to her about to-night, and wire me this afternoon. If all's well, I come for you at eleven."

The Duchess rustled away. Julie was left standing by the table, alone. Her face was very still, but her eyes shone, her teeth pressed her lip. Unconsciously her hand closed upon a delicate blossom of eucharis and crushed it.

"I'll go," she said, to herself. "Yes, I'll go."

Her letter of the morning, as it happened, had included the following sentences:

"I think to-night I must put in an appearance at the Hubert Delafields', though I own that neither the house nor the son of the house is very much to my liking. But I hear that he has gone back to the country. And there are a few people who frequent Lady Hubert, who might just now be of use."

Lady Henry gave her consent that Mademoiselle Le Breton should accompany the Duchess to Lady Hubert's party almost with effusion. "It will be very dull," she said. "My sister-in-law makes a desert and calls it society. But if you want to go, go. As to Evelyn Crowborough, I am engaged to my dentist to-morrow morning."

When at night this message was reported to the Duchess, as she and Julie were on their way to Rutland Gate, she laughed.

"How much leek shall I have to swallow? What's to-morrow? Wednesday. Hm--cards in the afternoon; in the evening I appear, sit on a stool at Lady Henry's feet, and look at you through my glasses as though I had never seen you before. On Thursday I leave a French book; on Friday I send the baby to see her. Goodness, what a time it takes!" said the Duchess, raising her very white and very small shoulders. "Well, for my life, I mustn't fail to-morrow night."

At Lady Hubert's they found a very tolerable, not to say lively, gathering, which quite belied Lady Henry's slanders. There was not the same conscious brilliance, the same thrill in the air, as pertained to the gatherings in Bruton Street. But there was a more solid social comfort, such as befits people untroubled by the certainty that the world is looking on. The guests of Bruton Street laughed, as well-bred people should, at the estimation in which Lady Henry's salon was held, by those especially who did not belong to it. Still, the mere knowledge of this outside estimate kept up a certain tension. At Lady Hubert's there was no tension, and the agreeable nobodies who found their way in were not made to blush for the agreeable nothings of their conversation.

Lady Hubert herself made for ease--partly, no doubt, for stupidity. She was fair, sleepy, and substantial. Her husband had spent her fortune, and ruffled all the temper she had. The Hubert Delafields were now, however, better off than they had been--investments had recovered--and Lady Hubert's temper was once more placid, as Providence had meant it to be. During the coming season it was her firm intention to marry her daughter, who now stood beside her as she received her guests--a blonde, sweet-featured girl, given, however, so it was said, to good works, and not at all inclined to trouble herself overmuch about a husband.

The rooms were fairly full; and the entry of the Duchess and Mademoiselle Le Breton was one of the incidents of the evening, and visibly quickened the pulses of the assembly. The little Dresden-china Duchess, with her clothes, her jewels, and her smiles, had been, since her marriage, one of the chief favorites of fashion. She had been brought up in the depths of the country, and married at eighteen. After six years she was not in the least tired of her popularity or its penalties. All the life in her dainty person, her glancing eyes, and small, smiling lips rose, as it were, to meet the stir that she evoked. She vaguely saw herself as Titania, and played the part with childish glee. And like Titania, as she had more than once ruefully reflected, she was liable to be chidden by her lord.

But the Duke was on this particular evening debating high subjects in the House of Lords, and the Duchess was amusing herself. Sir Wilfrid Bury, who arrived not long after his goddaughter, found her the centre first of a body-guard of cousins, including among them apparently a great many handsome young men, and then of a small crowd, whose vaguely smiling faces reflected the pleasure that was to be got, even at a distance, out of her young and merry beauty.

Julie Le Breton was not with her. But in the next room Sir Wilfrid soon perceived the form and face which, in their own way, exacted quite as much attention from the world as those of the Duchess. She was talking with many people, and, as usual, he could not help watching her. Never yet had he seen her wide, black eyes more vivid than they were to-night. Now, as on his first sight of her, he could not bring himself to call them beautiful. Yet beautiful they were, by every canon of form and color. No doubt it was something in their expression that offended his own well-drilled instincts.

He found himself thinking suspicious thoughts about most of the conversations in which he saw her engaged. Why was she bestowing those careful smiles on that intolerable woman, Lady Froswick? And what an acquaintance she seemed to have among these elderly soldiers, who might at all times be reckoned on at Lady Hubert's parties! One gray-haired veteran after another recalled himself to her attention, got his few minutes with her, and passed on smiling. Certain high officials, too, were no less friendly. Her court, it seemed to him, was mainly composed of the middle-aged; to-night, at any rate, she left the young to the Duchess. And it was on the whole a court of men. The women, as he now perceived, were a trifle more reserved. There was not, indeed, a trace of exclusion. They were glad to see her; glad, he thought, to be noticed by her. But they did not yield themselves--or so he fancied--with the same wholeness as their husbands.

"How old is she?" he asked himself. "About nine-and-twenty?... Jacob's age--or a trifle older."

After a time he lost sight of her, and in the amusement of his own evening forgot her. But as the rooms were beginning to thin he walked through them, looking for a famous collection of miniatures that belonged to Lady Hubert. English family history was one of his hobbies, and he was far better acquainted with the Delafield statesmen, and the Delafield beauties of the past, than were any of their modern descendants. Lady Hubert's Cosways and Plimers had made a lively impression upon him in days gone by, and he meant to renew acquaintance with them.

But they had been moved from the room in which he remembered them, and he was led on through a series of drawing-rooms, now nearly empty, till on the threshold of the last he paused suddenly.

A lady and gentleman rose from a sofa on which they had been sitting. Captain Warkworth stood still. Mademoiselle Le Breton advanced to the new-comer.

"Is it very late?" she said, gathering up her fan and gloves. "We have been looking at Lady Hubert's miniatures. That lady with the muff"--she pointed to the case which occupied a conspicuous position in the room--"is really wonderful. Can you tell me, Sir Wilfrid, where the Duchess is?"

"No, but I can help you find her," said that gentleman, forgetting the miniatures and endeavoring to look at neither of his companions.

"And I must rush," said Captain Warkworth, looking at his watch. "I told a man to come to my rooms at twelve. Heavens!"

He shook hands with Miss Le Breton and hurried away.

Sir Wilfrid and Julie moved on together. That he had disturbed a most intimate and critical conversation was somehow borne in upon Sir Wilfrid. But kind and even romantic as was the old man's inmost nature, his feelings were not friendly.

"How does the biography get on?" he asked his companion, with a smile.

A bright flush appeared in Mademoiselle Le Breton's cheek.

"I think Lady Henry has dropped it."

"Ah, well, I don't imagine she will regret it;" he said, dryly.

She made no reply. He mentally accused himself for a brute, and then shook off the charge. Surely a few pin-pricks were her desert! That she should defend her own secrets was, as Delafield had said, legitimate enough. But when a man offers you his services, you should not befool him beyond a certain point.

She must be aware of what he was thinking. He glanced at her curiously; at the stately dress gleaming with jet, which no longer affected anything of the girl; at the fine but old-fashioned necklace of pearls and diamonds--no doubt her mother's--which clasped her singularly slender throat. At any rate, she showed nothing. She began to talk again of the Delafield miniatures, using her fan the while with graceful deliberation; and presently they found the Duchess.

"Is she an adventuress, or is she not?" thought Bury, as his hansom carried him away from Rutland Gate. "If she marries Jacob, it will be a queer business."

VIII

Meanwhile the Duchess had dropped Julie Le Breton at Lady Henry's door. Julie groped her way up-stairs through the sleeping house. She found her room in darkness, and she turned on no light. There was still a last glimmer of fire, and she sank down by it, her long arms clasped round her knees, her head thrown back as though she listened still to words in her ears.

"Oh, such a child! Such a dear, simple-minded child! Report engaged her to at least ten different people at Simla. She had a crowd of cavaliers there--I was one of them. The whole place adored her. She is a very rare little creature, but well looked after, I can tell you--a long array of guardians in the background."

How was it possible not to trust that aspect and that smile? Her mind travelled back to the autumn days when she had seen them first; reviewed the steps, so little noticed at first, so rapid lately and full of fate, by which she had come into this bondage wherein she stood. She saw the first appearance of the young soldier in Lady Henry's drawing-room; her first conversation with him; and all the subtle development of that singular relation between them, into which so many elements had entered. The flattering sense of social power implied both in the homage of this young and successful man, and in the very services that she, on her side, was able to render him; impulsive gratitude for that homage, at a time when her very soul was smarting under Lady Henry's contemptuous hostility; and then the sweet advances of a "friendship" that was to unite them in a bond, secret and unique, a bond that took no account of the commonplaces of love and marriage, the link of equal and kindred souls in a common struggle with hard and sordid circumstance.

"I have neither family nor powerful friends," he had written to her a few weeks after their first meeting; "all that I have won, I have won for myself. Nobody ever made 'interest' for me but you. You, too, are alone in the world. You, too, have to struggle for yourself. Let us unite our forces--cheer each other, care for each other--and keep our friendship a sacred secret from the world that would misunderstand it. I will not fail you, I will give you all my confidence; and I will try and understand that noble, wounded heart of yours, with its memories, and all those singular prides and isolations that have been imposed on it by circumstance. I will not say, let me be your brother; there is something banal in that; 'friend' is good enough for us both; and there is between us a community of intellectual and spiritual interest which will enable us to add new meaning even to that sacred word. I will write to you every day; you shall know all that happens to me; and whatever grateful devotion can do to make your life smoother shall be done."

Five months ago was it, that that letter was written?

Its remembered phrases already rang bitterly in an aching heart. Since it reached her, she had put out all her powers as a woman, all her influence as an intelligence, in the service of the writer.

And now, here she sat in the dark, tortured by a passion of which she was ashamed, before which she was beginning to stand helpless in a kind of terror. The situation was developing, and she found herself wondering how much longer she would be able to control herself or it. Very miserably conscious, too, was she all the time that she was now playing for a reward that was secretly, tacitly, humiliatingly denied her. How could a poor man, with Harry Warkworth's ambitions, think for a moment of marriage with a woman in her ambiguous and dependent position? Her common-sense told her that the very notion was absurd. And yet, since the Duchess's gossip had given point and body to a hundred vague suspicions, she was no longer able to calm, to master herself.

Suddenly a thought of another kind occurred to her. It added to her smart that Sir Wilfrid, in their meeting at Lady Hubert's, had spoken to her and looked at her with that slight touch of laughing contempt. There had been no insincerity in that emotion with which she had first appealed to him as her mother's friend; she did truly value the old man's good opinion. And yet she had told him lies.

"I can't help it," she said to herself, with a little shiver. The story about the biography had been the invention of a moment. It had made things easy, and it had a small foundation in the fact that Lady Henry had talked vaguely of using the letters lent her by Captain Warkworth for the elucidation--perhaps in a Nineteenth Century article--of certain passages in her husband's Indian career.

Jacob Delafield, too. There also it was no less clear to her than to Sir Wilfrid that she had "overdone it." It was true, then, what Lady Henry said of her--that she had an overmastering tendency to intrigue--to a perpetual tampering with the plain fact?

"Well, it is the way in which such people as I defend themselves," she said, obstinately, repeating to herself what she had said to Sir Wilfrid Bury.

And then she set against it, proudly, that disinterestedness of which, as she vowed to herself, no one but she knew the facts. It was true, what she had said to the Duchess and to Sir Wilfrid. Plenty of people would give her money, would make her life comfortable, without the need for any daily slavery. She would not take it. Jacob Delafield would marry her, if she lifted her finger; and she would not lift it. Dr. Meredith would marry her, and she had said him nay. She hugged the thought of her own unknown and unapplauded integrity. It comforted her pride. It drew a veil over that wounding laughter which had gleamed for a moment through those long lashes of Sir Wilfrid Bury.

Last of all, as she sank into her restless sleep, came the remembrance that she was still under Lady Henry's roof. In the silence of the night the difficulties of her situation pressed upon and tormented her. What was she to do? Whom was she to trust?

"Dixon, how is Lady Henry?"

"Much too ill to come down-stairs, miss. She's very much put out; in fact, miss (the maid lowered her voice), you hardly dare go near her. But she says herself it would be absurd to attempt it."

"Has Hatton had any orders?"

"Yes, miss. I've just told him what her ladyship wishes. He's to tell everybody that Lady Henry's very sorry, and hoped up to the last moment to be able to come down as usual."

"Has Lady Henry all she wants, Dixon? Have you taken her the evening papers?"

"Oh yes, miss. But if you go in to her much her ladyship says you're disturbing her; and if you don't go, why, of course, everybody's neglecting her."

"Do you think I may go and say good-night to her, Dixon?"

The maid hesitated.

"I'll ask her, miss--I'll certainly ask her."

The door closed, and Julie was left alone in the great drawing-room of the Bruton Street house. It had been prepared as usual for the Wednesday--evening party. The flowers were fresh; the chairs had been arranged as Lady Henry liked to have them; the parquet floors shone under the electric light; the Gainsboroughs seemed to look down from the walls with a gay and friendly expectancy.

For herself, Julie had just finished her solitary dinner, still buoyed up while she was eating it by the hope that Lady Henry would be able to come down. The bitter winds of the two previous days, however, had much aggravated her chronic rheumatism. She was certainly ill and suffering; but Julie had known her make such heroic efforts before this to keep her Wednesdays going that not till Dixon appeared with her verdict did she give up hope.

So everybody would be turned away. Julie paced the drawing-room a solitary figure amid its lights and flowers--solitary and dejected. In a couple of hours' time all her particular friends would come to the door, and it would be shut against them. "Of course, expect me to-night," had been the concluding words of her letter of the morning. Several people also had announced themselves for this evening whom it was extremely desirable she should see. A certain eminent colonel, professor at the Staff College, was being freely named in the papers for the Mokembe mission. Never was it more necessary for her to keep all the threads of her influence in good working order. And these Wednesday evenings offered her the occasions when she was most successful, most at her ease--especially whenever Lady Henry was not well enough to leave the comparatively limited sphere of the back drawing-room.

Moreover, the gatherings themselves ministered to a veritable craving in Julie Le Breton--the craving for society and conversation. She shared it with Lady Henry, but in her it was even more deeply rooted. Lady Henry had ten talents in the Scriptural sense--money, rank, all sorts of inherited bonds and associations. Julie Le Breton had but this one. Society was with her both an instinct and an art. With the subtlest and most intelligent ambition she had trained and improved her natural gift for it during the last few years. And now, to the excitement of society was added the excitement of a new and tyrannous feeling, for which society was henceforth a mere weapon to be used.

She fumed and fretted for a while in silence. Every now and then she would pause in front of one of the great mirrors of the room, and look at the reflection of her tall thinness and the trailing satin of her gown.

"The girl--so pretty, in a gossamer sort of way," The words echoed in her mind, and vaguely, beside her own image in the glass, there rose a vision of girlhood--pale, gold hair, pink cheeks, white frock--and she turned away, miserable, from that conscious, that intellectual distinction with which, in general, she could persuade herself to be very fairly satisfied.

Hutton, the butler, came in to look at the fire.

"Will you be sitting here to-night, miss?"

"Oh no, Hutton. I shall go back to the library. I think the fire in my own room is out."

"I had better put out these lights, anyway," said the man, looking round the brilliant room.

"Oh, certainly," said Julie, and she began to assist him to do so.

Suddenly a thought occurred to her.

"Hutton!" She went up to him and spoke in a lower tone. "If the Duchess of Crowborough comes to-night, I should very much like to see her, and I know she wants to see me. Do you think it could possibly disturb Lady Henry if you were to show her into the library for twenty minutes?"

The man considered.

"I don't think there could be anything heard up-stairs, miss. I should, of course, warn her grace that her ladyship was ill."

"Well, then, Hutton, please ask her to come in," said Miss Le Breton, hurriedly. "And, Hutton, Dr. Meredith and Mr. Montresor, you know how disappointed they'll be not to find Lady Henry at home?"

"Yes, miss. They'll want to know how her ladyship is, no doubt. I'll tell them you're in the library. And Captain Warkworth, miss?--he's never missed a Wednesday evening for weeks."

"Oh, well, if he comes--you must judge for yourself, Hutton," said Miss Le Breton, occupying herself with the electric switches. "I should like to tell them all--the old friends--how Lady Henry is."

The butler's face was respectful discretion itself.

"Of course, miss. And shall I bring tea and coffee?"

"Oh no," said Miss Le Breton, hastily; and then, after reflection, "Well, have it ready; but I don't suppose anybody will ask for it. Is there a good fire in the library?"

"Oh yes, miss. I thought you would be coming down there again. Shall I take some of these flowers down? The room looks rather bare, if anybody's coming in."

Julie colored a little.

"Well, you might--not many. And, Hutton, you're sure we can't disturb Lady Henry?"

Hutton's expression was not wholly confident.

"Her ladyship's very quick of hearing, miss. But I'll shut those doors at the foot of the back stairs, and I'll ask every one to come in quietly."

"Thank you, Hutton--thank you. That'll be very good of you. And, Hutton--"

"Yes, miss." The man paused with a large vase of white arums in his hand.

"You'll say a word to Dixon, won't you? If anybody comes in, there'll be no need to trouble Lady Henry about it. I can tell her to-morrow."

"Very good, miss. Dixon will be down to her supper presently."

The butler departed. Julie was left alone in the now darkened room, lighted only by one lamp and the bright glow of the fire. She caught her breath--suddenly struck with the audacity of what she had been doing. Eight or ten of these people certainly would come in--eight or ten of Lady

Henry's "intimates." If Lady Henry discovered it--after this precarious truce between them had just been patched up!

Julie made a step towards the door as though to recall the butler, then stopped herself. The thought that in an hour's time Harry Warkworth might be within a few yards of her, and she not permitted to see him, worked intolerably in heart and brain, dulling the shrewd intelligence by which she was ordinarily governed. She was conscious, indeed, of some profound inner change. Life had been difficult enough before the Duchess had said those few words to her. But since!

Suppose he had deceived her at Lady Hubert's party! Through all her mounting passion her acute sense of character did not fail her. She secretly knew that it was quite possible he had deceived her. But the knowledge merely added to the sense of danger which, in this case, was one of the elements of passion itself.

"He must have money--of course he must have money," she was saying, feverishly, to herself. "But I'll find ways. Why should he marry yet--for years? It would be only hampering him."

Again she paused before the mirrored wall; and again imagination evoked upon the glass the same white and threatening image--her own near kinswoman--the child of her mother's sister! How strange! Where was the little gossamer creature now--in what safe haven of money and family affection, and all the spoiling that money brings? From the climbing paths of her own difficult and personal struggle Julie Le Breton looked down with sore contempt on such a degenerate ease of circumstance. She had heard it said that the mother and daughter were lingering abroad for a time on their way home from India. Yet was the girl all the while pining for England, thinking not of her garden, her horse, her pets, but only of this slim young soldier who in a few minutes, perhaps, would knock at Lady Henry's door, in quest of Aileen Moffatt's unknown, unguessed-of cousin? These thoughts sent wild combative thrills through Julie's pulses. She turned to one of the old French clocks. How much longer now--till he came?

"Her ladyship would like to see you, miss."

The voice was Dixon's, and Julie turned hurriedly, recalling all her self-possession. She climbed some steep stairs, still unmodernized, to Lady Henry's floor. That lady slept at the back of the house, so as to be out of noise. Her room was an old-fashioned apartment, furnished about the year Queen Victoria came to the throne, with furniture, chintzes, and carpet of the most approved early Victorian pattern. What had been ugly then was dingy now; and its strong mistress, who had known so well how to assimilate and guard the fine decorations and noble pictures of the drawing-rooms, would not have a thing in it touched. "It suits me," she would say, impatiently, when her stout sister-in-law pleaded placidly for white paint and bright colors. "If it's ugly, so am I."

Fierce, certainly, and forbidding she was on this February evening. She lay high on her pillow, tormented by her chronic bronchitis and by rheumatic pain, her brows drawn together, her vigorous hands clasped before her in an evident tension, as though she only restrained herself with difficulty from defying maid, doctor, and her own sense of prudence.

"Well, you have dressed?" she said, sharply, as Julie Le Breton entered her room.

"I did not get your message till I had finished dinner. And I dressed before dinner."

Lady Henry looked her up and down, like a cat ready to pounce.

"You didn't bring me those letters to sign?"

"No, I thought you were not fit for it."

"I said they were to go to-night. Kindly bring them at once."

Julie brought them. With groans and flinchings that she could not repress, Lady Henry read and signed them. Then she demanded to be read to. Julie sat down, trembling. How fast the hands of Lady Henry's clock were moving on!

Mercifully, Lady Henry was already somewhat sleepy, partly from weakness, partly from a dose of bromide.

"I hear nothing," she said, putting out an impatient hand. "You should raise your voice. I didn't mean you to shout, of course. Thank you--that'll do. Good-night. Tell Hutton to keep the house as quiet as he can. People must knock and ring, I suppose; but if all the doors are properly shut it oughtn't to bother me. Are you going to bed?"

"I shall sit up a little to write some letters. But--I sha'n't be late."

"Why should you be late?" said Lady Henry, tartly, as she turned away.

Julie made her way down-stairs with a beating heart. All the doors were carefully shut behind her. When she reached the hall it was already half-past ten o'clock. She hurried to the library, the large panelled room behind the dining-room. How bright Hutton had made it look! Up shot her spirits. With a gay and dancing step she went from chair to chair, arranging everything instinctively as she was accustomed to do in the drawing-room. She made the flowers less stiff; she put on another light; she drew one table forward and pushed its fellow back against the wall. What a charming old room, after all! What a pity Lady Henry so seldom used it! It was panelled in dark oak, while the drawing-room was white. But the pictures, of which there were two or three, looked even better here than up-stairs. That beautiful Lawrence--a "red boy" in gleaming satin--that pair of Hoppners, fine studies in blue, why, who had ever seen them before? And another light or two would show them still better.

A loud knock and ring. Julie held her breath. Ah! A distant voice in the hall. She moved to the fire, and stood quietly reading an evening paper.

"Captain Warkworth would be glad if you would see him for a few minutes, miss. He would like to ask you himself about her ladyship."

"Please ask him to come in, Hutton."

Hutton effaced himself, and the young man entered, Then Julie raised her voice.

"Remember, please, Hutton, that I particularly want to see the Duchess."

Hutton bowed and retired. Warkworth came forward.

"What luck to find you like this!"

He threw her one look--Julie knew it to be a look of scrutiny--and then, as she held out her hand, he stooped and kissed it.

"He wants to know that my suspicions are gone," she thought. "At any rate, he should believe it."

"The great thing," she said, with her finger to her lip, "is that Lady Henry should hear nothing."

She motioned her somewhat puzzled guest to a seat on one side of the fire, and, herself, fell into another opposite. A wild vivacity was in her face and manner.

"Isn't this amusing? Isn't the room charming? I think I should receive very well"--she looked round her--"in my own house."

"You would receive well in a garret--a stable," he said. "But what is the meaning of this? Explain."

"Lady Henry is ill and is gone to bed. That made her very cross--poor Lady Henry! She thinks I, too, am in bed. But you see--you forced your way in--didn't you?--to inquire with greater minuteness after Lady Henry's health."

She bent towards him, her eyes dancing.

"Of course I did. Will there presently be a swarm on my heels, all possessed with a similar eagerness, or--?"

He drew his chair, smiling, a little closer to her. She, on the contrary, withdrew hers.

"There will, no doubt, be six or seven," she said, demurely, "who will want personal news. But now, before they come"--her tone changed--"is there anything to tell me?"

"Plenty," he said, drawing a letter out of his pocket. "Your writ, my dear lady, runs as easily in the City as elsewhere." And he held up an envelope.

She flushed.

"You have got your allotment? But I knew you would. Lady Froswick promised."

"And a large allotment, too," he said, joyously. "I am the envy of all my friends. Some of them have got a few shares, and have already sold them--grumbling. I keep mine three days more on the best advice--the price may go higher yet. But, anyway, there"--he shook the envelope--"there it is--deliverance from debt--peace of mind for the first time since I was a lad at school--the power of going, properly fitted out and equipped, to Africa--if I go--and not like a beggar--all in that bit of paper, and all the work of--some one you and I know. Fairy godmother! tell me, please, how to say a proper thank you."

The young soldier dropped his voice. Those blue eyes which had done him excellent service in many different parts of the globe were fixed with brilliance on his companion; the lines of a full-lipped mouth quivered with what seemed a boyish pleasure. The comfort of money relief was never acknowledged more frankly or more handsomely.

Julie hurriedly repressed him. Did she feel instinctively that there are thanks which it sometimes humiliates a man to remember, lavishly as he may have poured them out at the moment--thanks which may easily count in the long run, not for, but against, the donor? She rather haughtily asked what she had done but say a chance word to Lady Froswick? The shares had to be allotted to somebody. She was glad, of course, very glad, if he were relieved from anxiety....

So did she free herself and him from a burdensome gratitude; and they passed to discussing the latest chances of the Mokembe appointment. The Staff-College Colonel was no doubt formidable; the Commander-in-Chief, who had hitherto allowed himself to be much talked to on the subject of young Warkworth's claims by several men in high place--General M'Gill among them--well known in Lady Henry's drawing-room, was perhaps inclining to the new suggestion, which was strongly supported by important people in Egypt; he had one or two recent appointments on his conscience not quite of the highest order, and the Staff-College man, in addition to a fine military record, was virtue, poverty, and industry embodied; was nobody's cousin, and would, altogether, produce a good effect.

Could anything more be done, and fresh threads set in motion?

They bandied names a little, Julie quite as subtly and minutely informed as the man with regard to all the sources of patronage. New devices, fresh modes of approach revealed themselves to the woman's quick brain. Yet she did not chatter about them; still less parade her own resources. Only, in talking with her, dead walls seemed to give way; vistas of hope and possibility opened in the very heart of discouragement. She found the right word, the right jest, the right spur to invention or effort; while all the time she was caressing and appeasing her companion's self-love--placing it like a hot-house plant in an atmosphere of expansion and content--with that art of hers, which, for the ambitious and irritable man, more conscious of the kicks than of the kisses of fortune, made conversation with her an active and delightful pleasure.

"I don't know how it is," Warkworth presently declared; "but after I have been talking to you for ten minutes the whole world seems changed. The sky was ink, and you have turned it rosy. But suppose it is all mirage, and you the enchanter?"

He smiled at her--consciously, superabundantly. It was not easy to keep quite cool with Julie Le Breton; the self-satisfaction she could excite in the man she wished to please recoiled upon the woman offering the incense. The flattered one was apt to be foolishly responsive.

"That is my risk," she said, with a little shrug. "If I make you confident, and nothing comes of it--"

"I hope I shall know how to behave myself," cried Warkworth. "You see, you hardly understand--forgive me!--your own personal effect. When people are face to face with you, they want to please you, to say what will please you, and then they go away, and--"

"Resolve not to be made fools of?" she said, smiling. "But isn't that the whole art--when you're guessing what will happen--to be able to strike the balance of half a dozen different attractions?"

"Montresor as the ocean," said Warkworth, musing, "with half a dozen different forces tugging at him? Well, dear lady, be the moon to these tides, while this humble mortal looks on--and hopes."

He bent forward, and across the glowing fire their eyes met. She looked so cool, so handsome, so little yielding at that moment, that, in addition to gratitude and flattered vanity, Warkworth was suddenly conscious of a new stir in the blood. It begat, however, instant recoil. Wariness!--let that be the word, both for her sake and his own. What had he to reproach himself with so far? Nothing. He had never offered himself as the lover, as the possible husband. They were both esprits faits--they understood each other. As for little Aileen, well, whatever had happened, or might happen, that was not his secret to give away. And a woman in Julie Le Breton's position, and with her intelligence, knows very well what the difficulties of her case are. Poor Julie! If she had been Lady Henry, what a career she would have made for herself! He was very curious as to her birth and antecedents, of which he knew little or nothing; with him she had always avoided the subject. She was the child, he understood, of English parents who had lived abroad; Lady Henry had come across her by chance. But there must be something in her past to account for this distinction, this ease with which she held her own in what passes as the best of English society.

Julie soon found herself unwilling to meet the gaze fixed upon her. She flushed a little and began to talk of other things.

"Everybody, surely, is unusually late. It will be annoying, indeed, if the Duchess doesn't come."

"The Duchess is a delicious creature, but not for me," said Warkworth, with a laugh. "She dislikes me. Ah, now then for the fray!"

For the outer bell rang loudly, and there were steps in the hall.

"Oh, Julie"--in swept a white whirlwind with the smallest white satin shoes twinkling in front of it--"how clever of you--you naughty angel! Aunt Flora in bed--and you down here! And I who came prepared for such a dose of humble-pie! What a relief! Oh, how do you do?"

The last words were spoken in quite another tone, as the Duchess, for the first time perceiving the young officer on the more shaded side of the fireplace, extended to him a very high wrist and a very stiff hand. Then she turned again to Julie.

"My dear, there's a small mob in the hall. Mr. Montresor--and General Somebody--and Jacob-- and Dr. Meredith with a Frenchman. Oh, and old Lord Lackington, and Heaven knows who! Hutton told me I might come in, so I promised to come first and reconnoitre. But what's Hutton to do? You really must take a line. The carriages are driving up at a fine rate."

"I'll go and speak to Hutton," said Julie.

And she hurried into the hall.

IX

When Miss Le Breton reached the hall, a footman was at the outer door reciting Lady Henry's excuses as each fresh carriage drove up; while in the inner vestibule, which was well screened from the view of the street, was a group of men, still in their hats and over-coats, talking and laughing in subdued voices.

Julie Le Breton came forward. The hats were removed, and the tall, stooping form of Montresor advanced.

"Lady Henry is so sorry," said Julie, in a soft, lowered voice. "But I am sure she would like me to give you her message and to tell you how she is. She would not like her old friends to be alarmed. Would you come in for a moment? There is a fire in the library. Mr. Delafield, don't you think that would be best?... Will you tell Hutton not to let in anybody else?"

She looked at him uncertainly, as though appealing to him, as a relation of Lady Henry's, to take the lead.

"By all means," said that young man, after perhaps a moment's hesitation, and throwing off his coat.

"Only please make no noise!" said Miss Le Breton, turning to the group. "Lady Henry might be disturbed."

Every one came in, as it were, on tiptoe. In each face a sense of the humor of the situation fought with the consciousness of its dangers. As soon as Montresor saw the little Duchess by the fire, he threw up his hands in relief.

"I breathe again," he said, greeting her with effusion. "Duchess, where thou goest, I may go. But I feel like a boy robbing a hen-roost. Let me introduce my friend, General Fergus. Take us both, pray, under your protection!"

"On the contrary," said the Duchess, as she returned General Fergus's bow, "you are both so magnificent that no one would dare to protect you."

For they were both in uniform, and the General was resplendent with stars and medals.

"We have been dining with royalty." said Montresor. "We want some relaxation."

He put on his eye-glasses, looked round the room, and gently rubbed his hands.

"How very agreeable this is! What a charming room! I never saw it before. What are we doing here? Is it a party? Why shouldn't it be? Meredith, have you introduced M. du Bartas to the Duchess? Ah, I see--"

For Julie Le Breton was already conversing with the distinguished Frenchman wearing the rosette of the Legion of Honor in his button-hole, who had followed Dr. Meredith into the room. As Montresor spoke, however, she came forward, and in a French which was a joy to the ear, she presented M. du Bartas, a tall, well-built Norman with a fair mustache, first to the Duchess and then to Lord Lackington and Jacob.

"The director of the French Foreign Office," said Montresor, in an aside to the Duchess. "He hates us like poison. But if you haven't already asked him to dinner--I warned you last week he was coming--pray do it at once!"

Meanwhile the Frenchman, his introductions over, looked curiously round the room, studied its stately emptiness, the books on the walls under a trellis-work, faintly gilt, the three fine pictures; then his eyes passed to the tall and slender lady who had addressed him in such perfect French, and to the little Duchess in her flutter of lace and satin, the turn of her small neck, and the blaze of her jewels. "These Englishwomen overdo their jewels," he thought, with distaste. "But they overdo everything. That is a handsome fellow, by-the-way, who was with la petite fée when we arrived."

And his shrewd, small eyes travelled from Warkworth to the Duchess, his mind the while instinctively assuming some hidden relation between them.

Meanwhile, Montresor was elaborately informing himself as to Lady Henry.

"This is the first time for twenty years that I have not found her on a Wednesday evening," he said, with a sudden touch of feeling which became him. "At our age, the smallest break in the old habit--"

He sighed, and then quickly threw off his depression.

"Nonsense! Next week she will be scolding us all with double energy. Meanwhile, may we sit down, mademoiselle? Ten minutes? And, upon my word, the very thing my soul was longing for--a cup of coffee!"

For at the moment Hutton and two footmen entered with trays containing tea and coffee, lemonade and cakes.

"Shut the door, Hutton, please," Mademoiselle Le Breton implored, and the door was shut at once.

"We mustn't, mustn't make any noise!" she said, her finger on her lip, looking first at Montresor and then at Delafield. The group laughed, moved their spoons softly, and once more lowered their voices.

But the coffee brought a spirit of festivity. Chairs were drawn up. The blazing fire shone out upon a semicircle of people representing just those elements of mingled intimacy and novelty which go to make conversation. And in five minutes Mademoiselle Le Breton was leading it as usual. A brilliant French book had recently appeared dealing with certain points of the Egyptian question in a manner so interesting, supple, and apparently impartial that the attention of Europe had been won. Its author had been formerly a prominent official of the French Foreign Office, and was now somewhat out of favor with his countrymen. Julie put some questions about him to M. du Bartas.

The Frenchman feeling himself among comrades worthy of his steel, and secretly pricked by the presence of an English cabinet minister, relinquished the half-disdainful reserve with which he had entered, and took pains. He drew the man in question, en silhouette, with a hostile touch so sure, an irony so light, that his success was instant and great.

Lord Lackington woke up. Handsome, white-haired dreamer that he was, he had been looking into the fire, half--smiling, more occupied, in truth, with his own thoughts than with his companions. Delafield had brought him in; he did not exactly know why he was there, except that he liked Mademoiselle Le Breton, and often wondered how the deuce Lady Henry had ever discovered such an interesting and delightful person to fill such an uncomfortable position. But this Frenchman challenged and excited him. He, too, began to talk French, and soon the whole room was talking it, with an advantage to Julie Le Breton which quickly made itself apparent. In English she was a link, a social conjunction; she eased all difficulties, she pieced all threads. But in French her tongue was loosened, though never beyond the point of grace, the point of delicate adjustment to the talkers round her.

So that presently, and by insensible gradations, she was the queen of the room. The Duchess in ecstasy pinched Jacob Delafield's wrist, and forgetting all that she ought to have remembered, whispered, rapturously, in his ear, "Isn't she enchanting--Julie--to-night?" That gentleman made no answer. The Duchess, remembering, shrank back, and spoke no more, till Jacob looked round upon her with a friendly smile which set her tongue free again.

M. du Bartas, meanwhile, began to consider this lady in black with more and more attention. The talk glided into a general discussion of the Egyptian position. Those were the days before Arabi, when elements of danger and of doubt abounded, and none knew what a month might bring forth. With perfect tact Julie guided the conversation, so that all difficulties, whether for the French official or the English statesman, were avoided with a skill that no one realized till each separate rock was safely passed. Presently Montresor looked from her to Du Bartas with a grin. The Frenchman's eyes were round with astonishment. Julie had been saying the lightest but the wisest things; she had been touching incidents and personalities known only to the initiated with a restrained gayety which often broke down into a charming shyness, which was ready to be scared away in a moment by a tone--too serious or too polemical--which jarred with the general key of the conversation, which never imposed itself, and was like the ripple on a summer sea. But the summer sea has its depths, and this modest gayety was the mark of an intimate and first-hand knowledge.

"Ah, I see," thought Montresor, amused. "P---- has been writing to her, the little minx. He seems to have been telling her all the secrets. I think I'll stop it. Even she mayn't quite understand what should and shouldn't be said before this gentleman."

So he gave the conversation a turn, and Mademoiselle Le Breton took the hint at once. She called others to the front--it was like a change of dancers in the ballet--while she rested, no less charming as a listener than as a talker, her black eyes turning from one to another and radiant with the animation of success.

But one thing--at last--she had forgotten. She had forgotten to impose any curb upon the voices round her. The Duchess and Lord Lackington were sparring like a couple of children, and Montresor broke in from time to time with his loud laugh and gruff throat voice. Meredith, the Frenchman, Warkworth, and General Fergus were discussing a grand review which had been held the day before. Delafield had moved round to the back of Julie's chair, and she was talking to him, while all the time her eyes were on General Fergus and her brain was puzzling as to how she was to secure the five minutes' talk with him she wanted. He was one of the intimates of the Commander-in-Chief. She herself had suggested to Montresor, of course in Lady Henry's name, that he should be brought to Bruton Street some Wednesday evening.

Presently there was a little shifting of groups. Julie saw that Montresor and Captain Warkworth were together by the fireplace, that the young man with his hands held out to the blaze and his back to her was talking eagerly, while Montresor, looking outward into the room, his great black head bent a little towards his companion, was putting sharp little questions from time to time, with as few words as might be. Julie understood that an important conversation was going on--that Montresor, whose mind various friends of hers had been endeavoring to make up for him, was now perhaps engaged in making it up for himself.

With a quickened pulse she turned to find General Fergus beside her. What a frank and soldierly countenance!--a little roughly cut, with a strong mouth slightly underhung, and a dogged chin, the whole lit by eyes that were the chosen homes of truth, humanity, and will. Presently she discovered, as they drew their chairs a little back from the circle, that she, too, was to be encouraged to talk about Warkworth. The General was, of course, intimately 'acquainted with his professional record; but there were certain additional Indian opinions--a few incidents in the young man's earlier career, including, especially, a shooting expedition of much daring in the very district to which the important Mokembe mission was now to be addressed, together with some quotations from private letters of her own, or Lady Henry's, which Julie, with her usual skill, was able to slip into his ear, all on the assumption, delicately maintained, that she was merely talking of a friend of Lady Henry's, as Lady Henry herself would have talked, to much better effect, had she been present.

The General gave her a grave and friendly attention. Few men had done sterner or more daring feats in the field. Yet here he sat, relaxed, courteous, kind, trusting his companions simply, as it was his instinct to trust all women. Julie's heart beat fast. What an exciting, what an important evening!...

Suddenly there was a voice in her ear.

"Do you know, I think we ought to clear out. It must be close on midnight."

She looked up, startled, to see Jacob Delafield. His expression--of doubt or discomfort--recalled her at once to the realities of her own situation.

But before she could reply, a sound struck on her ear. She sprang to her feet.

"What was that?" she said.

A voice was heard in the hall.

Julie Le Breton caught the chair behind her, and Delafield saw her turn pale. But before she or he could speak again, the door of the library was thrown open.

"Good Heavens!" said Montresor, springing to his feet. "Lady Henry!"

M. du Bartas lifted astonished eyes. On the threshold of the room stood an old lady, leaning heavily on two sticks. She was deathly pale, and her fierce eyes blazed upon the scene before her. Within the bright, fire-lit room the social comedy was being played at its best; but here surely was Tragedy--or Fate. Who was she? What did it mean?

The Duchess rushed to her, and fell, of course, upon the one thing she should not have said.

"Oh, Aunt Flora, dear Aunt Flora! But we thought you were too ill to come down!"

"So I perceive," said Lady Henry, putting her aside. "So you, and this lady"--she pointed a shaking finger at Julie--"have held my reception for me. I am enormously obliged. You have also"--she looked at the coffee-cups--"provided my guests with refreshment. I thank you. I trust my servants have given you satisfaction.

"Gentlemen"--she turned to the rest of the company, who stood stupefied--"I fear I cannot ask you to remain with me longer. The hour is late, and I am--as you see--indisposed. But I trust, on some future occasion, I may have the honor--"

She looked round upon them, challenging and defying them all.

Montresor went up to her.

"My dear old friend, let me introduce to you M. du Bartas, of the French Foreign Office."

At this appeal to her English hospitality and her social chivalry, Lady Henry looked grimly at the Frenchman.

"M. du Bartas, I am charmed to make your acquaintance. With your leave, I will pursue it when I am better able to profit by it. To-morrow I will write to you to propose another meeting--should my health allow."

"Enchanté, madame," murmured the Frenchman, more embarrassed than he had ever been in his life. "Permettez--moi de vous faire mes plus sincères excuses."

"Not at all, monsieur, you owe me none."

Montresor again approached her.

"Let me tell you," he said, imploringly, "how this has happened--how innocent we all are--"

"Another time, if you please," she said, with a most cutting calm. "As I said before, it is late. If I had been equal to entertaining you"--she looked round upon them all--"I should not have told my butler to make my excuses. As it is, I must beg you to allow me to bid you good-night. Jacob, will you kindly get the Duchess her cloak? Good-night. Good-night. As you see"--she pointed to the sticks which supported her--"I have no hands to-night. My infirmities have need of them."

Montresor approached her again, in real and deep distress.

"Dear Lady Henry--"

"Go!" she said, under her breath, looking him in the eyes, and he turned and went without a word. So did the Duchess, whimpering, her hand in Delafield's arm. As she passed Julie, who stood as though turned to stone, she made a little swaying movement towards her.

"Dear Julie!" she cried, imploringly.

But Lady Henry turned.

"You will have every opportunity to-morrow," she said. "As far as I am concerned, Miss Le Breton will have no engagements."

Lord Lackington quietly said, "Good-night, Lady Henry," and, without offering to shake hands, walked past her. As he came to the spot where Julie Le Breton stood, that lady made a sudden, impetuous movement towards him. Strange words were on her lips, a strange expression in her eyes.

"You must help me," she said, brokenly. "It is my right!"

Was that what she said? Lord Lackington looked at her in astonishment. He did not see that Lady Henry was watching them with eagerness, leaning heavily on her sticks, her lips parted in a keen expectancy.

Then Julie withdrew.

"I beg your pardon," she said, hurriedly. "I beg your pardon. Good-night."

Lord Lackington hesitated. His face took a puzzled expression. Then he held out his hand, and she placed hers in it mechanically.

"It will be all right," he whispered, kindly. "Lady Henry will soon be herself again. Shall I tell the butler to call for some one--her maid?"

Julie shook her head, and in another moment he, too, was gone. Dr. Meredith and General Fergus stood beside her. The General had a keen sense of humor, and as he said good-night to this unlawful hostess, whose plight he understood no more than his own, his mouth twitched with repressed laughter. But Dr. Meredith did not laugh. He pressed Julie's hand in both of his. Looking behind him, he saw that Jacob Delafield, who had just returned from the hall, was endeavoring to appease Lady Henry. He bent towards Julie.

"Don't deceive yourself," he said, quickly, in a low voice; "this is the end. Remember my letter. Let me hear to-morrow."

As Dr. Meredith left the room, Julie lifted her eyes. Only Jacob Delafield and Lady Henry were left.

Harry Warkworth, too, was gone--without a word? She looked round her piteously. She could not remember that he had spoken--that he had bade her farewell. A strange pang convulsed her. She scarcely heard what Lady Henry was saying to Jacob Delafield. Yet the words were emphatic enough.

"Much obliged to you, Jacob. But when I want your advice in my household affairs, I will ask it. You and Evelyn Crowborough have meddled a good deal too much in them already. Good-night. Hutton will get you a cab."

And with a slight but imperious gesture, Lady Henry motioned towards the door. Jacob hesitated, then quietly took his departure. He threw Julie a look of anxious appeal as he went out. But she did not see it; her troubled gaze was fixed on Lady Henry.

That lady eyed her companion with composure, though by now even the old lips were wholly blanched.

"There is really no need for any conversation between us, Miss Le Breton," said the familiar voice. "But if there were, I am not to-night, as you see, in a condition to say it. So--when you came up to say good-night to me--you had determined on this adventure? You had been good enough, I see, to rearrange my room--to give my servants your orders."

Julie stood stonily erect. She made her dry lips answer as best they could.

"We meant no harm," she said, coldly. "It all came about very simply. A few people came in to inquire after you. I regret they should have stayed talking so long."

Lady Henry smiled in contempt.

"You hardly show your usual ability by these remarks. The room you stand in"--she glanced significantly at the lights and the chairs--"gives you the lie. You had planned it all with Hutton, who has become your tool, before you came to me. Don't contradict. It distresses me to hear you.

Well, now we part."

"Of course. Perhaps to-morrow you will allow me a few last words?"

"I think not. This will cost me dear," said Lady Henry, her white lips twitching. "Say them now, mademoiselle."

"You are suffering." Julie made an uncertain step forward. "You ought to be in bed."

"That has nothing to do with it. What was your object to-night?"

"I wished to see the Duchess--"

"It is not worth while to prevaricate. The Duchess was not your first visitor."

Julie flushed.

"Captain Warkworth arrived first; that was a mere chance."

"It was to see him that you risked the whole affair. You have used my house for your own intrigues."

Julie felt herself physically wavering under the lash of these sentences. But with a great effort she walked towards the fireplace, recovered her gloves and handkerchief, which were on the mantel-piece, and then turned slowly to Lady Henry.

"I have done nothing in your service that I am ashamed of. On the contrary, I have borne what no one else would have borne. I have devoted myself to you and your interests, and you have trampled upon and tortured me. For you I have been merely a servant, and an inferior--"

Lady Henry nodded grimly.

"It is true," she said, interrupting, "I was not able to take your romantic view of the office of companion."

"You need only have taken a human view," said Julie, in a voice that pierced; "I was alone, poor--worse than motherless. You might have done what you would with me. A little indulgence, and I should have been your devoted slave. But you chose to humiliate and crush me; and in return, to protect myself, I, in defending myself, have been led, I admit it, into taking liberties. There is no way out of it. I shall, of course, leave you to-morrow morning."

"Then at last we understand each other," said Lady Henry, with a laugh. "Good-night, Miss Le Breton."

She moved heavily on her sticks. Julie stood aside to let her pass. One of the sticks slipped a little on the polished floor. Julie, with a cry, ran forward, but Lady Henry fiercely motioned her aside.

"Don't touch me! Don't come near me!"

She paused a moment to recover breath and balance. Then she resumed her difficult walk. Julie followed her.

"Kindly put out the electric lights," said Lady Henry, and Julie obeyed.

They entered the hall in which one little light was burning. Lady Henry, with great difficulty, and panting, began to pull herself up the stairs.

"Oh, do let me help you!" said Julie, in an agony. "You will kill yourself. Let me at least call Dixon."

"You will do nothing of the kind," said Lady Henry, indomitable, though tortured by weakness and rheumatism. "Dixon is in my room, where I bade her remain. You should have thought of the consequences of this before you embarked upon it. If I were to die in mounting these stairs, I would not let you help me."

"Oh!" cried Julie, as though she had been struck, and hid her eyes with her hand.

Slowly, laboriously, Lady Henry dragged herself from step to step. As she turned the corner of the staircase, and could therefore be no longer seen from below, some one softly opened the door of the dining-room and entered the hall.

Julie looked round her, startled. She saw Jacob Delafield, who put his finger to his lip.

Moved by a sudden impulse, she bowed her head on the banister of the stairs against which she was leaning and broke into stifled sobs.

Jacob Delafield came up to her and took her hand. She felt his own tremble, and yet its grasp was firm and supporting.

"Courage!" he said, bending over her. "Try not to give way. You will want all your fortitude."

"Listen!" She gasped, trying vainly to control herself, and they both listened to the sounds above them in the dark house--the labored breath, the slow, painful step.

"Oh, she wouldn't let me help her. She said she would rather die. Perhaps I have killed her. And I could--I could--yes, I could have loved her."

She was in an anguish of feeling--of sharp and penetrating remorse.

Jacob Delafield held her hand close in his, and when at last the sounds had died in the distance he lifted it to his lips.

"You know that I am your friend and servant," he said, in a queer, muffled voice. "You promised I should be."

She tried to withdraw her hand, but only feebly. Neither physically nor mentally had she the strength to repulse him. If he had taken her in his arms, she could hardly have resisted. But he did not attempt to conquer more than her hand. He stood beside her, letting her feel the whole mute, impetuous offer of his manhood--thrown at her feet to do what she would with.

Presently, when once more she moved away, he said to her, in a whisper:

"Go to the Duchess to-morrow morning, as soon as you can get away. She told me to say that-- Hutton gave me a little note from her. Your home must be with her till we can all settle what is best. You know very well you have devoted friends. But now good-night. Try to sleep. Evelyn and I will do all we can with Lady Henry."

Julie drew herself out of his hold. "Tell Evelyn I will come to see her, at any rate, as soon as I can put my things together. Good-night."

And she, too, dragged herself up-stairs sobbing, starting at every shadow. All her nerve and daring were gone. The thought that she must spend yet another night under the roof of this old woman who hated her filled her with terror. When she reached her room she locked her door and wept for hours in a forlorn and aching misery.

X

The Duchess was in her morning-room. On the rug, in marked and, as it seemed to her plaintive eyes, brutal contrast with the endless photographs of her babies and women friends which crowded her mantel-piece, stood the Duke, much out of temper. He was a powerfully built man, some twenty years older than his wife, with a dark complexion, enlivened by ruddy cheeks and prominent, red lips. His eyes were of a cold, clear gray; his hair very black, thick, and wiry. An extremely vigorous person, more than adequately aware of his own importance, tanned and seasoned by the life of his class, by the yachting, hunting, and shooting in which his own existence was largely spent, slow in perception, and of a sulky temper--so one might have read him at first sight. But these impressions only took you a certain way in judging the character of the Duchess's husband.

As to the sulkiness, there could be no question on this particular morning--though, indeed, his ill-humor deserved a more positive and energetic name.

"You have got yourself and me," he was declaring, "into a most disagreeable and unnecessary scrape. This letter of Lady Henry's"--he held it up--"is one of the most annoying that I have received for many a day. Lady Henry seems to me perfectly justified. You have been behaving in a quite unwarrantable way. And now you tell me that this woman, who is the cause of it all, of whose conduct I thoroughly and entirely disapprove, is coming to stay here, in my house, whether I like it or not, and you expect me to be civil to her. If you persist, I shall go down to Brackmoor till she is pleased to depart. I won't countenance the thing at all, and, whatever you may do, I shall apologize to Lady Henry."

"There's nothing to apologize for," cried the drooping Duchess, plucking up a little spirit. "Nobody meant any harm. Why shouldn't the old friends go in to ask after her? Hutton--that old butler that has been with Aunt Flora for twenty years--asked us to come in."

"Then he did what he had no business to do, and he deserves to be dismissed at a day's notice. Why, Lady Henry tells me that it was a regular party--that the room was all arranged for it by that most audacious young woman--that the servants were ordered about--that it lasted till nearly midnight, and that the noise you all made positively woke Lady Henry out of her sleep. Really, Evelyn, that you should have been mixed up in such an affair is more unpalatable to me than I can find words to describe." And he paced, fuming, up and down before her.

"Anybody else than Aunt Flora would have laughed," said the Duchess, defiantly. "And I declare, Freddie, I won't be scolded in such a tone. Besides, if you only knew--"

She threw back her head and looked at him, her cheeks flushed, her lips quivering with a secret that, once out, would perhaps silence him at once--would, at any rate, as children do when they give a shake to their spillikins, open up a number of new chances in the game.

"If I only knew what?"

The Duchess pulled at the hair of the little spitz on her lap without replying.

"What is there to know that I don't know?" insisted the Duke. "Something that makes the matter still worse, I suppose?"

"Well, that depends," said the Duchess, reflectively. A gleam of mischief had slipped into her face, though for a moment the tears had not been far off.

The Duke looked at his watch.

"Don't keep me here guessing riddles longer than you can help," he said, impatiently. "I have an appointment in the City at twelve, and I want to discuss with you the letter that must be written to Lady Henry."

"That's your affair," said the Duchess. "I haven't made up my mind yet whether I mean to write at all. And as for the riddle, Freddie, you've seen Miss Le Breton?"

"Once. I thought her a very pretentious person," said the Duke, stiffly.

"I know--you didn't get on. But, Freddie, didn't she remind you of somebody?"

The Duchess was growing excited. Suddenly she jumped up; the little spitz rolled off her lap; she ran to her husband and took him by the fronts of his coat.

"Freddie, you'll be very much astonished." And suddenly releasing him, she began to search among the photographs on the mantel-piece. "Freddie, you know who that is?" She held up a picture.

"Of course I know. What on earth has that got to do with the subject we have been discussing?"

"Well, it has a good deal to do with it," said the Duchess, slowly. "That's my uncle, George Chantrey, isn't it, Lord Lackington's second son, who married mamma's sister? Well--oh, you won't like it, Freddie, but you've got to know--that's--Julie's uncle, too!"

"What in the name of fortune do you mean?" said the Duke, staring at her.

His wife again caught him by the coat, and, so imprisoning him, she poured out her story very fast, very incoherently, and with a very evident uncertainty as to what its effect might be.

And indeed the effect was by no means easy to determine. The Duke was first incredulous, then bewildered by the very mixed facts which she poured out upon him. He tried to cross-examine her en route, but he gained little by that; she only shook him a little, insisting the more vehemently on telling the story her own way. At last their two impatiences had nearly come to a dead-lock. But the Duke managed to free himself physically, and so regained a little freedom of mind.

"Well, upon my word," he said, as he resumed his march up and down--"upon my word!" Then, as he stood still before her, "You say she is Marriott Dalrymple's daughter?"

"And Lord Lackington's granddaughter." said the Duchess, panting a little from her exertions. "And, oh, what a blind bat you were not to see it at once--from the likeness!"

"As if one had any right to infer such a thing from a likeness!" said the Duke, angrily. "Really, Evelyn, your talk is most--most unbecoming. It seems to me that Mademoiselle Le Breton has already done you harm. All that you have told me, supposing it to be true--oh, of course, I know you believe it to be true--only makes me"--he stiffened his back--"the more determined to break off the connection between her and you. A woman of such antecedents is not a fit companion for my wife, independently of the fact that she seems to be, in herself, an intriguing and dangerous character."

"How could she help her antecedents?" cried the Duchess.

"I didn't say she could help them. But if they are what you say, she ought--well, she ought to be all the more careful to live in a modest and retired way, instead of, as I understand, making herself the rival of Lady Henry. I never heard anything so preposterous--so--so indecent! She shows no proper sense, and, as for you, I deeply regret you should have been brought into any contact with such a disgraceful story."

"Freddie!" The Duchess went into a helpless, half-hysterical fit of laughter.

But the Duke merely expanded, as it seemed, still further--to his utmost height and bulk. "Oh, dear," thought the Duchess, in despair, "now he is going to be like his mother!" Her strictly Evangelical mother-in-law, with whom the Duke had made his bachelor home for many years, had been the scourge of her early married life; and though for Freddie's sake she had shed a few tears over her death, eighteen months before this date, the tears--as indeed the Duke had thought at the time--had been only too quickly dried.

There could be no question about it, the Duke was painfully like his mother as he replied:

"I fear that your education, Evelyn, has led you to take such things far more lightly than you ought. I am old-fashioned. Illegitimacy with me does carry a stigma, and the sins of the fathers are visited upon the children. At any rate, we who occupy a prominent social place have no right to do anything which may lead others to think lightly of God's law. I am sorry to speak plainly, Evelyn. I dare say you don't like these sentiments, but you know, at least, that I am quite honest in expressing them."

The Duke turned to her, not without dignity. He was and had been from his boyhood a person of irreproachable morals--earnest and religious according to his lights, a good son, husband, and father. His wife looked at him with mingled feelings.

"Well, all I know is," she said, passionately beating her little foot on the carpet before her, "that, by all accounts, the only thing to do with Colonel Delaney was to run away from him."

The Duke shrugged his shoulders.

"You don't expect me to be much moved by a remark of that kind? As to this lady, your story does not affect me in her favor in the smallest degree. She has had her education; Lord Lackington gives her one hundred pounds a year; if she is a self-respecting woman she will look after herself. I don't want to have her here, and I beg you won't invite her. A couple of nights, perhaps--I don't mind that--but not for longer."

"Oh, as to that, you may be very sure she won't stay here unless you're very particularly nice to her. There'll be plenty of people glad--enchanted--to have her! I don't care about that, but what I do want is"--the Duchess looked up with calm audacity--"that you should find her a house."

The Duke paused in his walk and surveyed his wife with amazement.

"Evelyn, are you quite mad?"

"Not in the least. You have more houses than you know what to do with, and a great deal more money than anybody in the world ought to have. If they ever do set up the guillotine at Hyde Park Corner, we shall be among the first--we ought to be!"

"What is the good of talking nonsense like this, Evelyn?" said the Duke, once more consulting his watch. "Let's go back to the subject of my letter to Lady Henry."

"It's most excellent sense!" cried the Duchess, springing up. "You have more houses than you know what to do with; and you have one house in particular--that little place at the back of Cureton Street where Cousin Mary Leicester lived so long--which is in your hands still, I know, for you told me so last week--which is vacant and furnished--Cousin Mary left you the furniture, as if we hadn't got enough!--and it would be the very thing for Julie, if only you'd lend it to her till she can turn round."

The Duchess was now standing up, confronting her lord, her hands grasping the chair behind her, her small form alive with eagerness and the feminine determination to get her own way, by fair means or foul.

"Cureton Street!" said the Duke, almost at the end of his tether. "And how do you propose that this young woman is to live--in Cureton Street, or anywhere else?"

"She means to write," said the Duchess, shortly. "Dr. Meredith has promised her work."

"Sheer lunacy! In six months time you'd have to step in and pay all her bills."

"I should like to see anybody dare to propose to Julie to pay her bills!" cried the Duchess, with scorn. "You see, the great pity is, Freddie, that you don't know anything at all about her. But that house--wasn't it made out of a stable? It has got six rooms, I know--three bedrooms up-stairs, and two sitting-rooms and a kitchen below. With one good maid and a boy Julie could be perfectly comfortable. She would earn four hundred pounds--Dr. Meredith has promised her--she has one hundred pounds a year of her own. She would pay no rent, of course. She would have just enough to live on, poor, dear thing! And she would be able to gather her old friends round her when she wanted them. A cup of tea and her delightful conversation--that's all they'd ever want."

"Oh, go on--go on!" said the Duke, throwing himself exasperated into an arm-chair; "the ease with which you dispose of my property on behalf of a young woman who has caused me most acute annoyance, who has embroiled us with a near relation for whom I have a very particular respect! Her friends, indeed! Lady Henry's friends, you mean. Poor Lady Henry tells me in this letter that her circle will be completely scattered. This mischievous woman in three years has destroyed what it has taken Lady Henry nearly thirty to build up. Now look here, Evelyn"--the Duke sat up and slapped his knee--"as to this Cureton Street plan, I will do nothing of the kind. You may have Miss Le Breton here for two or three nights if you like--I shall probably go down to the country--and, of course, I have no objection to make if you wish to help her find another situation--"

"Another situation!" cried the Duchess, beside herself. "Freddie, you really are impossible! Do you understand that I regard Julie Le Breton as my relation, whatever you may say--that I love her dearly--that there are fifty people with money and influence ready to help her if you won't, because she is one of the most charming and distinguished women in London--that you ought to be proud to do her a service--that I want you to have the honor of it--there! And if you won't do this little favor for me--when I ask and beg it of you--I'll make you remember it for a very long time to come--you may be sure of that!"

And his wife turned upon him as an image of war, her fair hair ruffling about her ears, her cheeks and eyes brilliant with anger--and something more.

The Duke rose in silent ferocity and sought for some letters which he had left on the mantel-piece.

"I had better leave you to come to your senses by yourself, and as quickly as possible," he said, as he put them into his pockets. "No good can come of any more discussion of this sort."

The Duchess said nothing. She looked out of the window busily, and bit her lip. Her silence served her better than her speech, for suddenly the Duke looked round, hesitated, threw down a book he carried, walked up to her, and took her in his arms.

"You are a very foolish child," he declared, as he held her by main force and kissed away her tears. "You make me lose my temper--and waste my time--for nothing."

"Not at all," said the sobbing Duchess, trying to push herself away, and denying him, as best she could, her soft, flushed face. "You don't, or you won't, understand! I was--I was very fond of Uncle George Chantrey. He would have helped Julie if he were alive. And as for you, you're Lord Lackington's godson, and you're always preaching what he's done for the army, and what the nation owes him--and--and--"

"Does he know?" said the Duke, abruptly, marvelling at the irrelevance of these remarks.

"No, not a word. Only six people in London know--Aunt Flora, Sir Wilfrid Bury"--the Duke made an exclamation--"Mr. Montresor, Jacob, you, and I."

"Jacob!" said the Duke. "What's he got to do with it?"

The Duchess suddenly saw her opportunity, and rushed upon it.

"Only that he's madly in love with her, that's all. And, to my knowledge, she has refused him both last year and this. Of course, naturally, if you won't do anything to help her, she'll probably marry him--simply as a way out."

"Well, of all the extraordinary affairs!"

The Duke released her, and stood bewildered. The Duchess watched him in some excitement. He was about to speak, when there was a sound in the anteroom. They moved hastily apart. The door was thrown open, and the footman announced, "Miss Le Breton."

Julie Le Breton entered, and stood a moment on the threshold, looking, not in embarrassment, but with a certain hesitation, at the two persons whose conversation she had disturbed. She was pale with sleeplessness; her look was sad and weary. But never had she been more composed, more elegant. Her closely fitting black cloth dress; her strangely expressive face, framed by a large hat, very simple, but worn as only the woman of fashion knows how; her miraculous yet most graceful slenderness; the delicacy of her hands; the natural dignity of her movements--these things produced an immediate, though, no doubt, conflicting impression upon the gentleman who had just been denouncing her. He bowed, with an involuntary deference which he had not at all meant to show to Lady Henry's insubordinate companion, and then stood frowning.

But the Duchess ran forward, and, quite heedless of her husband, threw herself into her friend's arms.

"Oh, Julie, is there anything left of you? I hardly slept a wink for thinking of you. What did that old--oh, I forgot--do you know my husband? Freddie, this is my great friend, Miss Le

Breton."

The Duke bowed again, silently. Julie looked at him, and then, still holding the Duchess by the hand, she approached him, a pair of very fine and pleading eyes fixed upon his face.

"You have probably heard from Lady Henry, have you not?" she said, addressing him. "In a note I had from her this morning she told me she had written to you. I could not help coming to-day, because Evelyn has been so kind. But--is it your wish that I should come here?"

The Christian name slipped out unawares, and the Duke winced at it. The likeness to Lord Lackington--it was certainly astonishing. There ran through his mind the memory of a visit paid long ago to his early home by Lord Lackington and two daughters, Rose and Blanche. He, the Duke, had then been a boy home from school. The two girls, one five or six years older than the other, had been the life and charm of the party. He remembered hunting with Lady Rose.

But the confusion in his mind had somehow to be mastered, and he made an effort.

"I shall be glad if my wife is able to be of any assistance to you, Miss Le Breton," he said, coldly; "but it would not be honest if I were to conceal my opinion--so far as I have been able to form it--that Lady Henry has great and just cause of complaint."

"You are quite right--quite right," said Julie, almost with eagerness. "She has, indeed."

The Duke was taken by surprise. Imperious as he was, and stiffened by a good many of those petty prides which the spoiled children of the world escape so hardly, he found himself hesitating--groping for his words.

The Duchess meanwhile drew Julie impulsively towards a chair.

"Do sit down. You look so tired."

But Julie's gaze was still bent upon the Duke. She restrained her friend's eager hand, and the Duke collected himself. He brought a chair, and Julie seated herself.

"I am deeply, deeply distressed about Lady Henry," she said, in a low voice, by which the Duke felt himself most unwillingly penetrated. "I don't--oh no, indeed, I don't defend last night. Only--my position has been very difficult lately. I wanted very much to see the Duchess--and--it was natural--wasn't it?--that the old friends should like to be personally informed about Lady Henry's illness? But, of course, they stayed too long; it was my fault--I ought to have prevented it."

She paused. This stern-looking man, who stood with his back to the mantel-piece regarding her, Philistine though he was, had yet a straight, disinterested air, from which she shrank a little. Honestly, she would have liked to tell him the truth. But how could she? She did her best, and her account certainly was no more untrue than scores of narratives of social incident which issue every day from lips the most respected and the most veracious. As for the Duchess, she thought it the height of candor and generosity. The only thing she could have wished, perhaps, in her inmost heart, was that she had not found Julie alone with Harry Warkworth. But her loyal lips would have suffered torments rather than accuse or betray her friend.

The Duke meanwhile went through various phases of opinion as Julie laid her story before him. Perhaps he was chiefly affected by the tone of quiet independence--as from equal to equal--in which she addressed him. His wife's cousin by marriage; the granddaughter of an old and intimate friend of his own family; the daughter of a man known at one time throughout Europe, and himself amply well born--all these facts, warm, living, and still efficacious, stood, as it were, behind this manner of hers, prompting and endorsing it. But, good Heavens! was illegitimacy to be as legitimacy?--to carry with it no stains and penalties? Was vice to be virtue, or as good? The Duke rebelled.

"It is a most unfortunate affair, of that there can be no doubt," he said, after a moment's silence, when Julie had brought her story to an end; and then, more sternly, "I shall certainly apologize for my wife's share in it."

"Lady Henry won't be angry with the Duchess long," said Julie Le Breton. "As for me"--her voice sank--"my letter this morning was returned to me unopened."

There was an uncomfortable pause; then Julie resumed, in another tone:

"But what I am now chiefly anxious to discuss is, how can we save Lady Henry from any further pain or annoyance? She once said to me in a fit of anger that if I left her in consequence of a quarrel, and any of her old friends sided with me, she would never see them again."

"I know," said the Duke, sharply. "Her salon will break up. She already foresees it."

"But why?--why?" cried Julie, in a most becoming distress. "Somehow, we must prevent it. Unfortunately I must live in London. I have the offer of work here--journalist's work which cannot be done in the country or abroad. But I would do all I could to shield Lady Henry."

"What about Mr. Montresor?" said the Duke, abruptly. Montresor had been the well-known Châteaubriand to Lady Henry's Madame Récamier for more than a generation.

Julie turned to him with eagerness.

"Mr. Montresor wrote to me early this morning. The letter reached me at breakfast. In Mrs. Montresor's name and his own, he asked me to stay with them till my plans developed. He--he was kind enough to say he felt himself partly responsible for last night."

"And you replied?" The Duke eyed her keenly.

Julie sighed and looked down.

"I begged him not to think any more of me in the matter, but to write at once to Lady Henry. I hope he has done so."

"And so you refused--excuse these questions--Mrs. Montresor's invitation?"

The working of the Duke's mind was revealed in his drawn and puzzled brows.

"Certainly." The speaker looked at him with surprise. "Lady Henry would never have forgiven that. It could not be thought of. Lord Lackington also"--but her voice wavered.

"Yes?" said the Duchess, eagerly, throwing herself on a stool at Julie's feet and looking up into her face.

"He, too, has written to me. He wants to help me. But--I can't let him."

The words ended in a whisper. She leaned back in her chair, and put her handkerchief to her eyes. It was very quietly done, and very touching. The Duchess threw a lightning glance at her husband; and then, possessing herself of one of Julie's hands, she kissed it and murmured over it.

"Was there ever such a situation?" thought the Duke, much shaken. "And she has already, if Evelyn is to be believed, refused the chance--the practical certainty--of being Duchess of

Chudleigh!"

He was a man with whom a gran rifiuto of this kind weighed heavily. His moral sense exacted such things rather of other people than himself. But, when made, he could appreciate them.

After a few turns up and down the room, he walked up to the two women.

"Miss Le Breton," he said, in a far more hurried tone than was usual to him, "I cannot approve--and Evelyn ought not to approve--of much that has taken place during your residence with Lady Henry. But I understand that your post was not an easy one, and I recognize the forbearance of your present attitude. Evelyn is much distressed about it all. On the understanding that you will do what you can to soften this breach for Lady Henry, I shall be, glad if you will allow me to come partially to your assistance."

Julie looked up gravely, her eyebrows lifting. The Duke found himself reddening as he went on.

"I have a little house near here--a little furnished house--Evelyn will explain to you. It happens to be vacant. If you will accept a loan of it, say for six months"--the Duchess frowned--"you will give me pleasure. I will explain my action to Lady Henry, and endeavor to soften her feelings."

He paused. Miss Le Breton's face was grateful, touched with emotion, but more than hesitating.

"You are very good. But I have no claim upon you at all. And I can support myself."

A touch of haughtiness slipped into her manner as she gently rose to her feet. "Thank God, I did not offer her money!" thought the Duke, strangely perturbed.

"Julie, dear Julie," implored the Duchess. "It's such a tiny little place, and it is quite musty for want of living in. Nobody has set foot in it but the caretaker for two years, and it would be really a kindness to us to go and live there--wouldn't it, Freddie? And there's all the furniture just as it was, down to the bellows and the snuffers. If you'd only use it and take care of it; Freddie hasn't liked to sell it, because it's all old family stuff, and he was very fond of Cousin Mary Leicester. Oh, do say yes, Julie! They shall light the fires, and I'll send in a few sheets and things, and you'll feel as though you'd been there for years. Do, Julie!"

Julie shook her head.

"I came here," she said, in a voice that was still unsteady, "to ask for advice, not favors. But it's very good of you."

And with trembling fingers she began to refasten her veil.

"Julie!--where are you going?" cried the Duchess "You're staying here."

"Staying here?" said Julie, turning round upon her. "Do you think I should be a burden upon you, or any one?"

"But, Julie, you told Jacob you would come."

"I have come. I wanted your sympathy, and your counsel. I wished also to confess myself to the Duke, and to point out to him how matters could be made easier for Lady Henry."

The penitent, yet dignified, sadness of her manner and voice completed the discomfiture--the temporary discomfiture--of the Duke.

"Miss Le Breton," he said, abruptly, coming to stand beside her, "I remember your mother."

Julie's eyes filled. Her hand still held her veil, but it paused in its task.

"I was a small school-boy when she stayed with us," resumed the Duke. "She was a beautiful girl. She let me go out hunting with her. She was very kind to me, and I thought her a kind of goddess. When I first heard her story, years afterwards, it shocked me awfully. For her sake, accept my offer. I don't think lightly of such actions as your mother's--not at all. But I can't bear to think of her daughter alone and friendless in London."

Yet even as he spoke he seemed to be listening to another person. He did not himself understand the feelings which animated him, nor the strength with which his recollections of Lady Rose had suddenly invaded him.

Julie leaned her arms on the mantel-piece, and hid her face. She had turned her back to them, and they saw that she was crying softly.

The Duchess crept up to her and wound her arms round her.

"You will, Julie!--you will! Lady Henry has turned you out-of-doors at a moment's notice. And it was a great deal my fault. You must let us help you!"

Julie did not answer, but, partially disengaging herself, and without looking at him, she held out her hand to the Duke.

He pressed it with a cordiality that amazed him.

"That's right--that's right. Now, Evelyn, I leave you to make the arrangements. The keys shall be here this afternoon. Miss Le Breton, of course, stays here till things are settled. As for me, I must really be off to my meeting. One thing, Miss Le Breton--"

"Yes."

"I think," he said, gravely, "you ought to reveal yourself to Lord Lackington."

She shrank.

"You'll let me take my own time for that?" was her appealing reply.

"Very well--very well. We'll speak of it again."

And he hurried away. As he descended his own stairs astonishment at what he had done rushed upon him and overwhelmed him.

"How on earth am I ever to explain the thing to Lady Henry?"

And as he went citywards in his cab, he felt much more guilty than his wife had ever done. What could have made him behave in this extraordinary, this preposterous way? A touch of foolish romance--immoral romance--of which he was already ashamed? Or the one bare fact that this woman had refused Jacob Delafield?

XI

"Here it is," said the Duchess, as the carriage stopped. "Isn't it an odd little place?"

And as she and Julie paused on the pavement, Julie looked listlessly at her new home. It was a two-storied brick house, built about 1780. The front door boasted a pair of Ionian columns and a classical canopy or pediment. The windows had still the original small panes; the mansarde roof, with its one dormer, was untouched. The little house had rather deep eaves; three windows above; two, and the front door, below. It wore a prim, old-fashioned air, a good deal softened and battered, however, by age, and it stood at the corner of two streets, both dingily quiet, and destined, no doubt, to be rebuilt before long in the general rejuvenation of Mayfair.

As the Duchess had said, it occupied the site of what had once--about 1740--been the westerly end of a mews belonging to houses in Cureton Street, long since pulled down. The space filled by these houses was now occupied by one great mansion and its gardens. The rest of the mews had been converted into three-story houses of a fair size, looking south, with a back road between them and the gardens of Cureton House. But at the southwesterly corner of what was now Heribert Street, fronting west and quite out of line and keeping with the rest, was this curious little place, built probably at a different date and for some special family reason. The big planes in the Cureton House gardens came close to it and overshadowed it; one side wall of the house, in fact, formed part of the wall of the garden.

The Duchess, full of nervousness, ran up the steps, put in the key herself, and threw open the door. An elderly Scotchwoman, the caretaker, appeared from the back and stood waiting to show them over.

"Oh, Julie, perhaps it's too queer and musty!" cried the Duchess, looking round her in some dismay. "I thought, you know, it would be a little out-of-the-way and quaint--unlike other people--just what you ought to have. But--"

"I think it's delightful," said Julie, standing absently before a case of stuffed birds, somewhat moth-eaten, which took up a good deal of space in the little hall. "I love stuffed birds."

The Duchess glanced at her uneasily. "What is she thinking about?" she wondered. But Julie roused herself.

"Why, it looks as though everything here had gone to sleep for a hundred years," she said, gazing in astonishment at the little hall, with its old clock, its two or three stiff hunting-pictures, its drab-painted walls, its poker-work chest.

And the drawing-room! The caretaker had opened the windows. It was a mild March day, and there were misty sun-gleams stealing along the lawns of Cureton House. None entered the room itself, for its two semi-circular windows looked north over the gardens. Yet it was not uncheerful. Its faded curtains of blue rep, its buff walls, on which the pictures and miniatures in their tarnished gilt frames were arranged at intervals in stiff patterns and groups; the Italian glass, painted with dilapidated Cupids, over the mantel-piece; the two or three Sheraton arm-chairs and settees, covered with threadbare needle-work from the days of "Evelina"; a carpet of old and well-preserved Brussels--blue arabesques on a white ground; one or two pieces of old satin-wood furniture, very fine and perfect; a heavy centre-table, its cloth garnished with some early Victorian wool-work, and a pair of pink glass vases; on another small table close by, of a most dainty and spindle-legged correctness, a set of Indian chessmen under a glass shade; and on another a collection of tiny animals, stags and dogs for the most part, deftly "pinched" out of soft paper, also under glass, and as perfect as when their slender limbs were first fashioned by Cousin Mary Leicester's mother, somewhere about the year that Marie Antoinette mounted the scaffold. These various elements, ugly and beautiful, combined to make a general effect--clean, fastidious, frugal, and refined--that was, in truth, full of a sort of acid charm.

"Oh, I like it! I like it so much!" cried Julie, throwing herself down into one of the straight-backed arm-chairs and looking first round the walls and then through the windows to the gardens outside.

"My dear," said the Duchess, flitting from one thing to another, frowning and a little fussed, "those curtains won't do at all. I must send some from home."

"No, no, Evelyn. Not a thing shall be changed. You shall lend it me just as it is or not at all. What a character it has! I taste the person who lived here."

"Cousin Mary Leicester?" said the Duchess. "Well, she was rather an oddity. She was Low Church, like my mother-in-law; but, oh, so much nicer! Once I let her come to Grosvenor Square and speak to the servants about going to church. The groom of the chambers said she was 'a dear old lady, and if she were his cousin he wouldn't mind her being a bit touched,' My maid said she had no idea poke-bonnets could be so sweet. It made her understand what the Queen looked like when she was young. And none of them have ever been to church since that I can make out. There was one very curious thing about Cousin Mary Leicester," added the Duchess, slowly-- "she had second sight. She saw her old mother, in this room, once or twice, after she had been dead for years. And she saw Freddie once, when he was away on a long voyage--"

"Ghosts, too!" said Julie, crossing her hands before her with a little shiver--"that completes it."

"Sixty years," said the Duchess, musing. "It was a long time--wasn't it?--to live in this little house, and scarcely ever leave it. Oh, she had quite a circle of her own. For many years her funny little sister lived here, too. And there was a time, Freddie says, when there was almost a rivalry between them and two other famous old ladies who lived in Bruton Street--what was their name? Oh, the Miss Berrys! Horace Walpole's Miss Berrys. All sorts of famous people, I believe, have sat in these chairs. But the Miss Berrys won."

"Not in years? Cousin Mary outlived them."

"Ah, but she was dead long before she died," said the Duchess as she came to perch on the arm of Julie's chair, and threw her arm round her friend's neck. "After her little sister departed this life she became a very silent, shrivelled thing--except for her religion--and very few people saw her. She took a fancy to me--which was odd, wasn't it, when I'm such a worldling?--and she let me come in and out. Every morning she read the Psalms and Lessons, with her old maid, who was just her own age--in this very chair. And two or three times a month Freddie would slip round and read them with her--you know Freddie's very religious. And then she'd work at flannel petticoats for the poor, or something of that kind, till lunch. Afterwards she'd go and read the

Bible to people in the workhouse or in hospital. When she came home, the butler brought her the Times; and sometimes you'd find her by the fire, straining her old eyes over 'a little Dante.' And she always dressed for dinner--everything was quite smart--and her old butler served her. Afterwards her maid played dominoes or spillikins with her--all her life she never touched a card--and they read a chapter, and Cousin Mary played a hymn on that funny little old piano there in the corner, and at ten they all went to bed. Then, one morning, the maid went in to wake her, and she saw her dear sharp nose and chin against the light, and her hands like that, in front of her--and--well, I suppose, she'd gone to play hymns in heaven--dear Cousin Mary! Julie, isn't it strange the kind of lives so many of us have to lead? Julie"--the little Duchess laid her cheek against her friend's--"do you believe in another life?"

"You forget I'm a Catholic," said Julie, smiling rather doubtfully.

"Are you, Julie? I'd forgotten."

"The good nuns at Bruges took care of that."

"Do you ever go to mass?"

"Sometimes."

"Then you're not a good Catholic, Julie?"

"No," said Julie, after a pause, "not at all. But it sometimes catches hold of me."

The old clock in the hall struck. The Duchess sprang up.

"Oh, Julie, I have got to be at Clarisse's by four. I promised her I'd go and settle about my Drawing-room dress to-day. Let's see the rest of the house."

And they went rapidly through it. All of it was stamped with the same character, representing, as it were, the meeting-point between an inherited luxury and a personal asceticism. Beautiful chairs, or cabinets transported sixty years before from one of the old Crowborough houses in the country to this little abode, side by side with things the cheapest and the commonest--all that Cousin Mary Leicester could ever persuade herself to buy with her own money. For all the latter part of her life she had been half a mystic and half a great lady, secretly hating the luxury from which she had not the strength to free herself, dressing ceremoniously, as the Duchess had said, for a solitary dinner, and all the while going in sore remembrance of a Master who "had not where to lay his head."

At any rate, there was an ample supply of household stuff for a single woman and her maids. In the china cupboard there were still the old-fashioned Crown Derby services, the costly cut glass, the Leeds and Wedgewood dessert dishes that Cousin Mary Leicester had used for half a century. The caretaker produced the keys of the iron-lined plate cupboard, and showed its old-world contents, clean and in order.

"Why, Julie! If we'd only ordered the dinner I might have come to dine with you to-night!" cried the Duchess, enjoying and peering into everything like a child with its doll's house. "And the linen--gracious!" as the doors of another cupboard were opened to her. "But now I remember, Freddie said nothing was to be touched till he made up his mind what to do with the little place. Why, there's everything!"

And they both looked in astonishment at the white, fragrant rows, at the worn monogram in the corners of the sheets, at the little bags of lavender and pot-pourri ranged along the shelves.

Suddenly Julie turned away and sat down by an open window, carrying her eyes far from the house and its stores.

"It is too much, Evelyn," she said, sombrely. "It oppresses me. I don't think I can live up to it."

"Julie!" and again the little Duchess came to stand caressingly beside her. "Why, you must have sheets--and knives and forks! Why should you get ugly new ones, when you can use Cousin Mary's? She would have loved you to have them."

"She would have hated me with all her strength," said Miss Le Breton, probably with much truth.

The two were silent a little. Through Julie's stormy heart there swept longings and bitternesses inexpressible. What did she care for the little house and all its luxuries! She was sorry that she had fettered herself with it.... Nearly four o'clock in the afternoon, and no letter--not a word!

"Julie," said the Duchess, softly, in her ear, "you know you can't live here alone. I'm afraid Freddie would make a fuss."

"I've thought of that," said Julie, wearily. "But, shall we really go on with it, Evelyn?"

The Duchess looked entreaty. Julie repented, and, drawing her friend towards her, rested her head against the chinchilla cloak.

"I'm tired, I suppose," she said, in a low voice. "Don't think me an ungrateful wretch. Well, there's my foster-sister and her child."

"Madame Bornier and the little cripple girl?" cried the Duchess. "Excellent! Where are they?"

"Léonie is in the French Governesses' Home, as it happens, looking out for a situation, and the child is in the Orthopædic Hospital. They've been straightening her foot. It's wonderfully better, and she's nearly ready to come out."

"Are they nice, Julie?"

"Thérèse is an angel--you must be the one thing or the other, apparently, if you're a cripple. And as for Léonie--well, if she comes here, nobody need be anxious about my finances. She'd count every crust and cinder. We couldn't keep any English servant; but we could get a Belgian one."

"But is she nice?" repeated the Duchess.

"I'm used to her," said Julie, in the same inanimate voice.

Suddenly the clock in the hall below struck four.

"Heavens!" cried the Duchess. "You don't know how Clarisse keeps you to your time. Shall I go on, and send the carriage back for you?"

"Don't trouble about me. I should like to look round me here a little longer."

"You'll remember that some of our fellow-criminals may look in after five? Dr. Meredith and Lord Lackington said, as we were getting away last night--oh, how that doorstep of Aunt Flora's burned my shoes!--that they should come round. And Jacob is coming; he'll stay and dine. And, Julie, I've asked Captain Warkworth to dine to-morrow night."

"Have you? That's noble of you--for you don't like him."

"I don't know him!" cried the Duchess, protesting. "If you like him--of course it's all right. Was he--was he very agreeable last night?" she added, slyly.

"What a word to apply to anybody or anything connected with last night!"

"Are you very sore, Julie?"

"Well, on this very day of being turned out it hurts. I wonder who is writing Lady Henry's letters for her this afternoon?"

"I hope they are not getting written," said the Duchess, savagely; "and that she's missing you abominably. Good-bye--au revoir! If I am twenty minutes late with Clarisse, I sha'n't get any fitting, duchess or no duchess."

And the little creature hurried off; not so fast, however, but that she found time to leave a number of parting instructions as to the house with the Scotch caretaker, on her way to her carriage.

Julie rose and made her way down to the drawing-room again. The Scotchwoman saw that she wanted to be alone and left her.

The windows were still open to the garden outside. Julie examined the paths, the shrubberies, the great plane-trees; she strained her eyes towards the mansion itself. But not much of it could be seen. The little house at the corner had been carefully planted out.

What wealth it implied--that space and size, in London! Evidently the house was still shut up. The people who owned it were now living the same cumbrous, magnificent life in the country which they would soon come up to live in the capital. Honors, parks, money, birth--all were theirs, as naturally as the sun rose. Julie envied and hated the big house and all it stood for; she flung a secret defiance at this coveted and elegant Mayfair that lay around her, this heart of all that is recognized, accepted, carelessly sovereign in our "materialized" upper class.

And yet all the while she knew that it was an unreal and passing defiance. She would not be able in truth to free herself from the ambition to live and shine in this world of the English rich and well born. For, after all, as she told herself with rebellious passion, it was or ought to be her world. And yet her whole being was sore from the experiences of these three years with Lady Henry--from those, above all, of the preceding twenty-four hours. She wove no romance about herself. "I should have dismissed myself long ago," she would have said, contemptuously, to any one who could have compelled the disclosure of her thoughts. But the long and miserable struggle of her self-love with Lady Henry's arrogance, of her gifts with her circumstances; the presence in this very world, where she had gained so marked a personal success, of two clashing estimates of herself, both of which she perfectly understood--the one exalting her, the other merely implying the cool and secret judgment of persons who see the world as it is--these things made a heat and poison in her blood.

She was not good enough, not desirable enough, to be the wife of the man she loved. Here was the plain fact that stung and stung.

Jacob Delafield had thought her good enough! She still felt the pressure of his warm, strong fingers, the touch of his kiss upon her hand. What a paradox was she living in! The Duchess might well ask: why, indeed, had she refused Jacob Delafield--that first time? As to the second refusal, that needed no explanation, at least for herself. When, upon that winter day, now some six weeks past, which had beheld Lady Henry more than commonly tyrannical, and her companion more than commonly weary and rebellious, Delafield's stammered words--as he and she were crossing Grosvenor Square in the January dusk--had struck for the second time upon her ear, she was already under Warkworth's charm. But before--the first time? She had come to Lady Henry firmly determined to marry as soon and as well as she could--to throw off the slur on her life--to regularize her name and place in the world. And then the possible heir of the Chudleighs proposes to her--and she rejects him!

It was sometimes difficult for her now to remember all the whys and wherefores of this strange action of which she was secretly so proud. But the explanation was in truth not far from that she had given to the Duchess. The wild strength in her own nature had divined and shrunk from a similar strength in Delafield's. Here, indeed, one came upon the fact which forever differentiated her from the adventuress, had Sir Wilfrid known. She wanted money and name; there were days when she hungered for them. But she would not give too reckless a price for them. She was a personality, a soul--not a vulgar woman--not merely callous or greedy. She dreaded to be miserable; she had a thirst for happiness, and the heart was, after all, stronger than the head.

Jacob Delafield? No! Her being contracted and shivered at the thought of him. A will tardily developed, if all accounts of his school and college days were true, but now, as she believed, invincible; a mystic; an ascetic; a man under whose modest or careless or self-mocking ways she, with her eye for character, divined the most critical instincts, and a veracity, iron, scarcely human--a man before whom one must be always posing at one's best--that was a personal risk too great to take for a Julie Le Breton.

Unless, indeed, if it came to this--that one must think no more of love--but only of power-- why, then--

A ring at the door, resounding through the quiet side street. After a minute the Scotchwoman opened the drawing-room door.

"Please, miss, is this meant for you?"

Julie took the letter in astonishment. Then through the door she saw a man standing in the hall and recognized Captain Warkworth's Indian servant.

"I don't understand him," said the Scotchwoman, shaking her head.

Julie went out to speak with him. The man had been sent to Crowborough House with instructions to inquire for Miss Le Breton and deliver his note. The groom of the chambers, misinterpreting the man's queer English, and thinking the matter urgent--the note was marked "immediate"--had sent him after the ladies to Heribert Street.

The man was soon feed and dismissed, and Miss Le Breton took the letter back to the drawing-room.

So, after all, he had not failed; there on her lap was her daily letter. Outside the scanty March sun, now just setting, was touching the garden with gold. Had it also found its way into Julie's eyes?

Now for his explanation:

/# "First, how and where are you? I called in Bruton Street at noon. Hutton told me you had just gone to Crowborough House. Kind--no, wise little Duchess! She honors herself in sheltering you.

"I could not write last night--I was too uncertain, too anxious. All I said might have jarred. This morning came your note, about eleven. It was angelic to think so kindly and thoughtfully of a friend--angelic to write such a letter at such a time. You announced your flight to Crowborough House, but did not say when, so I crept to Bruton Street, seeing Lady Henry in every lamp-post, got a few clandestine words with Hutton, and knew, at least, what had happened to you-- outwardly and visibly.

"Last night did you think me a poltroon to vanish as I did? It was the impulse of a moment. Mr. Montresor had pulled me into a corner of the room, away from the rest of the party, nominally to look at a picture, really that I might answer a confidential question he had just put to me with regard to a disputed incident in the Afridi campaign. We were in the dark and partly behind a screen. Then the door opened. I confess the sight of Lady Henry paralyzed me. A great, murderous, six-foot Afridi--that would have been simple enough. But a woman--old and ill and furious--with that Medusa's face--no! My nerves suddenly failed me. What right had I in her house, after all? As she advanced into the room, I slipped out behind her. General Fergus and M. du Bartas joined me in the hall. We walked to Bond Street together. They were divided between laughter and vexation. I should have laughed--if I could have forgotten you.

"But what could I have done for you, dear lady, if I had stayed out the storm? I left you with three or four devoted adherents, who had, moreover, the advantage over me of either relationship or old acquaintance with Lady Henry. Compared to them, I could have done nothing to shield you. Was it not best to withdraw? Yet all the way home I accused myself bitterly. Nor did I feel, when I reached home, that one who had not grasped your hand under fire had any right to rest or sleep. But anxiety for you, regrets for myself, took care of that; I got my deserts.

"After all, when the pricks and pains of this great wrench are over, shall we not all acknowledge that it is best the crash should have come? You have suffered and borne too much. Now we shall see you expand in a freer and happier life. The Duchess has asked me to dinner to-morrow--the note has just arrived--so that I shall soon have the chance of hearing from you some of those details I so much want to know. But before then you will write?

"As for me, I am full of alternate hopes and fears. General Fergus, as we walked home, was rather silent and bearish--I could not flatter myself that he had any friendly intentions towards me in his mind. But Montresor was more than kind, and gave me some fresh opportunities of which I was very glad to avail myself. Well, we shall know soon.

"You told me once that if, or when, this happened, you would turn to your pen, and that Dr. Meredith would find you openings. That is not to be regretted, I think. You have great gifts, which will bring you pleasure in the using. I have got a good deal of pleasure out of my small ones. Did you know that once, long ago, when I was stationed at Gibraltar, I wrote a military novel?

"No, I don't pity you because you will need to turn your intellect to account. You will be free, and mistress of your fate. That, for those who, like you and me, are the 'children of their works,' as the Spaniards say, is much.

"Dear friend--kind, persecuted friend!--I thought of you in the watches of the night--I think of you this morning. Let me soon have news of you." #/

Julie put the letter down upon her knee. Her face stiffened. Nothing that she had ever received from him yet had rung so false.

Grief? Complaint? No! Just a calm grasp of the game--a quick playing of the pieces--so long as the game was there to play. If he was appointed to this mission, in two or three weeks he would be gone--to the heart of Africa. If not--

Anyway, two or three weeks were hers. Her mind seemed to settle and steady itself.

She got up and went once more carefully through the house, giving her attention to it. Yes, the whole had character and a kind of charm. The little place would make, no doubt, an interesting and distinguished background for the life she meant to put into it. She would move in at once--in three days at most. Ways and means were for the moment not difficult. During her life with Lady Henry she had saved the whole of her own small rentes. Three hundred pounds lay ready to her hand in an investment easily realized. And she would begin to earn at once.

Thérèse--that should be her room--the cheerful, blue-papered room with the south window. Julie felt a strange rush of feeling as she thought of it. How curious that these two--Léonie and little Thérèse--should be thus brought back into her life! For she had no doubt whatever that they would accept with eagerness what she had to offer. Her foster-sister had married a school-master in one of the Communal schools of Bruges while Julie was still a girl at the convent. Léonie's lame child had been much with her grandmother, old Madame Le Breton. To Julie she had been at first unwelcome and repugnant. Then some quality in the frail creature had unlocked the girl's sealed and often sullen heart.

While she had been living with Lady Henry, these two, the mother and child, had been also in London; the mother, now a widow, earning her bread as an inferior kind of French governess, the child boarded out with various persons, and generally for long periods of the year in hospital or convalescent home. To visit her in her white hospital bed--to bring her toys and flowers, or merely kisses and chat--had been, during these years, the only work of charity on Julie's part which had been wholly secret, disinterested, and constant.

XII

It was a somewhat depressed company that found its straggling way into the Duchess's drawing-room that evening between tea and dinner.

Miss Le Breton did not appear at tea. The Duchess believed that, after her inspection of the house in Heribert Street, Julie had gone on to Bloomsbury to find Madame Bornier. Jacob Delafield was there, not much inclined to talk, even as Julie's champion. And, one by one, Lady Henry's oldest habitués, the "criminals" of the night before, dropped in.

Dr. Meredith arrived with a portfolio containing what seemed to be proof-sheets.

"Miss Le Breton not here?" he said, as he looked round him.

The Duchess explained that she might be in presently. The great man sat down, his portfolio carefully placed beside him, and drank his tea under what seemed a cloud of preoccupation.

Then appeared Lord Lackington and Sir Wilfrid Bury. Montresor had sent a note from the House to say that if the debate would let him he would dash up to Grosvenor Square for some dinner, but could only stay an hour.

"Well, here we are again--the worst of us!" said the Duchess, presently, with a sigh of bravado, as she handed Lord Lackington his cup of tea and sank back in her chair to enjoy her own.

"Speak for yourselves, please," said Sir Wilfrid's soft, smiling voice, as he daintily relieved his mustache of some of the Duchess's cream.

"Oh, that's all very well," said the Duchess, throwing up a hand in mock annoyance; "but why weren't you there?"

"I knew better."

"The people who keep out of scrapes are not the people one loves," was the Duchess's peevish reply.

"Let him alone," said Lord Lackington, coming for some more tea-cake. "He will get his deserts. Next Wednesday he will be tête-à-tête with Lady Henry."

"Lady Henry is going to Torquay to-morrow," said Sir Wilfrid, quietly.

"Ah!"

There was a general chorus of interrogation, amid which the Duchess made herself heard.

"Then you've seen her?"

"To-day, for twenty minutes--all she was able to bear. She was ill yesterday. She is naturally worse to-day. As to her state of mind--"

The circle of faces drew eagerly nearer.

"Oh, it's war," said Sir Wilfrid, nodding--"undoubtedly war--upon the Cave--if there is a Cave."

"Well, poor things, we must have something to shelter us!" cried the Duchess. "The Cave is being aired to-day."

The interrogating faces turned her way. The Duchess explained the situation, and drew the house in Heribert Street--with its Cyclops-eye of a dormer window, and its Ionian columns--on the tea-cloth with her nail.

"Ah," said Sir Wilfrid, crossing his knees reflectively. "Ah, that makes it serious."

"Julie must have a place to live in," said the Duchess, stiffly.

"I suppose Lady Henry would reply that there are still a few houses in London which do not belong to her kinsman, the Duke of Crowborough."

"Not perhaps to be had for the lending, and ready to step into at a day's notice," said Lord Lackington, with his queer smile, like the play of sharp sunbeams through a mist. "That's the worst of our class. The margin between us and calamity is too wide. We risk too little. Nobody goes to the workhouse."

Sir Wilfrid looked at him curiously. "Do I catch your meaning?" he said, dropping his voice; "is it that if there had been no Duchess, and no Heribert Street, Miss Le Breton would have managed to put up with Lady Henry?"

Lord Lackington smiled again. "I think it probable.... As it is, however, we are all the gainers. We shall now see Miss Julie at her ease and ours."

"You have been for some time acquainted with Miss Le Breton?"

"Oh, some time. I don't exactly remember. Lady Henry, of course, is an old friend of mine, as she is of yours. Sometimes she is rude to me. Then I stay away. But I always go back. She and I can discuss things and people that nobody else recollects--no, as far as that's concerned, you're not in it, Bury. Only this winter, somehow, I have often gone round to see Lady Henry, and have found Miss Le Breton instead so attractive--"

"Precisely," said Sir Wilfrid, laughing; "the whole case in a nutshell."

"What puzzles me," continued his companion, in a musing voice, "is how she can be so English as she is--with her foreign bringing up. She has a most extraordinary instinct for people--people in London--and their relations. I have never known her make a mistake. Yet it is only five years since she began to come to England at all; and she has lived but three with Lady Henry. It was clear, I thought, that neither she nor Lady Henry wished to be questioned. But, do you, for instance--I have no doubt Lady Henry tells you more than she tells me--do you know anything of Mademoiselle Julie's antecedents?"

Sir Wilfrid started. Through his mind ran the same reflection as that to which the Duke had given expression in the morning--"she ought to reveal herself!" Julie Le Breton had no right to leave this old man in his ignorance, while those surrounding him were in the secret. Thereby she made a spectacle of her mother's father--made herself and him the sport of curious eyes. For who could help watching them--every movement, every word? There was a kind of indelicacy in it.

His reply was rather hesitating. "Yes, I happen to know something. But I feel sure Miss Le Breton would prefer to tell you herself. Ask her. While she was with Lady Henry there were reasons for silence--"

"But, of course, I'll ask her," said his companion, eagerly, "if you suppose that I may. A more hungry curiosity was never raised in a human breast than in mine with regard to this dear lady. So charming, handsome, and well bred--and so forlorn! That's the paradox of it. The personality presupposes a milieu--else how produce it? And there is no milieu, save this little circle she has made for herself through Lady Henry.... Ah, and you think I may ask her? I will--that's flat--I will!"

And the old man gleefully rubbed his hands, face and form full of the vivacity of his imperishable youth.

"Choose your time and place," said Sir Wilfrid, hastily. "There are very sad and tragic circumstances--"

Lord Lackington looked at him and nodded gayly, as much as to say, "You distrust me with the sex? Me, who have had the whip-hand of them since my cradle!"

Suddenly the Duchess interrupted. "Sir Wilfrid, you have seen Lady Henry; which did she mind most--the coming-in or the coffee?"

Bury returned, smiling, to the tea-table.

"The coming-in would have been nothing if it had led quickly to the going-out. It was the coffee that ruined you."

"I see," said the Duchess, pouting--"it meant that it was possible for us to enjoy ourselves without Lady Henry. That was the offence."

"Precisely. It showed that you were enjoying yourselves. Otherwise there would have been no lingering, and no coffee."

"I never knew coffee so fatal before," sighed the Duchess. "And now"--it was evident that she shrank from the answer to her own question--"she is really irreconcilable?"

"Absolutely. Let me beg you to take it for granted."

"She won't see any of us--not me?"

Sir Wilfrid hesitated.

"Make the Duke your ambassador."

The Duchess laughed, and flushed a little.

"And Mr. Montresor?"

"Ah," said Sir Wilfrid in another tone, "that's not to be lightly spoken of."

"You don't mean--"

"How many years has that lasted?" said Sir Wilfrid, meditatively.

"Thirty, I think--if not more. It was Lady Henry who told him of his son's death, when his wife daren't do it."

There was a silence. Montresor had lost his only son, a subaltern in the Lancers, in the action of Alumbagh, on the way to the relief of Lucknow.

Then the Duchess broke out:

"I know that you think in your heart of hearts that Julie has been in fault, and that we have all behaved abominably!"

"My dear lady," said Sir Wilfrid, after a moment, "in Persia we believe in fate; I have brought the trick home."

"Yes, yes, that's it!" exclaimed Lord Lackington--it! When Lady Henry wanted a companion-- and fate brought her Miss Le Breton--"

"Last night's coffee was already drunk," put in Sir Wilfrid.

Meredith's voice, raised and a trifle harsh, made itself heard.

"Why you should dignify an ugly jealousy by fine words I don't know. For some women--women like our old friend--gratitude is hard. That is the moral of this tale."

"The only one?" said Sir Wilfrid, not without a mocking twist of the lip.

"The only one that matters. Lady Henry had found, or might have found, a daughter--"

"I understand she bargained for a companion."

"Very well. Then she stands upon her foolish rights, and loses both daughter and companion. At seventy, life doesn't forgive you a blunder of that kind."

Sir Wilfrid silently shook his head. Meredith threw back his blanched mane of hair, his deep eyes kindling under the implied contradiction.

"I am an old comrade of Lady Henry's," he said, quickly. "My record, you'll find, comes next to yours, Bury. But if Lady Henry is determined to make a quarrel of this, she must make it. I regret nothing."

"What madness has seized upon all these people?" thought Bury, as he withdrew from the discussion. The fire, the unwonted fire, in Meredith's speech and aspect, amazed him. From the corner to which he had retreated he studied the face of the journalist. It was a face subtly and strongly lined by much living--of the intellectual, however, rather than the physical sort; breathing now a studious dignity, the effect of the broad sweep of brow under the high-peaked lines of grizzled hair, and now broken, tempestuous, scornful, changing with the pliancy of an actor. The head was sunk a little in the shoulders, as though dragged back by its own weight. The form which it commanded had the movements of a man no less accustomed to rule in his own sphere than Montresor himself.

To Sir Wilfrid the famous editor was still personally mysterious, after many years of intermittent acquaintance. He was apparently unmarried; or was there perhaps a wife, picked up in a previous state of existence, and hidden away with her offspring at Clapham or Hornsey or Peckham? Bury could remember, years before, a dowdy old sister, to whom Lady Henry had been on occasion formally polite. Otherwise, nothing. What were the great man's origins and antecedents--his family, school, university? Sir Wilfrid did not know; he did not believe that any one knew. An amazing mastery of the German, and, it was said, the Russian tongues, suggested a foreign education; but neither on this ground nor any other connected with his personal history did Meredith encourage the inquirer. It was often reported that he was of Jewish descent, and there were certain traits, both of feature and character, that lent support to the notion. If so, the strain was that of Heine or Disraeli, not the strain of Commerce.

At any rate, he was one of the most powerful men of his day--the owner, through The New Rambler, of an influence which now for some fifteen years had ranked among the forces to be reckoned with. A man in whom politics assumed a tinge of sombre poetry; a man of hatreds, ideals, indignations, yet of habitually sober speech. As to passions, Sir Wilfrid could have sworn that, wife or no wife, the man who could show that significance of mouth and eye had not gone through life without knowing the stress and shock of them.

Was he, too, beguiled by this woman?--he, too? For a little behind him, beside the Duchess, sat Jacob Delafield; and, during his painful interview that day with Lady Henry, Sir Wilfrid had been informed of several things with regard to Jacob Delafield he had not known before. So she had refused him--this lady who was now the heart of this whirlwind? Permanently? Lady Henry had poured scorn on the notion. She was merely sure of him; could keep him in a string to play with as she chose. Meanwhile the handsome soldier was metal more attractive. Sir Wilfrid reflected, with an inward shrug, that, once let a woman give herself to such a fury as possessed Lady Henry, and there did not seem to be much to choose between her imaginings and those of the most vulgar of her sex.

So Jacob could be played with--whistled on and whistled off as Miss Le Breton chose? Yet his was not a face that suggested it, any more than the face of Dr. Meredith. The young man's countenance was gradually changing its aspect for Sir Wilfrid, in a somewhat singular way, as old impressions of his character died away and new ones emerged. The face, now, often recalled to Bury a portrait by some Holbeinesque master, which he had seen once in the Basle Museum and never forgotten. A large, thin-lipped mouth that, without weakness, suggested patience; the long chin of a man of will; nose, bluntly cut at the tip, yet in the nostril and bridge most delicate; grayish eyes, with a veil of reverie drawn, as it were, momentarily across them, and showing behind the veil a kind of stern sweetness; fair hair low on the brow, which was heavy, and made a massive shelter for the eyes. So looked the young German who had perhaps heard Melanchthon; so, in this middle nineteenth century, looked Jacob Delafield. No, anger makes obtuse; that, no doubt, was Lady Henry's case. At any rate, in Delafield's presence her theory did not commend itself.

But if Delafield had not echoed them, the little Duchess had received Meredith's remarks with enthusiasm.

"Regret! No, indeed! Why should we regret anything, except that Julie has been miserable so long? She has had a bad time. Every day and all day. Ah, you don't know--none of you. You haven't seen all the little things as I have."

"The errands, and the dogs," said Sir William, slyly.

The Duchess threw him a glance half conscious, half resentful, and went on:

"It has been one small torture after another. Even when a person's old you can't bear more than a certain amount, can you? You oughtn't to. No, let's be thankful it's all over, and Julie--our dear, delightful Julie--who has done everybody in this room all sorts of kindnesses, hasn't she?"

An assenting murmur ran round the circle.

"Julie's free! Only she's very lonely. We must see to that, mustn't we? Lady Henry can buy another companion to-morrow--she will. She has heaps of money and heaps of friends, and she'll tell her own story to them all. But Julie has only us. If we desert her--"

"Desert her!" said a voice in the distance, half amused, half electrical. Bury thought it was Jacob's.

"Of course we sha'n't desert her!" cried the Duchess. "We shall rally round her and carry her through. If Lady Henry makes herself disagreeable, then we'll fight. If not, we'll let her cool down. Oh, Julie, darling--here you are!"

The Duchess sprang up and caught her entering friend by the hand.

"And here are we," with a wave round the circle. "This is your court--your St. Germain."

"So you mean me to die in exile," said Julie, with a quavering smile, as she drew off her gloves. Then she looked at her friends. "Oh, how good of you all to come! Lord Lackington!" She went up to him impetuously, and he, taken by surprise, yielded his hands, which she took in both hers. "It was foolish, I know, but you don't think it was so bad, do you?"

She gazed up at him wistfully. Her lithe form seemed almost to cling to the old man. Instinctively, Jacob, Meredith, Sir Wilfrid Bury withdrew their eyes. The room held its breath. As for Lord Lackington, he colored like a girl.

"No, no; a mistake, perhaps, for all of us; but more ours than yours, mademoiselle--much more! Don't fret. Indeed, you look as if you hadn't slept, and that mustn't be. You must think that, sooner or later, it was bound to come. Lady Henry will soften in time, and you will know so well how to meet her. But now we have your future to think of. Only sit down. You mustn't look so tired. Where have you been wandering?"

And with a stately courtesy, her hand still in his, he took her to a chair and helped her to remove her heavy cloak.

"My future!" She shivered as she dropped into her seat.

How weary and beaten-down she looked--the heroine of such a turmoil! Her eyes travelled from face to face, shrinking--unconsciously appealing. In the dim, soft color of the room, her white face and hands, striking against her black dress, were strangely living and significant. They spoke command--through weakness, through sex. For that, in spite of intellectual distinction, was, after all, her secret. She breathed femininity--the old common spell upon the blood.

"I don't know why you're all so kind to me," she murmured. "Let me disappear. I can go into the country and earn my living there. Then I shall be no more trouble."

Unseen himself, Sir Wilfrid surveyed her. He thought her a consummate actress, and revelled in each new phase.

The Duchess, half laughing, half crying, began to scold her friend. Delafield bent over Julie Le Breton's chair.

"Have you had some tea?"

The smile in his eyes provoked a faint answer in hers. While she was declaring that she was in no need whatever of physical sustenance, Meredith advanced with his portfolio. He looked the editor merely, and spoke with a business-like brevity.

"I have brought the sheets of the new Shelley book, Miss Le Breton. It is due for publication on the 22d. Kindly let me have your review within a week. It may run to two columns--possibly even two and a half. You will find here also the particulars of one or two other things--let me know, please, what you will undertake."

Julie put out a languid hand for the portfolio.

"I don't think you ought to trust me."

"What do you want of her?" said Lord Lackington, briskly. "'Chatter about Harriet?' I could write you reams of that myself. I once saw Harriet."

"Ah!"

Meredith, with whom the Shelley cult was a deep-rooted passion, started and looked round; then sharply repressed the eagerness on his tongue and sat down by Miss Le Breton, with whom, in a lowered voice, he began to discuss the points to be noticed in the sheets handed over to her. No stronger proof could he have given of his devotion to her. Julie knew it, and, rousing herself, she met him with a soft attention and docility; thus tacitly relinquishing, as Bury noticed with amusement, all talk of "disappearance."

Only with himself, he suspected, was the fair lady ill at ease. And, indeed, it was so. Julie, by her pallor, her humility, had thrown herself, as it were, into the arms of her friends, and each was now vying with the other as to how best to cheer and console her. Meanwhile her attention was really bent upon her critic--her only critic in this assembly; and he discovered various attempts to draw him into conversation. And when Lord Lackington, discomfited by Meredith, had finished discharging his literary recollections upon him, Sir Wilfrid became complaisant; Julie slipped in and held him.

Leaning her chin on both hands, she bent towards him, fixing him with her eyes. And in spite of his antagonism he no longer felt himself strong enough to deny that the eyes were beautiful, especially with this tragic note in them of fatigue and pain.

"Sir Wilfrid"--she spoke in low entreaty--"you must help me to prevent any breach between Lady Henry and Mr. Montresor."

He looked at her gayly.

"I fear," he said, "you are too late. That point is settled, as I understand from herself."

"Surely not--so soon!"

"There was an exchange of letters this morning."

"Oh, but you can prevent it--you must!" She clasped her hands.

"No," he said, slowly, "I fear you must accept it. Their relation was a matter of old habit. Like other things old and frail, it bears shock and disturbance badly."

She sank back in her chair, raising her hands and letting them fall with a gesture of despair.

One little stroke of punishment--just one! Surely there was no cruelty in that. Sir Wilfrid caught the Horatian lines dancing through his head:

Yet here was Jacob interposing!--Jacob, who had evidently been watching his mild attempt at castigation, no doubt with disapproval. Lover or no lover--what did the man expect? Under his placid exterior, Sir Wilfrid's mind was, in truth, hot with sympathy for the old and helpless.

Delafield bent over Miss Le Breton.

"You will go and rest? Evelyn advises it."

She rose to her feet, and most of the party rose, too.

"Good-bye--good-bye," said Lord Lackington, offering her a cordial hand. "Rest and forget. Everything blows over. And at Easter you must come to me in the country. Blanche will be with me, and my granddaughter Aileen, if I can tempt them away from Italy. Aileen's a little fairy; you'd be charmed with her. Now mind, that's a promise. You must certainly come."

The Duchess had paused in her farewell nothings with Sir Wilfrid to observe her friend. Julie, with her eyes on the ground, murmured thanks; and Lord Lackington, straight as a dart to-night, carrying his seventy-five years as though they were the merest trifle, made a stately and smiling exit. Julie looked round upon the faces left. In her own heart she read the same judgment as in their eyes: "The old man must know!"

The Duke came into the drawing-room half an hour later in quest of his wife. He was about to leave town by a night train for the north, and his temper was, apparently, far from good.

The Duchess was stretched on the sofa in the firelight, her hands behind her head, dreaming. Whether it was the sight of so much ease that jarred on the Duke's ruffled nerves or no, certain it is that he inflicted a thorny good-bye. He had seen Lady Henry, he said, and the reality was even worse than he had supposed. There was absolutely nothing to be said for Miss Le Breton, and he was ashamed of himself to have been so weakly talked over in the matter of the house. His word once given, of course, there was an end of it--for six months. After that, Miss Le Breton must provide for herself. Meanwhile, Lady Henry refused to receive the Duchess, and would be some time before she forgave himself. It was all most annoying, and he was thankful to be going away, for, Lady Rose or no Lady Rose, he really could not have entertained the lady with civility.

"Oh, well, never mind, Freddie," said the Duchess, springing up. "She'll be gone before you come back, and I'll look after her."

The Duke offered a rather sulky embrace, walked to the door, and came back.

"I really very much dislike this kind of gossip," he said, stiffly, "but perhaps I had better say that Lady Henry believes that the affair with Delafield was only one of several. She talks of a certain Captain Warkworth--"

"Yes," said the Duchess, nodding. "I know; but he sha'n't have Julie."

Her smile completed the Duke's annoyance.

"What have you to do with it? I beg, Evelyn--I insist--that you leave Miss Le Breton's love affairs alone."

"You forget, Freddie, that she is my friend."

The little creature fronted him, all wilfulness and breathing hard, her small hands clasped on her breast.

With an angry exclamation the Duke departed.

At half-past eight a hansom dashed up to Crowborough House. Montresor emerged.

He found the two ladies and Jacob Delafield just beginning dinner, and stayed with them an hour; but it was not an hour of pleasure. The great man was tired with work and debate, depressed also by the quarrel with his old friend. Julie did not dare to put questions, and guiltily shrank into herself. She divined that a great price was being paid on her behalf, and must needs bitterly ask whether anything that she could offer or plead was worth it--bitterly suspect, also, that the query had passed through other minds than her own.

After dinner, as Montresor rose with the Duchess to take his leave, Julie got a word with him in the corridor.

"You will give me ten minutes' talk?" she said, lifting her pale face to him. "You mustn't, mustn't quarrel with Lady Henry because of me."

He drew himself up, perhaps with a touch of haughtiness.

"Lady Henry could end it in a moment. Don't, I beg of you, trouble your head about the matter. Even as an old friend, one must be allowed one's self-respect."

"But mayn't I--"

"Nearly ten o'clock!" he cried, looking at his watch. "I must be off this moment. So you are going to the house in Heribert Street? I remember Lady Mary Leicester perfectly. As soon as you are settled, tell me, and I will present myself. Meanwhile "--he smiled and bent his black head towards her--"look in to-morrow's papers for some interesting news."

He sprang into his hansom and was gone.

Julie went slowly up-stairs. Of course she understood. The long intrigue had reached its goal, and within twelve hours the Times would announce the appointment of Captain Warkworth, D.S.O., to the command of the Mokembe military mission. He would have obtained his heart's desire--through her.

How true were those last words, perhaps only Julie knew. She looked back upon all the manoeuvres and influences she had brought to bear--flattery here, interest or reciprocity there, the lures of Crowborough House, the prestige of Lady Henry's drawing-room. Wheel by wheel she had built up her cunning machine, and the machine had worked. No doubt the last completing touch had been given the night before. Her culminating offence against Lady Henry-- the occasion of her disgrace and banishment--had been to Warkworth the stepping-stone of fortune.

What "gossamer girl" could have done so much? She threw back her head proudly and heard the beating of her heart.

Lady Henry was fiercely forgotten. She opened the drawing-room door, absorbed in a counting of the hours till she and Warkworth should meet.

Then, amid the lights and shadows of the Duchess's drawing-room, Jacob Delafield rose and came towards her. Her exaltation dropped in a moment. Some testing, penetrating influence seemed to breathe from this man, which filled her with a moral discomfort, a curious restlessness. Did he guess the nature of her feeling for Warkworth? Was he acquainted with the efforts she had been making for the young soldier? She could not be sure; he had never given her the smallest sign. Yet she divined that few things escaped him where the persons who touched his feelings were concerned. And Evelyn--the dear chatterbox--certainly suspected.

"How tired you are!" he said to her, gently. "What a day it has been for you! Evelyn is writing letters. Let me bring you the papers--and please don't talk."

She submitted to a sofa, to an adjusted light, to the papers on her knee. Then Delafield withdrew and took up a book.

She could not rest, however; visions of the morrow and of Warkworth's triumphant looks kept flashing through her. Yet all the while Delafield's presence haunted her--she could not forget him, and presently she addressed him.

"Mr. Delafield!"

He heard the low voice and came.

"I have never thanked you for your goodness last night. I do thank you now--most earnestly."

"You needn't. You know very well what I would do to serve you if I could."

"Even when you think me in the wrong?" said Julie, with a little, hysterical laugh.

Her conscience smote her. Why provoke this intimate talk--wantonly--with the man she had made suffer? Yet her restlessness, which was partly nervous fatigue, drove her on.

Delafield flushed at her words.

"How have I given you cause to say that?"

"Oh, you are very transparent. One sees that you are always troubling yourself about the right and wrong of things."

"All very well for one's self," said Delafield, trying to laugh. "I hope I don't seem to you to be setting up as a judge of other people's right and wrong?"

"Yes, yes, you do!" she said, passionately. Then, as he winced, "No, I don't mean that. But you do judge--it is in your nature--and other people feel it."

"I didn't know I was such a prig," said Delafield, humbly. "It is true I am always puzzling over things."

Julie was silent. She was indeed secretly convinced that he no more approved the escapade of the night before than did Sir Wilfrid Bury. Through the whole evening she had been conscious of a watchful anxiety and resistance on his part. Yet he had stood by her to the end--so warmly, so faithfully.

He sat down beside her, and Julie felt a fresh pang of remorse, perhaps of alarm. Why had she called him to her? What had they to do with each other? But he soon reassured her. He began to talk of Meredith, and the work before her--the important and glorious work, as he naïvely termed it, of the writer.

And presently he turned upon her with sudden feeling.

"You accused me, just now, of judging what I have no business to judge. If you think that I regret the severance of your relation with Lady Henry, you are quite, quite mistaken. It has been the dream of my life this last year to see you free--mistress of your own life. It--it made me mad that you should be ordered about like a child--dependent upon another person's will."

She looked at him curiously.

"I know. That revolts you always--any form of command? Evelyn tells me that you carry it to curious lengths with your servants and laborers."

He drew back, evidently disconcerted.

"Oh, I try some experiments. They generally break down."

"You try to do without servants, Evelyn says, as much as possible."

"Well, if I do try, I don't succeed," he said, laughing. "But"--his eyes kindled--"isn't it worth while, during a bit of one's life, to escape, if one can, from some of the paraphernalia in which we are all smothered? Look there! What right have I to turn my fellow-creatures into bedizened automata like that?"

And he threw out an accusing hand towards the two powdered footmen, who were removing the coffee-cups and making up the fire in the next room, while the magnificent groom of the chambers stood like a statue, receiving some orders from the Duchess.

Julie, however, showed no sympathy.

"They are only automata in the drawing-room. Down-stairs they are as much alive as you or I."

"Well, let us put it that I prefer other kinds of luxury," said Delafield. "However, as I appear to have none of the qualities necessary to carry out my notions, they don't get very far."

"You would like to shake hands with the butler?" said Julie, musing. "I knew a case of that kind. But the butler gave warning."

Delafield laughed.

"Perhaps the simpler thing would be to do without the butler."

"I am curious," she said, smiling--"very curious. Sir Wilfrid, for instance, talks of going down to stay with you?"

"Why not? He'd come off extremely well. There's an ex-butler, and an ex-cook of Chudleigh's settled in the village. When I have a visitor, they come in and take possession. We live like fighting-cocks."

"So nobody knows that, in general, you live like a workman?"

Delafield looked impatient.

"Somebody seems to have been cramming Evelyn with ridiculous tales, and she's been spreading them. I must have it out with her."

"I expect there is a good deal in them," said Julie. Then, unexpectedly, she raised her eyes and gave him a long and rather strange look. "Why do you dislike having servants and being waited upon so much, I wonder? Is it--you won't be angry?--that you have such a strong will, and you do these things to tame it?"

Delafield made a sudden movement, and Julie had no sooner spoken the words than she regretted them.

"So you think I should have made a jolly tyrannical slave-owner?" said Delafield, after a moment's pause.

Julie bent towards him with a charming look of appeal--almost of penitence. "On the contrary, I think you would have been as good to your slaves as you are to your friends."

His eyes met hers quietly.

"Thank you. That was kind of you. And as to giving orders, and getting one's way, don't suppose I let Chudleigh's estate go to ruin! It's only"--he hesitated--"the small personal tyrannies of every day that I'd like to minimize. They brutalize half the fellows I know."

"You'll come to them," said Julie, absently. Then she colored, suddenly remembering the possible dukedom that awaited him.

His brow contracted a little, as though he understood. He made no reply. Julie, with her craving to be approved--to say what pleased--could not leave it there.

"I wish I understood," she said, softly, after a moment, "what, or who it was that gave you these opinions."

Getting still no answer, she must perforce meet the gray eyes bent upon her, more expressively, perhaps, than their owner knew. "That you shall understand," he said, after a minute, in a voice which was singularly deep and full, "whenever you choose to ask."

Julie shrank and drew back.

"Very well," she said, trying to speak lightly. "I'll hold you to that. Alack! I had forgotten a letter I must write."

And she pretended to write it, while Delafield buried himself in the newspapers.

XIII

Julie's curiosity--passing and perfunctory as it was--concerning the persons and influences that had worked upon Jacob Delafield since his college days, was felt in good earnest by not a few of Delafield's friends. For he was a person rich in friends, reserved as he generally was, and crotchety as most of them thought him. The mixture of self-evident strength and manliness in his physiognomy with something delicate and evasive, some hindering element of reflection or doubt, was repeated in his character. On the one side he was a robust, healthy Etonian, who could ride, shoot, and golf like the rest of his kind, who used the terse, slangy ways of speech of the ordinary Englishman, who loved the land and its creatures, and had a natural hatred for a poacher; and on another he was a man haunted by dreams and spiritual voices, a man for whom, as he paced his tired horse homeward after a day's run, there would rise on the grays and purples of the winter dusk far-shining "cities of God" and visions of a better life for man. He read much poetry, and the New Testament spoke to him imperatively, though in no orthodox or accustomed way. Ruskin, and the earlier work of Tolstoy, then just beginning to take hold of the English mind, had affected his thought and imagination, as the generation before him had been affected by Carlyle, Emerson, and George Sand.

This present phase of his life, however, was the outcome of much that was turbulent and shapeless in his first youth. He seemed to himself to have passed through Oxford under a kind of eclipse. All that he could remember of two-thirds of his time there was an immoderate amount of eating, drinking, and sleeping. A heavy animal existence, disturbed by moments of unhappiness and remorse, or, at best, lightened by intervals and gleams of friendship with two or three men who tried to prod him out of his lethargy, and cherished what appeared, to himself in particular, a strange and unreasonable liking for him. Such, to his own thinking, had been his Oxford life, up to the last year of his residence there.

Then, when he was just making certain of an ignominious failure in the final schools, he became more closely acquainted with one of the college tutors, whose influence was to be the spark which should at last fire the clay. This modest, heroic, and learned man was a paralyzed invalid, owing to an accident in the prime of life. He had lost the use of his lower limbs--"dead from the waist down." Yet such was the strength of his moral and intellectual life that he had become, since the catastrophe, one of the chief forces of his college. The invalid-chair on which he wheeled himself, recumbent, from room to room, and from which he gave his lectures, was, in the eyes of Oxford, a symbol not of weakness, but of touching and triumphant victory. He gave himself no airs of resignation or of martyrdom. He simply lived his life--except during those crises of weakness or pain when his friends were shut out--as though it were like any other life, save only for what he made appear an insignificant physical limitation. Scholarship, college business or college sports, politics and literature--his mind, at least, was happy, strenuous, and at home in them all. To have pitied him would have been a mere impertinence. While in his own heart, which never grieved over himself, there were treasures of compassion for the weak, the tempted, and the unsuccessful, which spent themselves in secret, simple ways, unknown to his most intimate friends.

This man's personality it was which, like the branch of healing on bitter waters, presently started in Jacob Delafield's nature obscure processes of growth and regeneration. The originator of them knew little of what was going on. He was Delafield's tutor for Greats, in the ordinary college routine; Delafield took essays to him, and occasionally lingered to talk. But they never became exactly intimate. A few conversations of "pith and moment"; a warm shake of the hand and a keen look of pleasure in the blue eyes of the recumbent giant when, after one year of superhuman but belated effort, Delafield succeeded in obtaining a second class; a little note of farewell, affectionate and regretful, when Delafield left the university; an occasional message through a common friend--Delafield had little more than these to look back upon, outside the discussions of historical or philosophical subjects which had entered into their relation as pupil and teacher.

And now the paralyzed tutor was dead, leaving behind him a volume of papers on classical subjects, the reputation of an admirable scholar, and the fragrance of a dear and honored name. His pupils had been many; they counted among the most distinguished of England's youth; and all of them owed him much. Few people thought of Delafield when the list of them was recited; and yet, in truth, Jacob's debt was greater than any; for he owed this man nothing less than his soul.

No doubt the period at Oxford had been rather a period of obscure conflict than of mere idleness and degeneracy, as it had seemed to be. But it might easily have ended in physical and moral ruin, and, as it was--thanks to Courtenay--Delafield went out to the business of life, a man singularly master of himself, determined to live his own life for his own ends.

In the first place, he was conscious, like many other young men of his time, of a strong repulsion towards the complexities and artificialities of modern society. As in the forties, a time of social stir was rising out of a time of stagnation. Social settlements were not yet founded, but the experiments which led to them were beginning. Jacob looked at the life of London, the clubs and the country-houses, the normal life of his class, and turned from it in aversion. He thought, sometimes, of emigrating, in search of a new heaven and a new earth, as men emigrated in the forties.

But his mother and sister were alone in the world--his mother a somewhat helpless being, his sister still very young and unmarried. He could not reconcile it to his conscience to go very far from them.

He tried the bar, amid an inner revolt that only increased with time. And the bar implied London, and the dinners and dances of London, which, for a man of his family, the probable heir to the lands and moneys of the Chudleighs, were naturally innumerable. He was much courted, in spite, perhaps because, of his oddities; and it was plain to him that with only a small exercise of those will-forces he felt accumulating within him, most of the normal objects of ambition were within his grasp. The English aristocratic class, as we all know, is no longer exclusive. It mingles freely with the commoner world on apparently equal terms. But all the while its personal and family cohesion is perhaps greater than ever. The power of mere birth, it seemed to Jacob, was hardly less in the England newly possessed of household suffrage than in the England of Charles James Fox's youth, though it worked through other channels. And for the persons in command of this power, a certain appareil de vie was necessary, taken for granted. So much income, so many servants, such and such habits--these things imposed themselves. Life became a soft and cushioned business, with an infinity of layers between it and any hard reality--a round pea in a silky pod.

And he meanwhile found himself hungry to throw aside these tamed and trite forms of existence, and to penetrate to the harsh, true, simple things behind. His imagination and his heart turned towards the primitive, indispensable labors on which society rests--the life of the husbandman, the laborer, the smith, the woodman, the builder; he dreamed the old, enchanted dream of living with nature; of becoming the brother not of the few, but of the many. He was still reading in chambers, however, when his first cousin, the Duke, a melancholy semi-invalid, a widower, with an only son tuberculous almost from his birth, arrived from abroad. Jacob was brought into new contact with him. The Duke liked him, and offered him the agency of his Essex property. Jacob accepted, partly that he might be quit of the law, partly that he might be in the country and among the poor, partly for reasons, or ghosts of reasons, unavowed even to himself. The one terror that haunted his life was the terror of the dukedom. This poor, sickly lad, the heir, with whom he soon made warm friends, and the silent, morbid Duke, with the face of Charles V. at St. Just--he became, in a short time, profoundly and pitifully attached to them. It pleased him to serve them; above all did it please him to do all he could, and to incite others to do all they could, to keep these two frail persons cheered and alive. His own passionate dread lest he should suddenly find himself in their place, gave a particular poignancy to the service he was always ready to render them of his best.

The Duke's confidence in him had increased rapidly. Delafield was now about to take over the charge of another of the Duke's estates, in the Midlands, and much of the business connected with some important London property was also coming into his hands. He had made himself a good man of business where another's interests were concerned, and his dreams did no harm to the Duke's revenues. He gave, indeed, a liberal direction to the whole policy of the estate, and, as he had said to Julie, the Duke did not forbid experiments.

As to his own money, he gave it away as wisely as he could, which is, perhaps, not saying very much for the schemes and Quixotisms of a young man of eight-and-twenty. At any rate, he gave it away--to his mother and sister first, then to a variety of persons and causes. Why should he save a penny of it? He had some money of his own, besides his income from the Duke. It was disgusting that he should have so much, and that it should be, apparently, so very easy for him to have indefinitely more if he wanted it.

He lived in a small cottage, in the simplest, plainest way compatible with his work and with the maintenance of two decently furnished rooms for any friend who might chance to visit him. He read much and thought much. But he was not a man of any commanding speculative or analytic ability. It would have been hard for him to give any very clear or logical account of himself and his deepest beliefs. Nevertheless, with every year that passed he became a more remarkable character--his will stronger, his heart gentler. In the village where he lived they wondered at him a good deal, and often laughed at him. But if he had left them, certainly the children and the old people would have felt as though the sun had gone out.

In London he showed little or nothing of his peculiar ways and pursuits; was, in fact, as far as anybody knew--outside half a dozen friends--just the ordinary, well-disposed young man, engaged in a business that every one understood. With Lady Henry, his relations, apart from his sympathy with Julie Le Breton, had been for some time rather difficult. She made gratitude hard for one of the most grateful of men. When the circumstances of the Hubert Delafields had been much straitened, after Lord Hubert's death, Lady Henry had come to their aid, and had, in particular, spent fifteen hundred pounds on Jacob's school and college education. But there are those who can make a gift burn into the bones of those who receive it. Jacob had now saved nearly the whole sum, and was about to repay her. Meanwhile his obligation, his relationship, and her age made it natural, or rather imperative, that he should be often in her house; but when he was with her the touch of arrogant brutality in her nature, especially towards servants and dependants, roused him almost to fury. She knew it, and would often exercise her rough tongue merely for the pleasure of tormenting him.

No sooner, therefore, had he come to know the fragile, distinguished creature whom Lady Henry had brought back with her one autumn as her companion than his sympathies were instantly excited, first by the mere fact that she was Lady Henry's dependant, and then by the confidence, as to her sad story and strange position, which she presently reposed in him and his cousin Evelyn. On one or two occasions, very early in his acquaintance with her, he was a witness of some small tyranny of Lady Henry's towards her. He saw the shrinking of the proud nature, and the pain thrilled through his own nerves as though the lash had touched himself. Presently it became a joy to him whenever he was in town to conspire with Evelyn Crowborough for her pleasure and relief. It was the first time he had ever conspired, and it gave him sometimes a slight shock to see how readily these two charming women lent themselves, on occasion, to devices that had the aspect of intrigue, and involved a good deal of what, in his own case, he would have roundly dubbed lying. And, in truth, if he had known, they did not find him a convenient ally, and he was by no means always in their confidence.

Once, about six months after Julie's arrival in Bruton Street, he met her on a spring morning crossing Kensington Gardens with the dogs. She looked startlingly white and ill, and when he spoke to her with eager sympathy her mouth quivered and her dark eyes clouded with tears. The sight produced an extraordinary effect on a man large-hearted and simple, for whom women still moved in an atmosphere of romance. His heart leaped within him as she let herself be talked with and comforted. And when her delicate hand rested in his as they said good-bye, he was conscious of feelings--wild, tumultuous feelings--to which, in his walk homeward through the spring glades of the park, he gave impetuous course.

Romantic, indeed, the position was, for romance rests on contrast. Jacob, who knew Julie Le Breton's secret, was thrilled or moved by the contrasts of her existence at every turn. Her success and her subjection; the place in Lady Henry's circle which Lady Henry had, in the first instance, herself forced her to take, contrasted with the shifts and evasions, the poor, tortuous ways by which, alas! she must often escape Lady Henry's later jealousy; her intellectual strength and her most feminine weaknesses; these things stirred and kept up in Jacob a warm and passionate pity. The more clearly he saw the specks in her glory, the more vividly did she appear to him a princess in distress, bound by physical or moral fetters not of her own making. None of the well-born, well-trained damsels who had been freely thrown across his path had so far beguiled him in the least. Only this woman of doubtful birth and antecedents, lonely, sad, and enslaved amid what people called her social triumphs, stole into his heart--beautified by what he chose to consider her misfortunes, and made none the less attractive by the fact that as he pursued, she retreated; as he pressed, she grew cold.

When, indeed, after their friendship had lasted about a year, he proposed to her and she refused him, his passion, instead of cooling, redoubled. It never occurred to him to think that she had done a strange thing from the worldly point of view--that would have involved an appreciation of himself, as a prize in the marriage market, he would have loathed to make. But he was one of the men for whom resistance enhances the value of what they desire, and secretly he said to himself, "Persevere!" When he was repelled or puzzled by certain aspects of her character, he would say to himself:

"It is because she is alone and miserable. Women are not meant to be alone. What soft, helpless creatures they are!--even when intellectually they fly far ahead of us. If she would but put her hand in mine I would so serve and worship her, she would have no need for these strange things she does--the doublings and ruses of the persecuted." Thus the touches of falsity that repelled Wilfrid Bury were to Delafield's passion merely the stains of rough travel on a fair garment.

But she refused him, and for another year he said no more. Then, as things got worse and worse for her, he spoke again--ambiguously--a word or two, thrown out to sound the waters. Her manner of silencing him on this second occasion was not what it had been before. His suspicions were aroused, and a few days later he divined the Warkworth affair.

When Sir Wilfrid Bury spoke to him of the young officer's relations to Mademoiselle Le Breton, Delafield's stiff defence of Julie's prerogatives in the matter masked the fact that he had just gone through a week of suffering, wrestling his heart down in country lanes; a week which had brought him to somewhat curious results.

In the first place, as with Sir Wilfrid, he stood up stoutly for her rights. If she chose to attach herself to this man, whose business was it to interfere? If he was worthy and loved her, Jacob himself would see fair play, would be her friend and supporter.

But the scraps of gossip about Captain Warkworth which the Duchess--who had disliked the man at first sight--gathered from different quarters and confided to Jacob were often disquieting. It was said that at Simla he had entrapped this little heiress, and her obviously foolish and incapable mother, by devices generally held to be discreditable; and it had taken two angry guardians to warn him off. What was the state of the case now no one exactly knew; though it was shrewdly suspected that the engagement was only dormant. The child was known to have been in love with him; in two years more she would be of age; her fortune was enormous, and

Warkworth was a poor and ambitious man.

There was also an ugly tale of a civilian's wife in a hill station, referring to a date some years back; but Delafield did not think it necessary to believe it.

As to his origins--there again, Delafield, making cautious inquiries, came across some unfavorable details, confided to him by a man of Warkworth's own regiment. His father had retired from the army immediately after the Mutiny, broken in health, and much straitened in means. Himself belonging to a family of the poorer middle class, he had married late, a good woman not socially his equal, and without fortune. They settled in the Isle of Wight, on his half-pay, and harassed by a good many debts. Their two children, Henry and Isabella, were then growing up, and the parents' hopes were fixed upon their promising and good-looking son. With difficulty they sent him to Charterhouse and a "crammer." The boy coveted a "crack" regiment; by dint of mustering all the money and all the interest they could, they procured him his heart's desire. He got unpardonably into debt; the old people's resources were lessening, not expanding; and ultimately the poor father died broken down by the terror of bankruptcy for himself and disgrace for Henry. The mother still survived, in very straitened circumstances.

"His sister," said Delafield's informant, "married one of the big London tailors, whom she met first on the Ryde pier. I happen to know the facts, for my father and I have been customers of his for years, and one day, hearing that I was in Warkworth's regiment, he told me some stories of his brother-in-law in a pretty hostile tone. His sister, it appears, has often financed him of late. She must have done. How else could he have got through? Warkworth may be a fine, showy fellow when there's fighting about. In private life he's one of the most self-indulgent dogs alive. And yet he's ashamed of the sister and her husband, and turns his back on them whenever he can. Oh, he's not a person of nice feeling, is Warkworth--but, mark my words, he'll be one of the most successful men in the army."

There was one side. On the other was to be set the man's brilliant professional record; his fine service in this recent campaign; the bull-dog defence of an isolated fort, which insured the safety of most important communications; contempt of danger, thirst, exposure; the rescue of a wounded comrade from the glacis of the fort, under a murderous fire; facts, all of them, which had fired the public imagination and brought his name to the front. No such acts as these could have been done by any mere self-indulgent pretender.

Delafield reserved his judgment. He set himself to watch. In his inmost heart there was a strange assumption of the right to watch, and, if need be, to act. Julie's instinct had told her truly. Delafield, the individualist, the fanatic for freedom--he, also, had his instinct of tyranny. She should not destroy herself, the dear, weak, beloved woman! He would prevent it.

Thus, during these hours of transition, Delafield thought much of Julie. Julie, on the other hand, had no sooner said good-night to him after the conversation described in the last chapter than she drove him from her thoughts--one might have said, with vehemence.

The Times of the following morning duly contained the announcement of the appointment of Captain Warkworth, D.S.O., of the Queen's Grays, to the command of the military mission to Mokembe recently determined on by her Majesty's government. The mission would proceed to

Mokembe as soon as possible, but of two officers who on the ground of especial knowledge would form part of it, under Captain Warkworth's command, one was at present in Canada and the other at the Cape. It would, therefore, hardly be possible for the mission to start from the coast for the interior before the beginning of May. In the same paper certain promotions and distinctions on account of the recent Mahsud campaign were reprinted from the Gazette. Captain Henry Warkworth's brevet majority was among them.

The Times leader on the announcement pointed out that the mission would be concerned with important frontier questions, still more with the revival of the prestige of England in regions where a supine government had allowed it to wither unaccountably. Other powers had been playing a filching and encroaching game at the expense of the British lion in these parts, and it was more than time that he should open his sleepy eyes upon what was going on. As to the young officer who was to command the mission, the great journal made a few civil though guarded remarks. His record in the recent campaign was indeed highly distinguished; still it could hardly be said that, take it as a whole, his history so far gave him a claim to promotion so important as that which he had now obtained.

Well, now he had his chance. English soldiers had a way of profiting by such chances. The Times courteously gave him the benefit of the doubt, prophesying that he would rise to the occasion and justify the choice of his superiors.

The Duchess looked over Julie's shoulder as she read.

"Schemer," she said, as she dropped a kiss on the back of Julie's neck, "I hope you're satisfied. The Times doesn't know what to make of it."

Julie put down the paper with a glowing cheek.

"They'll soon know," she said, quietly.

"Julie, do you believe in him so much?"

"What does it matter what I think? It is not I who have appointed him."

"Not so sure," laughed the Duchess. "As if he would have had a chance without you. Whom did he know last November when you took him up?"

Julie moved to and fro, her hands behind her. The tremor on her lip, the light in her eye showed her sense of triumph.

"What have I done," she said, laughing, "but push a few stones out of the way of merit?"

"Some of them were heavy," said the Duchess, making a little face. "Need I invite Lady Froswick any more?"

Julie threw her arms about her.

"Evelyn, what a darling you've been! Now I'll never worry you again."

"Oh, for some people I would do ten times as much!" cried the Duchess. "But, Julie, I wish I knew why you think so well of this man. I--I don't always hear very nice things about him."

"I dare say not," said Julie, flushing. "It is easy to hate success."

"No, come, we're not as mean as that!" cried the Duchess. "I vow that all the heroes I've ever known had a ripping time. Julie"--she kissed her friend impulsively--"Julie, don't like him too much. I don't think he's good enough."

"Good enough for what?" said Julie's bitter voice. "Make yourself easy about Captain Warkworth, Evelyn; but please understand--anything is good enough for me. Don't let your dear head be troubled about my affairs. They are never serious, and nothing counts--except," she added, recklessly, "that I get a little amusement by the way."

"Julie," cried the Duchess, "as if Jacob--"

Julie frowned and released herself; then she laughed.

"Nothing that one ever says about ordinary mortals applies to Mr. Delafield. He is, of course, hors concours."

"Julie!"

"It is you, Evelyn, who make me méchante. I could be grateful--and excellent friends with that young man--in my own way."

The Duchess sighed, and held her tongue with difficulty.

When the successful hero arrived that night for dinner he found a solitary lady in the drawing-room.

Was this, indeed, Julie Le Breton--this soft, smiling vision in white?

He expected to have found a martyr, pale and wan from the shock of the catastrophe which had befallen her, and, even amid the intoxication of his own great day, he was not easy as to how she might have taken his behavior on the fatal night. But here was some one, all joy, animation, and indulgence--a glorified Julie who trod on air. Why? Because good-fortune had befallen her friend? His heart smote him. He had never seen her so touching, so charming. Since the incubus of Lady Henry's house and presence had been removed she seemed to have grown years younger. A white muslin dress of her youth, touched here and there by the Duchess's maid, replaced the familiar black satin. When Warkworth first saw her he paused unconsciously in surprise.

Then he advanced to meet her, broadly smiling, his blue eyes dancing.

"You got my note this morning?"

"Yes," she said, demurely. "You were much too kind, and much--much too absurd. I have done nothing."

"Oh, nothing, of course." Then, after a moment: "Are you going to tie me to that fiction, or am I to be allowed a little decent sincerity? You know perfectly well that you have done it all. There, there; give me your hand."

She gave it, shrinking, and he kissed it joyously.

"Isn't it jolly!" he said, with a school-boy's delight as he released her hand. "I saw Lord M---- this morning." He named the Prime Minister. "Very civil, indeed. Then the Commander-in-Chief--and Montresor gave me half an hour. It is all right. They are giving me a capital staff. Excellent fellows, all of them. Oh, you'll see, I shall pull it through--I shall pull it through. By George! it is a chance!"

And he stood radiant, rubbing his hands over the blaze.

The Duchess came in accompanied by an elderly cousin of the Duke's, a white-haired, black-gowned spinster, Miss Emily Lawrence--one of those single women, travelled, cultivated, and good, that England produces in such abundance.

"Well, so you're going," said the Duchess, to Warkworth. "And I hear that we ought to think you a lucky man."

"Indeed you ought, and you must," he said, gayly. "If only the climate will behave itself. The blackwater fever has a way of killing you in twenty-four hours if it gets hold of you; but short of that--"

"Oh, you will be quite safe," said the Duchess. "Let me introduce you to Miss Lawrence. Emily, this is Captain Warkworth."

The elderly lady gave a sudden start. Then she quietly put on her spectacles and studied the young soldier with a pair of intelligent gray eyes.

Nothing could have been more agreeable than Warkworth at dinner. Even the Duchess admitted as much. He talked easily, but not too much, of the task before him; told amusing tales of his sporting experience of years back in the same regions which were now to be the scene of his mission; discussed the preparations he would have to make at Denga, the coast town, before starting on his five weeks' journey to the interior; drew the native porter and the native soldier, not to their advantage, and let fall, by the way, not a few wise or vivacious remarks as to the races, resources, and future of this illimitable and mysterious Africa--this cavern of the unknown, into which the waves of white invasion, one upon another, were now pressing fast and ceaselessly, towards what goal, only the gods knew.

A few other men were dining; among them two officers from the staff of the Commander-in-Chief. Warkworth, much their junior, treated them with a skilful deference; but through the talk that prevailed his military competence and prestige appeared plainly enough, even to the women. His good opinion of himself was indeed sufficiently evident; but there was no crude vainglory. At any rate, it was a vainglory of youth, ability, and good looks, ratified by these budding honors thus fresh upon him, and no one took it amiss.

When the gentlemen returned to the drawing-room, Warkworth and Julie once more found themselves together, this time in the Duchess's little sitting-room at the end of the long suite of rooms.

"When do you go?" she asked him, abruptly.

"Not for about a month." He mentioned the causes of delay.

"That will bring you very late--into the worst of the heat?" Her voice had a note of anxiety.

"Oh, we shall all be seasoned men. And after the first few days we shall get into the uplands."

"What do your home people say?" she asked him, rather shyly. She knew, in truth, little about them.

"My mother? Oh, she will be greatly pleased. I go down to the Isle of Wight for a day or two to see her to-morrow. But now, dear lady, that is enough of my wretched self. You--do you stay on here with the Duchess?"

She told him of the house in Heribert Street. He listened with attention.

"Nothing could be better. You will have a most distinguished little setting of your own, and Lady Henry will repent at leisure. You won't be lonely?"

"Oh no!" But her smile was linked with a sigh.

He came nearer to her.

"You should never be lonely if I could help it," he said, in a low voice.

"When people are nameless and kinless," was her passionate reply, in the same undertone as his, "they must be lonely."

He looked at her with eagerness. She lay back in the firelight, her beautiful brow and eyes softly illuminated. He felt within him a sudden snapping of restraints. Why--why refuse what was so clearly within his grasp? Love has many manners--many entrances--and many exits.

"When will you tell me all that I want to know about you?" he said, bending towards her with tender insistence. "There is so much I have to ask."

"Oh, some time," she said, hurriedly, her pulses quickening. "Mine is not a story to be told on a great day like this."

He was silent a moment, but his face spoke for him.

"Our friendship has been a beautiful thing, hasn't it?" he said, at last, in a voice of emotion. "Look here!" He thrust his hand into his breast-pocket and half withdrew it. "Do you see where I carry your letters?"

"You shouldn't--they are not worthy."

"How charming you are in that dress--in that light! I shall always see you as you are to-night."

A silence. Excitement mounted in their veins. Suddenly he stooped and kissed her hands. They looked into each other's eyes, and the seconds passed like hours.

Presently, in the nearer drawing-room, there was a sound of approaching voices and they moved apart.

"Julie, Emily Lawrence is going," said the Duchess's voice, pitched in what seemed to Julie a strange and haughty note. "Captain Warkworth, Miss Lawrence thinks that you and she have common friends--Lady Blanche Moffatt and her daughter."

Captain Warkworth murmured some conventionality, and passed into the next drawing-room with Miss Lawrence.

Julie rose to her feet, the color dying out of her face, her passionate eyes on the Duchess, who stood facing her friend, guiltily pale, and ready to cry.

XIV

On the morning following these events, Warkworth went down to the Isle of Wight to see his mother. On the journey he thought much of Julie. They had parted awkwardly the night before. The evening, which had promised so well, had, after all, lacked finish and point. What on earth had that tiresome Miss Lawrence wanted with him? They had talked of Simla and the Moffatts. The conversation had gone in spurts, she looking at him every now and then with eyes that seemed to say more than her words. All that she had actually said was perfectly insignificant and trivial. Yet there was something curious in her manner, and when the time came for him to take his departure she had bade him a frosty little farewell.

She had described herself once or twice as a great friend of Lady Blanche Moffatt. Was it possible?

But if Lady Blanche, whose habits of sentimental indiscretion were ingrained, had gossiped to this lady, what then? Why should he be frowned on by Miss Lawrence, or anybody else? That malicious talk at Simla had soon exhausted itself. His present appointment was a triumphant answer to it all. His slanderers--including Aileen's ridiculous guardians--could only look foolish if they pursued the matter any further. What "trap" was there--what mésalliance? A successful soldier was good enough for anybody. Look at the first Lord Clyde, and scores besides.

The Duchess, too. Why had she treated him so well at first, and so cavalierly after dinner? Her manners were really too uncertain.

What was the matter, and why did she dislike him? He pondered over it a good deal, and with much soreness of spirit. Like many men capable of very selfish or very cruel conduct, he was extremely sensitive, and took keen notice of the fact that a person liked or disliked him.

If the Duchess disliked him it could not be merely on account of the Simla story, even though the old maid might conceivably have given her a jaundiced account. The Duchess knew nothing of Aileen, and was little influenced, so far as he had observed her, by considerations of abstract justice or propriety, affecting persons whom she had never seen.

No, she was Julie's friend, the little wilful lady, and it was for Julie she ruffled her feathers, like an angry dove.

So his thoughts had come back to Julie, though, indeed, it seemed to him that they were never far from her. As he looked absently from the train windows on the flying landscape, Julie's image hovered between him and it--a magic sun, flooding soul and senses with warmth. How unconsciously, how strangely his feelings had changed towards her! That coolness of temper and nerve he had been able to preserve towards her for so long was, indeed, breaking down. He recognized the danger, and wondered where it would lead him. What a fascinating, sympathetic creature!--and, by George! what she had done for him!

Aileen! Aileen was a little sylph, a pretty child-angel, white-winged and innocent, who lived in a circle of convent thoughts, knowing nothing of the world, and had fallen in love with him as the first man who had ever made love to her. But this intelligent, full-blooded woman, who could understand at a word, or a half word, who had a knowledge of affairs which many a high-placed man might envy, with whom one never had a dull moment--this courted, distinguished Julie Le Breton--his mind swelled with half-guilty pride at the thought that for six months he had absorbed all her energies, that a word from him could make her smile or sigh, that he could force her to look at him with eyes so melting and so troubled as those with which she had given him her hands--her slim, beautiful hands--that night in Grosvenor Square.

How freedom became her! Dependency had dropped from her, like a cast-off cloak, and beside her fresh, melancholy charm, the airs and graces of a child of fashion and privilege like the little Duchess appeared almost cheap and trivial. Poor Julie! No doubt some social struggle was before her. Lady Henry was strong, after all, in this London world, and the solider and stupider people who get their way in the end were not, she thought, likely to side with Lady Henry's companion in a quarrel where the facts of the story were unquestionably, at first sight, damaging to Miss Le Breton. Julie would have her hours of bitterness and humiliation; and she would conquer by boldness, if she conquered at all--by originality, by determining to live her own life. That would preserve for her the small circle, if it lost her the large world. And the small circle was what she lived for, what she ought, at any rate, to live for.

It was not likely she would marry. Why should she desire it? From any blundering tragedy a woman of so acute a brain would, of course, know how to protect herself. But within the limits of her life, why should she refuse herself happiness, intimacy, love?

His heart beat fast; his thoughts were in a whirl. But the train was nearing Portsmouth, and with an effort he recalled his mind to the meeting with his mother, which was then close upon him.

He spent nearly a week in the little cottage at Sea View, and Mrs. Warkworth got far more pleasure than usual, poor lady, out of his visit. She was a thin, plain woman, not devoid of either ability or character. But life had gone hardly with her, and since her husband's death what had been reserve had become melancholy. She had always been afraid of her only son since they had sent him to Charterhouse, and he had become so much "finer" than his parents. She knew that he must consider her a very ignorant and narrow-minded person; when he was with her she was humiliated in her own eyes, though as soon as he was gone she resumed what was in truth a leading place among her own small circle.

She loved him, and was proud of him; yet at the bottom of her heart she had never absolved him from his father's death. But for his extravagance, and the misfortunes he had brought upon them, her old general would be alive still--pottering about in the spring sunshine, spudding the daisies from the turf, or smoking his pipe beneath the thickening trees. Silently her heart still yearned and hungered for the husband of her youth; his son did not replace him.

Nevertheless, when he came down to her with this halo of glory upon him, and smoked up and down her small garden through the mild spring days, gossiping to her of all the great things that had befallen him, repeating to her, word for word, his conversation with the Prime Minister, and his interview with the Commander-in-Chief, or making her read all the letters of congratulation he had received, her mother's heart thawed within her as it had not done for long. Her ears told her that he was still vain and a boaster; her memory held the indelible records of his past selfishness; but as he walked beside her, his fair hair blown back from his handsome brow, and eyes that were so much younger than the rest of the face, his figure as spare and boyish now as when he had worn the colors of the Charterhouse eleven, she said to herself, in that inward and unsuspected colloquy she was always holding with her own heart about him, that if his father could have seen him now he would have forgiven him everything. According to her secret Evangelical faith, God "deals" with every soul he has created--through joy or sorrow, through good or evil fortune. He had dealt with herself through anguish and loss. Henry, it seemed, was to be moulded through prosperity. His good fortune was already making a better man of him.

Certainly he was more affectionate and thoughtful than before. He would have liked to give her money, of which he seemed to have an unusual store; but she bade him keep what he had for his own needs. Her own little bit of money, saved from the wreck of their fortunes, was enough for her. Then he went into Ryde and brought her back a Shetland shawl and a new table-cloth for her little sitting-room, which she accepted with a warmer kiss than she had given him for years.

He left her on a bright, windy morning which flecked the blue Solent with foam and sent the clouds racing to westward. She walked back along the sands, thinking anxiously of the African climate and the desert hard-ships he was going to face. And she wondered what significance there might be in the fact that he had written twice during his stay with her to a Miss Le Breton, whose name, nevertheless, he had not mentioned in their conversations. Well, he would marry soon, she supposed, and marry well, in circles out of her ken. With the common prejudice of the English middle class, she hoped that if this Miss Le Breton were his choice, she might be only French in name and not in blood.

Meanwhile, Warkworth sped up to London in high spirits, enjoying the comforts of a good conscience.

He drove first to his club, where a pile of letters awaited him--some letters of congratulation, others concerned with the business of his mission. He enjoyed the first, noticing jealously who had and who had not written to him; then he applied himself to the second. His mind worked vigorously and well; he wrote his replies in a manner that satisfied him. Then throwing himself into a chair, with a cigar, he gave himself up to the close and shrewd planning of the preparations necessary for his five weeks' march, or to the consideration of two or three alternative lines of action which would open before him as soon as he should find himself within the boundaries of Mokembe. Some five years before, the government of the day had sent a small expedition to this Debatable Land, which had failed disastrously, both from the diplomatic and the military points of view. He went backward and forward to the shelves of the fine "Service" library which surrounded him, taking down the books and reports which concerned this expedition. He buried himself in them for an hour, then threw them aside with contempt. What blunders and short-sight everywhere! The general public might well talk of the stupidity of English officers. And blunders so easily avoided, too! It was sickening. He felt within himself a fulness of energy and intelligence, a perspicacity of brain which judged mistakes of this kind unpardonable.

As he was replacing some of the books he had been using in the shelves, the club began to fill up with men coming in to lunch. A great many congratulated him; and a certain number who of old had hardly professed to know him greeted him with cordiality. He found himself caught in a series of short but flattering conversations, in which he bore himself well--neither over-discreet nor too elate. "I declare that fellow's improved," said one man, who might certainly have counted as Warkworth's enemy the week before, to his companion at table. "The government's been beastly remiss so far. Hope he'll pull it off. Ripping chance, anyway. Though what they gave it to him for, goodness knows! There were a dozen fellows, at least, did as well as he in the Mahsud business. And the Staff-College man had a thousand times more claim."

Nevertheless, Warkworth felt the general opinion friendly, a little surprised, no doubt, but showing that readiness to believe in the man coming to the front, which belongs much more to the generous than to the calculating side of the English character. Insensibly his mental and moral stature rose. He exchanged a few words on his way out with one of the most distinguished members of the club, a man of European reputation, whom he had seen the week before in the Commander-in-Chief's room at the War Office. The great man spoke to him with marked friendliness, and Warkworth walked on air as he went his way. Potentially he felt himself the great man's equal; the gates of life seemed to be opening before him.

And with the rise of fortune came a rush of magnanimous resolution. No more shady episodes; no more mean devices; no more gambling, and no more debt. Major Warkworth's sheet was clean, and it should remain so. A man of his prospects must run straight.

He felt himself at peace with all the world. By-the-way, just time to jump into a cab and get to Park Crescent in time for his sister's luncheon. His last interview with his brother-in-law had not been agreeable. But now--he felt for the check-book in his pocket--he was in a position to repay at least half the last sum of money which Bella had lent him. He would go and give it her now, and report news of the mother. And if the two chicks were there--why, he had a free hour and he would take them to the Zoo--he vowed he would!--give them something pleasant to remember their uncle by.

And a couple of hours later a handsome, soldierly man might have been seen in the lion-house at the Zoo, leading a plump little girl by either hand. Rose and Katie Mullins enjoyed a golden time, and started a wholly new adoration for the uncle who had so far taken small notice of them, and was associated in their shrewd, childish minds rather with tempests at home than buns abroad. But this time buns, biscuits, hansom-drives and elephant-rides were showered upon them by an uncle who seemed to make no account of money, while his gracious and captivating airs set their little hearts beating in a common devotion.

"Now go home--go home, little beggars!" said that golden gentleman, as he packed them into a hansom and stood on the step to accept a wet kiss on his mustache from each pink mouth. "Tell your mother all about it, and don't forget your uncle Harry. There's a shilling for each of you. Don't you spend it on sweets. You're quite fat enough already. Good-bye!"

"That's the hardest work I've done for many a long day," he said to himself, with a sigh of relief, as the hansom drove away. "I sha'n't turn nurse-maid when other trades fail. But they're nice little kids all the same.

"Now, then, Cox's--and the City"--he ran over the list of his engagements for the afternoon--

"and by five o'clock shall I find my fair lady--at home--and established? Where on earth is Heribert Street?"

He solved the question, for a few minutes after five he was on Miss Le Breton's doorstep. A quaint little house--and a strange parlor-maid! For the door was opened to him by a large-eyed, sickly child, who looked at him with the bewilderment of one trying to follow out instructions still strange to her.

"HE ENTERED UPON A MERRY SCENE"

"Yes, sir, Miss Le Breton is in the drawing-room," she said, in a sweet, deliberate voice with a foreign accent, and she led the way through the hall.

Poor little soul--what a twisted back, and what a limp! She looked about fourteen, but was probably older. Where had Julie discovered her?

Warkworth looked round him at the little hall with its relics of country-house sports and amusements; his eye travelled through an open door to the little dining-room and the Russell pastels of Lady Mary's parents, as children, hanging on the wall. The character of the little dwelling impressed itself at once. Smiling; he acknowledged its congruity with Julie. Here was a lady who fell on her feet!

The child, leading him, opened the door to the left.

"Please walk in, sir," she said, shyly, and stood aside.

As the door opened, Warkworth was conscious of a noise of tongues.

So Julie was not alone? He prepared his manner accordingly.

He entered upon a merry scene. Jacob Delafield was standing on a chair, hanging a picture, while Dr. Meredith and Julie, on either side, directed or criticised the operation. Meredith carried picture-cord and scissors; Julie the hammer and nails. Meredith was expressing the profoundest disbelief in Jacob's practical capacities; Jacob was defending himself hotly; and Julie laughed at both.

Towards the other end of the room stood the tea-table, between the fire and an open window. Lord Lackington sat beside it, smiling to himself, and stroking a Persian kitten. Through the open window the twinkling buds on the lilacs in the Cureton House garden shone in the still lingering sun. A recent shower had left behind it odors of earth and grass. Even in this London air they spoke of the spring--the spring which already in happier lands was drawing veils of peach and cherry blossom, over the red Sienese earth or the green terraces of Como. The fire crackled in the grate. The pretty, old-fashioned room was fragrant with hyacinth and narcissus; Julie's books lay on the tables; Julie's hand and taste were already to be felt everywhere. And Lord Lackington with the kitten, beside the fire, gave the last touch of home and domesticity.

"So I find you established?" said Warkworth, smiling, to the lady with the nails, while Delafield nodded to him from the top of the steps and Meredith ceased to chatter.

"I haven't a hand, I fear," said Julie. "Will you have some tea? Ah, Léonie, tu vas en faire de nouveau, n'est-ce pas, pour ce monsieur?"

A little woman in black, with a shawl over her shoulders, had just glided into the room. She had a small, wrinkled face, bright eyes, and a much-flattened nose.

"Tout de suite, monsieur," she said, quickly, and disappeared with the teapot. Warkworth guessed, of course, that she was Madame Bornier, the foster-sister--the "Propriety" of this ménage.

"Can't I help?" he said to Julie, with a look at Delafield.

"It's just done," she said, coldly, handing a nail to Delafield. "Just a trifle more to the right. Ecco! Perfection!"

"Oh, you spoil him," said Meredith, "And not one word of praise for me!"

"What have you done?" she said, laughing. "Tangled the cord--that's all!"

Warkworth turned away. His face, so radiant as he entered, had settled into sharp, sudden lines. What was the meaning of this voice, this manner? He remembered that to his three letters he had received no word of reply. But he had interpreted that to mean that she was in the throes of moving and could find no time to write.

As he neared the tea-table, Lord Lackington looked up. He greeted the new-comer with the absent stateliness he generally put on when his mind was in a state of confusion as to a person's identity.

"Well, so they're sending you to D----? There'll be a row there before long. Wish you joy of the missionaries!"

"No, not D----," said Warkworth, smiling. "Nothing so amusing. Mokembe's my destination."

"Oh, Mokembe!" said Lord Lackington, a little abashed. "That's where Cecil Ray, Lord R's second son, was killed last year--lion-hunting? No, it was of fever that he died. By-the-way, a vile climate!"

"In the plains, yes," said Warkworth, seating himself. "As to the uplands, I understand they are to be the Switzerland of Africa."

Lord Lackington did not appear to listen.

"Are you a homoeopath?" he said, suddenly, rising to his full and immense stature and looking down with eagerness on Warkworth.

"No. Why?"

"Because it's your only chance, for those parts. If Cecil Ray had had their medicines with him he'd be alive now. Look here; when do you start?" The speaker took out his note-book.

"In rather less than a month I start for Denga."

"All right. I'll send you a medicine-case--from Epps. If you're ill, take 'em."

"You're very good."

"Not at all. It's my hobby--one of the last." A broad, boyish smile flashed over the handsome old face. "Look at me; I'm seventy-five, and I can tire out my own grandsons at riding and shooting. That comes of avoiding all allopathic messes like the devil. But the allopaths are such mean fellows they filch all our ideas."

The old man was off. Warkworth submitted to five minutes' tirade, stealing a glance sometimes at the group of Julie, Meredith, and Delafield in the farther window--at the happy ease and fun that seemed to prevail in it. He fiercely felt himself shut out and trampled on.

Suddenly, Lord Lackington pulled up, his instinct for declamation qualified by an equally instinctive dread of boring or being bored. "What did you think of Montresor's statement?" he said, abruptly, referring to a batch of army reforms that Montresor the week before had endeavored to recommend to a sceptical House of Commons.

"All very well, as far as it goes," said Warkworth, with a shrug.

"Precisely! We English want an army and a navy; we don't like it when those fellows on the Continent swagger in our faces, and yet we won't pay either for the ships or the men. However, now that they've done away with purchase--Gad! I could fight them in the streets for the way in which they've done it!--now that they've turned the army into an examination-shop, tempered with jobbery, whatever we do, we shall go to the deuce. So it don't matter."

"You were against the abolition?"

"I was, sir--with Wellington and Raglan and everybody else of any account. And as for the violence, the disgraceful violence with which it was carried--"

"Oh no, no," said Warkworth, laughing. "It was the Lords who behaved abominably, and it'll do a deal of good."

Lord Lackington's eyes flashed.

"I've had a long life," he said, pugnaciously. "I began as a middy in the American war of 1812, that nobody remembers now. Then I left the sea for the army. I knocked about the world. I commanded a brigade in the Crimea--"

"Who doesn't remember that?" said Warkworth, smiling.

The old man acknowledged the homage by a slight inclination of his handsome head.

"And you may take my word for it that this new system will not give you men worth a tenth part of those fellows who bought and bribed their way in under the old. The philosophers may like it, or lump it, but so it is."

Warkworth dissented strongly. He was a good deal of a politician, himself a "new man," and on the side of "new men." Lord Lackington warmed to the fight, and Warkworth, with bitterness in his heart--because of that group opposite--was nothing loath to meet him. But presently he found the talk taking a turn that astonished him. He had entered upon a drawing-room discussion of a subject which had, after all, been settled, if only by what the Tories were pleased to call the coup d'état of the Royal Warrant, and no longer excited the passions of a few years back. What he had really drawn upon himself was a hand-to-hand wrestle with a man who had no sooner provoked contradiction than he resented it with all his force, and with a determination to crush the contradictor.

Warkworth fought well, but with a growing amazement at the tone and manner of his opponent. The old man's eyes darted war-flames under his finely arched brows. He regarded the younger with a more and more hostile, even malicious air; his arguments grew personal, offensive; his shafts were many and barbed, till at last Warkworth felt his face burning and his temper giving way.

"What are you talking about?" said Julie Le Breton, at last, rising and coming towards them.

Lord Lackington broke off suddenly and threw himself into his chair.

Warkworth rose from his.

"We had better have been handing nails," he said, "but you wouldn't give us any work." Then, as Meredith and Delafield approached, he seized the opportunity of saying, in a low voice:

"Am I not to have a word?"

She turned with composure, though it seemed to him she was very pale.

"Have you just come back from the Isle of Wight?"

"This morning." He looked her in the eyes. "You got my letters?"

"Yes, but I have had no time for writing. I hope you found your mother well."

"Very well, thank you. You have been hard at work?"

"Yes, but the Duchess and Mr. Delafield have made it all easy."

And so on, a few more insignificant questions and answers.

"I must go," said Delafield, coming up to them, "unless there is any more work for me to do. Good-bye, Major, I congratulate you. They have given you a fine piece of work."

Warkworth made a little bow, half ironical. Confound the fellow's grave and lordly ways! He did not want his congratulations.

He lingered a little, sorely, full of rage, yet not knowing how to go.

Lord Lackington's eyes ceased to blaze, and the kitten ventured once more to climb upon his knee. Meredith, too, found a comfortable arm-chair, and presently tried to beguile the kitten from his neighbor. Julie sat erect between them, very silent, her thin, white hands on her lap, her head drooped a little, her eyes carefully restrained from meeting Warkworth's. He meanwhile leaned against the mantel-piece, irresolute.

Meredith, it was clear, made himself quite happy and at home in the little drawing-room. The lame child came in and took a stool beside him. He stroked her head and talked nonsense to her in the intervals of holding forth to Julie on the changes necessary in some proofs of his which he had brought back. Lord Lackington, now quite himself again, went back to dreams, smiling over them, and quite unaware that the kitten had been slyly ravished from him. The little woman in black sat knitting in the background. It was all curiously intimate and domestic, only Warkworth had no part in it.

"Good-bye, Miss Le Breton," he said, at last, hardly knowing his own voice. "I am dining out."

She rose and gave him her hand. But it dropped from his like a thing dead and cold. He went out in a sudden suffocation of rage and pain; and as he walked in a blind haste to Cureton Street, he still saw her standing in the old-fashioned, scented room, so coldly graceful, with those proud, deep eyes.

When he had gone, Julie moved to the window and looked out into the gathering dusk. It seemed to her as if those in the room must hear the beating of her miserable heart.

When she rejoined her companions, Dr. Meredith had already risen and was stuffing various letters and papers into his pockets with a view to departure.

"Going?" said Lord Lackington. "You shall see the last of me, too, Mademoiselle Julie."

And he stood up. But she, flushing, looked at him with a wistful smile.

"Won't you stay a few minutes? You promised to advise me about Thérèse's drawings."

"By all means."

Lord Lackington sat down again. The lame child, it appeared, had some artistic talent, which Miss Le Breton wished to cultivate. Meredith suddenly found his coat and hat, and, with a queer look at Julie, departed in a hurry.

"Thérèse, darling," said Julie, "will you go up-stairs, please, and fetch me that book from my room that has your little drawings inside it?"

The child limped away on her errand. In spite of her lameness she moved with wonderful lightness and swiftness, and she was back again quickly with a calf-bound book in her hand.

"Léonie!" said Julie, in a low voice, to Madame Bornier.

The little woman looked up startled, nodded, rolled up her knitting in a moment, and was gone.

"Take the book to his lordship, Thérèse," she said, and then, instead of moving with the child, she again walked to the window, and, leaning her head against it, looked out. The hand hanging against her dress trembled violently.

"What did you want me to look at, my dear?" said Lord Lackington, taking the book in his hand and putting on his glasses.

But the child was puzzled and did not know. She gazed at him silently with her sweet, docile look.

"Run away, Thérèse, and find mother," said Julie, from the window.

The child sped away and closed the door behind her.

Lord Lackington adjusted his glasses and opened the book. Two or three slips of paper with drawings upon them fluttered out and fell on the table beneath. Suddenly there was a cry. Julie turned round, her lips parted.

Lord Lackington walked up to her.

"Tell me what this means," he said, peremptorily. "How did you come by it?"

It was a volume of George Sand. He pointed, trembling, to the name and date on the fly-leaf-- "Rose Delaney, 1842."

"It is mine," she said, softly, dropping her eyes.

"But how--how, in God's name, did you come by it?"

"My mother left it to me, with all her other few books and possessions."

There was a pause. Lord Lackington came closer.

"Who was your mother?" he said, huskily.

The words in answer were hardly audible. Julie stood before him like a culprit, her beautiful head humbly bowed.

Lord Lackington dropped the book and stood bewildered.

"Rose's child?" he said--"Rose's child?"

Then, approaching her, he placed his hand on her arm.

"Let me look at you," he commanded.

Julie raised her eyes to him, and at the same time dumbly held out to him a miniature she had been keeping hidden in her hand. It was one of the miniatures from the locked triptych.

He took it, looked from the pictured to the living face, then, turning away with a groan, he covered his face with his hands and fell again into the chair from which he had risen.

Julie hurried to him. Her own eyes were wet with tears. After a moment's hesitation she knelt down beside him.

"I ought to ask your pardon for not having told you before," she murmured.

It was some time before Lord Lackington looked up. When at last his hands dropped, the face they uncovered was very white and old.

"So you," he said, almost in a whisper, "are the child she wrote to me about before she died?"

Julie made a sign of assent.

"How old are you?"

"Twenty-nine."

"She was thirty-two when I saw her last."

There was a silence. Julie lifted one of his hands and kissed it. But he took no notice.

"You know that I was going to her, that I should have reached her in time"--the words seemed wrung from him--"but that I was myself dangerously ill?"

"I know. I remember it all."

"Did she speak of me?"

"Not often. She was very reserved, you remember. But not long before she died--she seemed half asleep--I heard her say, 'Papa!--Blanche!' and she smiled."

Lord Lackington's face contracted, and the slow tears of old age stood in his eyes.

"You are like her in some ways," he said, brusquely, as though to cover his emotion; "but not very like her."

"She always thought I was like you."

A cloud came over Lord Lackington's face. Julie rose from her knees and sat beside him. He lost himself a few moments amid the painful ghosts of memory. Then, turning to her abruptly, he said:

"You have wondered, I dare say, why I was so hard--why, for seventeen years, I cast her off?"

"Yes, often. You could have come to see us without anybody knowing. Mother loved you very much."

Her voice was low and sad. Lord Lackington rose, fidgeted restlessly with some of the small ornaments on the mantel-piece, and at last turned to her.

"She brought dishonor," he said, in the same stifled voice, "and the women of our family have always been stainless. But that I could have forgiven. After a time I should have resumed relations--private relations--with her. But it was your father who stood in the way. I was then--I am now--you saw me with that young fellow just now--quarrelsome and hot-tempered. It is my nature." He drew himself up obstinately. "I can't help it. I take great pains to inform myself, then I cling to my opinions tenaciously, and in argument my temper gets the better of me. Your father, too, was hot-tempered. He came, with my consent, once to see me--after your mother had left her husband--to try and bring about some arrangement between us. It was the Chartist time. He was a Radical, a Socialist of the most extreme views. In the course of our conversation something was said that excited him. He went off at score. I became enraged, and met him with equal violence. We had a furious argument, which ended in each insulting the other past forgiveness. We parted enemies for life. I never could bring myself to see him afterwards, nor to run the risk of seeing him. Your mother took his side and espoused his opinions while he lived. After his death, I suppose, she was too proud and sore to write to me. I wrote to her once--it was not the letter it might have been. She did not reply till she felt herself dying. That is the explanation of what, no doubt, must seem strange to you."

"'FOR MY ROSE'S CHILD,' HE SAID, GENTLY"

He turned to her almost pleadingly. A deep flush had replaced the pallor of his first emotion, as though in the presence of these primal realities of love, death, and sorrow which she had recalled to him, his old quarrel, on a political difference, cut but a miserable figure.

"No," she said, sadly, "not very strange. I understood my father--my dear father," she added, with soft, deliberate tenderness.

Lord Lackington was silent a little, then he threw her a sudden, penetrating look.

"You have been in London three years. You ought to have told me before."

It was Julie's turn to color.

"Lady Henry bound me to secrecy."

"Lady Henry did wrong," he said, with emphasis. Then he asked, jealously, with a touch of his natural irascibility, "Who else has been in the secret?"

"Four people, at most--the Duchess, first of all. I couldn't help it," she pleaded. "I was so unhappy with Lady Henry."

"You should have come to me. It was my right."

"But"--she dropped her head--"you had made it a condition that I should not trouble you."

He was silenced; and once more he leaned against the mantel-piece and hid his face from her, till, by a secret impulse, both moved. She rose and approached him; he laid his hands on her arms. With his persistent instinct for the lovely or romantic he perceived, with sudden pleasure, the grave, poetic beauty of her face and delicate form. Emotion had softened away all that was harsh; a quivering charm hovered over the features. With a strange pride, and a sense of mystery, he recognized his daughter and his race.

"For my Rose's child," he said, gently, and, stooping, he kissed her on the brow. She broke out into weeping, leaning against his shoulder, while the old man comforted and soothed her.

XV

After the long conversation between herself and Lord Lackington which followed on the momentous confession of her identity, Julie spent a restless and weary evening, which passed into a restless and weary night. Was she oppressed by this stirring of old sorrows?--haunted afresh by her parents' fate?

Ah! Lord Lackington had no sooner left her than she sank motionless into her chair, and, with the tears excited by the memories of her mother still in her eyes, she gave herself up to a desperate and sombre brooding, of which Warkworth's visit of the afternoon was, in truth, the sole cause, the sole subject.

Why had she received him so? She had gone too far--much too far. But, somehow, she had not been able to bear it--that buoyant, confident air, that certainty of his welcome. No! She would show him that she was not his chattel, to be taken or left on his own terms. The, careless good-humor of his blue eyes was too much, after those days she had passed through.

He, apparently, to judge from his letters to her from the Isle of Wight, had been conscious of no crisis whatever. Yet he must have seen from the little Duchess's manner, as she bade farewell to him that night at Crowborough House, that something was wrong. He must have realized that Miss Lawrence was an intimate friend of the Moffatts, and that--Or was he really so foolish as to suppose that his quasi-engagement to this little heiress, and the encouragement given him, in defiance of the girl's guardians, by her silly and indiscreet mother, were still hidden and secret matters?--that he could still conceal them from the world, and deny them to Julie?

Her whole nature was sore yet from her wrestle with the Duchess on that miserable evening.

"Julie, I can't help it! I know it's impertinent--but--Julie, darling!--do listen! What business has that man to make love to you as he does, when all the time--Yes, he does make love to you--he does! Freddie had a most ill-natured letter from Lady Henry this morning. Of course he had--and of course she'll write that kind of letter to as many people as she can. And it wouldn't matter a bit, if--But, you see, you have been moving heaven and earth for him! And now his manner to you" (while the sudden flush burned her cheek, Julie wondered whether by chance the Duchess had seen anything of the yielded hands and the kiss) "and that ill-luck of his being the first to arrive, last night, at Lady Henry's! Oh, Julie, he's a wretch--he is! Of course he is in love with you. That's natural enough. But all the time--listen, that nice woman told me the whole story-- he's writing regularly to that little girl. She and her mother, in spite of the guardians, regard it as an engagement signed and sealed, and all his friends believe he's quite determined to marry her because of the money. You may think me an odious little meddler, Julie, if you like, but I vow I could stab him to the heart, with all the pleasure in life!"

And neither the annoyance, nor the dignity, nor the ridicule of the supposed victim--not Julie's angry eyes, nor all her mocking words from tremulous lips--had availed in the least to silence the tumult of alarmed affection in the Duchess's breast. Her Julie had been flouted and trifled with; and if she was so blind, so infatuated, as not to see it, she should at least be driven to realize what other people felt about it.

So she had her say, and Julie had been forced, willy-nilly, upon discussion and self-defence--nay, upon a promise also. Pale, and stiffly erect, yet determined all the same to treat it as a laughing matter, she had vouchsafed the Duchess some kind of assurance that she would for the future observe a more cautious behavior towards Warkworth. "He is my friend, and whatever any one may say, he shall remain so," she had said, with a smiling stubbornness which hid something before which the little Duchess shrank. "But, of course, if I can do anything to please you, Evelyn--you know I like to please you."

But she had never meant, she had never promised to forswear his society, to ban him from the new house. In truth she would rather have left home and friends and prospects, at one stroke, rather than have pledged herself to anything of the sort. Evelyn should never bind her to that.

Then, during his days of absence, she had passed through wave after wave of feeling, while all the time to the outer eye she was occupied with nothing but the settlement into Lady Mary's strange little house. She washed, dusted, placed chairs and tables. And meanwhile a wild expectancy of his first letter possessed her. Surely there would be some anxiety in it, some fear, some disclosure of himself, and of the struggle in his mind between interest and love?

Nothing of the kind. His first letter was the letter of one sure of his correspondent, sure of his reception and of his ground; a happy and intimate certainty shone through its phrases; it was the letter, almost, of a lover whose doubts are over.

The effect of it was to raise a tempest, sharp and obscure, in Julie's mind. The contrast between the pose of the letter and the sly reality behind bred a sudden anguish of jealousy, concerned not so much with Warkworth as with this little, unknown creature, who, without any effort, any desert--by the mere virtue of money and blood--sat waiting in arrogant expectancy till what she desired should come to her. How was it possible to feel any compunction towards her? Julie felt none.

As to the rest of Miss Lawrence's gossip--that Warkworth was supposed to have "behaved badly," to have led the pretty child to compromise herself with him at Simla in ways which Simla society regarded as inadmissible and "bad form"; that the guardians had angrily intervened, and that he was under a promise, habitually broken by the connivance of the girl's mother, not to see or correspond with the heiress till she was twenty-one, in other words, for the next two years--what did these things matter to her? Had she ever supposed that Warkworth, in regard to money or his career, was influenced by any other than the ordinary worldly motives? She knew very well that he was neither saint nor ascetic. These details--or accusations--did not, properly speaking, concern her at all. She had divined and accepted his character, in all its average human selfishness and faultiness, long ago. She loved him passionately in spite of it--perhaps, if the truth were known, because of it.

As for the marrying, or rather the courting, for money, that excited in her no repulsion whatever. Julie, in her own way, was a great romantic; but owing to the economic notions of marriage, especially the whole conception of the dot, prevailing in the French or Belgian minds amid whom she had passed her later girlhood, she never dreamed for a moment of blaming Warkworth for placing money foremost in his plans of matrimony. She resembled one of the famous amoureuses of the eighteenth century, who in writing to the man she loved but could not marry, advises him to take a wife to mend his fortunes, and proposes to him various tempting morsels--une jeune personne, sixteen, with neither father nor mother, only a brother. "They will give her on her marriage thirteen thousand francs a year, and the aunt will be quite content to keep her and look after her for some time." And if that won't do--"I know a man who would be only too happy to have you for a son-in-law; but his daughter is only eleven; she is an only child, however, and she will be very rich. You know, mon ami, I desire your happiness above all things; how to procure it--there lies the chief interest of my life."

This notion of things, more or less disguised, was to Julie customary and familiar; and it was no more incompatible in her with the notions and standards of high sentiment, such as she might be supposed to have derived from her parents, than it is in the Latin races generally.

No doubt it had been mingled in her, especially since her settlement in Lady Henry's house, with the more English idea of "falling in love"--the idea which puts personal choice first in marriage, and makes the matter of dowry subordinate to that mysterious election and affinity which the Englishman calls "love." Certainly, during the winter, Julie had hoped to lead Warkworth to marry her. As a poor man, of course, he must have money. But her secret feeling had been that her place in society, her influence with important people, had a money value, and that he would perceive this.

Well, she had been a mere trusting fool, and he had deceived her. There was his crime--not in seeking money and trusting to money. He had told her falsehoods and misled her. He was doing it still. His letter implied that he loved her? Possibly. It implied to Julie's ear still more plainly that he stood tacitly and resolutely by Aileen Moffatt and her money, and that all he was prepared to offer to the dear friend of his heart was a more or less ambiguous relation, lasting over two years perhaps--till his engagement might be announced.

A dumb and bitter anger mounted within her. She recalled the manner in which he had evaded her first questions, and her opinion became very much that of the Duchess. She had, indeed, been mocked, and treated like a child. So she sent no answer to his first letter, and when his second came she forbade herself to open it. It lay there on her writing-table. At night she transferred it to the table beside her bed, and early in the spring dawn her groping fingers drew it trembling towards her and slipped it under her pillow. By the time the full morning had come she had opened it, read and reread it--had bathed it, indeed, with her tears.

But her anger persisted, and when Warkworth appeared on her threshold it flamed into sudden expression. She would make him realize her friends, her powerful friends--above all, she would make him realize Delafield.

Well, now it was done. She had repelled her lover. She had shown herself particularly soft and gracious to Delafield. Warkworth now would break with her--might, perhaps, be glad of the chance to return safely and without further risks to his heiress.

She sat on in the dark, thinking over every word, every look. Presently Thérèse stole in.

"Mademoiselle, le souper sera bientôt prêt."

Julie rose wearily, and the child slipped a thin hand into hers.

"J'aime tant ce vieux monsieur," she said, softly. "Je l'aime tant!"

Julie started. Her thoughts had wandered far, indeed, from Lord Lackington.

As she went up-stairs to her little room her heart reproached her. In their interview the old man had shown great sweetness of feeling, a delicate and remorseful tenderness, hardly to have been looked for in a being so fantastic and self-willed. The shock of their conversation had deepened the lines in a face upon which age had at last begun to make those marks which are not another beauty, but the end of beauty. When she had opened the door for him in the dusk, Julie had longed, indeed, to go with him and soothe his solitary evening. His unmarried son, William, lived with him intermittently; but his wife was dead. Lady Blanche seldom came to town, and, for the most part, he lived alone in the fine house in St. James's Square, of which she had heard her mother talk.

He liked her--had liked her from the first. How natural that she should tend and brighten his old age--how natural, and how impossible! He was not the man to brave the difficulties and discomforts inseparable from the sudden appearance of an illegitimate granddaughter in his household, and if he had been, Julie, in her fierce, new-born independence, would have shrunk from such a step. But she had been drawn to him; her heart had yearned to her kindred.

No; neither love nor kindred were for her. As she entered the little, bare room over the doorway, which she had begun to fill with books and papers, and all the signs of the literary trade, she miserably bid herself be content with what was easily and certainly within her grasp. The world was pleased to say that she had a remarkable social talent. Let her give her mind to the fight with Lady Henry, and prove whether, after all, the salon could not be acclimatized on English soil. She had the literary instinct and aptitude, and she must earn money. She looked at her half-written article, and sighed to her books to save her.

That evening Thérèse, who adored her, watched her with a wistful and stealthy affection. Her idol was strangely sad and pale. But she asked no questions. All she could do was to hover about "mademoiselle" with soft, flattering services, till mademoiselle went to bed, and then to lie awake herself, quietly waiting till all sounds in the room opposite had died away, and she might comfort her dumb and timid devotion with the hope that Julie slept.

Sleep, however, or no sleep, Julie was up early next day. Before the post arrived she was already dressed, and on the point of descending to the morning coffee, which, in the old, frugal, Bruges fashion, she and Léonie and the child took in the kitchen together. Lady Henry's opinion of her as a soft and luxurious person dependent on dainty living was, in truth, absurdly far from the mark. After those years of rich food and many servants in Lady Henry's household, she had resumed the penurious Belgian ways at once, without effort--indeed, with alacrity. In the morning she helped Léonie and Thérèse with the housework. Her quick fingers washed and rubbed and dusted. In less than a week she knew every glass and cup in Cousin Mary Leicester's well-filled china cupboard, and she and Thérèse between them kept the two sitting-rooms spotless. She who had at once made friends and tools of Lady Henry's servants, disdained, so it appeared, to be served beyond what was absolutely necessary in her own house. A charwoman, indeed, came in the morning for the roughest work, but by ten o'clock she was gone, and Julie,

Madame Bornier, and the child remained in undisputed possession. Little, flat-nosed, silent Madame Bornier bought and brought in all they ate. She denounced the ways, the viands, the brigand's prices of English fournisseurs, but it seemed to Julie, all the same, that she handled them with a Napoleonic success. She bought as the French poor buy, so far as the West End would let her, and Julie had soon perceived that their expenditure, even in this heart of Mayfair, would be incredibly small. Whereby she felt herself more and more mistress of her fate. By her own unaided hands would she provide for herself and her household. Each year there should be a little margin, and she would owe no man anything. After six months, if she could not afford to pay the Duke a fair rent for his house--always supposing he allowed her to remain in it--she would go elsewhere.

As she reached the hall, clad in an old serge dress, which was a survival from Bruges days, Thérèse ran up to her with the letters.

Julie looked through them, turned and went back to her room. She had expected the letter which lay on the top, and she must brace herself to read it.

It began abruptly:

/# "You will hardly wonder that I should write at once to ask if you have no explanation to give me of your manner of this afternoon. Again and again I go over what happened, but no light comes. It was as though you had wiped out all the six months of our friendship; as though I had become for you once more the merest acquaintance. It is impossible that I can have been mistaken. You meant to make me--and others?--clearly understand--what? That I no longer deserved your kindness--that you had broken altogether with the man on whom you had so foolishly bestowed it?

"My friend, what have I done? How have I sinned? Did that sour lady, who asked me questions she had small business to ask, tell you tales that have set your heart against me? But what have incidents and events that happened, or may have happened, in India, got to do with our friendship, which grew up for definite reasons and has come to mean so much--has it not?--to both of us? I am not a model person, Heaven knows!--very far from it. There are scores of things in my life to be ashamed of. And please remember that last year I had never seen you; if I had, much might have gone differently.

"But how can I defend myself? I owe you so much. Ought not that, of itself, to make you realize how great is your power to hurt me, and how small are my powers of resistance? The humiliations you can inflict upon me are infinite, and I have no rights, no weapons, against you.

"I hardly know what I am saying. It is very late, and I am writing this after a dinner at the club given me by two or three of my brother officers. It was a dinner in my honor, to congratulate me on my good fortune. They are good fellows, and it should have been a merry time. But my half hour in your room had killed all power of enjoyment for me. They found me a wretched companion, and we broke up early. I came home through the empty streets, wishing myself, with all my heart, away from England--facing the desert. Let me just say this. It is not of good omen that now, when I want all my faculties at their best, I should suddenly find myself invaded by this distress and despondency. You have some responsibility now in my life and career; if you would, you cannot get rid of it. You have not increased the chances of your friend's success in his great task.

"You see how I restrain myself. I could write as madly as I feel--violently and madly. But of set purpose we pitched our relation in a certain key and measure; and I try, at least, to keep the measure, if the music and the charm must go. But why, in God's name, should they go? Why have you turned against me? You have listened to slanderers; you have secretly tried me by tests that are not in the bargain, and you have judged and condemned me without a hearing, without a word. I can tell you I am pretty sore.

"I will come and see you no more in company for the present. You gave me a footing with you, which has its own dignity. I'll guard it; not even from you will I accept anything else. But-- unless, indeed, the grove is cut down and the bird flown forever--let me come when you are alone. Then charge me with what you will. I am an earthy creature, struggling through life as I best can, and, till I saw you, struggling often, no doubt, in very earthy ways. I am not a philosopher, nor an idealist, with expectations, like Delafield. This rough-and-tumble world is all I know. It's good enough for me--good enough to love a friend in, as--I vow to God, Julie!--I have loved you.

"There, it's out, and you must put up with it. I couldn't help it. I am too miserable.

"But--

"But I won't write any more. I shall stay in my rooms till twelve o'clock. You owe me promptness." #/

Julie put down the letter.

She looked round her little study with a kind of despair--the despair perhaps of the prisoner who had thought himself delivered, only to find himself caught in fresh and stronger bonds. As for ambition, as for literature--here, across their voices, broke this voice of the senses, this desire of "the moth for the star." And she was powerless to resist it. Ah, why had he not accepted his dismissal--quarrelled with her at once and forever?

She understood the letter perfectly--what it offered, and what it tacitly refused. An intimate and exciting friendship--for two years. For two years he was ready to fill up such time as he could spare from his clandestine correspondence with her cousin, with this romantic, interesting, but unprofitable affection. And then?

She fell again upon his letter. Ah, but there was a new note in it--a hard, strained note, which gave her a kind of desperate joy. It seemed to her that for months she had been covetously listening for it in vain.

She was beginning to be necessary to him; he had suffered--through her. Never before could she say that to herself. Pleasure she had given him, but not pain; and it is pain that is the test and consecration of--

Of what?... Well, now for her answer. It was short.

/# "I am very sorry you thought me rude. I was tired with talking and unpacking, and with literary work--housework, too, if the truth were known. I am no longer a fine lady, and must slave for myself. The thought, also, of an interview with Lord Lackington which faced me, which I went through as soon as you, Dr. Meredith, and Mr. Delafield had gone, unnerved me. You were good to write to me, and I am grateful indeed. As to your appointment, and your career, you owe no one anything. Everything is in your own hands. I rejoice in your good fortune, and I beg that you will let no false ideas with regard to me trouble your mind.

"This afternoon at five, if you can forgive me, you will find me. In the early afternoon I shall be in the British Museum, for my work's sake." #/

She posted her letter, and went about her daily housework, oppressed the while by a mental and moral nausea. As she washed and tidied and dusted, a true housewife's love growing up in her for the little house and its charming, old-world appointments--a sort of mute relation between her and it, as though it accepted her for mistress, and she on her side vowed it a delicate and prudent care--she thought how she could have delighted in this life which had opened upon her had it come to her a year ago. The tasks set her by Meredith were congenial and within her power. Her independence gave her the keenest pleasure. The effort and conquests of the intellect--she had the mind to love them, to desire them; and the way to them was unbarred.

What plucked her back?

A tear fell upon the old china cup that she was dusting. A sort of maternal element had entered into her affection for Warkworth during the winter. She had upheld him and fought for him. And now, like a mother, she could not tear the unworthy object from her heart, though all the folly of their pseudo-friendship and her secret hopes lay bare before her.

Warkworth came at five.

He entered in the dusk; a little pale, with his graceful head thrown back, and that half-startled, timid look in his wide, blue eyes--that misleading look--which made him the boy still, when he chose.

Julie was standing near the window as he came in. As she turned and saw him there, a flood of tenderness and compunction swept over her. He was going away. What if she never saw him again?

She shuddered and came forward rapidly, eagerly. He read the meaning of her movement, her face; and, wringing her hands with a violence that hurt her, he drew a long breath of relief.

"Why--why"--he said, under his breath--"have you made me so unhappy?"

The blood leaped in her veins. These, indeed, were new words in a new tone.

"Don't let us reproach each other," she said. "There is so much to say. Sit down."

To-day there were no beguiling spring airs. The fire burned merrily in the grate; the windows were closed.

A scent of narcissus--the Duchess had filled the tables with flowers--floated in the room. Amid its old-fashioned and distinguished bareness--tempered by flowers, and a litter of foreign books-- Julie seemed at last to have found her proper frame. In her severe black dress, opening on a delicate vest of white, she had a muselike grace; and the wreath made by her superb black hair round the fine intelligence of her brow had never been more striking. Her slender hands busied themselves with Cousin Mary Leicester's tea-things; and every movement had in Warkworth's eyes a charm to which he had never yet been sensible, in this manner, to this degree.

"Am I really to say no more of yesterday?" he said, looking at her nervously.

Her flush, her gesture, appealed to him.

"Do you know what I had before me--that day--when you came in?" she said, softly.

"No. I cannot guess. Ah, you said something about Lord Lackington?"

She hesitated. Then her color deepened.

"You don't know my story. You suppose, don't you, that I am a Belgian with English connections, whom Lady Henry met by chance? Isn't that how you explain me?"

Warkworth had pushed aside his cup.

"I thought--"

He paused in embarrassment, but there was a sparkle of astonished expectancy in his eyes.

"My mother"--she looked away into the blaze of the fire, and her voice choked a little--"my mother was Lord Lackington's daughter."

"Lord Lackington's daughter?" echoed Warkworth, in stupefaction. A rush of ideas and inferences sped through his mind. He thought of Lady Blanche--things heard in India--and while he stared at her in an agitated silence the truth leaped to light.

"Not--not Lady Rose Delaney?" he said, bending forward to her.

She nodded.

"My father was Marriott Dalrymple. You will have heard of him. I should be Julie Dalrymple, but--they could never marry--because of Colonel Delaney."

Her face was still turned away.

All the details of that famous scandal began to come back to him. His companion, her history, her relations to others, to himself, began to appear to him in the most astonishing new lights. So, instead of the mere humble outsider, she belonged all the time to the best English blood? The society in which he had met her was full of her kindred. No doubt the Duchess knew--and Montresor.... He was meshed in a net of thoughts perplexing and confounding, of which the total result was perhaps that she appeared to him as she sat there, the slender outline so quiet and still, more attractive and more desirable than ever. The mystery surrounding her in some way glorified her, and he dimly perceived that so it must have been for others.

"How did you ever bear the Bruton Street life?" he said, presently, in a low voice of wonder. "Lady Henry knew?"

"Oh yes!"

"And the Duchess?"

"Yes. She is a connection of my mother's."

Warkworth's mind went back to the Moffatts. A flush spread slowly over the face of the young officer. It was indeed an extraordinary imbroglio in which he found himself.

"How did Lord Lackington take it?" he asked, after a pause.

"He was, of course, much startled, much moved. We had a long talk. Everything is to remain just the same. He wishes to make me an allowance, and, if he persists, I suppose I can't hurt him by refusing. But for the present I have refused. It is more amusing to earn one's own living." She turned to him with a sharp brightness in her black eyes. "Besides, if Lord Lackington gives me money, he will want to give me advice. And I would rather advise myself."

Warkworth sat silent a moment. Then he took a great resolve.

"I want to speak to you," he said, suddenly, putting out his hand to hers, which lay on her knee. She turned to him, startled.

"I want to have no secrets from you," he said, drawing his breath quickly. "I told you lies one day, because I thought it was my duty to tell lies. Another person was concerned. But now I can't. Julie!--you'll let me call you so, won't you? The name is already"--he hesitated; then the words rushed out--"part of my life! Julie, it's quite true, there is a kind of understanding between your little cousin Aileen and me. At Simla she attracted me enormously. I lost my head one day in the woods, when she--whom we were all courting--distinguished me above two or three other men who were there. I proposed to her upon a sudden impulse, and she accepted me. She is a charming, soft creature. Perhaps I wasn't justified. Perhaps she ought to have had more chance of seeing the world. Anyway, there was a great row. Her guardians insisted that I had behaved badly. They could not know all the details of the matter, and I was not going to tell them. Finally I promised to withdraw for two years."

He paused, anxiously studying her face. It had grown very white, and, he thought, very cold. But she quickly rose, and, looking down upon him, said:

"Nothing of that is news to me. Did you think it was?"

And moving to the tea-table, she began to make provision for a fresh supply of tea.

Both words and manner astounded him. He, too, rose and followed her.

"How did you first guess?" he said, abruptly.

"Some gossip reached me." She looked up with a smile. "That's what generally happens, isn't it?"

"There are no secrets nowadays," he said, sorely. "And then, there was Miss Lawrence?"

"Yes, there was Miss Lawrence."

"Did you think badly of me?"

"Why should I? I understand Aileen is very pretty, and--"

"And will have a large fortune. You understand that?" he said, trying to carry it off lightly.

"The fact is well known, isn't it?"

He sat down, twisting his hat between his hands. Then with an exclamation he dashed it on the floor, and, rising, he bent over Julie, his hands in his pockets.

"Julie," he said, in a voice that shook her, "don't, for God's sake, give me up! I have behaved abominably, but don't take your friendship from me. I shall soon be gone. Our lives will go different ways. That was settled--alack!--before we met. I am honorably bound to that poor child. She cares for me, and I can't get loose. But these last months have been happy, haven't they? There are just three weeks left. At present the strongest feeling in my heart is--" He paused for his word, and he saw that she was looking through the window to the trees of the garden, and that, still as she was, her lip quivered.

"What shall I say?" he resumed, with emotion. "It seems to me our case stands all by itself, alone in the world. We have three weeks--give them to me. Don't let's play at cross purposes any more. I want to be sincere--I want to hide nothing from you in these days. Let us throw aside convention and trust each other, as friends may, so that when I go we may say to each other, 'Well, it was worth the pain. These have been days of gold--we shall get no better if we live to be a hundred.'"

She turned her face to him in a tremulous amazement and there were tears on her cheek. Never had his aspect been so winning. What he proposed was, in truth, a mean thing; all the same, he proposed it nobly.

It was in vain that something whispered in her ear: "This girl to whom he describes himself as 'honorably bound' has a fortune of half a million. He is determined to have both her money and my heart." Another inward voice, tragically generous, dashed down the thought, and, at the moment, rightly; for as he stood over her, breathless and imperious, to his own joy, to his own exaltation, Warkworth was conscious of a new sincerity flowing in a tempestuous and stormy current through all the veins of being.

With a sombre passion which already marked an epoch in their relation, and contained within itself the elements of new and unforeseen developments, she gazed silently into his face. Then, leaning back in her chair, she once more held out to him both her hands.

He gave an exclamation of joy, kissed the hands tenderly, and sat down beside her.

"Now, then, all your cares, all your thoughts, all your griefs are to be mine--till fate call us. And I have a thousand things to tell you, to bless you for, to consult you about. There is not a thought in my mind that you shall not know--bad, good, and indifferent--if you care to turn out the rag-bag. Shall I begin with the morning--my experiences at the club, my little nieces at the Zoo?" He laughed, but suddenly grew serious again. "No, your story first; you owe it me. Let me know all that concerns you. Your past, your sorrows, ambitions--everything."

He bent to her imperiously. With a faint, broken smile, her hands still in his, she assented. It was difficult to begin, then difficult to control the flood of memory; and it had long been dark when Madame Bornier, coming in to light the lamp and make up the fire, disturbed an intimate and searching conversation, which had revealed the two natures to each other with an agitating fulness.

Yet the results of this memorable evening upon Julie Le Breton were ultimately such as few could have foreseen.

When Warkworth had left her, she went to her own room and sat for a long while beside the window, gazing at the dark shrubberies of the Cureton House garden, at the few twinkling, distant lights.

The vague, golden hopes she had cherished through these past months of effort and scheming were gone forever. Warkworth would marry Aileen Moffatt, and use her money for an ambitious career. After these weeks now lying before them--weeks of dangerous intimacy, dangerous emotion--she and he would become as strangers to each other. He would be absorbed by his profession and his rich marriage. She would be left alone to live her life.

A sudden terror of her own weakness overcame her. No, she could not be alone. She must place a barrier between herself and this--this strange threatening of illimitable ruin that sometimes rose upon her from the dark. "I have no prejudices," she had said to Sir Wilfrid. There were many moments when she felt a fierce pride in the element of lawlessness, of defiance, that seemed to be her inheritance from her parents. But to-night she was afraid of it.

Again, if love was to go, power, the satisfaction of ambition, remained. She threw a quick glance into the future--the future beyond these three weeks. What could she make of it? She knew well that she was not the woman to resign herself to a mere pining obscurity.

Jacob Delafield? Was it, after all, so impossible?

For a few minutes she set herself deliberately to think out what it would mean to marry him; then suddenly broke down and wept, with inarticulate cries and sobs, with occasional reminiscences of her old convent's prayers, appeals half conscious, instinctive, to a God only half believed.

XVI

Delafield was walking through the Park towards Victoria Gate. A pair of beautiful roans pulled up suddenly beside him, and a little figure with a waving hand bent to him from a carriage.

"Jacob, where are you off to? Let me give you a lift?"

The gentleman addressed took off his hat.

"Much obliged to you, but I want some exercise. I say, where did Freddie get that pair?"

"I don't know, he doesn't tell me. Jacob, you must get in. I want to speak to you."

Rather unwillingly, Delafield obeyed, and away they sped.

"J'ai un tas de choses à vous dire," she said, speaking low, and in French, so as to protect herself from the servants in front. "Jacob, I'm very unhappy about Julie."

Delafield frowned uncomfortably.

"Why? Hadn't you better leave her alone?"

"Oh, of course, I know you think me a chatterbox. I don't care. You must let me tell you some fresh news about her. It isn't gossip, and you and I are her best friends. Oh, Freddie's so disagreeable about her. Jacob, you've got to help and advise a little. Now, do listen. It's your duty--your downright catechism duty."

And she poured into his reluctant ear the tale which Miss Emily Lawrence nearly a fortnight before had confided to her.

"Of course," she wound up, "you'll say it's only what we knew or guessed long ago. But you see, Jacob, we didn't know. It might have been just gossip. And then, besides"--she frowned and dropped her voice till it was only just audible--"this horrid man hadn't made our Julie so--so conspicuous, and Lady Henry hadn't turned out such a toad--and, altogether, Jacob, I'm dreadfully worried."

"Don't be," said Jacob, dryly.

"And what a creature!" cried the Duchess, unheeding. "They say that poor Moffatt child will soon have fretted herself ill, if the guardians don't give way about the two years."

"What two years?"

"The two years that she must wait--till she is twenty-one. Oh, Jacob, you know that!" exclaimed the Duchess, impatient with him. "I've told you scores of times."

"I'm not in the least interested in Miss Moffatt's affairs."

"But you ought to be, for they concern Julie," cried the Duchess. "Can't you imagine what kind of things people are saying? Lady Henry has spread it about that it was all to see him she bribed the Bruton Street servants to let her give the Wednesday party as usual--that she had been flirting with him abominably for months, and using Lady Henry's name in the most impertinent ways. And now, suddenly, everybody seems to know something about this Indian engagement. You may imagine it doesn't look very well for our poor Julie. The other night at Chatton House I was furious. I made Julie go. I wanted her to show herself, and keep up her friends. Well, it was horrid! One or two old frights, who used to be only too thankful to Julie for reminding Lady Henry to invite them, put their noses in the air and behaved odiously. And even some of the nicer ones seemed changed--I could see Julie felt it."

"Nothing of all that will do her any real harm," said Jacob, rather contemptuously.

"Well, no. I know, of course, that her real friends will never forsake her--never, never! But, Jacob"--the Duchess hesitated, her charming little face furrowed with thought--"if only so much of it weren't true. She herself--"

"Please, Evelyn," said Delafield, with decision, "don't tell me anything she may have said to you."

The Duchess flushed.

"I shouldn't have betrayed any confidence," she said, proudly. "And I must consult with some one who cares about her. Dr. Meredith lunched with me to-day, and he said a few words to me afterwards. He's quite anxious, too--and unhappy. Captain Warkworth's always there--always! Even I have been hardly able to see her the last few days. Last Sunday they took the little lame child and went into the country for the whole day--"

"Well, what is there to object to in that?" cried Jacob.

"I didn't say there was anything to object to," said the Duchess, looking at him with eyes half angry, half perplexed. "Only it's so unlike her. She had promised to be at home that afternoon for several old friends, and they found her flown, without a word. And think how sweet Julie is always about such things--what delicious notes she writes, how she hates to put anybody out or disappoint them! And now, not a word of excuse to anybody. And she looks so ill--so white, so fixed--like a person in a dream which she can't shake off. I'm just miserable about her. And I hate, hate that man--engaged to her own cousin all the time!" cried the little Duchess, under her breath, as she passionately tore some violets at her waist to pieces and flung them out of the carriage. Then she turned to Jacob.

"But, of course, if you don't care twopence about all this, Jacob, it's no good talking to you!"

Her taunt fell quite unnoticed. Jacob turned to her with smiling composure.

"You have forgotten, my dear Evelyn, all this time, that Warkworth goes away--to mid-Africa--in little more than two weeks."

"I wish it was two minutes," said the Duchess, fuming.

Delafield made no reply for a while. He seemed to be studying the effect of a pale shaft of sunlight which had just come stealing down through layers of thin gray cloud to dance upon the Serpentine. Presently, as they left the Serpentine behind them, he turned to his companion with more apparent sympathy.

"We can't do anything, Evelyn, and we've no right whatever to talk of alarm, or anxiety--to talk of it, mind! It's--it's disloyal. Forgive me," he added, hastily, "I know you don't gossip. But it fills me with rage that other people should be doing it."

The brusquerie of his manner disconcerted the little lady beside him. She recovered herself, however, and said, with a touch of sarcasm, tempered by a rather trembling lip:

"Your rage won't prevent their gossiping, Mr. Jacob, I thought, perhaps, your friendship might have done something to stop it--to--to influence Julie," she added, uncertainly.

"My friendship, as you call it, is of no use whatever," he said, obstinately. "Warkworth will go away, and if you and others do their best to protect Miss Le Breton, talk will soon die out. Behave as if you had never heard the man's name before--stare the people down. Why, good Heavens! you have a thousand arts! But, of course, if the little flame is to be blown into a blaze by a score of so-called friends--"

He shrugged his shoulders.

The Duchess did not take his rebukes kindly, not having, in truth, deserved them.

"You are rude and unkind, Jacob," she said, almost with the tears in her eyes. "And you don't understand--it is because I myself am so anxious--"

"For that reason, play the part with all your might," he said, unyieldingly. "Really, even you and I oughtn't to talk of it any more. But there is one thing I want very much to know about Miss Le Breton."

He bent towards her, smiling, though in truth he was disgusted with himself, vexed with her, and out of tune with all the world.

The Duchess made a little face.

"All very well, but after such a lecture as you have indulged in, I think I prefer not to say any more about Julie."

"Do. I'm ashamed of myself--except that I don't retract one word, not one. Be kind, all the same, and tell me--if you know--has she spoken to Lord Lackington?"

The Duchess still frowned, but a few more apologetic expressions on his part restored a temper that had always a natural tendency to peace. Indeed, Jacob's boutades never went long unpardoned. An only child herself, he, her first cousin, had played the part of brother in her life, since the days when she first tottered in long frocks, and he had never played it in any mincing fashion. His words were often blunt. She smarted and forgave--much more quickly than she forgave her husband. But then, with him, she was in love.

So she presently vouchsafed to give Jacob the news that Lord Lackington at last knew the secret--that he had behaved well--had shown much feeling, in fact--so that poor Julie--

But Jacob again cut short the sentimentalisms, the little touching phrases in which the woman delighted.

"What is he going to do for her?" he said, impatiently. "Will he make any provision for her? Is there any way by which she can live in his house--take care of him?"

The Duchess shook her head.

"At seventy-five one can't begin to explain a thing as big as that. Julie perfectly understands, and doesn't wish it."

"But as to money?" persisted Jacob.

"Julie says nothing about money. How odd you are, Jacob! I thought that was the last thing needful in your eyes."

Jacob did not reply. If he had, he would probably have said that what was harmful or useless for men might be needful for women--for the weakness of women. But he kept silence, while the vague intensity of the eyes, the pursed and twisted mouth, showed that his mind was full of thoughts.

Suddenly he perceived that the carriage was nearing Victoria Gate. He called to the coachman to stop, and jumped out.

"Good-bye, Evelyn. Don't bear me malice. You're a good friend," he said in her ear--"a real good friend. But don't let people talk to you--not even elderly ladies with the best intentions. I tell you it will be a fight, and one of the best weapons is"--he touched his lips significantly, smiled at her, and was gone.

The Duchess passed out of the Park. Delafield turned as though in the direction of the Marble Arch, but as soon as the carriage was out of sight he paused and quickly retraced his steps towards Kensington Gardens. Here, in this third week of March, some of the thorns and lilacs were already in leaf. The grass was springing, and the chatter of many sparrows filled the air. Faint patches of sun flecked the ground between the trees, and blue hazes, already redeemed from the dreariness of winter, filled the dim planes of distance and mingled with the low, silvery clouds. He found a quiet spot, remote from nursery-maids and children, and there he wandered to and fro, indefinitely, his hands behind his back. All the anxieties for which he had scolded his cousin possessed him, only sharpened tenfold; he was in torture, and he was helpless.

However, when at last he emerged from his solitude, and took a hansom to the Chudleigh estate office in Spring Gardens, he resolutely shook off the thoughts which had been weighing upon him. He took his usual interest in his work, and did it with his usual capacity.

Towards five o'clock in the afternoon, Delafield found himself in Cureton Street. As he turned down Heribert Street he saw a cab in front of him. It stopped at Miss Le Breton's door, and Warkworth jumped out. The door was quickly opened to him, and he went in without having turned his eyes towards the man at the far corner of the street.

Delafield paused irresolute. Finally he walked back to his club in Piccadilly, where he dawdled over the newspapers till nearly seven.

Then he once more betook himself to Heribert Street.

"Is Miss Le Breton at home?"

Thérèse looked at him with a sudden flickering of her clear eyes.

"I think so, sir," she said, with soft hesitation, and she slowly led him across the hall.

The drawing-room door opened. Major Warkworth emerged.

"Ah, how do you do?" he said, shortly, staring in a kind of bewilderment as he saw Delafield. Then he hurriedly looked for his hat, ran down the stairs, and was gone.

"Announce me, please," said Delafield, peremptorily, to the little girl. "Tell Miss Le Breton that I am here." And he drew back from the open door of the drawing-room. Thérèse slipped in, and reappeared.

"Please to walk in, sir," she said, in her shy, low voice, and Delafield entered. From the hall he had caught one involuntary glimpse of Julie, standing stiff and straight in the middle of the room, her hands clasped to her breast--a figure in pain. When he went in, she was in her usual seat by the fire, with her embroidery frame in front of her.

"May I come in? It is rather late."

"Oh, by all means! Do you bring me any news of Evelyn? I haven't seen her for three days."

He seated himself beside her. It was hard, indeed, for him to hide all signs of the tumult within. But he held a firm grip upon himself.

"I saw Evelyn this afternoon. She complained that you had had no time for her lately."

Julie bent over her work. He saw that her fingers were so unsteady that she could hardly make them obey her.

"There has been a great deal to do, even in this little house. Evelyn forgets; she has an army of servants; we have only our hands and our time."

She looked up, smiling. He made no reply, and the smile died from her face, suddenly, as though some one had blown out a light. She returned to her work, or pretended to. But her aspect had left him inwardly shaken. The eyes, disproportionately large and brilliant, were of an emphasis almost ghastly, the usually clear complexion was flecked and cloudy, the mouth dry-lipped. She looked much older than she had done a fortnight before. And the fact was the more noticeable because in her dress she had now wholly discarded the touch of stateliness--almost old-maidishness--which had once seemed appropriate to the position of Lady Henry's companion. She was wearing a little gown of her youth, a blue cotton, which two years before had been put aside as too slight and juvenile. Never had the form within it seemed so girlish, so appealing. But the face was heart-rending.

After a pause he moved a little closer to her.

"Do you know that you are looking quite ill?"

"Then my looks are misleading. I am very well."

"I am afraid I don't put much faith in that remark. When do you mean to take a holiday?"

"Oh, very soon. Léonie, my little housekeeper, talks of going to Bruges to wind up all her affairs there and bring back some furniture that she has warehoused. I may go with her. I, too, have some property stored there. I should go and see some old friends--the soeurs, for instance, with whom I went to school. In the old days I was a torment to them, and they were tyrants to me. But they are quite nice to me now--they give me patisserie, and stroke my hands and spoil me."

And she rattled on about the friends she might revisit, in a hollow, perfunctory way, which set him on edge.

"I don't see that anything of that kind will do you any good. You want rest of mind and body. I expect those last scenes with Lady Henry cost you more than you knew. There are wounds one does not notice at the time--"

"Which afterwards bleed inwardly?" She laughed. "No, no, I am not bleeding for Lady Henry. By-the-way, what news of her?"

"Sir Wilfrid told me to-day that he had had a letter. She is at Torquay, and she thinks there are too many curates at Torquay. She is not at all in a good temper."

Julie looked up.

"You know that she is trying to punish me. A great many people seem to have been written to."

"That will blow over."

"I don't know. How confident I was at one time that, if there was a breach, it would be Lady

Henry that would suffer! It makes me hot to remember some things I said--to Sir Wilfrid, in particular. I see now that I shall not be troubled with society in this little house."

"It is too early for you to guess anything of that kind."

"Not at all! London is pretty full. The affair has made a noise. Those who meant to stand by me would have called, don't you think?"

The quivering bitterness of her face was most pitiful in Jacob's eyes.

"Oh, people take their time," he said, trying to speak lightly.

She shook her head.

"It's ridiculous that I should care. One's self-love, I suppose--that bleeds! Evelyn has made me send out cards for a little house-warming. She said I must. She made me go to that smart party at Chatton House the other night. It was a great mistake. People turned their backs on me. And this, too, will be a mistake--and a failure."

"You were kind enough to send me a card."

"Yes--and you must come?"

She looked at him with a sudden nervous appeal, which made another tug on his self-control.

"Of course I shall come."

"Do you remember your own saying--that awful evening--that I had devoted friends? Well, we shall soon see."

"That depends only on yourself," he replied, with gentle deliberation.

She started--threw him a doubtful look.

"If you mean that I must take a great deal of trouble, I am afraid I can't. I am too tired."

And she sank back in her chair.

The sigh that accompanied the words seemed to him involuntary, unconscious.

"I didn't mean that--altogether," he said, after a moment.

She moved restlessly.

"Then, really, I don't know what you meant. I suppose all friendship depends on one's self."

She drew her embroidery frame towards her again, and he was left to wonder at his own audacity. "Do you know," she said, presently, her eyes apparently busy with her silks, "that I have told Lord Lackington?"

"Yes. Evelyn gave me that news. How has the old man behaved?"

"Oh, very well--most kindly. He has already formed a habit, almost, of 'dropping in' upon me at all hours. I have had to appoint him times and seasons, or there would be no work done. He sits here and raves about young Mrs. Delaray--you know he is painting her portrait, for the famous series?--and draws her profile on the backs of my letters. He recites his speeches to me; he asks my advice as to his fights with his tenants or his miners. In short, I'm adopted--I'm almost the real thing."

She smiled, and then again, as she turned over her silks, he heard her sigh--a long breath of weariness. It was strange and terrible in his ear--the contrast between this unconscious sound, drawn as it were from the oppressed heart of pain, and her languidly, smiling words.

"Has he spoken to you of the Moffatts?" he asked her, presently, not looking at her.

A sharp crimson color rushed over her face.

"Not much. He and Lady Blanche are not great friends. And I have made him promise to keep my secret from her till I give him leave to tell it."

"It will have to be known to her some time, will it not?"

"Perhaps," she said, impatiently. "Perhaps, when I can make up my mind."

Then she pushed aside her frame and would talk no more about Lord Lackington. She gave him, somehow, the impression of a person suffocating, struggling for breath and air. And yet her hand was icy, and she presently went to the fire, complaining of the east wind; and as he put on the coal he saw her shiver.

"Shall I force her to tell me everything?" he thought to himself.

Did she divine the obscure struggle in his mind? At any rate she seemed anxious to cut short their tête-à-tête. She asked him to come and look at some engravings which the Duchess had sent round for the embellishment of the dining-room. Then she summoned Madame Bornier, and asked him a number of questions on Léonie's behalf, with reference to some little investment of the ex-governess's savings, which had been dropping in value. Meanwhile, as she kept him talking, she leaned herself against the lintel of the door, forgetting every now and then that any one else was there, and letting the true self appear, like some drowned thing floating into sight. Delafield disposed of Madame Bornier's affairs, hardly knowing what he said, but showing in truth his usual conscience and kindness. Then when Léonie was contented, Julie saw the little cripple crossing the hall, and called to her.

"Ah, ma chérie! How is the poor little foot?"

And turning to Delafield, she explained volubly that Thérèse had given herself a slight twist on the stairs that morning, pressing the child to her side the while with a tender gesture. The child nestled against her.

"Shall maman keep back supper?" Thérèse half whispered, looking at Delafield.

"No, no, I must go!" cried Delafield, rousing himself and looking for his hat.

"I would ask you to stay," said Julie, smiling, "just to show off Léonie's cooking; but there wouldn't be enough for a great big man. And you're probably dining with dukes."

Delafield disclaimed any such intention, and they went back to the drawing-room to look for his hat and stick. Julie still had her arm round Thérèse and would not let the child go. She clearly avoided being left alone with him; and yet it seemed, even to his modesty, that she was loath to see him depart. She talked first of her little ménage, as though proud of their daily economies and contrivances; then of her literary work and its prospects; then of her debt to Meredith. Never before had she thus admitted him to her domestic and private life. It was as though she leaned upon his sympathy, his advice, his mere neighborhood. And her pale, changed face had never seemed to him so beautiful--never, in fact, truly beautiful till now. The dying down of the brilliance and energy of the strongly marked character, which had made her the life of the Bruton Street salon, into this mildness, this despondency, this hidden weariness, had left her infinitely more lovely in his eyes. But how to restrain himself much longer from taking the sad, gracious woman in his arms and coercing her into sanity and happiness!

At last he tore himself away.

"You won't forget Wednesday?" she said to him, as she followed him into the hall.

"No. Is there anything else that you wish--that I could do?"

"No, nothing. But if there is I will ask."

Then, looking up, she shrank from something in his face--something accusing, passionate, profound.

He wrung her hand.

"Promise that you will ask."

She murmured something, and he turned away.

She came back alone into the drawing-room.

"Oh, what a good man!" she said, sighing. "What a good man!"

And then, all in a moment, she was thankful that he was gone--that she was alone with and mistress of her pain.

The passion and misery which his visit had interrupted swept back upon her in a rushing swirl, blinding and choking every sense. Ah, what a scene, to which his coming had put an end--scene of bitterness, of recrimination, not restrained even by this impending anguish of parting!

It came as a close to a week during which she and Warkworth had been playing the game which they had chosen to play, according to its appointed rules--the delicacies and restraints of friendship masking, and at the same time inflaming, a most unhappy, poisonous, and growing love. And, finally, there had risen upon them a storm-wave of feeling--tyrannous, tempestuous--bursting in reproach and agitation, leaving behind it, bare and menacing, the old, ugly facts, unaltered and unalterable.

Warkworth was little less miserable than herself. That she knew. He loved her, as it were, to his own anger and surprise. And he suffered in deserting her, more than he had ever suffered yet through any human affection.

But his purpose through it all remained stubbornly fixed; that, also, she knew. For nearly a year Aileen Moffatt's fortune and Aileen Moffatt's family connections had entered into all his calculations of the future. Only a few more years in the army, then retirement with ample means, a charming wife, and a seat in Parliament. To jeopardize a plan so manifestly desirable, so easy to carry out, so far-reaching in its favorable effects upon his life, for the sake of those hard and doubtful alternatives in which a marriage with Julie would involve him, never seriously entered his mind. When he suffered he merely said to himself, steadily, that time would heal the smart for both of them.

"Only one thing would be absolutely fatal for all of us--that I should break with Aileen."

Julie read these obscure processes in Warkworth's mind with perfect clearness. She was powerless to change them; but that afternoon she had, at any rate, beaten her wings against the bars, and the exhaustion and anguish of her revolt, her reproaches, were still upon her.

The spring night had fallen. The room was hot, and she threw a window open. Some thorns in the garden beneath had thickened into leaf. They rose in a dark mass beneath the window. Overhead, beyond the haze of the great city, a few stars twinkled, and the dim roar of London life beat from all sides upon this quiet corner which still held Lady Mary's old house.

Julie's eyes strained into the darkness; her head swam with weakness and weariness. Suddenly she gave a cry--she pressed her hands to her heart. Upon the darkness outside there rose a face, so sharply drawn, so life-like, that it printed itself forever upon the quivering tissues of the brain. It was Warkworth's face, not as she had seen it last, but in some strange extremity of physical ill--drawn, haggard, in a cold sweat--the eyes glazed, the hair matted, the parched lips open as though they cried for help. She stood gazing. Then the eyes turned, and the agony in them looked out upon her.

Her whole sense was absorbed by the phantom; her being hung upon it. Then, as it faded on the quiet trees, she tottered to a chair and hid her face. Common sense told her that she was the victim of her own tired nerves and tortured fancy. But the memory of Cousin Mary Leicester's second sight, of her "visions" in this very room, crept upon her and gripped her heart. A ghostly horror seized her of the room, the house, and her own tempestuous nature. She groped her way out, in blind and hurrying panic--glad of the lamp in the hall, glad of the sounds in the house, glad, above all, of Thérèse's thin hands as they once more stole lovingly round her own.

XVII

The Duchess and Julie were in the large room of Burlington House. They had paused before a magnificent Turner of the middle period, hitherto unseen by the public, and the Duchess was reading from the catalogue in Julie's ear.

She had found Julie alone in Heribert Street, surrounded by books and proofs, endeavoring, as she reported, to finish a piece of work for Dr. Meredith. Distressed by her friend's pale cheeks, the Duchess had insisted on dragging her from the prison-house and changing the current of her thoughts. Julie, laughing, hesitating, indignant, had at last yielded--probably in order to avoid another tête-à-tête and another scene with the little, impetuous lady, and now the Duchess had her safe and was endeavoring to amuse her.

But it was not easy. Julie, generally so instructed and sympathetic, so well skilled in the difficult art of seeing pictures with a friend, might, to-day, never have turned a phrase upon a Constable or a Romney before. She tried, indeed, to turn them as usual; but the Duchess, sharply critical and attentive where her beloved Julie was concerned, perceived the difference acutely! Alack, what languor, what fatigue! Evelyn became more and more conscious of an inward consternation.

"But, thank goodness, he goes to-morrow--the villain! And when that's over, it will be all right."

Julie, meanwhile, knew that she was observed, divined, and pitied. Her pride revolted, but it could wring from her nothing better than a passive resistance. She could prevent Evelyn from expressing her thoughts; she could not so command her own bodily frame that the Duchess should not think. Days of moral and mental struggle, nights of waking, combined with the serious and sustained effort of a new profession, had left their mark. There are, moreover, certain wounds to self-love and self-respect which poison the whole being.

"Julie! you must have a holiday!" cried the Duchess, presently, as they sat down to rest.

Julie replied that she, Madame Bornier, and the child were going to Bruges for a week.

"Oh, but that won't be comfortable enough! I'm sure I could arrange something. Think of all our tiresome houses--eating their heads off!"

Julie firmly refused. She was going to renew old friendships at Bruges; she would be made much of; and the prospect was as pleasant as any one need wish.

"Well, of course, if you have made up your mind. When do you go?"

"In three or four days--just before the Easter rush. And you?"

"Oh, we go to Scotland to fish. We must, of course, be killing something. How long, darling, will you be away?"

"About ten days." Julie pressed the Duchess's little hand in acknowledgment of the caressing word and look.

"By-the-way, didn't Lord Lackington invite you? Ah, there he is!"

And suddenly, Lord Lackington, examining with fury a picture of his own which some rascally critic had that morning pronounced to be "Venetian school" and not the divine Giorgione himself, lifted an angry countenance to find the Duchess and Julie beside him.

The start which passed through him betrayed itself. He could not yet see Julie with composure. But when he had pressed her hand and inquired after her health, he went back to his grievance, being indeed rejoiced to have secured a pair of listeners.

"Really, the insolence of these fellows in the press! I shall let the Academy know what I think of it. Not a rag of mine shall they ever see here again. Ears and little fingers, indeed! Idiots and owls!"

Julie smiled. But it had to be explained to the Duchess that a wise man, half Italian, half German, had lately arisen who proposed to judge the authenticity of a picture by its ears, assisted by any peculiarities of treatment in the little fingers.

"What nonsense!" said the Duchess, with a yawn. "If I were an artist, I should always draw them different ways."

"Well, not exactly," said Lord Lackington, who, as an artist himself, was unfortunately debarred from statements of this simplicity. "But the ludicrous way in which these fools overdo their little discoveries!"

And he walked on, fuming, till the open and unmeasured admiration of the two ladies for his great Rembrandt, the gem of his collection, now occupying the place of honor in the large room of the Academy, restored him to himself.

"Ah, even the biggest ass among them holds his tongue about that!" he said, exultantly. "But, hallo! What does that call itself?" He looked at a picture in front of him, then at the catalogue, then at the Duchess.

"That picture is ours," said the Duchess. "Isn't it a dear? It's a Leonardo da Vinci."

"Leonardo fiddlesticks!" cried Lord Lackington. "Leonardo, indeed! What absurdity! Really, Duchess, you should tell Crowborough to be more careful about his things. We mustn't give handles to these fellows."

"What do you mean?" said the Duchess, offended. "If it isn't a Leonardo, pray what is it?"

"Why, a bad school copy, of course!" said Lord Lackington, hotly. "Look at the eyes"--he took out a pencil and pointed--"look at the neck, look at the fingers!"

The Duchess pouted.

"Oh!" she said. "Then there is something in fingers!"

Lord Lackington's face suddenly relaxed. He broke into a shout of laughter, bon enfant that he was; and the Duchess laughed, too; but under cover of their merriment she, mindful of quite other things, drew him a little farther away from Julie.

"I thought you had asked her to Nonpareil for Easter?" she said, in his ear, with a motion of her pretty head towards Julie in the distance.

"Yes, but, my dear lady, Blanche won't come home! She and Aileen put it off, and put it off. Now she says they mean to spend May in Switzerland--may perhaps be away the whole summer! I had counted on them for Easter. I am dependent on Blanche for hostess. It is really too bad of her. Everything has broken down, and William and I (he named his youngest son) are going to the Uredales' for a fortnight."

Lord Uredale, his eldest son, a sportsman and farmer, troubled by none of his father's originalities, reigned over the second family "place," in Herefordshire, beside the Wye.

"Has Aileen any love affairs yet?" said the Duchess, abruptly, raising her face to his.

Lord Lackington looked surprised.

"Not that I know of. However, I dare say they wouldn't tell me. I'm a sieve, I know. Have you heard of any? Tell me." He stooped to her with roguish eagerness. "I like to steal a march on Blanche."

So he knew nothing--while half their world was talking! It was very characteristic, however. Except for his own hobbies, artistic, medical, or military, Lord Lackington had walked through life as a Johnny Head-in-Air, from his youth till now. His children had not trusted him with their secrets, and he had never discovered them for himself.

"Is there any likeness between Julie and Aileen?" whispered the Duchess.

Lord Lackington started. Both turned their eyes towards Julie, as she stood some ten yards away from them, in front of a refined and mysterious profile of the cinque-cento--some lady, perhaps, of the d'Este or Sforza families, attributed to Ambrogio da Predis. In her soft, black dress, delicately folded and draped to hide her excessive thinness, her small toque fitting closely over her wealth of hair, her only ornaments a long and slender chain set with uncut jewels which Lord Lackington had brought her the day before, and a bunch of violets which the Duchess had just slipped into her belt, she was as rare and delicate as the picture. But she turned her face towards them, and Lord Lackington made a sudden exclamation.

"No! Good Heavens, no! Aileen was a dancing-sprite when I saw her last, and this poor girl!-- Duchess, why does she look like that? So sad, so bloodless!"

He turned upon her impetuously, his face frowning and disturbed.

The Duchess sighed.

"You and I have just got to do all we can for her," she said, relieved to see that Julie had wandered farther away, as though it pleased her to be left to herself.

"But I would do anything--everything!" cried Lord Lackington. "Of course, none of us can undo the past. But I offered yesterday to make full provision for her. She has refused. She has the most Quixotic notions, poor child!"

"No, let her earn her own living yet awhile. It will do her good. But--shall I tell you secrets?" The Duchess looked at him, knitting her small brows.

"Tell me what I ought to know--no more," he said, gravely, with a dignity contrasting oddly with his school-boy curiosity in the matter of little Aileen's lover.

The Duchess hesitated. Just in front of her was a picture of the Venetian school representing St. George, Princess Saba, and the dragon. The princess, a long and slender victim, with bowed head and fettered hands, reminded her of Julie. The dragon--perfidious, encroaching wretch!--he was easy enough of interpretation. But from the blue distance, thank Heaven! spurs the champion. Oh, ye heavenly powers, give him wings and strength! "St. George--St. George to the rescue!"

"Well," she said, slowly, "I can tell you of some one who is very devoted to Julie--some one worthy of her. Come with me."

And she took him away into the next room, still talking in his ear.

When they returned, Lord Lackington was radiant. With a new eagerness he looked for Julie's distant figure amid the groups scattered about the central room. The Duchess had sworn him to secrecy, indeed; and he meant to be discretion itself. But--Jacob Delafield! Yes, that, indeed, would be a solution. His pride was acutely pleased; his affection--of which he already began to feel no small store for this charming woman of his own blood, this poor granddaughter de la main gauche--was strengthened and stimulated. She was sad now and out of spirits, poor thing, because, no doubt, of this horrid business with Lady Henry, to whom, by-the-way, he had written his mind. But time would see to that--time--gently and discreetly assisted by himself and the Duchess. It was impossible that she should finally hold out against such a good fellow-- impossible, and most unreasonable. No. Rose's daughter would be brought back safely to her mother's world and class, and poor Rose's tragedy would at last work itself out for good. How strange, romantic, and providential!

In such a mood did he now devote himself to Julie. He chattered about the pictures; he gossiped about their owners; he excused himself for the absence of "that gad-about Blanche"; he made her promise him a Whitsuntide visit instead, and whispered in her ear, "You shall have her room"; he paid her the most handsome and gallant attentions, natural to the man of fashion par excellence, mingled with something intimate, brusque, capricious, which marked her his own, and of the family. Seventy-five!--with that step, that carriage of the shoulders, that vivacity! Ridiculous!

And Julie could not but respond.

Something stole into her heart that had never yet lodged there. She must love the old man--she did. When he left her for the Duchess her eyes followed him--her dark-rimmed, wistful eyes.

"I must be off," said Lord Lackington, presently, buttoning up his coat. "This, ladies, has been dalliance. I now go to my duties. Read me in the Times to-morrow. I shall make a rattling speech. You see, I shall rub it in."

"Montresor?" said the Duchess.

Lord Lackington nodded. That afternoon he proposed to strew the floor of the House of Lords with the débris of Montresor's farcical reforms.

Suddenly he pulled himself up.

"Duchess, look round you, at those two in the doorway. Isn't it--by George, it is!--Chudleigh and his boy!"

"Yes--yes, it is," said the Duchess, in some excitement. "Don't recognize them. Don't speak to him. Jacob implored me not."

And she hurried her companions along till they were well out of the track of the new-comers; then on the threshold of another room she paused, and, touching Julie on the arm, said, in a whisper:

"Now look back. That's Jacob's Duke, and his poor, poor boy!"

Julie threw a hurried glance towards the two figures; but that glance impressed forever upon her memory a most tragic sight.

A man of middle height, sallow, and careworn, with jet-black hair and beard, supported a sickly lad, apparently about seventeen, who clung to his arm and coughed at intervals. The father moved as though in a dream. He looked at the pictures with unseeing, lustreless eyes, except when the boy asked him a question. Then he would smile, stoop his head and answer, only to resume again immediately his melancholy passivity. The boy, meanwhile, his lips gently parted over his white teeth, his blue eyes wide open and intent upon the pictures, his emaciated cheeks deeply flushed, wore an aspect of patient suffering, of docile dependence, peculiarly touching.

It was evident the father and son thought of none but each other. From time to time the man would make the boy rest on one of the seats in the middle of the room, and the boy would look up and chatter to his companion standing before him. Then again they would resume their walk, the boy leaning on his father. Clearly the poor lad was marked for death; clearly, also, he was the desire of his father's heart.

"The possessor, and the heir, of perhaps the finest houses and the most magnificent estates in England," said Lord Lackington, with a shrug of pity. "And Chudleigh would gladly give them all to keep that boy alive."

Julie turned away. Strange thoughts had been passing and repassing through her brain.

Then, with angry loathing, she flung her thoughts from her. What did the Chudleigh inheritance matter to her? That night she said good-bye to the man she loved. These three miserable, burning weeks were done. Her heart, her life, would go with Warkworth to Africa and the desert. If at the beginning of this period of passion--so short in prospect, and, to look back upon, an eternity--she had ever supposed that power or wealth could make her amends for the loss of her lover, she was in no mood to calculate such compensations to-day. Parting was too near, the anguish in her veins too sharp.

"Jacob takes them to Paris to-morrow," said the Duchess to Lord Lackington. "The Duke has heard of some new doctor."

An hour or two later, Sir Wilfrid Bury, in the smoking-room of his club, took out a letter which he had that morning received from Lady Henry Delafield and gave it a second reading.

/# "So I hear that mademoiselle's social prospects are not, after all, so triumphant as both she and I imagined. I gave the world credit for more fools than it seems actually to possess; and she-- well, I own I am a little puzzled. Has she taken leave of her senses? I am told that she is constantly seen with this man; that in spite of all denials there can be no doubt of his engagement to the Moffatt girl; and that en somme she has done herself no good by the whole affair. But, after all, poor soul, she is disinterested. She stands to gain nothing, as I understand; and she risks a good deal. From this comfortable distance, I really find something touching in her behavior.

"She gives her first 'Wednesday,' I understand, to-morrow. 'Mademoiselle Le Breton at home!' I confess I am curious. By all means go, and send me a full report. Mr. Montresor and his wife will certainly be there. He and I have been corresponding, of course. He wishes to persuade me that he feels himself in some way responsible for mademoiselle's position, and for my dismissal of her; that I ought to allow him in consequence full freedom of action. I cannot see matters in the same light. But, as I tell him, the change will be all to his advantage. He exchanges a fractious old woman, always ready to tell him unpleasant truths, for one who has made flattery her métier. If he wants quantity she will give it him. Quality he can dispense with--as I have seen for some time past.

"Lord Lackington has written me an impertinent letter. It seems she has revealed herself, and il s'en prend à moi, because I kept the secret from him, and because I have now dared to dismiss his granddaughter. I am in the midst of a reply which amuses me. He is to cast off his belongings as he pleases; but when a lady of the Chantrey blood--no matter how she came by it-- condescends to enter a paid employment, legitimate or illegitimate, she must be treated en reine, or Lord L. will know the reason why. 'Here is one hundred pounds a year, and let me hear no more of you,' he says to her at sixteen. Thirteen years later I take her in, respect his wishes, and keep the secret. She misbehaves herself, and I dismiss her. Where is the grievance? He himself made her a lectrice, and now complains that she is expected to do her duty in that line of life. He himself banished her from the family, and now grumbles that I did not at once foist her upon him. He would like to escape the odium of his former action by blaming me; but I am not meek, and I shall make him regret his letter.

"As for Jacob Delafield, don't trouble yourself to write me any further news of him. He has insulted me lately in a way I shall not soon forgive--nothing to do, however, with the lady who says she refused him. Whether her report be veracious or no matters nothing to me, any more than his chances of succeeding to the Captain's place. He is one of the ingenious fools who despise the old ways of ruining themselves, and in the end achieve it as well as the commoner sort. He owes me a good deal, and at one time it pleased me to imagine that he was capable both of affection and gratitude. That is the worst of being a woman; we pass from one illusion to another; love is only the beginning; there are a dozen to come after.

"You will scold me for a bitter tongue. Well, my dear Wilfrid, I am not gay here. There are too many women, too many church services, and I see too much of my doctor. I pine for London, and I don't see why I should have been driven out of it by an intrigante.

"Write to me, my dear Wilfrid. I am not quite so bad as I paint myself; say to yourself she has arthritis, she is sixty-five, and her new companion reads aloud with a twang; then you will only wonder at my moderation." #/

Sir Wilfrid returned the letter to his pocket. That day, at luncheon with Lady Hubert, he had had the curiosity to question Susan Delafield, Jacob's fair-haired sister, as to the reasons for her brother's quarrel with Lady Henry.

It appeared that being now in receipt of what seemed to himself, at any rate, a large salary as his cousin's agent, he had thought it his duty to save up and repay the sums which Lady Henry had formerly spent upon his education.

His letter enclosing the money had reached that lady during the first week of her stay at Torquay. It was, no doubt, couched in terms less cordial or more formal than would have been the case before Miss Le Breton's expulsion. "Not that he defends her altogether," said Susan Delafield, who was herself inclined to side with Lady Henry; "but as Lady Henry has refused to see him since, it was not much good being friendly, was it?"

Anyway, the letter and its enclosure had completed a breach already begun. Lady Henry had taken furious offence; the check had been insultingly returned, and had now gone to swell the finances of a London hospital.

Sir Wilfrid was just reflecting that Jacob's honesty had better have waited for a more propitious season, when, looking up, he saw the War Minister beside him, in the act of searching for a newspaper.

"Released?" said Bury, with a smile.

"Yes, thank Heaven. Lackington is, I believe, still pounding at me in the House of Lords. But that amuses him and doesn't hurt me."

"You'll carry your resolutions?"

"Oh, dear, yes, with no trouble at all," said the Minister, almost with sulkiness, as he threw himself into a chair and looked with distaste at the newspaper he had taken up.

Sir Wilfrid surveyed him.

"We meet to-night?" he said, presently.

"You mean in Heribert Street? I suppose so," said Montresor, without cordiality.

"I have just got a letter from her ladyship."

"Well, I hope it is more agreeable than those she writes to me. A more unreasonable old woman--"

The tired Minister took up Punch, looked at a page, and flung it down again. Then he said: "Are you going?"

"I don't know. Lady Henry gives me leave, which makes me feel myself a kind of spy."

"Oh, never mind. Come along. Mademoiselle Julie will want all our support. I don't hear her as kindly spoken of just now as I should wish."

"No. Lady Henry has more personal hold than we thought."

"And Mademoiselle Julie less tact. Why, in the name of goodness, does she go and get herself talked about with the particular man who is engaged to her little cousin? You know, by-the-way, that the story of her parentage is leaking out fast? Most people seem to know something about it."

"Well, that was bound to come. Will it do her good or harm?"

"Harm, for the present. A few people are straitlaced, and a good many feel they have been taken in. But, anyway, this flirtation is a mistake."

"Nobody really knows whether the man is engaged to the Moffatt girl or no. The guardians have forbidden it."

"At any rate, everybody is kind enough to say so. It's a blunder on Mademoiselle Julie's part. As to the man himself, of course, there is nothing to say. He is a very clever fellow." Montresor looked at his companion with a sudden stiffness, as though defying contradiction. "He will do this piece of work that we have given him to do extremely well."

"The Mokembe mission?"

Montresor nodded.

"He had very considerable claims, and was appointed entirely on his military record. All the tales as to Mademoiselle's influence--with me, for instance--that Lady Henry has been putting into circulation are either absurd fiction or have only the very smallest foundation in fact."

Sir Wilfrid smiled amicably and diverted the conversation.

"Warkworth starts at once?"

"He goes to Paris to-morrow. I recommended him to see Pattison, the Military Secretary there, who was in the expedition of five years back."

"This hasn't gone as well as it ought," said Dr. Meredith, in the ear of the Duchess.

They were standing inside the door of Julie's little drawing-room. The Duchess, in a dazzling frock of white and silver, which placed Clarisse among the divinities of her craft, looked round her with a look of worry.

"What's the matter with the tiresome creatures? Why is everybody going so early? And there are not half the people here who ought to be here."

Meredith shrugged his shoulders.

"I saw you at Chatton House the other night," he said, in the same tone.

"Well?" said the Duchess, sharply.

"It seemed to me there was something of a demonstration."

"Against Julie? Let them try it!" said the little lady, with evasive defiance. "We shall be too strong for them."

"Lady Henry is putting her back into it. I confess I never thought she would be either so venomous or so successful."

"Julie will come out all right."

"She would--triumphantly--if--"

The Duchess glanced at him uneasily.

"I believe you are overworking her. She looks skin and bone."

Dr. Meredith shook his head.

"On the contrary, I have been holding her back. But it seems she wants to earn a good deal of money."

"That's so absurd," cried the Duchess, "when there are people only pining to give her some of theirs."

"No, no," said the journalist, brusquely. "She is quite right there. Oh, it would be all right if she were herself. She would make short work of Lady Henry. But, Mademoiselle Julie"--for she glided past them, and he raised his voice--"sit down and rest yourself. Don't take so much trouble."

She flung them a smile.

"Lord Lackington is going," and she hurried on.

Lord Lackington was standing in a group which contained Sir Wilfrid Bury and Mr. Montresor.

"Well, good-bye, good-bye," he said, as she came up to him. "I must go. I'm nearly asleep."

"Tired with abusing me?" said Montresor, nonchalantly, turning round upon him.

"No, only with trying to make head or tail of you," said Lackington, gayly. Then he stooped over Julie.

"Take care of yourself. Come back rosier--and fatter."

"I'm perfectly well. Let me come with you."

"No, don't trouble yourself." For she had followed him into the hall and found his coat for him. All the arrangements for her little "evening" had been of the simplest. That had been a point of pride with her. Madame Bornier and Thérèse dispensing tea and coffee in the dining-room, one hired parlor-maid, and she herself active and busy everywhere. Certain French models were in her head, and memories of her mother's bare little salon in Bruges, with its good talk, and its thinnest of thin refreshments--a few cups of weak tea, or glasses of eau sucrée, with a plate of patisserie.

The hired parlor-maid was whistling for a cab in the service of some other departing guest; so Julie herself put Lord Lackington into his coat, much to his discomfort.

"I don't think you ought to have come," she said to him, with soft reproach. "Why did you have that fainting fit before dinner?"

"I say! Who's been telling tales?"

"Sir Wilfrid Bury met your son, Mr. Chantrey, at dinner."

"Bill can never hold his tongue. Oh, it was nothing; not with the proper treatment, mind you. Of course, if the allopaths were to get their knives into me--but, thank God! I'm out of that galère. Well, in a fortnight, isn't it? We shall both be in town again. I don't like saying good-bye."

And he took both her hands in his.

"It all seems so strange to me still--so strange!" he murmured.

"Next week I shall see mamma's grave," said Julie, under her breath. "Shall I put some flowers there for you?"

The fine blue eyes above her wavered. He bent to her.

"Yes. And write to me. Come back soon. Oh, you'll see. Things will all come right, perfectly right, in spite of Lady Henry."

Confidence, encouragement, a charming raillery, an enthusiastic tenderness--all these beamed upon her from the old man's tone and gesture. She was puzzled. But with another pressure of the hand he was gone. She stood looking after him. And as the carriage drove away, the sound of the wheels hurt her. It was the withdrawal of something protecting--something more her own, when all was said, than anything else which remained to her.

As she returned to the drawing-room, Dr. Meredith intercepted her.

"You want me to send you some work to take abroad?" he said, in a low voice. "I shall do nothing of the kind."

"Why?"

"Because you ought to have a complete holiday."

"Very well. Then I sha'n't be able to pay my way," she said, with a tired smile.

"Remember the doctor's bills if you fall ill."

"Ill! I am never ill," she said, with scorn. Then she looked round the room deliberately, and her gaze returned to her companion. "I am not likely to be fatigued with society, am I?" she added, in a voice that did not attempt to disguise the bitterness within.

"My dear lady, you are hardly installed."

"I have been here a month--the critical month. Now was the moment to stand by me, or throw me over--n'est-ce pas? This is my first party, my house-warming. I gave a fortnight's notice; I asked about sixty people, whom I knew well. Some did not answer at all. Of the rest, half declined--rather curtly, in many instances. And of those who accepted, not all are here. And, oh, how it dragged!"

Meredith looked at her rather guiltily, not knowing what to say. It was true the evening had dragged. In both their minds there rose the memory of Lady Henry's "Wednesdays," the beautiful rooms, the varied and brilliant company, the power and consideration which had attended Lady Henry's companion.

"I suppose," said Julie, shrugging her shoulders, "I had been thinking of the French maîtresses de salon, like a fool; of Mademoiselle de l'Espinasse--or Madame Mohl--imagining that people would come to me for a cup of tea and an agreeable hour. But in England, it seems, people must be paid to talk. Talk is a business affair--you give it for a consideration."

"No, no! You'll build it up," said Meredith. In his heart of hearts he said to himself that she had not been herself that night. Her wonderful social instincts, her memory, her adroitness, had somehow failed her. And from a hostess strained, conscious, and only artificially gay, the little gathering had taken its note.

"You have the old guard, anyway," added the journalist, with a smile, as he looked round the room. The Duchess, Delafield, Montresor and his wife, General McGill, and three or four other old habitués of the Bruton Street evenings were scattered about the little drawing-room. General Fergus, too, was there--had arrived early, and was staying late. His frank soldier's face, the accent, cheerful, homely, careless, with which he threw off talk full of marrow, talk only possible--for all its simplicity--to a man whose life had been already closely mingled with the fortunes of his country, had done something to bind Julie's poor little party together. Her eye rested on him with gratitude. Then she replied to Meredith.

"Mr. Montresor will scarcely come again."

"What do you mean? Ungrateful lady! Montresor! who has already sacrificed Lady Henry and the habits of thirty years to your beaux yeux!"

"That is what he will never forgive me," said Julie, sadly. "He has satisfied his pride, and I--have lost a friend."

"Pessimist! Mrs. Montresor seemed to me most friendly."

Julie laughed.

"She, of course, is enchanted. Her husband has never been her own till now. She married him, subject to Lady Henry's rights. But all that she will soon forget--and my existence with it."

"I won't argue. It only makes you more stubborn," said Meredith. "Ah, still they come!"

For the door opened to admit the tall figure of Major Warkworth.

"Am I very late?" he said, with a surprised look as he glanced at the thinly scattered room. Julie greeted him, and he excused himself on the ground of a dinner which had begun just an hour late, owing to the tardiness of a cabinet minister.

Meredith observed the young man with some attention, from the dark corner in which Julie had left him. The gossip of the moment had reached him also, but he had not paid much heed to it. It seemed to him that no one knew anything first-hand of the Moffatt affair. And for himself, he found it difficult to believe that Julie Le Breton was any man's dupe.

She must marry, poor thing! Of course she must marry. Since it had been plain to him that she would never listen to his own suit, this great-hearted and clear-brained man had done his best to stifle in himself all small or grasping impulses. But this fellow--with his inferior temper and morale--alack! why are the clever women such fools?

If only she had confided in him--her old and tried friend--he thought he could have put things before her, so as to influence without offending her. But he suffered--had always suffered--from the jealous reserve which underlay her charm, her inborn tendency to secretiveness and intrigue.

Now, as he watched her few words with Warkworth, it seemed to him that he saw the signs of some hidden relation. How flushed she was suddenly, and her eyes so bright!

He was not allowed much time or scope, however, for observation. Warkworth took a turn round the room, chatted a little with this person and that, then, on the plea that he was off to Paris early on the following morning, approached his hostess again to take his leave.

"Ah, yes, you start to-morrow," said Montresor, rising. "Well, good luck to you--good luck to you."

General Fergus, too, advanced. The whole room, indeed, awoke to the situation, and all the remaining guests grouped themselves round the young soldier. Even the Duchess was thawed a little by this actual moment of departure. After all, the man was going on his country's service.

"No child's play, this mission, I can assure you," General McGill had said to her. "Warkworth will want all the powers he has--of mind or body."

The slim, young fellow, so boyishly elegant in his well-cut evening-dress, received the ovation offered to him with an evident pleasure which tried to hide itself in the usual English ways. He had been very pale when he came in. But his cheek reddened as Montresor grasped him by the hand, as the two generals bade him a cordial godspeed, as Sir Wilfrid gave him a jesting message for the British representative in Egypt, and as the ladies present accorded him those flattering and admiring looks that woman keeps for valor.

Julie counted for little in these farewells. She stood apart and rather silent. "They have had their good-bye," thought the Duchess, with a thrill she could not help.

"Three days in Paris?" said Sir Wilfrid. "A fortnight to Denga--and then how long before you start for the interior?"

"Oh, three weeks for collecting porters and supplies. They're drilling the escort already. We should be off by the middle of May."

"A bad month," said General Fergus, shrugging his shoulders.

"Unfortunately, affairs won't wait. But I am already stiff with quinine," laughed Warkworth--"or I shall be by the time I get to Denga. Good-bye--good-bye."

And in another moment he was gone. Miss Le Breton had given him her hand and wished him "Bon voyage," like everybody else.

The party broke up. The Duchess kissed her Julie with peculiar tenderness; Delafield pressed her hand, and his deep, kind eyes gave her a lingering look, of which, however, she was quite unconscious; Meredith renewed his half-irritable, half-affectionate counsels of rest and recreation; Mrs. Montresor was conventionally effusive; Montresor alone bade the mistress of the house a somewhat cold and perfunctory farewell. Even Sir Wilfrid was a little touched, he knew not why; he vowed to himself that his report to Lady Henry on the morrow should contain no food for malice, and inwardly he forgave Mademoiselle Julie the old romancings.

XVIII

It was twenty minutes since the last carriage had driven away. Julie was still waiting in the little hall, pacing its squares of black-and-white marble, slowly, backward and forward.

There was a low knock on the door.

She opened it. Warkworth appeared on the threshold, and the high moon behind him threw a bright ray into the dim hall, where all but one faint light had been extinguished. She pointed to the drawing-room.

"I will come directly. Let me just go and ask Léonie to sit up."

Warkworth went into the drawing-room. Julie opened the dining-room door. Madame Bornier was engaged in washing and putting away the china and glass which had been used for Julie's modest refreshments.

"Léonie, you won't go to bed? Major Warkworth is here."

Madame Bornier did not raise her head.

"How long will he be?"

"Perhaps half an hour."

"It is already past midnight."

"Léonie, he goes to-morrow."

"Très bien. Mais--sais-tu, ma chère, ce n'est pas convenable, ce que tu fais là!"

And the older woman, straightening herself, looked her foster-sister full in the face. A kind of watch-dog anxiety, a sulky, protesting affection breathed from her rugged features.

Julie went up to her, not angrily, but rather with a pleading humility.

The two women held a rapid colloquy in low tones--Madame Bornier remonstrating, Julie softly getting her way.

Then Madame Bornier returned to her work, and Julie went to the drawing-room.

Warkworth sprang up as she entered. Both paused and wavered. Then he went up to her, and roughly, irresistibly, drew her into his arms. She held back a moment, but finally yielded, and clasping her hands round his neck she buried her face on his breast.

They stood so for some minutes, absolutely silent, save for her hurried breathing, his head bowed upon hers.

"Julie, how can we say good-bye?" he whispered, at last.

She disengaged herself, and, seeing his face, she tried for composure.

"Come and sit down."

She led him to the window, which he had thrown open as he entered the room, and they sat beside it, hand in hand. A mild April night shone outside. Gusts of moist air floated in upon them. There were dim lights and shadows in the garden and on the shuttered facade of the great house.

"Is it forever?" said Julie, in a low, stifled voice. "Good-bye--forever?"

She felt his hand tremble, but she did not look at him. She seemed to be reciting words long since spoken in the mind.

"You will be away--perhaps a year? Then you go back to India, and then--"
She paused.

Warkworth was physically conscious, as it were, of a letter he carried in his coat-pocket--a letter from Lady Blanche Moffatt which had reached him that morning, the letter of a grande dame, reduced to undignified remonstrance by sheer maternal terror--terror for the health and life of a child as fragile and ethereal as a wild rose in May. Reports had reached her; but no--they could not be true! She bade him be thankful that not a breath of suspicion had yet touched Aileen. As for herself, let him write and reassure her at once. Otherwise--

And the latter part of the letter conveyed a veiled menace that Warkworth perfectly understood.

No--in that direction, no escape; his own past actions closed him in. And henceforth, it was clear, he must walk more warily.

But how blame himself for these feelings of which he was now conscious towards Julie Le Breton--the strongest, probably, that a man not built for passion would ever know. His relation towards her had grown upon him unawares, and now their own hands were about to cut it at the root. What blame to either of them? Fate had been at work; and he felt himself glorified by a situation so tragically sincere, and by emotions of which a month before he would have secretly held himself incapable.

Resolutely, in this last meeting with Julie, he gave these emotions play. He possessed himself of her cold hands as she put her desolate question--"And then?"--and kissed them fervently.

"Julie, if you and I had met a year ago, what happened in India would never have happened. You know that!"

"Do I? But it only hurts me to think it away like that. There it is--it has happened."
She turned upon him suddenly.

"Have you any picture of her?"
He hesitated.

"Yes," he said, at last.

"Have you got it here?"

"Why do you ask, dear one? This one evening is ours."
And again he tried to draw her to him. But she persisted.

"I feel sure you have it. Show it me."

"Julie, you and you only are in my thoughts!"

"Then do what I ask." She bent to him with a wild, entreating air; her lips almost touched his cheek. Unwillingly he drew out a letter-case from his breast-pocket, and took from it a little photograph which he handed to her.

She looked at it with eager eyes. A face framed, as it were, out of snow and fire lay in her hand, a thing most delicate, most frail, yet steeped in feeling and significance--a child's face with its soft curls of brown hair, and the upper lip raised above the white, small teeth, as though in a young wonder; yet behind its sweetness, what suggestions of a poetic or tragic sensibility! The slender neck carried the little head with girlish dignity; the clear, timid eyes seemed at once to shrink from and trust the spectator.

Julie returned the little picture, and hid her face with her hands. Warkworth watched her uncomfortably, and at last drew her hands away.

"What are you thinking of?" he said, almost with violence. "Don't shut me out!"

"I am not jealous now," she said, looking at him piteously. "I don't hate her. And if she knew all--she couldn't--hate me."

"No one could hate her. She is an angel. But she is not my Julie!" he said, vehemently, and he thrust the little picture into his pocket again.

"Tell me," she said, after a pause, laying her hand on his knee, "when did you begin to think of me--differently? All the winter, when we used to meet, you never--you never loved me then?"

"How, placed as I was, could I let myself think of love? I only knew that I wanted to see you, to talk to you, to write to you--that the day when we did not meet was a lost day. Don't be so proud!" He tried to laugh at her. "You didn't think of me in any special way, either. You were much too busy making bishops, or judges, or academicians. Oh, Julie, I was so afraid of you in those early days!"

"The first night we met," she said, passionately, "I found a carnation you had worn in your button-hole. I put it under my pillow, and felt for it in the dark like a talisman. You had stood between me and Lady Henry twice. You had smiled at me and pressed my hand--not as others did, but as though you understood me, myself--as though, at least, you wished to understand. Then came the joy of joys, that I could help you--that I could do something for you. Ah, how it altered life for me! I never turned the corner of a street that I did not count on the chance of seeing you beyond--suddenly--on my path. I never heard your voice that it did not thrill me from head to foot. I never made a new friend or acquaintance that I did not ask myself first how I could thereby serve you. I never saw you come into the room that my heart did not leap. I never slept but you were in my dreams. I loathed London when you were out of it. It was paradise when you were there."

Straining back from him as he still held her hands, her whole face and form shook with the energy of her confession. Her wonderful hair, loosened from the thin gold bands in which it had been confined during the evening, fell in a glossy confusion about her brow and slender neck; its black masses, the melting brilliance of the eyes, the tragic freedom of the attitude gave both to form and face a wild and poignant beauty.

Warkworth, beside her, was conscious first of amazement, then of a kind of repulsion--a kind of fear--till all else was lost in a hurry of joy and gratitude.

The tears stood on his cheek. "Julie, you shame me--you trample me into the earth!"

He tried to gather her in his arms, but she resisted, Caresses were not what those eyes demanded--eyes feverishly bright with the memory of her own past dreams, Presently, indeed, she withdrew herself from him. She rose and closed the window; she put the lamp in another place; she brought her rebellious hair into order.

"We must not be so mad," she said, with a quivering smile, as she again seated herself, but at some distance from him. "You see, for me the great question is "--her voice became low and rapid--"What am I going to do with the future? For you it is all plain. We part to-night. You have your career, your marriage. I withdraw from your life--absolutely. But for me--"

She paused. It was the manner of one trying to see her way in the dark.

"Your social gifts," said Warkworth, in agitation, "your friends, Julie--these will occupy your mind. Then, of course, you will, you must marry! Oh, you'll soon forget me, Julie! I pray you may!"

"My social gifts?" she repeated, disregarding the rest of his speech. "I have told you already they have broken down. Society sides with Lady Henry. I am to be made to know my place--I do know it!"

"The Duchess will fight for you."

She laughed.

"The Duke won't let her--nor shall I."

"You'll marry," he repeated, with emotion. "You'll find some one worthy of you--some one who will give you the great position for which you were born."

"I could have it at any moment," she said, looking him quietly in the eyes.

Warkworth drew back, conscious of a disagreeable shock. He had been talking in generalities, giving away the future with that fluent prodigality, that easy prophecy which costs so little. What did she mean?

"Delafield?" he cried.

And he waited for her reply--which lingered--in a tense and growing eagerness. The notion had crossed his mind once or twice during the winter, only to be dismissed as ridiculous. Then, on the occasion of their first quarrel, when Julie had snubbed him in Delafield's presence and to Delafield's advantage, he had been conscious of a momentary alarm. But Julie, who on that one and only occasion had paraded her intimacy with Delafield, thenceforward said not a word of him, and Warkworth's jealousy had died for lack of fuel. In relation to Julie, Delafield had been surely the mere shadow and agent of his little cousin the Duchess--a friendly, knight-errant sort of person, with a liking for the distressed. What! the heir-presumptive of Chudleigh Abbey, and one of the most famous of English dukedoms, when even he, the struggling, penurious officer, would never have dreamed of such a match?

Julie, meanwhile, heard only jealousy in his exclamation, and it caressed her ear, her heart. She was tempted once more, woman-like, to dwell upon the other lover, and again something compelling and delicate in her feeling towards Delafield forbade.

"No, you mustn't make me tell you any more," she said, putting the name aside with a proud gesture. "It would be poor and mean. But it's true. I have only to put out my hand for what you call 'a great position,' I have refused to put it out. Sometimes, of course, it has dazzled me. To-night it seems to me--dust and ashes. No; when we two have said good-bye, I shall begin life again. And this time I shall live it in my own way, for my own ends. I'm very tired. Henceforth 'I'll walk where my own nature would be leading--it vexes me to choose another guide.'"

And as she spoke the words of one of the chainless souls of history, in a voice passionately full and rich, she sprang to her feet, and, drawing her slender form to its full height, she locked her hands behind her, and began to pace the room with a wild, free step.

Every nerve in Warkworth's frame was tingling. He was carried out of himself, first by the rebellion of her look and manner, then by this fact, so new, so astounding, which her very evasion had confirmed. During her whole contest with Lady Henry, and now, in her present ambiguous position, she had Delafield, and through Delafield the English great world, in the hollow of her hand? This nameless woman--no longer in her first youth. And she had refused? He watched her in a speechless wonder and incredulity.

The thought leaped. "And this sublime folly--this madness--was for me?"

It stirred and intoxicated him. Yet she was not thereby raised in his eyes. Nay, the contrary. With the passion which was rapidly mounting in his veins there mingled--poor Julie!--a curious diminution of respect.

"Julie!" He held out his hand to her peremptorily. "Come to me again. You are so wonderful to-night, in that white dress--like a wild muse. I shall always see you so. Come!"

She obeyed, and gave him her hands, standing beside his chair. But her face was still absorbed.

"To be free," she said, under her breath--"free, like my parents, from all these petty struggles and conventions!"

Then she felt his kisses on her hands, and her expression changed.

"How we cheat ourselves with words!" she whispered, trembling, and, withdrawing one hand, she smoothed back the light-brown curls from his brow with that protecting tenderness which had always entered into her love for him. "To-night we are here--together--this one last night! And to-morrow, at this time, you'll be in Paris; perhaps you'll be looking out at the lights--and the crowds on the Boulevard--and the chestnut-trees. They'll just be in their first leaf--I know so well!--and the little thin leaves will be shining so green under the lamps--and I shall be here--and it will be all over and done with--forever. What will it matter whether I am free or not free? I shall be alone! That's all a woman knows."

Her voice died away. Warkworth rose. He put his arms round her, and she did not resist.

"Julie," he said in her ear, "why should you be alone?"

A silence fell between them.

"I--I don't understand," she said, at last.

"Julie, listen! I shall be three days in Paris, but my business can be perfectly done in one. What if you met me there after to-morrow? What harm would it be? We are not babes, we two. We understand life. And who would have any right to blame or to meddle? Julie, I know a little inn in the valley of the Bièvre, quite near Paris, but all wood and field. No English tourists ever go there. Sometimes an artist or two--but this is not the time of year. Julie, why shouldn't we spend our last two days there--together--away from all the world, before we say good-bye? You've been afraid here of prying people--of the Duchess even--of Madame Bornier--how she scowls at me sometimes! Why shouldn't we sweep all that away--and be happy! Nobody should ever-- nobody could ever know." His voice dropped, became still more hurried and soft. "We might go as brother and sister--that would be quite simple. You are practically French. I speak French well. Who is to have an idea, a suspicion of our identity? The spring there is mild and warm. The Bois de Verrières close by is full of flowers. When my father was alive, and I was a child, we went once, to economize, for a year, to a village a mile or two away. But I knew this place quite well. A lovely, green, quiet spot! With your poetical ideas, Julie, you would delight in it. Two days--wandering in the woods--together! Then I put you into the train for Brussels, and I go my way. But to all eternity, Julie, those days will have been ours!"

At the first words, almost, Julie had disengaged herself. Pushing him from her with both hands, she listened to him in a dumb amazement. The color first deserted her face, then returned in a flood.

"So you despise me?" she said, catching her breath.

"No. I adore you."

She fell upon a chair and hid her eyes. He first knelt beside her, arguing and soothing; then he paced up and down before her, talking very fast and low, defending and developing the scheme, till it stood before them complete and tempting in all its details.

Julie did not look up, nor did she speak. At last, Warkworth, full of tears, and stifled with his own emotions, threw open the window again in a craving for air and coolness. A scent of fresh leaves and moistened earth floated up from the shrubbery beneath the window. The scent, the branching trees, the wide, mild spaces of air brought relief. He leaned out, bathing his brow in the night. A tumult of voices seemed to be echoing through his mind, dominated by one which held the rest defiantly in check.

"Is she a mere girl, to be 'led astray'? A moment of happiness--what harm?--for either of us?" Then he returned to Julie.

"Julie!" He touched her shoulder, trembling. Had she banished him forever? It seemed to him that in these minutes he had passed through an infinity of experience. Was he not the nobler, the more truly man? Let the moralists talk.

"Julie!" he repeated, in an anguish.

She raised her head, and he saw that she had been crying. But there was in her face a light, a wildness, a yearning that reassured him. She put her arm round him and pressed her cheek to his. He divined that she, too, had lived and felt a thousand hours in one. With a glow of ecstatic joy he began to talk to her again, her head resting on his shoulder, her slender hands crushed in his.

And Julie, meanwhile, was saying to herself, "Either I go to him, as he asks, or in a few minutes I must send him away--forever."

And then as she clung to him, so warm and near, her strength failed her. Nothing in the world mattered to her at that moment but this handsome, curly head bowed upon her own, this voice that called her all the names of love, this transformation of the man's earlier prudence, or ambition, or duplicity, into this eager tenderness, this anguish in separation....

"Listen, dear!" He whispered to her. "All my business can be got through the day before you come. I have two men to see. A day will be ample. I dine at the Embassy to-morrow night--that is arranged; the day after I lunch with the Military Secretary; then--a thousand regrets, but I must hurry on to meet some friends in Italy. So I turn my back on Paris, and for two days I belong to Julie--and she to me. Say yes, Julie--my Julie!"

He bent over her, his hands framing her face.

"Say yes," he urged, "and put off for both of us that word--alone!"

His low voice sank into her heart. He waited, till his strained sense caught the murmured words which conveyed to him the madness and the astonishment of victory.

Léonie had shut up the house, in a grim silence, and had taken her way up-stairs to bed.

Julie, too, was in her room. She sat on the edge of her bed, her head drooped, her hands clasped before her absently, like Hope still listening for the last sounds of the harp of life. The candle beside her showed her, in the big mirror opposite, her grace, the white confusion of her dress.

She had expected reaction, but it did not come. She was still borne on a warm tide of will and energy. All that she was about to do seemed to her still perfectly natural and right. Petty scruples, conventional hesitations, the refusal of life's great moments--these are what are wrong, these are what disgrace!

Romance beckoned to her, and many a secret tendency towards the lawless paths of conduct, infused into her by the associations and affections of her childhood. The horror naturalis which protects the great majority of women from the wilder ways of passion was in her weakened or dormant. She was the illegitimate child of a mother who had defied law for love, and of that fact she had been conscious all her life.

A sharp contempt, indeed, arose within her for the interpretation that the common mind would be sure to place upon her action.

"What matter! I am my own mistress--responsible to no one. I choose for myself--I dare for myself!"

And when at last she rose, first loosening and then twisting the black masses of her hair, it seemed to her that the form in the glass was that of another woman, treading another earth. She trampled cowardice under foot; she freed herself from--"was uns alle bändigt, das Gemeine!"

Then as she stood before the oval mirror in a classical frame, which adorned the mantel-piece of what had once been Lady Mary Leicester's room, her eye was vaguely caught by the little family pictures and texts which hung on either side of it. Lady Mary and her sister as children, their plain faces emerging timidly from their white, high-waisted frocks; Lady 'Mary's mother, an old lady in a white coif and kerchief, wearing a look austerely kind; on the other side a clergyman, perhaps the brother of the old lady, with a similar type of face, though gentler--a face nourished on the Christian Year; and above and below them two or three card-board texts, carefully illuminated by Lady Mary Leicester herself:

"Thou, Lord, knowest my down-sitting and my uprising."

"Wash me, and I shall be whiter than snow."

"Fear not, little flock. It is your Father's good pleasure to give you the kingdom."

Julie observed these fragments, absently at first, then with repulsion. This Anglican pietism, so well fed, so narrowly sheltered, which measured the universe with its foot-rule, seemed to her quasi-Catholic eye merely fatuous and hypocritical. It is not by such forces, she thought, that the true world of men and women is governed.

As she turned away she noticed two little Catholic pictures, such as she had been accustomed in her convent days to carry in her books of devotion, carefully propped up beneath the texts.

"Ah, Thérèse!" she said to herself, with a sudden feeling of pain. "Is the child asleep?"

She listened. A little cough sounded from the neighboring room. Julie crossed the landing.

"Thérèse! tu ne dors pas encore?"

A voice said, softly, in the darkness, "Je t'attendais, mademoiselle."

Julie went to the child's bed, put down her candle, and stooped to kiss her.

The child's thin hand caressed her cheek.

"Ah, it will be good--to be in Bruges--with mademoiselle."

Julie drew herself away.

"I sha'n't be there to-morrow, dear."

"Not there! Oh, mademoiselle!"

The child's voice was pitiful.

"I shall join you there. But I find I must go to Paris first. I--I have some business there."

"But maman said--"

"Yes, I have only just made up my mind. I shall tell maman to-morrow morning,"

"You go alone, mademoiselle?"

"Why not, dear goose?"

"Vous êtes fatiguée. I would like to come with you, and carry your cloak and the umbrellas."

"You, indeed!" said Julie. "It would end, wouldn't it, in my carrying you--besides the cloak and the umbrellas?"

Then she knelt down beside the child and took her in her arms.

"Do you love me, Thérèse?"

The child drew a long breath. With her little, twisted hands she stroked the beautiful hair so close to her.

"Do you, Thérèse?"

A kiss fell on Julie's cheek.

"Ce soir, j'ai beaucoup prié la Sainte Vierge pour vous!" she said, in a timid and hurried whisper.

Julie made no immediate reply. She rose from her knees, her hand still clasped in that of the crippled girl.

"Did you put those pictures on my mantel-piece, Thérèse?"

"Yes."

"Why?"

The child hesitated.

"It does one good to look at them--n'est-ce pas?--when one is sad?"

"Why do you suppose I am sad?"

Thérèse was silent a moment; then she flung her little skeleton arms round Julie, and Julie felt her crying.

"Well, I won't be sad any more," said Julie, comforting her. "When we're all in Bruges together, you'll see."

And smiling at the child, she tucked her into her white bed and left her.

Then from this exquisite and innocent affection she passed back into the tumult of her own thoughts and plans. Through the restless night her parents were often in her mind. She was the child of revolt, and as she thought of the meeting before her she seemed to be but entering upon a heritage inevitable from the beginning. A sense of enfranchisement, of passionate enlargement, upheld her, as of a life coming to its fruit.

"Creil!"

A flashing vision of a station and its lights, and the Paris train rushed on through cold showers of sleet and driving wind, a return of winter in the heart of spring.

On they sped through the half-hour which still divided them from the Gare du Nord. Julie, in her thick veil, sat motionless in her corner. She was not conscious of any particular agitation. Her mind was strained not to forget any of Warkworth's directions. She was to drive across immediately to the Gare de Sceaux, in the Place Denfert-Rochereau, where he would meet her. They were to dine at an obscure inn near the station, and go down by the last train to the little town in the wooded valley of the Bièvre, where they were to stay.

She had her luggage with her in the carriage. There would be no custom-house delays.

Ah, the lights of Paris beginning! She peered into the rain, conscious of a sort of home-coming joy. She loved the French world and the French sights and sounds--these tall, dingy houses of the banlieue, the dregs of a great architecture; the advertisements; the look of the streets.

The train slackened into the Nord Station. The blue-frocked porters crowded into the carriages.

"C'est tout, madame? Vous n'avez pas de grands bagages?"

"No, nothing. Find me a cab at once."

There was a great crowd outside. She hurried on as quickly as she could, revolving what was to be said if any acquaintance were to accost her. By great good luck, and by travelling second class both in the train and on the boat, she had avoided meeting anybody she knew. But the Nord Station was crowded with English people, and she pushed her way through in a nervous terror.

"Miss Le Breton!"

She turned abruptly. In the white glare of the electric lights she did not at first recognize the man who had spoken to her. Then she drew back. Her heart beat wildly. For she had distinguished the face of Jacob Delafield.

He came forward to meet her as she passed the barrier at the end of the platform, his aspect full of what seemed to her an extraordinary animation, significance, as though she were expected.

"Miss Le Breton! What an astonishing, what a fortunate meeting! I have a message for you from Evelyn."

"From Evelyn?" She echoed the words mechanically as she shook hands.

"Wait a moment," he said, leading her aside towards the waiting-room, while the crowd that was going to the douane passed them by. Then he turned to Julie's porter.

"Attendez un instant."

The man sulkily shook his head, dropped Julie's bag at their feet, and hurried off in search of a more lucrative job.

"I am going back to-night," added Delafield, hurriedly. "How strange that I should have met you, for I have very sad news for you! Lord Lackington had an attack this morning, from which he cannot recover. The doctors give him perhaps forty-eight hours. He has asked for you-- urgently. The Duchess tells me so in a long telegram I had from her to-day. But she supposed you to be in Bruges. She has wired there. You will go back, will you not?"

"Go back?" said Julie, staring at him helplessly. "Go back to-night?"

"The evening train starts in little more than an hour. You would be just in time, I think, to see the old man alive."

She still looked at him in bewilderment, at the blue eyes under the heavily moulded brows, and the mouth with its imperative, and yet eager--or tremulous?--expression. She perceived that he hung upon her answer.

She drew her hand piteously across her eyes as though to shut out the crowds, the station, and the urgency of this personality beside her. Despair was in her heart. How to consent? How to refuse?

"But my friends," she stammered--"the friends with whom I was going to stay--they will be alarmed."

"Could you not telegraph to them? They would understand, surely. The office is close by."

She let herself be hurried along, not knowing what to do. Delafield walked beside her. If she had been able to observe him, she must have been struck afresh by the pale intensity, the controlled agitation of his face.

"Is it really so serious?" she asked, pausing a moment, as though in resistance.

"It is the end. Of that there can be no question. You have touched his heart very deeply. He longs to see her, Evelyn says. And his daughter and granddaughter are still abroad--Miss Moffatt, indeed, is ill at Florence with a touch of diphtheria. He is alone with his two sons. You will go?"

Even in her confusion, the strangeness of it all was borne in upon her--his insistence, the extraordinary chance of their meeting, his grave, commanding manner.

"How could you know I was here?" she said, in bewilderment.

"I didn't know," he said, slowly. "But, thank God, I have met you. I dread to think of your fatigue, but you will be glad just to see him again--just to give him his last wish--won't you?" he said, pleadingly. "Here is the telegraph-office. Shall I do it for you?"

"No, thank you. I--I must think how to word it. Please wait."

She went in alone. As she took the pencil into her hands a low groan burst from her lips. The man writing in the next compartment turned round in astonishment. She controlled herself and began to write. There was no escape. She must submit; and all was over.

She telegraphed to Warkworth, care of the Chef de Gare, at the Sceaux Station, and also to the country inn.

"Have met Mr. Delafield by chance at Nord Station. Lord Lackington dying. Must return to- night. Where shall I write? Good-bye."

When it was done she could hardly totter out of the office. Delafield made her take his arm.

"You must have some food. Then I will go and get a sleeping-car for you to Calais. There will be no crowd to-night. At Calais I will look after you if you will allow me."

"You are crossing to-night?" she said, vaguely. Her lips framed the words with difficulty.

"Yes. I came over with my cousins yesterday."

She asked nothing more. It did not occur to her to notice that he had no luggage, no bag, no rug, none of the paraphernalia of travel. In her despairing fatigue and misery she let him guide her as he would.

He made her take some soup, then some coffee, all that she could make herself swallow. There was a dismal period of waiting, during which she was hardly conscious of where she was or of what was going on round her.

Then she found herself in the sleeping-car, in a reserved compartment, alone. Once more the train moved through the night. The miles flew by--the miles that forever parted her from Warkworth.

XIX

The train was speeding through the forest country of Chantilly. A pale moon had risen, and beneath its light the straight forest roads, interminably long, stretched into the distance; the vaporous masses of young and budding trees hurried past the eye of the traveller; so, also, the white hamlets, already dark and silent; the stations with their lights and figures; the great wood-piles beside the line.

Delafield, in his second-class carriage, sat sleepless and erect. The night was bitterly cold. He wore the light overcoat in which he had left the Hôtel du Rhin that afternoon for a stroll before dinner, and had no other wrap or covering. But he felt nothing, was conscious of nothing but the rushing current of his own thoughts.

The events of the two preceding days, the meaning of them, the significance of his own action and its consequences--it was with these materials that his mind dealt perpetually, combining, interpreting, deducing, now in one way, now in another. His mood contained both excitement and dread. But with a main temper of calmness, courage, invincible determination, these elements did not at all interfere.

The day before, he had left London with his cousins, the Duke of Chudleigh, and young Lord Elmira, the invalid boy. They were bound to Paris to consult a new doctor, and Jacob had offered to convey them there. In spite of all the apparatus of servants and couriers with which they were surrounded, they always seemed to him, on their journeys, a singularly lonely and hapless pair, and he knew that they leaned upon him and prized his company.

On the way to Paris, at the Calais buffet, he had noticed Henry Warkworth, and had given him a passing nod. It had been understood the night before in Heribert Street that they would both be crossing on the morrow.

On the following day--the day of Julie's journey--Delafield, who was anxiously awaiting the return of his two companions from their interview with the great physician they were consulting, was strolling up the Rue de la Paix, just before luncheon, when, outside the Hôtel Mirabeau, he ran into a man whom he immediately perceived to be Warkworth.

Politeness involved the exchange of a few sentences, although a secret antagonism between the two men had revealed itself from the first day of their meeting in Lady Henry's drawing-room. Each word of their short conversation rang clearly through Delafield's memory.

"You are at the 'Rhin'?" said Warkworth.

"Yes, for a couple more days. Shall we meet at the Embassy to-morrow?"

"No. I dined there last night. My business here is done. I start for Rome to-night."

"Lucky man. They have put on a new fast train, haven't they?"

"Yes. You leave the Gare de Lyon at 7.15, and you are at Rome the second morning, in good time."

"Magnificent! Why don't we all rush south? Well, good-bye again, and good luck."

They touched hands perfunctorily and parted.

This happened about mid-day. While Delafield and his cousins were lunching, a telegram from the Duchess of Crowborough was handed to Jacob. He had wired to her early in the morning to ask for the address in Paris of an old friend of his, who was also a cousin of hers. The telegram contained:

/# "Thirty-six Avenue Friedland. Lord Lackington heart-attack this morning. Dying. Has asked urgently for Julie. Blanche Moffatt detained Florence by daughter's illness. All circumstances most sad. Woman Heribert Street gave me Bruges address. Have wired Julie there." #/

The message set vibrating in Delafield's mind the tender memory which already existed there of his last talk with Julie, of her strange dependence and gentleness, her haunting and pleading personality. He hoped with all his heart she might reach the old man in time, that his two sons, Uredale and William, would treat her kindly, and that it would be found when the end came that he had made due provision for her as his granddaughter.

But he had small leisure to give to thoughts of this kind. The physician's report in the morning had not been encouraging, and his two travelling companions demanded all the sympathy and support he could give them. He went out with them in the afternoon to the Hôtel de la Terrasse at St. Germain. The Duke, a nervous hypochondriac, could not sleep in the noise of Paris, and was accustomed to a certain apartment in this well-known hotel, which was often reserved for him. Jacob left them about six o'clock to return to Paris. He was to meet one of the Embassy attachés-- an old Oxford friend--at the Café Gaillard for dinner. He dressed at the "Rhin," put on an overcoat, and set out to walk to the Rue Gaillard about half-past seven. As he approached the "Mirabeau," he saw a cab with luggage standing at the door. A man came out with the hotel concierge. To his astonishment, Delafield recognized Warkworth.

The young officer seemed in a hurry and out of temper. At any rate, he jumped into the cab without taking any notice of the two sommeliers and the concierge who stood round expectant of francs, and when the concierge in his stiffest manner asked where the man was to drive, Warkworth put his head out of the window and said, hastily, to the cocher:

"D'abord, à la Gare de Sceaux! Puis, je vous dirai. Mais dépêchez-vous!"

The cab rolled away, and Delafield walked on.

Half-past seven, striking from all the Paris towers! And Warkworth's intention in the morning was to leave the Gare de Lyon at 7.15. But it seemed he was now bound, at 7.30, for the Gare de Sceaux, from which point of departure it was clear that no reasonable man would think of starting for the Eternal City.

"D'abord, à la Gare de Sceaux!"

Then he was not catching a train?--at any rate, immediately. He had some other business first, and was perhaps going to the station to deposit his luggage?

Suddenly a thought, a suspicion, flashed through Delafield's mind, which set his heart thumping in his breast. In after days he was often puzzled to account for its origin, still more for the extraordinary force with which it at once took possession of all his energies. In his more mystical moments of later life he rose to the secret belief that God had spoken to him.

At any rate, he at once hailed a cab, and, thinking no more of his dinner engagement, he drove post-haste to the Nord Station. In those days the Calais train arrived at eight. He reached the station a few minutes before it appeared. When at last it drew up, amid the crowd on the platform it took him only a few seconds to distinguish the dark and elegant head of Julie Le Breton.

A pang shot through him that pierced to the very centre of life. He was conscious of a prayer for help and a clear mind. But on his way to the station he had rapidly thought out a plan on which to act should this mad notion in his brain turn out to have any support in reality.

It had so much support that Julie Le Breton was there--in Paris--and not at Bruges, as she had led the Duchess to suppose. And when she turned her startled face upon him, his wild fancy became, for himself, a certainty.

"Amiens! Cinq minutes d'arrêt."

Delafield got out and walked up and down the platform. He passed the closed and darkened windows of the sleeping-car; and it seemed to his abnormally quickened sense that he was beside her, bending over her, and that he said to her:

"Courage! You are saved! Let us thank God!"

A boy from the refreshment-room came along, wheeling a barrow on which were tea and coffee.

Delafield eagerly drank a cup of tea and put his hand into his pocket to pay for it. He found there three francs and his ticket. After paying for the tea he examined his purse. That contained an English half-crown.

So he had had with him just enough to get his own second-class ticket, her first-class, and a sleeping-car. That was good fortune, seeing that the bulk of his money, with his return ticket, was reposing in his dressing-case at the Hôtel du Rhin.

"En voiture! En voiture, s'il vous plaît!"

He settled himself once more in his corner, and the train rushed on. This time it was the strange hour at the Gare du Nord which he lived through again, her white face opposite to him in the refreshment-room, the bewilderment and misery she had been so little able to conceal, her spasmodic attempts at conversation, a few vague words about Lord Lackington or the Duchess, and then pauses, when her great eyes, haggard and weary, stared into vacancy, and he knew well enough that her thoughts were with Warkworth, and that she was in fierce rebellion against his presence there, and this action into which he had forced her.

As for him, he perfectly understood the dilemma in which she stood. Either she must accept the duty of returning to the death-bed of the old man, her mother's father, or she must confess her appointment with Warkworth.

Yet--suppose he had been mistaken? Well, the telegram from the Duchess covered his whole action. Lord Lackington was dying; and apart from all question of feeling, Julie Le Breton's friends must naturally desire that he should see her, acknowledge her before his two sons, and, with their consent, provide for her before his death.

But, ah, he had not been mistaken! He remembered her hurried refusal when he had asked her if he should telegraph for her to her Paris "friends"--how, in a sudden shame, he had turned away that he might not see the beloved false face as she spoke, might not seem to watch or suspect her.

He had just had time to send off a messenger, first to his friend at the Café Gaillard, and then to the Hôtel du Rhin, before escorting her to the sleeping-car.

Ah, how piteous had been that dull bewilderment with which she had turned to him!

"But--my ticket?"

"Here they are. Oh, never mind--we will settle in town. Try to sleep. You must be very tired."

And then it seemed to him that her lips trembled, like those of a miserable child; and surely, surely, she must hear that mad beating of his pulse!

Boulogne was gone in a flash. Here was the Somme, stretched in a pale silver flood beneath the moon--a land of dunes and stunted pines, of wide sea-marshes, over which came the roar of the Channel. Then again the sea was left behind, and the rich Picard country rolled away to right and left. Lights here and there, in cottage or villa--the lights, perhaps, of birth or death--companions of hope or despair.

Calais!

The train moved slowly up to the boat-side. Delafield jumped out. The sleeping-car was yielding up its passengers. He soon made out the small black hat and veil, the slender form in the dark travelling-dress.

Was she fainting? For she seemed to him to waver as he approached her, and the porter who had taken her rugs and bag was looking at her in astonishment. In an instant he had drawn her arm within his, and was supporting her as he best could,

"The car was very hot, and I am so tired. I only want some air."

They reached the deck.

"You will go down-stairs?"

"No, no--some air!" she murmured, and he saw that she could hardly keep her feet.

But in a few moments they had reached the shelter on the upper deck usually so well filled with chairs and passengers on a day crossing. Now it was entirely deserted. The boat was not full, the night was cold and stormy, and the stream of passengers had poured down into the shelter of the lower deck.

Julie sank into a chair. Delafield hurriedly loosened the shawl she carried with her from its attendant bag and umbrella, and wrapped it round her.

"It will be a rough crossing," he said, in her ear. "Can you stand it on deck?"

"I am a good sailor. Let me stay here."

Her eyes closed. He stooped over her in an anguish. One of the boat officials approached him.

"Madame ferait mieux de descendre, monsieur. La traversée ne sera pas bonne."

Delafield explained that the lady must have air, and was a good sailor. Then he pressed into the man's hand his three francs, and sent him for brandy and an extra covering of some kind. The man went unwillingly.

During the whole bustle of departure, Delafield saw nothing but Julie's helpless and motionless form; he heard nothing but the faint words by which, once or twice, she tried to convey to him that she was not unconscious.

The brandy came. The man who brought it again objected to Julie's presence on deck. Delafield took no heed. He was absorbed in making Julie swallow some of the brandy.

At last they were off. The vessel glided slowly out of the old harbor, and they were immediately in rough water.

Delafield was roused by a peremptory voice at his elbow.

"This lady ought not to stay here, sir. There is plenty of room in the ladies' cabin."

Delafield looked up and recognized the captain of the boat, the same man who, thirty-six hours before, had shown special civilities to the Duke of Chudleigh and his party.

"Ah, you are Captain Whittaker," he said.

The shrewd, stout man who had accosted him raised his eyebrows in astonishment.

Delafield drew him aside a moment. After a short conversation the captain lifted his cap and departed, with a few words to the subordinate officer who had drawn his attention to the matter. Henceforward they were unmolested, and presently the officer brought a pillow and striped blanket, saying they might be useful to the lady. Julie was soon comfortably placed, lying down on the seat under the wooden shelter. Delicacy seemed to suggest that her companion should leave her to herself.

Jacob walked up and down briskly, trying to shake off the cold which benumbed him. Every now and then he paused to look at the lights on the receding French coast, at its gray phantom line sweeping southward under the stormy moon, or disappearing to the north in clouds of rain. There was a roar of waves and a dashing of spray. The boat, not a large one, was pitching heavily, and the few male passengers who had at first haunted the deck soon disappeared.

Delafield hung over the surging water in a strange exaltation, half physical, half moral. The wild salt strength and savor of the sea breathed something akin to that passionate force of will which had impelled him to the enterprise in which he stood. No mere man of the world could have dared it; most men of the world, as he was well aware, would have condemned or ridiculed it. But for one who saw life and conduct sub specie æternitatis it had seemed natural enough.

The wind blew fierce and cold. He made his way back to Julie's side. To his surprise, she had raised herself and was sitting propped up against the corner of the seat, her veil thrown back.

"You are better?" he said, stooping to her, so as to be heard against the boom of the waves. "This rough weather does not affect you?"

She made a negative sign. He drew his camp-stool beside her. Suddenly she asked him what time it was. The haggard nobleness of her pale face amid the folds of black veil, the absent passion of the eye, thrilled to his heart. Where were her thoughts?

"Nearly four o'clock." He drew out his watch. "You see it is beginning to lighten,"

And he pointed to the sky, in which that indefinable lifting of the darkness which precedes the dawn was taking place, and to the far distances of sea, where a sort of livid clarity was beginning to absorb and vanquish that stormy play of alternate dark and moonlight which had prevailed when they left the French shore.

He had hardly spoken, when he felt that her eyes were fixed upon him.

To look at his watch, he had thrown open his long Newmarket coat, forgetting that in so doing he disclosed the evening-dress in which he had robed himself at the Hôtel du Rhin for his friend's dinner at the Café Gaillard.

He hastily rebuttoned his coat, and turned his face seaward once more. But he heard her voice, and was obliged to come close to her that he might catch the words.

"You have given me your wraps," she said, with difficulty. "You will suffer."

"Not at all. You have your own rug, and one that the captain provided. I keep myself quite warm with moving about."

There was a pause. His mind began to fill with alarm. He was not of the men who act a part with ease; but, having got through so far, he had calculated on preserving his secret.

Flight was best, and he was just turning away when a gesture of hers arrested him. Again he stooped till their faces were near enough to let her voice reach him.

"Why are you in evening-dress?"

"I had intended to dine with a friend. There was not time to change."

"Then you did not mean to cross to-night?"

He delayed a moment, trying to collect his thoughts.

"Not when I dressed for dinner, but some sudden news decided me."

Her head fell back wearily against the support behind it. The eyes closed, and he, thinking she would perhaps sleep, was about to rise from his seat, when the pressure of her hand upon his arm detained him. He sat still and the hand was withdrawn.

There was a lessening of the roar in their ears. Under the lee of the English shore the wind was milder, the "terror-music" of the sea less triumphant. And over everything was stealing the first discriminating touch of the coming light. Her face was clear now; and Delafield, at last venturing to look at her, saw that her eyes were open again, and trembled at their expression. There was in them a wild suspicion. Secretly, steadily, he nerved himself to meet the blow that he foresaw.

"Mr. Delafield, have you told me all the truth?"

She sat up as she spoke, deadly pale but rigid. With an impatient hand she threw off the wraps which had covered her. Her face commanded an answer.

"Certainly I have told you the truth."

"Was it the whole truth? It seems--it seems to me that you were not prepared yourself for this journey--that there is some mystery--which I do not understand--which I resent!"

"But what mystery? When I saw you, I of course thought of Evelyn's telegram."

"I should like to see that telegram."

He hesitated. If he had been more skilled in the little falsehoods of every day he would simply have said that he had left it at the hotel. But he lost his chance. Nor at the moment did he clearly perceive what harm it would do to show it to her. The telegram was in his pocket, and he handed it to her.

There was a dim oil-lamp in the shelter. With difficulty she held the fluttering paper up and just divined the words. Then the wind carried it away and blew it overboard. He rose and leaned against the edge of the shelter, looking down upon her. There was in his mind a sense of something solemn approaching, round which this sudden lull of blast and wave seemed to draw a "wind-warm space," closing them in.

"Why did you come with me?" she persisted, in an agitation she could now scarcely control. "It is evident you had not meant to travel. You have no luggage, and you are in evening-dress. And I remember now--you sent two letters from the station!"

"I wished to be your escort."

Her gesture was almost one of scorn at the evasion.

"Why were you at the station at all? Evelyn had told you I was at Bruges. And--you were dining out. I--I can't understand!"

She spoke with a frowning intensity, a strange queenliness, in which was neither guilt nor confusion.

A voice spoke in Delafield's heart. "Tell her!" it said.

He bent nearer to her.

"Miss Le Breton, with what friends were you going to stay in Paris?"

She breathed quick.

"I am not a school-girl, I think, that I should be asked questions of that kind."

"But on your answer depends mine."

She looked at him in amazement. His gentle kindness had disappeared. She saw, instead, that Jacob Delafield whom her instinct had divined from the beginning behind the modest and courteous outer man, the Jacob Delafield of whom she had told the Duchess she was afraid.

But her passion swept every other thought out of its way. With dim agony and rage she began to perceive that she had been duped.

"Mr. Delafield"--she tried for calm--"I don't understand your attitude, but, so far as I do understand it, I find it intolerable. If you have deceived me--"

"I have not deceived you. Lord Lackington is dying."

"But that is not why you were at the station," she repeated, passionately. "Why did you meet the English train?"

Her eyes, clear now in the cold light, shone upon him imperiously.

Again the inner voice said: "Speak--get away from conventionalities. Speak--soul to soul!"

He sat down once more beside her. His gaze sought the ground. Then, with sharp suddenness, he looked her in the face.

"Miss Le Breton, you were going to Paris to meet Major Warkworth?"

She drew back.

"And if I was?" she said, with a wild defiance.

"I had to prevent it, that was all."

His tone was calm and resolution itself.

"Who--who gave you authority over me?"

"One may save--even by violence. You were too precious to be allowed to destroy yourself."

His look, so sad and strong, the look of a deep compassion, fastened itself upon her. He felt himself, indeed, possessed by a force not his own, that same force which in its supreme degree made of St. Francis "the great tamer of souls."

"Who asked you to be our judge? Neither I nor Major Warkworth owe you anything."

"No. But I owed you help--as a man--as your friend. The truth was somehow borne in upon me. You were risking your honor--I threw myself in the way."

Every word seemed to madden her.

"What--what could you know of the circumstances?" cried her choked, laboring voice. "It is unpardonable--an outrage! You know nothing either of him or of me."

She clasped her hands to her breast in a piteous, magnificent gesture, as though she were defending her lover and her love.

"I know that you have suffered much," he said, dropping his eyes before her, "but you would suffer infinitely more if--"

"If you had not interfered." Her veil had fallen over her face again. She flung it back in impatient despair. "Mr. Delafield, I can do without your anxieties."

"But not"--he spoke slowly--"without your own self-respect."

Julie's face trembled. She hid it in her hands.

"Go!" she said. "Go!"

He went to the farther end of the ship and stood there motionless, looking towards the land but seeing nothing. On all sides the darkness was lifting, and in the distance there gleamed already the whiteness that was Dover. His whole being was shaken with that experience which comes so rarely to cumbered and superficial men--the intimate wrestle of one personality with another. It seemed to him he was not worthy of it.

After some little time, when only a quarter of an hour lay between the ship and Dover pier, he went back to Julie.

She was sitting perfectly still, her hands clasped in front of her, her veil drawn down.

"May I say one word to you?" he said, gently.

She did not speak.

"It is this. What I have confessed to you to-night is, of course, buried between us. It is as though it had never been said. I have given you pain. I ask your pardon from the bottom of my heart, and, at the same time"--his voice trembled--"I thank God that I had the courage to do it!"

She threw him a glance that showed her a quivering lip and the pallor of intense emotion.

"I know you think you were right," she said, in a voice dull and strained, "but henceforth we can only be enemies. You have tyrannized over me in the name of standards that you revere and I reject. I can only beg you to let my life alone for the future."

He said nothing. She rose, dizzily, to her feet. They were rapidly approaching the pier.

"HER HANDS CLASPED IN FRONT OF HER"

With the cold aloofness of one who feels it more dignified to submit than to struggle, she allowed him to assist her in landing. He put her into the Victoria train, travelling himself in another carriage.

As he walked beside her down the platform of Victoria Station, she said to him:

"I shall be obliged if you will tell Evelyn that I have returned."

"I go to her at once."

She suddenly paused, and he saw that she was looking helplessly at one of the newspaper placards of the night before. First among its items appeared: "Critical state of Lord Lackington."

He hardly knew how far she would allow him to have any further communication with her, but her pale exhaustion made it impossible not to offer to serve her.

"It would be early to go for news now," he said, gently. "It would disturb the house. But in a couple of hours from now"--the station clock pointed to 6.15--"if you will allow me, I will leave the morning bulletin at your door."

She hesitated.

"You must rest, or you will have no strength for nursing," he continued, in the same studiously guarded tone. "But if you would prefer another messenger--"

"I have none," and she raised her hand to her brow in mute, unconscious confession of an utter weakness and bewilderment.

"Then let me go," he said, softly.

It seemed to him that she was so physically weary as to be incapable either of assent or resistance. He put her into her cab, and gave the driver his directions. She looked at him uncertainly. But he did not offer his hand. From those blue eyes of his there shot out upon her one piercing glance--manly, entreating, sad. He lifted his hat and was gone.

XX

"Jacob, what brings you back so soon?" The Duchess ran into the room, a trim little figure in her morning dress of blue-and-white cloth, with her small spitz leaping beside her.

Delafield advanced.

"I came to tell you that I got your telegram yesterday, and that in the evening, by an extraordinary and fortunate chance, I met Miss Le Breton in Paris--"

"You met Julie in Paris?" echoed the Duchess, in astonishment.

"She had come to spend a couple of days with some friends there before going on to Bruges. I gave her the news of Lord Lackington's illness, and she at once turned back. She was much fatigued and distressed, and the night was stormy. I put her into the sleeping-car, and came back myself to see if I could be any assistance to her. And at Calais I was of some use. The crossing was very rough."

"Julie was in Paris?" repeated the Duchess, as though she had heard nothing else of what he had been saying.

Her eyes, so blue and large in her small, irregular face, sought those of her cousin and endeavored to read them.

"It seems to have been a rapid change of plan. And it was a great stroke of luck my meeting her."

"But how--and where?"

"Oh, there is no time for going into that," said Delafield, impatiently. "But I knew you would like to know that she was here--after your message yesterday. We arrived a little after six this morning. About nine I went for news to St. James's Square. There is a slight rally."

"Did you see Lord Uredale? Did you say anything about Julie?" asked the Duchess, eagerly.

"I merely asked at the door, and took the bulletin to Miss Le Breton. Will you see Uredale and arrange it? I gather you saw him yesterday."

"By all means," said the Duchess, musing. "Oh, it was so curious yesterday. Lord Lackington had just told them. You should have seen those two men."

"The sons?"

The Duchess nodded.

"They don't like it. They were as stiff as pokers. But they will do absolutely the right thing. They see at once that she must be provided for. And when he asked for her they told me to telegraph, if I could find out where she was. Well, of all the extraordinary chances."

She looked at him again, oddly, a spot of red on either small cheek. Delafield took no notice. He was pacing up and down, apparently in thought.

"Suppose you take her there?" he said, pausing abruptly before her.

"To St. James's Square? What did you tell her?"

"That he was a trifle better, and that you would come to her."

"Yes, it would be hard for her to go alone," said the Duchess, reflectively. She looked at her watch. "Only a little after eleven. Ring, please, Jacob."

The carriage was ordered. Meanwhile the little lady inquired eagerly after her Julie. Had she been exhausted by the double journey? Was she alone in Paris, or was Madame Bornier with her?

Jacob had understood that Madame Bornier and the little girl had gone straight to Bruges.

The Duchess looked down and then looked up.

"Did--did you come across Major Warkworth?"

"Yes, I saw him for a moment in the Rue de la Paix, He was starting for Rome."

The Duchess turned away as though ashamed of her question, and gave her orders for the carriage. Then her attention was suddenly drawn to her cousin. "How pale you look, Jacob," she said, approaching him. "Won't you have something--some wine?"

Delafield refused, declaring that all he wanted was an hour or two's sleep.

"I go back to Paris to-morrow," he said, as he prepared to take his leave. "Will you be here to-night if I look in?"

"Alack! we go to Scotland to-night! It was just a piece of luck that you found me this morning. Freddie is fuming to get away."

Delafield paused a moment. Then he abruptly shook hands and went.

"He wants news of what happens at St. James's Square," thought the Duchess, suddenly, and she ran after him to the top of the stairs. "Jacob! If you don't mind a horrid mess to-night, Freddie and I shall be dining alone--of course we must have something to eat. Somewhere about eight. Do look in. There'll be a cutlet--on a trunk--anyway."

Delafield laughed, hesitated, and finally accepted.

The Duchess went back to the drawing-room, not a little puzzled and excited.

"It's very, very odd," she said to herself. "And what is the matter with Jacob?"

Half an hour later she drove to the splendid house in St. James's Square where Lord Lackington lay dying.

She asked for Lord Uredale, the eldest son, and waited in the library till he came.

He was a tall, squarely built man, with fair hair already gray, and somewhat absent and impassive manners.

At sight of him the Duchess's eyes filled with tears. She hurried to him, her soft nature dissolved in sympathy.

"How is your father?"

"A trifle easier, though the doctors say there is no real improvement. But he is quite conscious--knows us all. I have just been reading him the debate."

"You told me yesterday he had asked for Miss Le Breton," said the Duchess, raising herself on tiptoe as though to bring her low tones closer to his ear. "She's here--in town, I mean. She came back from Paris last night."

Lord Uredale showed no emotion of any kind. Emotion was not in his line.

"Then my father would like to see her," he said, in a dry, ordinary voice, which jarred upon the sentimental Duchess.

"When shall I bring her?"

"He is now comfortable and resting. If you are free--"

The Duchess replied that she would go to Heribert Street at once. As Lord Uredale took her to her carriage a young man ran down the steps hastily, raised his hat, and disappeared.

Lord Uredale explained that he was the husband of the famous young beauty, Mrs. Delaray, whose portrait Lord Lackington had been engaged upon at the time of his seizure. Having been all his life a skilful artist, a man of fashion, and a harmless haunter of lovely women, Lord Lackington, as the Duchess knew, had all but completed a gallery of a hundred portraits, representing the beauty of the reign. Mrs. Delaray's would have been the hundredth in a series of which Mrs. Norton was the first.

"He has been making arrangements with the husband to get it finished," said Lord Uredale; "it has been on his mind."

The Duchess shivered a little.

"He knows he won't finish it?"

"Quite well."

"And he still thinks of those things?"

"Yes--or politics," said Lord Uredale, smiling faintly. "I have written to Mr. Montresor. There are two or three points my father wants to discuss with him."

"And he is not depressed, or troubled about himself?"

"Not in the least. He will be grateful if you will bring him Miss Le Breton."

"Julie, my darling, are you fit to come with me?"

The Duchess held her friend in her arms, soothing and caressing her. How forlorn was the little house, under its dust-sheets, on this rainy, spring morning! And Julie, amid the dismantled drawing-room, stood spectrally white and still, listening, with scarcely a word in reply, to the affection, or the pity, or the news which the Duchess poured out upon her.

"Shall we go now? I am quite ready."

And she withdrew herself from the loving grasp which held her, and put on her hat and gloves.

"You ought to be in bed," said the Duchess. "Those night journeys are too abominable. Even Jacob looks a wreck. But what an extraordinary chance, Julie, that Jacob should have found you! How did you come across each other?"

"At the Nord Station," said Julie, as she pinned her veil before the glass over the mantel-piece.

Some instinct silenced the Duchess. She asked no more questions, and they started for St. James's Square.

"You won't mind if I don't talk?" said Julie, leaning back and closing her eyes. "I seem still to have the sea in my ears."

The Duchess looked at her tenderly, clasping her hand close, and the carriage rolled along. But just before they reached St. James's Square, Julie hastily raised the fingers which held her own and kissed them.

"Oh, Julie," said the Duchess, reproachfully, "I don't like you to do that!"

She flushed and frowned. It was she who ought to pay such acts of homage, not Julie.

"Father, Miss Le Breton is here."

"Let her come in, Jack--and the Duchess, too."

Lord Uredale went back to the door. Two figures came noiselessly into the room, the Duchess in front, with Julie's hand in hers.

Lord Lackington was propped up in bed, and breathing fast. But he smiled as they approached him.

"This is good-bye, dear Duchess," he said, in a whisper, as she bent over him. Then, with a spark of his old gayety in the eyes, "I should be a cur to grumble. Life has been very agreeable. Ah, Julie!"

Julie dropped gently on her knees beside him and laid her cheek against his arm. At the mention of her name the old man's face had clouded as though the thoughts she called up had suddenly rebuked his words to the Duchess. He feebly moved his hands towards hers, and there was silence in the room for a few moments.

"Uredale!"

"Yes, father."

"This is Rose's daughter."

His eyes lifted themselves to those of his son.

"I know, father. If Miss Le Breton will allow us, we will do what we can to be of service to her."

Bill Chantrey, the younger brother, gravely nodded assent. They were both men of middle age, the younger over forty. They did not resemble their father, nor was there any trace in either of them of his wayward fascination. They were a pair of well-set-up, well-bred Englishmen, surprised at nothing, and quite incapable of showing any emotion in public; yet just and kindly men. As Julie entered the house they had both solemnly shaken hands with her, in a manner which showed at once their determination, as far as they were concerned, to avoid anything sentimental or in the nature of a scene, and their readiness to do what could be rightly demanded of them.

Julie hardly listened to Lord Uredale's little speech. She had eyes and ears only for her grandfather. As she knelt beside him, her face bowed upon his hand, the ice within her was breaking up, that dumb and straitening anguish in which she had lived since that moment at the Nord Station in which she had grasped the meaning and the implications of Delafield's hurried words. Was everything to be swept away from her at once--her lover, and now this dear old man, to whom her heart, crushed and bleeding as it was, yearned with all its strength?

Lord Lackington supposed that she was weeping.

"Don't grieve, my dear," he murmured. "It must come to an end some time--'cette charmante promenade à travers la réalité!'"

And he smiled at her, agreeably vain to the last of that French accent and that French memory which--so his look implied--they two could appreciate, each in the other. Then he turned to the Duchess.

"Duchess, you knew this secret before me. But I forgive you, and thank you. You have been very good to Rose's child. Julie has told me--and--I have observed--"

"Oh, dear Lord Lackington!" Evelyn bent over him. "Trust her to me," she said, with a lovely yearning to comfort and cheer him breathing from her little face.

He smiled.

"To you--and--"

He did not finish the sentence.

After a pause he made a little gesture of farewell which the Duchess understood. She kissed his hand and turned away weeping.

"Nurse--where is nurse?" said Lord Lackington.

Both the nurse and the doctor, who had withdrawn a little distance from the family group, came forward.

"Doctor, give me some strength," said the laboring voice, not without its old wilfulness of accent.

He moved his arm towards the young homoeopath, who injected strychnine. Then he looked at the nurse.

"Brandy--and--lift me."

All was done as he desired.

"Now go, please," he said to his sons. "I wish to be left with Julie."

For some moments, that seemed interminable to Julie, Lord Lackington lay silent. A feverish flush, a revival of life in the black eyes had followed on the administration of the two stimulants. He seemed to be gathering all his forces.

At last he laid his hand on her arm. "You shouldn't be alone," he said, abruptly.

His expression had grown anxious, even imperious. She felt a vague pang of dread as she tried to assure him that she had kind friends, and that her work would be her resource.

Lord Lackington frowned.

"That won't do," he said, almost vehemently. "You have great talents, but you are weak--you are a woman--you must marry."

Julie stared at him, whiter even than when she had entered his room--helpless to avert what she began to foresee.

"Jacob Delafield is devoted to you. You should marry him, dear--you should marry him."

The room seemed to swim around her. But his face was still plain--the purpled lips and cheeks, the urgency in the eyes, as of one pursued by an overtaking force, the magnificent brow, the crown of white hair.

She summoned all her powers and told him hurriedly that he was mistaken--entirely mistaken. Mr. Delafield had, indeed, proposed to her, but, apart from her own unwillingness, she had reason to know that his feelings towards her were now entirely changed. He neither loved her nor thought well of her.

Lord Lackington lay there, obstinate, patient, incredulous. At last he interrupted her.

"You make yourself believe these things. But they are not true. Delafield is attached to you. I know it."

He nodded to her with his masterful, affectionate look. And before she could find words again he had resumed.

"He could give you a great position. Don't despise it. We English big-wigs have a good time."

A ghostly, humorous ray shot out upon her; then he felt for her hand.

"Dear Julie, why won't you?"

"If you were to ask him," she cried, in despair, "he would tell you as I do."

And across her miserable thoughts there flashed two mingled images--Warkworth waiting, waiting for her at the Sceaux Station, and that look of agonized reproach in Delafield's haggard face as he had parted from her in the dawn of this strange, this incredible day.

And here beside her, with the tyranny of the dying, this dear babbler wandered on in broken words, with painful breath, pleading, scolding, counselling. She felt that he was exhausting himself. She begged him to let her recall nurse and doctor. He shook his head, and when he could no longer speak, he clung to her hand, his gaze solemnly, insistently, fixed upon her.

Her spirit writhed and rebelled. But she was helpless in the presence of this mortal weakness, this affection, half earthly, half beautiful, on its knees before her.

A thought struck her. Why not content him? Whatever pledges she gave would die with him. What did it matter? It was cruelty to deny him the words--the mere empty words--he asked of her.

"I--I would do anything to please you!" she said, with a sudden burst of uncontrollable tears, as she laid her head down beside him on the pillow. "If he were to ask me again, of course, for your sake, I would consider it once more. Dear, dear friend, won't that satisfy you?"

Lord Lackington was silent a few moments, then he smiled.

"That's a promise?"

She raised herself and looked at him, conscious of a sick movement of terror. What was there in his mind, still so quick, fertile, ingenious, under the very shadow of death?

He waited for her answer, feebly pressing her hand.

"Yes," she said, faintly, and once more hid her face beside him.

Then, for some little time, the dying man neither stirred nor spoke. At last Julie heard:

"I used to be afraid of death--that was in middle life. Every night it was a torment. But now, for many years, I have not been afraid at all.... Byron--Lord Byron--said to me, once, he would not change anything in his life; but he would have preferred not to have lived at all. I could not say that. I have enjoyed it all--being an Englishman, and an English peer--pictures, politics, society--everything. Perhaps it wasn't fair. There are so many poor devils."

Julie pressed his hand to her lips. But in her thoughts there rose the sudden, sharp memory of her mother's death--of that bitter stoicism and abandonment in which the younger life had closed, in comparison with this peace, this complacency.

Yet it was a complacency rich in sweetness. His next words were to assure her tenderly that he had made provision for her. "Uredale and Bill--will see to it. They're good fellows. Often-- they've thought me--a pretty fool. But they've been kind to me--always."

Then, after another interval, he lifted himself in bed, with more strength than she had supposed he could exert, looked at her earnestly, and asked her, in the same painful whisper, whether she believed in another life.

"Yes," said Julie. But her shrinking, perfunctory manner evidently distressed him. He resumed, with a furrowed brow:

"You ought. It is good for us to believe it."

"I must hope, at any rate, that I shall see you again--and mamma," she said, smiling on him through her tears.

"I wonder what it will be like," he replied, after a pause. His tone and look implied a freakish, a whimsical curiosity, yet full of charm. Then, motioning to her to come nearer, and speaking into her ear:

"Your poor mother, Julie, was never happy--never! There must be laws, you see--and churches--and religious customs. It's because--we're made of such wretched stuff. My wife, when she died--made me promise to continue going to church--and praying. And--without it--I should have been a bad man. Though I've had plenty of sceptical thoughts--plenty. Your poor parents rebelled--against all that. They suffered--they suffered. But you'll make up--you're a noble woman--you'll make up."

He laid his hand on her head. She offered no reply; but through the inner mind there rushed the incidents, passions, revolts of the preceding days.

But for that strange chance of Delafield's appearance in her path--a chance no more intelligible to her now, after the pondering of several feverish hours, than it had been at the moment of her first suspicion--where and what would she be now? A dishonored woman, perhaps, with a life-secret to keep; cut off, as her mother had been, from the straight-living, law-abiding world.

The touch of the old man's hand upon her hair roused in her a first recoil, a first shattering doubt of the impulse which had carried her to Paris. Since Delafield left her in the early dawn she had been pouring out a broken, passionate heart in a letter to Warkworth. No misgivings while she was writing it as to the all-sufficing legitimacy of love!

But here, in this cold neighborhood of the grave--brought back to gaze in spirit; on her mother's tragedy--she shrank, she trembled. Her proud intelligence denied the stain, and bade her hate and despise her rescuer. And, meanwhile, things also inherited and inborn, the fruit of a remoter ancestry, rising from the dimmest and deepest caverns of personality, silenced the clamor of the naturalist mind. One moment she felt herself seized with terror lest anything should break down the veil between her real self and this unsuspecting tenderness of the dying man; the next she rose in revolt against her own fear. Was she to find herself, after all, a mere weak penitent--meanly grateful to Jacob Delafield? Her heart cried out to Warkworth in a protesting anguish.

So absorbed in thought was she that she did not notice how long the silence had lasted.

"He seems to be sleeping," said a low voice beside her.

She looked up to see the doctor, with Lord Uredale. Gently releasing herself, she kissed Lord Lackington's forehead, and rose to her feet.

Suddenly the patient opened his eyes, and as he seemed to become aware of the figures beside him, he again lifted himself in bed, and a gleam most animated, most vivacious, passed over his features.

"Brougham's not asked," he said, with a little chuckle of amusement. "Isn't it a joke?"

The two men beside him looked at each other. Lord Uredale approached the bed.

"Not asked to what, father?" he said, gently.

"Why, to the Queen's fancy ball, of course," said Lord Lackington, still smiling. "Such a to-do! All the elderly sticks practising minuets for their lives!"

A voluble flow of talk followed--hardly intelligible. The words "Melbourne" and "Lady Holland" emerged--the fragment, apparently, of a dispute with the latter, in which "Allen" intervened--the names of "Palmerston" and "that dear chap, Villiers."

Lord Uredale sighed. The young doctor looked at him interrogatively.

"He is thinking of his old friends," said the son. "That was the Queen's ball, I imagine, of '42. I have often heard him describe my mother's dress."

But while he was speaking the fitful energy died away. The old man ceased to talk; his eyelids fell. But the smile still lingered about his mouth, and as he settled himself on his pillows, like one who rests, the spectators were struck by the urbane and distinguished beauty of his aspect. The purple flush had died again into mortal pallor. Illness had masked or refined the weakness of mouth and chin; the beautiful head and countenance, with their characteristic notes of youth, impetuosity, a kind of gay detachment, had never been more beautiful.

The young doctor looked stealthily from the recumbent figure to the tall and slender woman standing absorbed and grief-stricken beside the bed. The likeness was as evident to him as it had been, in the winter, to Sir Wilfrid Bury.

As he was escorting her down-stairs, Lord Uredale said to his companion, "Foster thinks he may still live twenty-four hours."

"If he asks for me again," said Julie, now shrouded once more behind a thick, black veil, "you will send?"

He gravely assented.

"It is a great pity," he said, with a certain stiffness--did it unconsciously mark the difference between her and his legitimate kindred?--"that my sister Lady Blanche and her daughter cannot be with us."

"They are in Italy?"

"At Florence. My niece has had an attack of diphtheria. She could neither travel nor could her mother leave her."

Then pausing in the hall, he added in a low voice, and with some embarrassment:

"My father has told you, I believe, of the addition he has made to his will?"

Julie drew back.

"I neither asked for it nor desired it," she said, in her coldest and clearest voice.

"That I quite understand," said Lord Uredale. "But--you cannot hurt him by refusing."

She hesitated.

"No. But afterwards--I must be free to follow my own judgment."

"We cannot take what does not belong to us," he said, with some sharpness. "My brother and I are named as your trustees. Believe me, we will do our best."

Meanwhile the younger brother had come out of the library to bid her farewell. She felt that she was under critical observation, though both pairs of gray eyes refrained from any appearance of scrutiny. Her pride came to her aid, and she did not shrink from the short conversation which the two brothers evidently desired. When it was over, and the brothers returned to the hall after putting her into the Duchess's carriage, the younger said to the elder:

"She can behave herself, Johnnie."

They looked at each other, with their hands in their pockets. A little nod passed between them-- an augur-like acceptance of this new and irregular member of the family.

"Yes, she has excellent manners," said Uredale. "And really, after the tales Lady Henry has been spreading--that's something!"

"Oh, I always thought Lady Henry an old cat," said Bill, tranquilly. "That don't matter."

The Chantrey brothers had not been among Lady Henry's habitués. In her eyes, they were the dull sons of an agreeable father. They were humorously aware of it, and bore her little malice.

"No," said Uredale, raising his eyebrows; "but the 'affaire Warkworth'? If there's any truth in what one hears, that's deuced unpleasant."

Bill Chantrey whistled.

"It's hard luck on that poor child Aileen that it should be her own cousin interfering with her preserves. By-the-way"--he stooped to look at the letters on the hall table--"do you see there's a letter for father from Blanche? And in a letter I got from her by the same post, she says that she has told him the whole story. According to her, Aileen's too ill to be thwarted, and she wants the governor to see the guardians. I say, Johnnie"--he looked at his brother--"we'll not trouble the father with it now?"

"Certainly not," said Uredale, with a sigh. "I saw one of the trustees--Jack Underwood-- yesterday. He told me Blanche and the child were more infatuated than ever. Very likely what one hears is a pack of lies. If not, I hope this woman will have the good taste to drop it. Father has charged me to write to Blanche and tell her the whole story of poor Rose, and of this girl's revealing herself. Blanche, it appears, is just as much in the dark as we were."

"If this gossip has got round to her, her feelings will be mixed. Oh, well, I've great faith in the money," said Bill Chantrey, carelessly, as they began to mount the stairs again. "It sounds disgusting; but if the child wants him I suppose she must have him. And, anyway, the man's off to Africa for a twelvemonth at least. Miss Le Breton will have time to forget him. One can't say that either he or she has behaved with delicacy--unless, indeed, she knew nothing of Aileen, which is quite probable."

"Well, don't ask me to tackle her," said Uredale. "She has the ways of an empress."

Bill Chantrey shrugged his shoulders. "And, by George! she looks as if she could fall in love," he said, slowly. "Magnificent eyes, Johnnie. I propose to make a study of our new niece."

"Lord Uredale!" said a voice on the stairs.

The young doctor descended rapidly to meet them.

"His lordship is asking for some one," he said. "He seems excited. But I cannot catch the name."

Lord Uredale ran up-stairs.

Later in the day a man emerged from Lackington House and walked rapidly towards the Mall. It was Jacob Delafield.

He passed across the Mall and into St. James's Park. There he threw himself on the first seat he saw, in an absorption so deep that it excited the wondering notice of more than one passer-by.

After about half an hour he roused himself, and walked, still in the same brown study, to his lodgings in Jermyn Street. There he found a letter which he eagerly opened.

"DEAR JACOB,--Julie came back this morning about one o'clock. I waited for her--and at first she seemed quite calm and composed. But suddenly, as I was sitting beside her, talking, she fainted away in her chair, and I was terribly alarmed. We sent for a doctor at once. He shakes his head over her, and says there are all the signs of a severe strain of body and mind. No wonder, indeed--our poor Julie! Oh, how I loathe some people! Well, there she is in bed, Madame Bornier away, and everybody. I simply can't go to Scotland. But Freddie is just mad. Do, Jacob, there's a dear, go and dine with him to-night and cheer him up. He vows he won't go north without me. Perhaps I'll come to-morrow. I could no more leave Julie to-night than fly.

"She'll be ill for weeks. What I ought to do is to take her abroad. She's very dear and good; but, oh, Jacob, as she lies there I feel her heart's broken. And it's not Lord Lackington. Oh no! though I'm sure she loved him. Do go to Freddie, there's a dear."

"No, that I won't!" said Delafield, with a laugh that choked him, as he threw the letter down.

He tried to write an answer, but could not achieve even the simplest note. Then he began a pacing of his room, which lasted till he dropped into his chair, worn out with the sheer physical exhaustion of the night and day. When his servant came in he found his master in a heavy sleep. And, at Crowborough House, the Duke dined and fumed alone.

XXI

"Why does any one stay in England who can make the trip to Paradise?" said the Duchess, as she leaned lazily back in the corner of the boat and trailed her fingers in the waters of Como.

It was a balmy April afternoon, and she and Julie were floating through a scene enchanted, incomparable. When spring descends upon the shores of the Lago di Como, she brings with her all the graces, all the beauties, all the fine, delicate, and temperate delights of which earth and sky are capable, and she pours them forth upon a land of perfect loveliness. Around the shores of other lakes--Maggiore, Lugano, Garda--blue mountains rise, and the vineyards spread their green and dazzling terraces to the sun. Only Como can show in unmatched union a main composition, incomparably grand and harmonious, combined with every jewelled, or glowing, or exquisite detail. Nowhere do the mountains lean towards each other in such an ordered splendor as that which bends round the northern shores of Como. Nowhere do buttressed masses rise behind each other, to right and left of a blue water-way, in lines statelier or more noble than those kept by the mountains of the Lecco Lake, as they marshal themselves on either hand, along the approaches to Lombardy and Venetia; bearing aloft, as though on the purple pillars of some majestic gateway, the great curtain of dazzling cloud which, on a sunny day, hangs over the Brescian plain--a glorious drop-scene, interposed between the dwellers on the Como Mountains, and those marble towns, Brescia, Verona, Padua, which thread the way to Venice.

And within this divine frame-work, between the glistening snows which still, in April, crown and glorify the heights, and those reflections of them which lie encalmed in the deep bosom of the lake, there's not a foot of pasture, not a shelf of vineyard, not a slope of forest where the spring is not at work, dyeing the turf with gentians, starring it with narcissuses, or drawing across it the first golden net-work of the chestnut leaves; where the mere emerald of the grass is not in itself a thing to refresh the very springs of being; where the peach-blossom and the wild-cherry and the olive are not perpetually weaving patterns on the blue, which ravish the very heart out of your breast. And already the roses are beginning to pour over the walls; the wistaria is climbing up the cypresses; a pomp of camellias and azaleas is in all the gardens; while in the grassy bays that run up into the hills the primrose banks still keep their sweet austerity, and the triumph of spring over the just banished winter is still sharp and new.

And in the heart and sense of Julie Le Breton, as she sat beside the Duchess, listening absently to the talk of the old boatman, who, with his oars resting idly in his hands, was chattering to the ladies, a renewing force akin to that of the spring was also at its healing and life-giving work. She had still the delicate, tremulous look of one recovering from a sore wrestle with physical ill; but in her aspect there were suggestions more intimate, more moving than this. Those who have lain down and risen up with pain; those who have been face to face with passion and folly and self-judgment; those who have been forced to seek with eagerness for some answer to those questions which the majority of us never ask, "Whither is my life leading me--and what is it worth to me or to any other living soul?"--these are the men and women who now and then touch or startle us with the eyes and the voice of Julie, if, at least, we have the capacity that responds.

Sir Wilfrid Bury, for instance, prince of self-governed and reasonable men, was not to be touched by Julie. For him, in spite of her keen intelligence, she was the type passionné, from which he instinctively recoiled--the Duke of Crowborough the same. Such men feel towards such women as Julie Le Breton hostility or satire; for what they ask, above all, of the women of their world is a kind of simplicity, a kind of lightness which makes life easier for men.

But for natures like Evelyn Crowborough--or Meredith--or Jacob Delafield--the Julie-type has perennial attractions. For these are all children of feeling, allied in this, however different in intelligence or philosophy. They are attracted by the storm-tossed temperament in itself; by mere sensibility; by that which, in the technical language of Catholicism, suggests or possesses "the gift of tears." At any rate, pity and love for her poor Julie--however foolish, however faulty--lay warm in Evelyn Crowborough's breast; they had brought her to Como; they kept her now battling on the one hand with her husband's angry letters and on the other with the melancholy of her most perplexing, most appealing friend.

"I had often heard" [wrote the sore-tried Duke] "of the ravages wrought in family life by these absurd and unreasonable female friendships, but I never thought that it would be you, Evelyn, who would bring them home to me. I won't repeat the arguments I have used a hundred times in vain. But once again I implore and demand that you should find some kind, responsible person to look after Miss Le Breton--I don't care what you pay--and that you yourself should come home to me and the children and the thousand and one duties you are neglecting.

"As for the spring month in Scotland, which I generally enjoy so much, that has been already entirely ruined. And now the season is apparently to be ruined also. On the Shropshire property there is an important election coming on, as I am sure you know; and the Premier said to me only yesterday that he hoped you were already up and doing. The Grand Duke of C---- will be in London within the next fortnight. I particularly want to show him some civility. But what can I do without you--and how on earth am I to explain your absence?

"Once more, Evelyn, I beg and I demand that you should come home."

To which the Duchess had rushed off a reply without a post's delay.

"Oh, Freddie, you are such a wooden-headed darling! As if I hadn't explained till I'm black in the face. I'm glad, anyway, you didn't say command; that would really have made difficulties.

"As for the election, I'm sure if I was at home I should think it very good fun. Out here I am extremely doubtful whether we ought to do such things as you and Lord M---- suggest. A duke shouldn't interfere in elections. Anyway, I'm sure it's good for my character to consider it a little--though I quite admit you may lose the election.

"The Grand Duke is a horrid wretch, and if he wasn't a grand duke you'd be the first to cut him. I had to spend a whole dinner-time last year in teaching him his proper place. It was very humiliating, and not at all amusing. You can have a men's dinner for him. That's all he's fit for.

"And as for the babies, Mrs. Robson sends me a telegram every morning. I can't make out that they have had a finger-ache since I went away, and I am sure mothers are entirely superfluous. All the same, I think about them a great deal, especially at night. Last night I tried to think about their education--if only I wasn't such a sleepy creature! But, at any rate, I never in my life tried to think about it at home. So that's so much to the good.

"Indeed, I'll come back to you soon, you poor, forsaken, old thing! But Julie has no one in the world, and I feel like a Newfoundland dog who has pulled some one out of the water. The water was deep; and the life's only just coming back; and the dog's not much good. But he sits there, for company, till the doctor comes, and that's just what I'm doing.

"I know you don't approve of the notions I have in my head now. But that's because you don't understand. Why don't you come out and join us? Then you'd like Julie as much as I do; everything would be quite simple; and I shouldn't be in the least jealous.

"Dr. Meredith is coming here, probably to-night, and Jacob should arrive to-morrow on his way to Venice, where poor Chudleigh and his boy are."

The breva, or fair-weather wind, from the north was blowing freshly yet softly down the lake. The afternoon sun was burning on Bellaggio, on the long terrace of the Melzi villa, on the white mist of fruit-blossom that lay lightly on the green slopes above San Giovanni.

Suddenly the Duchess and the boatman left the common topics of every day by which the Duchess was trying to improve her Italian--such as the proposed enlargement of the Bellevue Hotel, the new villas that were springing up, the gardens of the Villa Carlotta, and so forth. Evelyn had carelessly asked the old man whether he had been in any of the fighting of '59, and in an instant, under her eyes, he became another being. Out rolled a torrent of speech; the oars lay idly on the water; and through the man's gnarled and wrinkled face there blazed a high and illumining passion. Novara and its beaten king, in '49; the ten years of waiting, when a whole people bode its time, in a gay, grim silence; the grudging victory of Magenta; the fivefold struggle that wrenched the hills of San Martino from the Austrians; the humiliations and the rage of Villafranca--of all these had this wasted graybeard made a part. And he talked of them with the Latin eloquence and facility, as no veteran of the north could have talked; he was in a moment the equal of these great affairs in which he had mingled; so that one felt in him the son of a race which had been rolled and polished--a pebble, as it were, from rocks which had made the primeval frame-work of the world--in the main course and stream of history.

Then from the campaign of '59 he fell back on the Five Days of Milan in '48--the immortal days, when a populace drove out an army, and what began almost in jest ended in a delirium, a stupefaction of victory. His language was hot, broken, confused, like the street fighting it chronicled. Afterwards--a further sharpening and blanching of the old face--and he had carried them deep into the black years of Italy's patience and Austria's revenge. Throwing out a thin arm, he pointed towards town after town on the lake shores, now in the brilliance of sunset, now in the shadow of the northern slope--Gravedona, Varenna, Argegno--towns which had each of them given their sons to the Austrian bullet and the Austrian lash for the ransom of Italy.

He ran through the sacred names--Stazzonelli, Riccini, Crescieri, Ronchetti, Ceresa, Previtali-- young men, almost all of them, shot for the possession of a gun or a knife, for helping their comrades in the Austrian army to desert, for "insulting conduct" towards an Austrian soldier or officer.

Of one of these executions, which he had himself witnessed at Varese--the shooting of a young fellow of six-and-twenty, his own friend and kinsman--he gave an account which blanched the Duchess's cheeks and brought the big tears into her eyes. Then, when he saw the effect he had produced, the old man trembled.

"Ah, eccellenza," he cried, "but it had to be! The Italians had to show they knew how to die; then God let them live. Ecco, eccellenza!"

And he drew from his breast-pocket, with shaking hands, an old envelope tied round with string. When he had untied it, a piece of paper emerged, brown with age and worn with much reading. It was a rudely printed broadsheet containing an account of the last words and sufferings of the martyrs of Mantua--those conspirators of 1852--from whose graves and dungeons sprang, tenfold renewed, the regenerating and liberating forces which, but a few years later, drove out the Austrian with the Bourbon, together.

"See here, eccellenza," he said, as he tenderly spread out its tattered folds and gave it into the Duchess's hand. "Have the goodness to look where is that black mark. There you will find the last words of Don Enrico Tazzoli, the half-brother of my father. He was a priest, eccellenza. Ah, it was not then as it is now! The priests were then for Italy. They hanged three of them at Mantua alone. As for Don Enrico, first they stripped him of his priesthood, and then they hanged him. And those were his last words, and the last words of Scarsellini also, who suffered with him. Veda eccellenza! As for me, I know them from a boy."

And while the Duchess read, the old man repeated tags and fragments under his breath, as he once more resumed the oars and drove the boat gently towards Menaggio.

"The multitude of victims has not robbed us of courage in the past, nor will it so rob us in the future--till victory dawns. The cause of the people is like the cause of religion--it triumphs only through its martyrs.... You--who survive--will conquer, and in your victory we, the dead, shall live....

"Take no thought for us; the blood of the forerunners is like the seed which the wise husbandman scatters on the fertile ground.... Teach our young men how to adore and how to suffer for a great idea. Work incessantly at that; so shall our country come to birth; and grieve not for us!... Yes, Italy shall be one! To that all things point. WORK! There is no obstacle that cannot be overcome, no opposition that cannot be destroyed. The HOW and the WHEN only remain to be solved. You, more fortunate than we, will find the clew to the riddle, when all things are accomplished, and the times are ripe.... Hope!--my parents, and my brothers--hope always!--waste no time in weeping."

The Duchess read aloud the Italian, and Julie stooped over her shoulder to follow the words.

"Marvellous!" said Julie, in a low voice, as she sank back into her place. "A youth of twenty-seven, with the rope round his neck, and he comforts himself with 'Italy.' What's 'Italy' to him, or he to 'Italy'?" Not even an immediate paradise. "Is there anybody capable of it now?"

Her face and attitude had lost their languor. As the Duchess returned his treasure to the old man she looked at Julie with joy. Not since her illness had there been any such sign of warmth and energy.

And, indeed, as they floated on, past the glow of Bellaggio, towards the broad gold and azure of the farther lake, the world-defying passion that breathed from these words of dead and murdered Italians played as a bracing and renewing power on Julie's still feeble being. It was akin to the high snows on those far Alps that closed in the lake--to the pure wind that blew from them--to the "gleam, the shadow, and the peace supreme," amid which their little boat pressed on towards the shore.

"What matter," cried the intelligence, but as though through sobs--"what matter the individual struggle and misery? These can be lived down. The heart can be silenced--nerves steadied--strength restored. Will and idea remain--the eternal spectacle of the world, and the eternal thirst of man to see, to know, to feel, to realize himself, if not in one passion, then in another. If not in love, then in patriotism--art--thought."

The Duchess and Julie landed presently beneath the villa of which they were the passing tenants. The Duchess mounted the double staircase where the banksia already hung in a golden curtain over the marble balustrade. Her face was thoughtful. She had to write her daily letter to the absent and reproachful Duke.

Julie parted from her with a caress, and paused awhile to watch the small figure till it mounted out of sight. Her friend had become very dear to her. A new humility, a new gratitude filled her heart. Evelyn should not sacrifice herself much longer. When she had insisted on carrying her patient abroad, Julie had neither mind nor will wherewith to resist. But now--the Duke should soon come to his own again.

She herself turned inland for that short walk by which each day she tested her returning strength. She climbed the winding road to Criante, the lovely village above Cadenabbia; then, turning to the left, she mounted a path that led to the woods which overhang the famous gardens of the Villa Carlotta.

Such a path! To the left hand, and, as it seemed, steeply beneath her feet, all earth and heaven--the wide lake, the purple mountains, the glories of a flaming sky. On the calm spaces of water lay a shimmer of crimson and gold, repeating the noble splendor of the clouds; the midgelike boats crept from shore to shore; and, midway between Bellaggio and Cadenabbia, the steamboat, a white speck, drew a silver furrow. To her right a green hill-side--each blade of grass, each flower, each tuft of heath, enskied, transfigured, by the broad light that poured across it from the hidden west. And on the very hill-top a few scattered olives, peaches, and wild cherries scrawled upon the blue, their bare, leaning stems, their pearly whites, their golden pinks and feathery grays all in a glory of sunset that made of them things enchanted, aerial, fantastical, like a dance of Botticelli angels on the height.

And presently a sheltered bank in a green hollow, where Julie sat down to rest. But nature, in this tranquil spot, had still new pageants, new sorceries wherewith to play upon the nerves of wonder. Across the hollow a great crag clothed in still leafless chestnut-trees reared itself against the lake. The innumerable lines of stem and branch, warm brown or steely gray, were drawn sharp on silver air, while at the very summit of the rock one superb tree with branching limbs, touched with intense black, sprang high above the rest, the proud plume or ensign of the wood. Through the trunks the blaze of distant snow and the purples of craggy mountains; in front the glistening spray of peach or cherry blossom, breaking the still wintry beauty of that majestic grove. And in all the air, dropping from the heaven, spread on the hills, or shimmering on the lake, a diffusion of purest rose and deepest blue, lake and cloud and mountain each melting into the other, as though heaven and earth conspired merely to give value and relief to the year's new birth, to this near sparkle of young leaf and blossom which shone like points of fire on the deep breast of the distance.

On the green ledge which ran round the hollow were children tugging at a goat. Opposite was a contadino's house of gray stone. A water-wheel turned beside it, and a stream, brought down from the hills, ran chattering past, a white and dancing thread of water. Everything was very still and soft. The children and the river made their voices heard; and there were nightingales singing in the woods below. Otherwise all was quiet. With a tranquil and stealthy joy the spring was taking possession. Nay--the Angelus! It swung over the lake and rolled from village to village....

The tears were in Julie's eyes. Such beauty as this was apt now to crush and break her. All her being was still sore, and this appeal of nature was sometimes more than she could bear.

Only a few short weeks since Warkworth had gone out of her life--since Delafield at a stroke had saved her from ruin--since Lord Lackington had passed away.

One letter had reached her from Warkworth, a wild and incoherent letter, written at night in a little room of a squalid hotel near the Gare de Sceaux. Her telegram had reached him, and for him, as for her, all was over.

But the letter was by no means a mere cry of baffled passion. There was in it a new note of moral anguish, as fresh and startling in her ear, coming from him, as the cry of passion itself. In the language of religion, it was the utterance of a man "convicted of sin."

/# "How long is it since that man gave me your telegram? I was pacing up and down the departure platform, working myself into an agony of nervousness and anxiety as the time went by, wondering what on earth had happened to you, when the chef de gare came up: 'Monsieur attend une dépêche?' There were some stupid formalities--at last I got it. It seemed to me I had already guessed what it contained.

"So it was Delafield who met you--Delafield who turned you back?

"I saw him outside the hotel yesterday, and we exchanged a few words. I have always disliked his long, pale face and his high and mighty ways--at any rate, towards plain fellows, who don't belong to the classes, like me. Yesterday I was more than usually anxious to get rid of him.

"So he guessed?

"It can't have been chance. In some way he guessed. And you have been torn from me. My God! If I could only reach him--if I could fling his contempt in his face! And yet--

"I have been walking up and down this room all night. The longing for you has been the sharpest suffering I suppose that I have ever known. For I am not one of the many people who enjoy pain. I have kept as free of it as I could. This time it caught and gripped me. Yet that isn't all. There has been something else.

"What strange, patched creatures we are! Do you know, Julie, that by the time the dawn came I was on my knees--thanking God that we were parted--that you were on your way home--safe--

out of my reach? Was I mad, or what? I can't explain it. I only know that one moment I hated Delafield as a mortal enemy--whether he was conscious of what he had done or no--and the next I found myself blessing him!

"I understand now what people mean when they talk of conversion. It seems to me that in the hours I have just passed through things have come to light in me that I myself never suspected. I came of an Evangelical stock--I was brought up in a religious household. I suppose that one can't, after all, get away from the blood and the life that one inherits. My poor, old father--I was a bad son, and I know I hastened his death--was a sort of Puritan saint, with very stern ideas. I seem to have been talking with him this night, and shrinking under his condemnation. I could see his old face, as he put before me the thoughts I had dared to entertain, the risks I had been ready to take towards the woman I loved--the woman to whom I owed a deep debt of eternal gratitude.

"Julie, it is strange how this appointment affects me. Last night I saw several people at the Embassy--good fellows--who seemed anxious to do all they could for me. Such men never took so much notice of me before. It is plain to me that this task will make or mar me. I may fail. I may die. But if I succeed England will owe me something, and these men at the top of the tree--

"Good God! how can I go on writing this to you? It's because I came back to the hotel and tossed about half the night brooding over the difference between what these men--these honorable, distinguished fellows--were prepared to think of me, and the blackguard I knew myself to be. What, take everything from a woman's hand, and then turn and try and drag her in the mire--propose to her what one would shoot a man for proposing to one's sister! Thief and cur.

"Julie--kind, beloved Julie--forget it all! For God's sake, let's cast it all behind us! As long as I live, your name, your memory will live in my heart. We shall not meet, probably, for many years. You'll marry and be happy yet. Just now I know you're suffering. I seem to see you in the train--on the steamer--your pale face that has lighted up life for me--your dear, slender hands that folded so easily into one of mine. You are in pain, my darling. Your nature is wrenched from its natural supports. And you gave me all your fine, clear mind, and all your heart. I ought to be damned to the deepest hell!

"Then, again, I say to myself, if only she were here! If only I had her here, with her arms round my neck, surely I might have found the courage and the mere manliness to extricate both herself and me from these entanglements. Aileen might have released and forgiven one.

"No, no! It's all over! I'll go and do my task. You set it me. You sha'n't be ashamed of me there.

"Good-bye, Julie, my love--good-bye--forever!" #/

These were portions of that strange document composed through the intervals of a long night, which showed in Warkworth's mind the survival of a moral code, inherited from generations of scrupulous and God-fearing ancestors, overlaid by selfish living, and now revived under the stress, the purification partly of deepening passion, partly of a high responsibility. The letter was incoherent, illogical; it showed now the meaner, now the nobler elements of character; but it was human; it came from the warm depths of life, and it had exerted in the end a composing and appeasing force upon the woman to whom it was addressed. He had loved her--if only at the moment of parting--he had loved her! At the last there had been feeling, sincerity, anguish, and to these all things may be forgiven.

And, indeed, what in her eyes there was to forgive, Julie had long forgiven. Was it his fault if, when they met first, he was already pledged--for social and practical reasons which her mind perfectly recognized and understood--to Aileen Moffatt? Was it his fault if the relations between herself and him had ripened into a friendship which in its turn could only maintain itself by passing into love? No! It was she, whose hidden, insistent passion--nourished, indeed, upon a tragic ignorance--had transformed what originally he had a perfect right to offer and to feel.

So she defended him; for in so doing she justified herself. And as to the Paris proposal, he had a right to treat her as a woman capable of deciding for herself how far love should carry her; he had a right to assume that her antecedents, her training, and her circumstances were not those of the ordinary sheltered girl, and that for her love might naturally wear a bolder and wilder aspect than for others. He blamed himself too severely, too passionately; but for this very blame her heart remembered him the more tenderly. For it meant that his mind was torn and in travail for her, that his thoughts clung to her in a passionate remorse; and again she felt herself loved, and forgave with all her heart.

All the same, he was gone out of her life, and through the strain and the unconscious progress to other planes and phases of being, wrought by sickness and convalescence, her own passion for him even was now a changed and blunted thing.

Was she ashamed of the wild impulse which had carried her to Paris? It is difficult to say. She was often seized with the shuddering consciousness of an abyss escaped, with wonder that she was still in the normal, accepted world, that Evelyn might still be her companion, that Thérèse still adored her more fervently than any saint in the calendar. Perhaps, if the truth were known, she was more abased in her own eyes by the self-abandonment which had preceded the assignation with Warkworth. She had much intellectual arrogance, and before her acquaintance with Warkworth she had been accustomed to say and to feel that love was but one passion among many, and to despise those who gave it too great a place. And here she had flung herself into it, like any dull or foolish girl for whom a love affair represents the only stirring in the pool of life that she is ever likely to know.

Well, she must recapture herself and remake her life. As she sat there in the still Italian evening she thought of the old boatman, and those social and intellectual passions to which his burst of patriotism had recalled her thoughts. Society, literature, friends, and the ambitions to which these lead--let her go back to them and build her days afresh. Dr. Meredith was coming. In his talk and companionship she would once more dip and temper the tools of mind and taste. No more vain self-arraignment, no more useless regrets. She looked back with bitterness upon a moment of weakness when, in the first stage of convalescence, in mortal weariness and loneliness, she had slipped one evening into the Farm Street church and unburdened her heart in confession. As she had told the Duchess, the Catholicism instilled into her youth by the Bruges nuns still laid upon her at times its ghostly and compelling hand. Now in her renewed strength she was inclined to look upon it as an element of weakness and disintegration in her nature. She resolved, in future, to free herself more entirely from a useless Aberglaube.

But Meredith was not the only visitor expected at the villa in the next few days. She was already schooling herself to face the arrival of Jacob Delafield.

It was curious how the mere thought of Delafield produced an agitation, a shock of feeling, which seemed to spread through all the activities of being. The faint, renascent glamour which had begun to attach to literature and social life disappeared. She fell into a kind of brooding, the sombre restlessness of one who feels in the dark the recurrent presence of an attacking and pursuing power, and is in a tremulous uncertainty where or how to meet it.

The obscure tumult within her represented, in fact, a collision between the pagan and Christian conceptions of life. In self-dependence, in personal pride, in her desire to refer all things to the arbitrament of reason, Julie, whatever her practice, was theoretically a stoic and a pagan. But Delafield's personality embodied another "must," another "ought," of a totally different kind. And it was a "must" which, in a great crisis of her life, she also had been forced to obey. There was the thought which stung and humiliated. And the fact was irreparable; nor did she see how she was ever to escape from the strange, silent, penetrating relation it had established between her and the man who loved her and had saved her, against her will.

During her convalescence at Crowborough House, Delafield had been often admitted. It would have been impossible to exclude him, unless she had confided the whole story of the Paris journey to the Duchess. And whatever Evelyn might tremblingly guess, from Julie's own mouth she knew nothing. So Delafield had come and gone, bringing Lord Lackington's last words, and the account of his funeral, or acting as intermediary in business matters between Julie and the Chantrey brothers. Julie could not remember that she had ever asked him for these services. They fell to him, as it were, by common consent, and she had been too weak to resist.

At first, whenever he entered the room, whenever he approached her, her sense of anger and resentment had been almost unbearable. But little by little his courtesy, tact, and coolness had restored a relation between them which, if not the old one, had still many of the outward characters of intimacy. Not a word, not the remotest allusion reminded her of what had happened. The man who had stood before her transfigured on the deck of the steamer, stammering out, "I thank God I had the courage to do it!"--it was often hard for her to believe, as she stole a look at Delafield, chatting or writing in the Duchess's drawing-room, that such a scene had ever taken place.

The evening stole on. How was it that whenever she allowed the thought of Delafield to obtain a real lodgment in the mind, even the memory of Warkworth was for the time effaced? Silently, irresistibly, a wild heat of opposition would develop within her. These men round whom, as it were, there breathes an air of the heights; in whom one feels the secret guard that religion keeps over thoughts and words and acts--her passionate yet critical nature flung out against them. How are they better than others, after all? What right have they over the wills of others?

Nevertheless, as the rose of evening burned on the craggy mountain face beyond Bellaggio, retreating upward, step by step, till the last glorious summit had died into the cool and already starlit blues of night, Julie, held, as it were, by a reluctant and half-jealous fascination, sat dreaming on the hill-side, not now of Warkworth, not of the ambitions of the mind, or society, but simply of the goings and comings, the aspects and sayings of a man in whose eyes she had once read the deepest and sternest things of the soul--a condemnation and an anguish above and beyond himself.

Dr. Meredith arrived in due time, a jaded Londoner athirst for idleness and fresh air. The Duchess and Julie carried him hither and thither about the lake in the four-oar boat which had been hired for the Duchess's pleasure. Here, enthroned between the two ladies, he passed luxurious hours, and his talk of politics, persons, and books brought just that stimulus to Julie's intelligence and spirits for which the Duchess had been secretly longing.

A first faint color returned to Julie's cheeks. She began to talk again; to resume certain correspondences; to show herself once more--at any rate intermittently--the affectionate, sympathetic, and beguiling friend.

As for Meredith, he knew little, but he suspected a good deal. There were certain features in her illness and convalescence which suggested to him a mental cause; and if there were such a cause, it must, of course, spring from her relations to Warkworth.

The name of that young officer was never mentioned. Once or twice Meredith was tempted to introduce it. It rankled in his mind that Julie had never been frank with him, freely as he had poured his affection at her feet. But a moment of languor or of pallor disarmed him.

"She is better," he said to the Duchess one day, abruptly. "Her mind is full of activity. But why, at times, does she still look so miserable--like a person without hope or future?"

The Duchess looked pensive. They were sitting in the corner of one of the villa's terraced walks, amid a scented wilderness of flowers. Above them was a canopy of purple and yellow-- rose and wistaria; while through the arches of the pergola which ran along the walk gleamed all those various blues which make the spell of Como--the blue and white of the clouds, the purple of the mountains, the azure of the lake.

"Well, she was in love with him. I suppose it takes a little time," said the Duchess, sighing.

"Why was she in love with him?" said Meredith, impatiently. "As to the Moffatt engagement, naturally, she was kept in the dark?"

"At first," said the Duchess, hesitating. "And when she knew, poor dear, it was too late!"

"Too late for what?"

"Well, when one falls in love one doesn't all at once shake it off because the man deceives you."

"One should," said Meredith, with energy. "Men are not worth all that women spend upon them."

"Oh, that's true!" cried the Duchess--"so dreadfully true! But what's the good of preaching? We shall go on spending it to the end of time."

"Well, at any rate, don't choose the dummies and the frauds."

"Ah, there you talk sense," said the Duchess. "And if only we had the French system in England! If only one could say to Julie: 'Now look here, there's your husband! It's all settled-- down to plate and linen--and you've got to marry him!' how happy we should all be."

Dr. Meredith stared.

"You have the man in your eye," he said.

The Duchess hesitated.

"Suppose you come a little walk with me in the wood," she said, at last, gathering up her white skirts.

Meredith obeyed her. They were away for half an hour, and when they returned the journalist's face, flushed and furrowed with thought, was not very easy to read.

Nor was his temper in good condition. It required a climb to the very top of Monte Crocione to send him back, more or less appeased, a consenting player in the Duchess's game. For if there are men who are flirts and egotists--who ought to be, yet never are, divined by the sensible woman at a glance--so also there are men too well equipped for this wicked world, too good, too well born, too desirable.

It was in this somewhat flinty and carping mood that Meredith prepared himself for the advent of Jacob Delafield.

But when Delafield appeared, Meredith's secret antagonisms were soon dissipated. There was certainly no challenging air of prosperity about the young man.

At first sight, indeed, he was his old cheerful self, always ready for a walk or a row, on easy terms at once with the Italian servants or boatmen. But soon other facts emerged--stealthily, as it were, from the concealment in which a strong man was trying to keep them.

"That young man's youth is over," said Meredith, abruptly, to the Duchess one evening. He pointed to the figure of Delafield, who was pacing, alone with his pipe, up and down one of the lower terraces of the garden.

The Duchess showed a teased expression.

"It's like something wearing through," she said, slowly. "I suppose it was always there, but it didn't show."

"Name your 'it.'"

"I can't." But she gave a little shudder, which made Meredith look at her with curiosity.

"You feel something ghostly--unearthly?"

She nodded assent; crying out, however, immediately afterwards, as though in compunction, that he was one of the dearest and best of fellows.

"Of course he is," said Meredith. "It is only the mystic in him coming out. He is one of the men who have the sixth sense."

"Well, all I know is, he has the oddest power over people," said Evelyn, with another shiver. "If Freddie had it, my life wouldn't be worth living. Thank goodness, he hasn't a vestige!"

"At bottom it's the power of the priest," said Meredith. "And you women are far too susceptible towards it. Nine times out of ten it plays the mischief."

The Duchess was silent a moment. Then she bent towards her companion, finger on lip, her charming eyes glancing significantly towards the lower terrace. The figures on it were now two. Julie and Delafield paced together.

"But this is the tenth!" she said, in an eager whisper.

Meredith smiled at her, then flung her a dubious "Chi sa?" and changed the subject.

Delafield, who was a fine oar, had soon taken command of the lake expeditions; and by the help of two stalwart youths from Tremezzo, the four-oar was in use from morning till night. Through the broad lake which lies between Menaggio and Varenna it sped northward to Gravedona; or beneath the shadowy cliffs of the Villa Serbelloni it slipped over deep waters, haunted and dark, into the sunny spaces of Lecco; or it coasted along the steep sides of Monte Primo, so that the travellers in it might catch the blue stain of the gentians on the turf, where it sloped into the lucent wave below, or watch the fishermen on the rocks, spearing their prey in the green or golden shallows.

The weather was glorious--a summer before its time. The wild cherries shook down their snow upon the grass; but the pears were now in bridal white, and a warmer glory of apple-blossom was just beginning to break upon the blue. The nights were calm and moonlit; the dawns were visions of mysterious and incredible beauty, wherein mountain and forest and lake were but the garments, diaphanous, impalpable, of some delicate, indwelling light and fire spirit, which breathed and pulsed through the solidity of rock, no less visibly than through the crystal leagues of air or the sunlit spaces of water.

Yet presently, as it were, a hush of waiting, of tension, fell upon their little party. Nature offered her best; but there was only an apparent acceptance of her bounties. Through the outward flow of talk and amusement, of wanderings on lake or hill, ugly hidden forces of pain and strife, regret, misery, resistance, made themselves rarely yet piercingly felt.

Julie drooped again. Her cheeks were paler even than when Meredith arrived. Delafield, too, began to be more silent, more absent. He was helpful and courteous as ever, but it began to be seen that his gayety was an effort, and now and then there were sharp or bitter notes in voice or manner, which jarred, and were not soon forgotten.

Presently, Meredith and the Duchess found themselves looking on, breathless and astonished, at the struggle of two personalities, the wrestle between two wills. They little knew that it was a renewed struggle--second wrestle. But silently, by a kind of tacit agreement, they drew away from Delafield and Julie. They dimly understood that he pursued and she resisted; and that for him life was becoming gradually absorbed into the two facts of her presence and her resistance.

"On ne s'appuie que sur ce qui résiste." For both of them these words were true. Fundamentally, and beyond all passing causes of grief and anger, each was fascinated by the full strength of nature in the other. Neither could ever forget the other. The hours grew electric, and every tiny incident became charged with spiritual meaning.

Often for hours together Julie would try to absorb herself in talk with Meredith. But the poor fellow got little joy from it. Presently, at a word or look of Delafield's she would let herself be recaptured, as though with a proud reluctance; they wandered away together; and once more Meredith and the Duchess became the merest by-standers.

The Duchess shrugged her shoulders over it, and, though she laughed, sometimes the tears were in her eyes. She felt the hovering of passion, but it was no passion known to her own blithe nature.

And if only this strange state of things might end, one way or other, and set her free to throw her arms round her Duke's neck, and beg his pardon for all these weeks of desertion! She said to herself, ruefully, that her babies would indeed have forgotten her.

Yet she stood stoutly to her post, and the weeks passed quickly by. It was the dramatic energy of the situation--so much more dramatic in truth than either she or Meredith suspected--that made it such a strain upon the onlookers.

One evening they had left the boat at Tremezzo, that they might walk back along that most winning of paths that skirts the lake between the last houses of Tremezzo and the inn at Cadenabbia. The sunset was nearly over, but the air was still suffused with its rose and pearl, and fragrant with the scent of flowering laurels. Each mountain face, each white village, either couched on the water's edge or grouped about its slender campanile on some shoulder of the hills, each house and tree and figure seemed still penetrated with light, the glorified creatures of some just revealed and already fading world. The echoes of the evening bell were floating on the lake, and from a boat in front, full of peasant-folk, there rose a sound of singing, some litany of saint or virgin, which stole in harmonies, rudely true, across the water.

"They have been to the pilgrimage church above Lenno," said Julie, pointing to the boat, and in order to listen to the singing, she found a seat on a low wall above the lake.

There was no reply, and, looking round her, she saw with a start that only Delafield was beside her, that the Duchess and Meredith had already rounded the corner of the Villa Carlotta and were out of sight.

Delafield's gaze was fixed upon her. He was very pale, and suddenly Julie's breath seemed to fail her.

"I don't think I can bear it any longer," he said, as he came close to her.

"Bear what?"

"That you should look as you do now."

Julie made no reply. Her eyes, very sad and bitter, searched the blue dimness of the lake in silence.

Delafield sat down on the wall beside her. Not a soul was in sight. At the Cadenabbia Hotel, the table d'hôte had gathered in the visitors; a few boats passed and repassed in the distance, but on land all was still.

Suddenly he took her hand with a firm grasp.

"Are you never going to forgive me?" he said, in a low voice.

"I suppose I ought to bless you."

Her face seemed to him to express the tremulous misery of a heart deeply, perhaps irrevocably, wounded. Emotion rose in a tide, but he crushed it down.

He bent over her, speaking with deliberate tenderness.

"Julie, do you remember what you promised Lord Lackington when he was dying?"

"Oh!" cried Julie.

She sprang to her feet, speechless and suffocated. Her eyes expressed a mingled pride and terror.

He paused, confronting her with a pale resolution.

"You didn't know that I had seen him?"

"Know!"

She turned away fiercely, choking with sobs she could hardly control, as the memory of that by-gone moment returned upon her.

"I thought as much," said Delafield, in a low voice. "You hoped never to hear of your promise again."

She made no answer; but she sank again upon the seat beside the lake, and supporting herself on one delicate hand, which clung to the coping of the wall, she turned her pale and tear-stained face to the lake and the evening sky. There was in her gesture an unconscious yearning, a mute and anguished appeal, as though from the oppressions of human character to the broad strength of nature, that was not lost on Delafield. His mind became the centre of a swift and fierce debate. One voice said: "Why are you persecuting her? Respect her weakness and her grief." And another replied: "It is because she is weak that she must yield--must allow herself to be guided and adored."

He came close to her again. Any passer-by might have supposed that they were both looking at the distant boat and listening to the pilgrimage chant.

"Do you think I don't understand why you made that promise?" he said, very gently, and the mere self-control of his voice and manner carried a spell with it for the woman beside him. "It was wrung out of you by kindness for a dying man. You thought I should never know, or I should never claim it. Well, I am selfish. I take advantage. I do claim it. I saw Lord Lackington only a few hours before his death. 'She mustn't be alone,' he said to me, several times. And then, almost at the last, 'Ask her again. She'll consider it--she promised.'"

Julie turned impetuously.

"Neither of us is bound by that--neither of us."

Delafield smiled.

"Does that mean that I am asking you now because he bade me?"

A pause. Julie must needs raise her eyes to his. She flushed red and withdrew them.

"No," he said, with a long breath, "you don't mean that, and you don't think it. As for you--yes, you are bound! Julie, once more I bring you my plea, and you must consider it."

"How can I be your wife?" she said, her breast heaving. "You know all that has happened. It would be monstrous."

"Not at all," was his quiet reply. "It would be natural and right. Julie, it is strange that I should be talking to you like this. You're so much cleverer than I--in some ways, so much stronger. And yet, in others--you'll let me say it, won't you?--I could help you. I could protect you. It's all I care for in the world."

"How can I be your wife?" she repeated, passionately, wringing her hands.

"Be what you will--at home. My friend, comrade, housemate. I ask nothing more--nothing." His voice dropped, and there was a pause. Then he resumed. "But, in the eyes of the world, make me your servant and your husband!"

"I can't condemn you to such a fate," she cried. "You know where my heart is."

Delafield did not waver.

"I know where your heart was," he said, with firmness. "You will banish that man from your thoughts in time. He has no right to be there. I take all the risks--all."

"Well, at least for you, I am no hypocrite," she said, with a quivering lip. "You know what I am."

"Yes, I know, and I am at your feet."

The tears dropped from Julie's eyes. She turned away and hid her face against one of the piers of the wall.

Delafield attempted no caress. He quietly set himself to draw the life that he had to offer her, the comradeship that he proposed to her. Not a word of what the world called his "prospects" entered in. She knew very well that he could not bring himself to speak of them. Rather, a sort of ascetic and mystical note made itself heard in all he said of the future, a note that before now had fascinated and controlled a woman whose ambition was always strangely tempered with high, poetical imagination.

Yet, ambitious she was, and her mind inevitably supplied what his voice left unsaid.

"He will have to fill his place whether he wishes it or no," she said to herself. "And if, in truth, he desires my help--"

Then she shrank from her own wavering. Look where she would into her life, it seemed to her that all was monstrous and out of joint.

"You don't realize what you ask," she said, at last, in despair. "I am not what you call a good woman--you know it too well. I don't measure things by your standards. I am capable of such a journey as you found me on. I can't find in my own mind that I repent it at all. I can tell a lie-- you can't. I can have the meanest and most sordid thoughts--you can't. Lady Henry thought me an intriguer--I am one. It is in my blood. And I don't know whether, in the end, I could understand your language and your life. And if I don't, I shall make you miserable."

She looked up, her slender frame straightening under what was, in truth, a noble defiance.

Delafield bent over her and took both her hands forcibly in his own.

"If all that were true, I would rather risk it a thousand times over than go out of your life again- -a stranger. Julie, you have done mad things for love--you should know what love is. Look in my face--there--your eyes in mine! Give way! The dead ask it of you--and it is God's will."

And as, drawn by the last, low-spoken words, Julie looked up into his face, she felt herself enveloped by a mystical and passionate tenderness that paralyzed her resistance. A force, superhuman, laid its grasp upon her will. With a burst of tears, half in despair, half in revolt, she submitted.

XXII

In the first week of May, Julie Le Breton married Jacob Delafield in the English Church at Florence. The Duchess was there. So was the Duke--a sulky and ill-resigned spectator of something which he believed to be the peculiar and mischievous achievement of his wife.

At the church door Julie and Delafield left for Camaldoli.

"Well, if you imagine that I intend to congratulate you or anybody else upon that performance you are very much mistaken," said the Duke, as he and his wife drove back to the "Grand Bretagne" together.

"I don't deny it's--risky," said the Duchess, her hands on her lap, her eyes dreamily following the streets.

"Risky!" repeated the Duke, shrugging his shoulders. "Well, I don't want to speak harshly of your friends, Evelyn, but Miss Le Breton--"

"Mrs. Delafield," said the Duchess.

"Mrs. Delafield, then"--the name was evidently a difficult mouthful--"seems to me a most undisciplined and unmanageable woman. Why does she look like a tragedy queen at her marriage? Jacob is twice too good for her, and she'll lead him a life. And how you can reconcile it to your conscience to have misled me so completely as you have in this matter, I really can't imagine."

"Misled you?" said Evelyn.

Her innocence was really a little hard to bear, and not even the beauty of her blue eyes, now happily restored to him, could appease the mentor at her side.

"You led me plainly to believe," he repeated, with emphasis, "that if I helped her through the crisis of leaving Lady Henry she would relinquish her designs on Delafield."

"Did I?" said the Duchess. And putting her hands over her face she laughed rather hysterically. "But that wasn't why you lent her the house, Freddie."

"You coaxed me into it, of course," said the Duke.

"No, it was Julie herself got the better of you," said Evelyn, triumphantly. "You felt her spell, just as we all do, and wanted to do something for her."

"Nothing of the sort," said the Duke, determined to admit no recollection to his disadvantage. "It was your doing entirely."

The Duchess thought it discreet to let him at least have the triumph of her silence, smiling, and a little sarcastic though it were.

"And of all the undeserved good fortune!" he resumed, feeling in his irritable disapproval that the moral order of the universe had been somehow trifled with. "In the first place, she is the daughter of people who flagrantly misconducted themselves--that apparently does her no harm. Then she enters the service of Lady Henry in a confidential position, and uses it to work havoc in Lady Henry's social relations. That, I am glad to say, has done her a little harm, although not nearly as much as she deserves. And finally she has a most discreditable flirtation with a man already engaged--to her own cousin, please observe!--and pulls wires for him all over the place in the most objectionable and unwomanly manner."

"As if everybody didn't do that!" cried the Duchess. "You know, Freddie, that your own mother always used to boast that she had made six bishops and saved the Establishment."

The Duke took no notice.

"And yet there she is! Lord Lackington has left her a fortune--a competence, anyway. She marries Jacob Delafield--rather a fool, I consider, but all the same one of the best fellows in the world. And at any time, to judge from what one hears of the health both of Chudleigh and his boy, she may find herself Duchess of Chudleigh."

The Duke threw himself back in the carriage with the air of one who waits for Providence to reply.

"Oh, well, you see, you can't make the world into a moral tale to please you," said the Duchess, absently.

Then, after a pause, she asked, "Are you still going to let them have the house, Freddie?"

"I imagine that if Jacob Delafield applies to me to let it to him, that I shall not refuse him," said the Duke, stiffly.

The Duchess smiled behind her fan. Yet her tender heart was not in reality very happy about her Julie. She knew well enough that it was a strange marriage of which they had just been witnesses--a marriage containing the seeds of many untoward things only too likely to develop unless fate were kinder than rash mortals have any right to expect.

"I wish to goodness Delafield weren't so religious," murmured the Duchess, fervently, pursuing her own thoughts.

"Evelyn!"

"Well, you see, Julie isn't, at all," she added, hastily.

"You need not have troubled yourself to tell me that," was the Duke's indignant reply.

After a fortnight at Camaldoli and Vallombrosa the Delafields turned towards Switzerland. Julie, who was a lover of Rousseau and Obermann, had been also busy with the letters of Byron. She wished to see with her own eyes St. Gingolphe and Chillon, Bevay and Glion.

So one day at the end of May they found themselves at Montreux. But Montreux was already hot and crowded, and Julie's eyes turned in longing to the heights. They found an old inn at Charnex, whereof the garden commanded the whole head of the lake, and there they settled themselves for a fortnight, till business, in fact, should recall Delafield to England. The Duke of Chudleigh had shown all possible kindness and cordiality with regard to the marriage, and the letter in which he welcomed his cousin's new wife had both touched Julie's feelings and satisfied her pride. "You are marrying one of the best of men," wrote this melancholy father of a dying son. "My boy and I owe him more than can be written. I can only tell you that for those he loves he grudges nothing--no labor, no sacrifice of himself. There are no half-measures in his affections. He has spent himself too long on sick and sorry creatures like ourselves. It is time he had a little happiness on his own account. You will give it him, and Mervyn and I will be most grateful to you. If joy and health can never be ours, I am not yet so vile as to grudge them to others. God bless you! Jacob will tell you that my house is not a gay one; but if you and he will sometimes visit it, you will do something to lighten its gloom."

Julie wondered, as she wrote her very graceful reply, how much the Duke might know about herself. Jacob had told his cousin, as she knew, the story of her parentage and of Lord Lackington's recognition of his granddaughter. But as soon as the marriage was announced it was not likely that Lady Henry had been able to hold her tongue.

A good many interesting tales of his cousin's bride had, indeed, reached the melancholy Duke. Lady Henry had done all that she conceived it her duty to do, filling many pages of note-paper with what the Duke regarded as most unnecessary information.

At any rate, he had brushed it all aside with the impatience of one for whom nothing on earth had now any savor or value beyond one or two indispensable affections. "What's good enough for Jacob is good for me," he wrote to Lady Henry, "and if I may offer you some advice, it is that you should not quarrel with Jacob about a matter so vital as his marriage. Into the rights and wrongs of the story you tell me, I really cannot enter; but rather than break with Jacob I would welcome anybody he chose to present to me. And in this case I understand the lady is very clever, distinguished, and of good blood on both sides. Have you had no trouble in your life, my dear Flora, that you can make quarrels with a light heart? If so, I envy you; but I have neither the energy nor the good spirits wherewith to imitate you."

Julie, of course, knew nothing of this correspondence, though from the Duke's letters to Jacob she divined that something of the kind had taken place. But it was made quite plain to her that she was to be spared all the friction and all the difficulty which may often attend the entrance of a person like herself within the circle of a rich and important family like the Delafields. With Lady Henry, indeed, the fight had still to be fought. But Jacob's mother, influenced on one side by her son and on the other by the head of the family, accepted her daughter-in-law with the facile kindliness and good temper that were natural to her; while his sister, the fair-haired and admirable Susan, owed her brother too much and loved him too well to be other than friendly to his wife.

No; on the worldly side all was smooth. The marriage had been carried through with ease and quietness The Duke, in spite of Jacob's remonstrances, had largely increased his cousin's salary, and Julie was already enjoying the income left her by Lord Lackington. She had only to reappear in London as Jacob's wife to resume far more than her old social ascendency. The winning cards had all passed into her hands, and if now there was to be a struggle with Lady Henry, Lady Henry would be worsted.

All this was or should have been agreeable to the sensitive nerves of a woman who knew the worth of social advantages. It had no effect, however, on the mortal depression which was constantly Julie's portion during the early weeks of her marriage.

As for Delafield, he had entered upon this determining experiment of his life--a marriage, which was merely a legalized comradeship, with the woman he adored--in the mind of one resolved to pay the price of what he had done. This graceful and stately woman, with her high intelligence and her social gifts, was now his own property. She was to be the companion of his days and the mistress of his house. But although he knew well that he had a certain strong hold upon her, she did not love him, and none of the fusion of true marriage had taken place or could take place. So be it. He set himself to build up a relation between them which should justify the violence offered to natural and spiritual law. His own delicacy of feeling and perception combined with the strength of his passion to make every action of their common day a symbol and sacrament. That her heart regretted Warkworth, that bitterness and longing, an unspent and baffled love, must be constantly overshadowing her--these things he not only knew, he was forever reminding himself of them, driving them, as it were, into consciousness, as the ascetic drives the spikes into his flesh. His task was to comfort her, to make her forget, to bring her back to common peace and cheerfulness of mind.

To this end he began with appealing as much as possible to her intelligence. He warmly encouraged her work for Meredith. From the first days of their marriage he became her listener, scholar, and critic. Himself interested mainly in social, economical, or religious discussion, he humbly put himself to school in matters of belles-lettres. His object was to enrich Julie's daily life with new ambitions and new pleasures, which might replace the broodings of her illness and convalescence, and then, to make her feel that she had at hand, in the companion of that life, one who felt a natural interest in all her efforts, a natural pride in all her successes.

Alack! the calculation was too simple--and too visible. It took too little account of the complexities of Julie's nature, of the ravages and the shock of passion. Julie herself might be ready enough to return to the things of the mind, but they were no sooner offered to her, as it were, in exchange for the perilous delights of love, than she grew dumbly restive. She felt herself, also, too much observed, too much thought over, made too often, if the truth were known, the subject of religious or mystical emotion.

More and more, also, was she conscious of strangeness and eccentricity in the man she had married. It often seemed to that keen and practical sense which in her mingled so oddly with the capacity for passion that, as they grew older, and her mind recovered tone and balance, she would probably love the world disastrously more and he disastrously less. And if so, the gulf between them, instead of closing, could but widen.

One day--a showery day in early June--she was left alone for an hour, while Delafield went down to Montreux to change some circular notes. Julie took a book from the table and strolled out along the lovely road that slopes gently downward from Charnex to the old field-embowered village of Brent.

The rain was just over. It had been a cold rain, and the snow had crept downward on the heights, and had even powdered the pines of the Cubly. The clouds were sweeping low in the west. Towards Geneva the lake was mere wide and featureless space--a cold and misty water, melting into the fringes of the rain-clouds. But to the east, above the Rhône valley, the sky was lifting; and as Julie sat down upon a midway seat and turned herself eastward, she was met by the full and unveiled glory of the higher Alps--the Rochers de Naye, the Velan, the Dent du Midi. On the jagged peaks of the latter a bright shaft of sun was playing, and the great white or rock-ribbed mass raised itself above the mists of the lower world, once more unstained and triumphant.

But the cold bise was still blowing, and Julie, shivering, drew her wrap closer round her. Her heart pined for Como and the south; perhaps for the little Duchess, who spoiled and petted her in the common, womanish ways.

The spring--a second spring--was all about her; but in this chilly northern form it spoke to her with none of the ravishment of Italy. In the steep fields above her the narcissuses were bent and bowed with rain; the red-browns of the walnuts glistened in the wet gleams of sun; the fading apple-blossom beside her wore a melancholy beauty; only in the rich, pushing grass, with its wealth of flowers and its branching cow-parsley, was there the stubborn life and prophecy of summer.

Suddenly Julie caught up the book that lay beside her and opened it with a hasty hand. It was one of that set of Saint-Simon which had belonged to her mother, and had already played a part in her own destiny.

She turned to the famous "character" of the Dauphin, of that model prince, in whose death Saint-Simon, and Fénelon, and France herself, saw the eclipse of all great hopes.

"A prince, affable, gentle, humane, patient, modest, full of compunctions, and, as much as his position allowed--sometimes beyond it--humble, and severe towards himself."

Was it not to the life? "Affable, doux, humain--patient, modeste--humble et austère pour soi"-- beyond what was expected, beyond, almost, what was becoming?

She read on to the mention of the Dauphine, terrified, in her human weakness, of so perfect a husband, and trying to beguile or tempt him from the heights; to the picture of Louis Quatorze, the grandfather, shamed in his worldly old age by the presence beside him of this saintly and high-minded youth; of the Court, looking forward with dismay to the time when it should find itself under the rule of a man who despised and condemned both its follies and its passions, until she reached that final rapture, where, in a mingled anguish and adoration, Saint-Simon bids eternal farewell to a character and a heart of which France was not worthy.

The lines passed before her, and she was conscious, guiltily conscious, of reading them with a double mind.

Then she closed the book, held by the thought of her husband--in a somewhat melancholy reverie.

There is a Catholic word with which in her convent youth she had been very familiar--the word recueilli--"recollected." At no time had it sounded kindly in her ears; for it implied fetters and self--suppressions--of the voluntary and spiritual sort--wholly unwelcome to and unvalued by her own temperament. But who that knew him well could avoid applying it to Delafield? A man of "recollection" living in the eye of the Eternal; keeping a guard over himself in the smallest matters of thought and action; mystically possessed by the passion of a spiritual ideal; in love with charity, purity, simplicity of life.

She bowed her head upon her hands in dreariness of spirit. Ultimately, what could such a man want with her? What had she to give him? In what way could she ever be necessary to him? And a woman, even in friendship, must feel herself that to be happy.

Already this daily state in which she found herself--of owing everything and giving nothing--

produced in her a secret irritation and repulsion; how would it be in the years to come?

"He never saw me as I am," she thought to herself, looking fretfully back to their past acquaintance. "I am neither as weak as he thinks me--nor as clever. And how strange it is--this tension in which he lives!"

And as she sat there idly plucking at the wet grass, her mind was overrun with a motley host of memories--some absurd, some sweet, some of an austerity that chilled her to the core. She thought of the difficulty she had in persuading Delafield to allow himself even necessary comforts and conveniences; a laugh, involuntary, and not without tenderness, crossed her face as she recalled a tale he had told her at Camaldoli, of the contempt excited in a young footman of a smart house by the mediocrity and exiguity of his garments and personal appointments generally. "I felt I possessed nothing that he would have taken as a gift," said Delafield, with a grin. "It was chastening."

Yet though he laughed, he held to it; and Julie was already so much of the wife as to be planning how to coax him presently out of a portmanteau and a top-hat that were in truth a disgrace to their species.

And all the time she must have the best of everything--a maid, luxurious travelling, dainty food. They had had one or two wrestles on the subject already. "Why are you to have all the high thinking and plain living to yourself?" she had asked him, angrily, only to be met by the plea, "Dear, get strong first--then you shall do what you like."

But it was at La Verna, the mountain height overshadowed by the memories of St. Francis, that she seemed to have come nearest to the ascetic and mystical tendency in Delafield. He went about the mountain-paths a transformed being, like one long spiritually athirst who has found the springs and sources of life. Julie felt a secret terror. Her impression was much the same as Meredith's--as of "something wearing through" to the light of day. Looking back she saw that this temperament, now so plain to view, had been always there; but in the young and capable agent of the Chudleigh property, in the Duchess's cousin, or Lady Henry's nephew, it had passed for the most part unsuspected. How remarkably it had developed!--whither would it carry them both in the future? When thinking about it, she was apt to find herself seized with a sudden craving for Mayfair, "little dinners," and good talk.

"What a pity you weren't born a Catholic!--you might have been a religious," she said to him one night at La Verna, when he had been reading her some of the Fioretti with occasional comments of his own.

But he had shaken his head with a smile.

"You see, I have no creed--or next to none."

The answer startled her. And in the depths of his blue eyes there seemed to her to be hovering a swarm of thoughts that would not let themselves loose in her presence, but were none the less the true companions of his mind. She saw herself a moment as Elsa, and her husband as a modern Lohengrin, coming spiritually she knew not whence, bound on some quest mysterious and unthinkable.

"What will you do," she said, suddenly, "when the dukedom comes to you?"

Delafield's aspect darkened in an instant. If he could have shown anger to her, anger there would have been.

"That is a subject I never think of or discuss, if I can help it," he said, abruptly; and, rising to his feet, he pointed out that the sun was declining fast towards the plain of the Casentino, and they were far from their hotel.

"Inhuman!--unreasonable!" was the cry of the critical sense in her as she followed him in silence.

Innumerable memories of this kind beat on Julie's mind as she sat dreamily on her bench among the Swiss meadows. How natural that in the end they should sweep her by reaction into imaginations wholly indifferent--of a drum-and-trumpet history, in the actual fighting world.

... Far, far in the African desert she followed the march of Warkworth's little troop.

Ah, the blinding light--the African scrub and sand--the long, single line--the native porters with their loads--the handful of English officers with that slender figure at their head--the endless, waterless path with its palms and mangoes and mimosas--the scene rushed upon the inward eye and held it. She felt the heat, the thirst, the weariness of bone and brain--all the spell and mystery of the unmapped, unconquered land.

Did he think of her sometimes, at night, under the stars, or in the blaze and mirage of noon? Yes, yes; he thought of her. Each to the other their thoughts must travel while they lived.

In Delafield's eyes, she knew, his love for her had been mere outrage and offence.

Ah, well, he, at least, had needed her. He had desired only very simple, earthy things--money, position, success--things it was possible for a woman to give him, or get for him; and at the last, though it were only as a traitor to his word and his fiancée, he had asked for love--asked commonly, hungrily, recklessly, because he could not help it--and then for pardon! And those are things the memory of which lies deep, deep in the pulsing, throbbing heart.

At this point she hurriedly checked and scourged herself, as she did a hundred times a day.

No, no, no! It was all over, and she and Jacob would still make a fine thing of their life together. Why not?

And all the time there were burning hot tears in her eyes; and as the leaves of Saint-Simon passed idly through her fingers, the tears blotted out the meadows and the flowers, and blurred the figure of a young girl who was slowly mounting the long slope of road that led from the village of Brent towards the seat on which Julie was sitting.

Gradually the figure approached. The mist cleared from Julie's eyes. Suddenly she found herself giving a close and passionate attention to the girl upon the road.

Her form was slight and small; under her shady hat there was a gleam of fair hair arranged in smooth, shining masses about her neck and temples. As she approached Julie she raised her eyes absently, and Julie saw a face of singular and delicate beauty, marred, however, by the suggestion of physical fragility, even sickliness, which is carried with it. One might have thought it a face blanched by a tropical climate, and for the moment touched into faint color by the keen Alpine air. The eyes, indeed, were full of life; they were no sooner seen but they defined and enforced a personality. Eager, intent, a little fretful, they expressed a nervous energy out of all proportion to their owner's slender physique. In this, other bodily signs concurred. As she perceived Julie on the bench, for instance, the girl's slight, habitual frown sharply deepened; she looked at the stranger with keen observation, both glance and gesture betraying a quick and restless sensibility.

As for Julie, she half rose as the girl neared her. Her cheeks were flushed, her lips parted; she had the air of one about to speak. The girl looked at her in a little surprise and passed on.

She carried a book under her arm, into which were thrust a few just-opened letters. She had scarcely passed the bench when an envelope fell out of the book and lay unnoticed on the road.

Julie drew a long breath. She picked up the envelope. It lay in her hand, and the name she had expected to see was written upon it.

For a moment she hesitated. Then she ran after the owner of the letter.

"You dropped this on the road."

The girl turned hastily.

"Thank you very much. I am sorry to have given you the trouble--"

Then she paused, arrested evidently by the manner in which Julie stood regarding her.

"Did--did you wish to speak to me?" she said, uncertainly.

"You are Miss Moffatt?"

"Yes. That is my name. But, excuse me. I am afraid I don't remember you." The words were spoken with a charming sweetness and timidity.

"I am Mrs. Delafield."

The girl started violently.

"Are you? I--I beg your pardon!"

She stood in a flushed bewilderment, staring at the lady who had addressed her, a troubled consciousness possessing itself of her face and manner more and more plainly with every moment.

Julie asked herself, hurriedly: "How much does she know? What has she heard?" But aloud she gently said: "I thought you must have heard of me. Lord Uredale told me he had written--his father wished it--to Lady Blanche. Your mother and mine were sisters."

The girl shyly withdrew her eyes.

"Yes, mother told me."

There was a moment's silence. The mingled fear and recklessness which had accompanied Julie's action disappeared from her mind. In the girl's manner there was neither jealousy nor hatred, only a young shrinking and reserve.

"May I walk with you a little?"

"Please do. Are you staying at Montreux?"

"No; we are at Charnex--and you?"

"We came up two days ago to a little pension at Brent. I wanted to be among the fields, now the narcissuses are out. If it were warm weather we should stay, but mother is afraid of the cold for me. I have been ill."

"I heard that," said Julie, in a voice gravely kind and winning. "That was why your mother could not come home."

The girl's eyes suddenly filled with tears.

"No; poor mother! I wanted her to go--we had a good nurse--but she would not leave me, though she was devoted to my grandfather. She--"

"She is always anxious about you?"

"Yes. My health has been a trouble lately, and since father died--"

"She has only you."

They walked on a few paces in silence. Then the girl looked up eagerly.

"You saw grandfather at the last? Do tell me about it, please. My uncles write so little."

Julie obeyed with difficulty. She had not realized how hard it would be for her to talk of Lord Lackington. But she described the old man's gallant dying as best she could; while Aileen Moffatt listened with that manner at once timid and rich in feeling which seemed to be her characteristic.

As they neared the top of the hill where the road begins to incline towards Charnex, Julie noticed signs of fatigue in her companion.

"You have been an invalid," she said. "You ought not to go farther. May I take you home? Would your mother dislike to see me?"

The girl paused perceptibly. "Ah, there she is!"

They had turned towards Brent, and Julie saw coming towards them, with somewhat rapid steps, a small, elderly lady, gray-haired, her features partly hidden by her country hat.

A thrill passed through Julie. This was the sister whose name her mother had mentioned in her last hour. It was as though something of her mother, something that must throw light upon that mother's life and being, were approaching her along this Swiss road.

But the lady in question, as she neared them, looked with surprise, not unmingled with hauteur, upon her daughter and the stranger beside her.

"Aileen, why did you go so far? You promised me only to be a quarter of an hour."

"I am not tired, mother. Mother, this is Mrs. Delafield. You remember, Uncle Uredale wrote--"

Lady Blanche Moffatt stood still. Once more a fear swept through Julie's mind, and this time it stayed. After an evident hesitation, a hand was coldly extended.

"How do you do? I heard from my brothers of your marriage, but they said you were in Italy."

"We have just come from there."

"And your husband?"

"He has gone down to Montreux, but he should be home very soon now. We are only a few steps from our little inn. Would you not rest there? Miss Moffatt looks very tired."

There was a pause. Lady Blanche was considering her daughter. Julie saw the trembling of her wide, irregular mouth, of which the lips were slightly turned outward. Finally she drew her daughter's hand into her arm, and bent anxiously towards her, scrutinizing her face.

"Thank you. We will rest a quarter of an hour. Can we get a carriage at Charnex?"

"Yes, I think so, if you will wait a little on our balcony."

They walked on towards Charnex. Lady Blanche began to talk resolutely of the weather, which was, indeed, atrocious. She spoke as she would have done to the merest acquaintance. There was not a word of her father; not a word, either, of her brother's letter, or of Julie's relationship to herself. Julie accepted the situation with perfect composure, and the three kept up some sort of a conversation till they reached the paved street of Charnex and the old inn at its lower end.

Julie guided her companions through its dark passages, till they reached an outer terrace where there were a few scattered seats, and among them a deck-chair with cushions.

"Please," said Julie, as she kindly drew the girl towards it. Aileen smiled and yielded. Julie placed her among the cushions, then brought out a shawl, and covered her warmly from the sharp, damp air. Aileen thanked her, and lightly touched her hand. A secret sympathy seemed to have suddenly sprung up between them.

Lady Blanche sat stiffly beside her daughter, watching her face. The warm touch of friendliness in Aileen's manner towards Mrs. Delafield seemed only to increase the distance and embarrassment of her own. Julie appeared to be quite unconscious. She ordered tea, and made no further allusion of any kind to the kindred they had in common. She and Lady Blanche talked as strangers.

Julie said to herself that she understood. She remembered the evening at Crowborough House, the spinster lady who had been the Moffatts' friend, her own talk with Evelyn. In that way, or in some other, the current gossip about herself and Warkworth, gossip they had been too mad and miserable to take much account of, had reached Lady Blanche. Lady Blanche probably abhorred her; though, because of her marriage, there was to be an outer civility. Meanwhile no sign whatever of any angry or resentful knowledge betrayed itself in the girl's manner. Clearly the mother had shielded her.

Julie felt the flutter of an exquisite relief. She stole many a look at Aileen, comparing the reality with that old, ugly notion her jealousy had found so welcome--of the silly or insolent little creature, possessing all that her betters desired, by the mere brute force of money or birth. And all the time the reality was this--so soft, suppliant, ethereal! Here, indeed, was the child of Warkworth's picture--the innocent, unknowing child, whom their passion had sacrificed and betrayed. She could see the face now, as it lay piteous, in Warkworth's hand. Then she raised her eyes to the original. And as it looked at her with timidity and nascent love her own heart beat wildly, now in remorse, now in a reviving jealousy.

Secretly, behind this mask of convention, were they both thinking of him? A girl's thoughts are never far from her lover; and Julie was conscious, this afternoon, of a strange and mysterious preoccupation, whereof Warkworth was the centre.

Gradually the great mountains at the head of the lake freed themselves from the last wandering cloud-wreaths. On the rock faces of the Rochers de Naye the hanging pine-woods, brushed with snow, came into sight. The white walls of Glion shone faintly out, and a pearly gold, which was but a pallid reflection of the Italian glory, diffused itself over mountain and lake. The sun was grudging; there was no caress in the air. Aileen shivered a little in her shawls, and when Julie spoke of Italy the girl's enthusiasm and longing sprang, as it were, to meet her, and both were conscious of another slight link between them.

Suddenly a sound of steps came to them from below.

"My husband," said Julie, rising, and, going to the balustrade, she waved to Delafield, who had come up from Montreux by one of the steep vineyard paths. "I will tell him you are here," she added, with what might have been taken for the shyness of the young wife.

She ran down the steps leading from the terrace to the lower garden. Aileen looked at her mother.

"Isn't she wonderful?" she said, in an ardent whisper. "I could watch her forever. She is the most graceful person I ever saw. Mother, is she like Aunt Rose?"

Lady Blanche shook her head.

"Not in the least," she said, shortly. "She has too much manner for me."

"Oh, mother!" And the girl caught her mother's hand in caressing remonstrance, as though to say: "Dear little mother, you must like her, because I do; and you mustn't think of Aunt Rose, and all those terrible things, except for pity."

"Hush!" said Lady Blanche, smiling at her a little excitedly. "Hush; they're coming!"

Delafield and Julie emerged from the iron staircase. Lady Blanche turned and looked at the tall, distinguished pair, her ugly lower lip hardening ungraciously. But she and Delafield had a slight previous acquaintance, and she noticed instantly the charming and solicitous kindness with which he greeted her daughter.

"Julie tells me Miss Moffatt is still far from strong," he said, returning to the mother.

Lady Blanche only sighed for answer. He drew a chair beside her, and they fell into the natural talk of people who belong to the same social world, and are travelling in the same scenes.

Meanwhile Julie was sitting beside the heiress. Not much was said, but each was conscious of a lively interest in the other, and every now and then Julie would put out a careful hand and draw the shawls closer about the girl's frail form. The strain of guilty compunction that entered into Julie's feeling did but make it the more sensitive. She said to herself in a vague haste that now she would make amends. If only Lady Blanche were willing--

But she should be willing! Julie felt the stirrings of the old self-confidence, the old trust in a social ingenuity which had, in truth, rarely failed her. Her intriguing, managing instinct made itself felt--the mood of Lady Henry's companion.

Presently, as they were talking, Aileen caught sight of an English newspaper which Delafield had brought up from Montreux. It lay still unopened on one of the tables of the terrace.

"Please give it me," said the girl, stretching out an eager hand. "It will have Tiny's marriage, mamma! A cousin of mine," she explained to Julie, who rose to hand it to her. "A very favorite cousin. Oh, thank you."

She opened the paper. Julie turned away, that she might relieve Lady Blanche of her teacup.

Suddenly a cry rang out--a cry of mortal anguish. Two ladies who had just stepped out upon the terrace from the hotel drawing-room turned in terror; the gardener who was watering the flower-boxes at the farther end stood arrested.

"Aileen!" shrieked Lady Blanche, running to her. "What--what is it?"

The paper had dropped to the floor, but the child still pointed to it, gasping.

"Mother--mother!"

Some intuition woke in Julie. She stood dead-white and dumb, while Lady Blanche threw herself on her daughter.

"Aileen, darling, what is it?"

The girl, in her agony, threw her arms frantically round her mother, and dragged herself to her feet. She stood tottering, her hand over her eyes.

"He's dead, mother! He's--dead!"

The last word sank into a sound more horrible even than the first cry. Then she swayed out of her mother's arms. It was Julie who caught her, who laid her once more on the deck-chair--a broken, shrunken form, in whom all the threads and connections of life had suddenly, as it were, fallen to ruin. Lady Blanche hung over her, pushing Julie away, gathering the unconscious girl madly in her arms. Delafield rushed for water-and-brandy. Julie snatched the paper and looked at the telegrams.

High up in the first column was the one she sought.

/# "CAIRO, June 12.--Great regret is felt here at the sudden and tragic news of Major Warkworth's death from fever, which seems to have occurred at a spot some three weeks' distance from the coast, on or about May 25. Letters from the officer who has succeeded him in the command of the Mokembe expedition have now reached Denga. A fortnight after leaving the coast Major Warkworth was attacked with fever; he made a brave struggle against it, but it was of a deadly type, and in less than a week he succumbed. The messenger brought also his private papers and diaries, which have been forwarded to his representatives in England. Major Warkworth was a most promising and able officer, and his loss will be keenly felt." #/

Julie fell on her knees beside her swooning cousin. Lady Blanche, meanwhile, was loosening her daughter's dress, chafing her icy hands, or moaning over her in a delirium of terror.

"My darling--my darling! Oh, my God! Why did I allow it? Why did I ever let him come near her? It was my fault--my fault! And it's killed her!"

And clinging to her child's irresponsive hands, she looked down upon her in a convulsion of grief, which included not a shadow of regret, not a gleam of pity for anything or any one else in the world but this bone of her bone and flesh of her flesh, which lay stricken there.

But Julie's mind had ceased to be conscious of the tragedy beside her. It had passed for the second time into the grasp of an illusion which possessed itself of the whole being and all its perceptive powers. Before her wide, terror-stricken gaze there rose once more the same piteous vision which had tortured her in the crisis of her love for Warkworth. Against the eternal snows which close in the lake the phantom hovered in a ghastly relief--emaciated, with matted hair, and purpled cheeks, and eyes--not to be borne!--expressing the dumb anger of a man, still young, who parts unwillingly from life in a last lonely spasm of uncomforted pain.

XXIII

It was midnight in the little inn at Charnex. The rain which for so many nights in this miserable June had been beating down upon the village had at last passed away. The night was clear and still--a night when the voice of mountain torrents, far distant, might reach the ear suddenly--sharply pure--from the very depths of silence.

Julie was in bed. She had been scarcely aware of her maid's help in undressing. The ordinary life was, as it were, suspended. Two scenes floated alternately before her--one the creation of memory, the other of imagination; and the second was, if possible, the more vivid, the more real of the two. Now she saw herself in Lady Henry's drawing-room; Sir Wilfrid Bury and a white-haired general were beside her. The door opened and Warkworth entered--young, handsome, soldierly, with that boyish, conquering air which some admired and others disliked. His eyes met hers, and a glow of happiness passed through her.

Then, at a stroke, the London drawing-room melted away. She was in a low bell-tent. The sun burned through its sides; the air was stifling. She stood with two other men and the doctor beside the low camp-bed; her heart was wrung by every movement, every sound; she heard the clicking of the fan in the doctor's hands, she saw the flies on the poor, damp brow.

And still she had no tears. Only, existence seemed to have ended in a gulf of horror, where youth and courage, repentance and high resolve, love and pleasure were all buried and annihilated together.

That poor girl up-stairs! It had not been possible to take her home. She was there with nurse and doctor, her mother hanging upon every difficult breath. The attack of diphtheria had left a weakened heart and nervous system; the shock had been cruel, and the doctor could promise nothing for the future.

"Mother--mother!... Dead!"

The cry echoed in Julie's ears. It seemed to fill the old, low-ceiled room in which she lay. Her fancy, preternaturally alive, heard it thrown back from the mountains outside--returned to her in wailing from the infinite depths of the lake. She was conscious of the vast forms and abysses of nature, there in the darkness, beyond the walls of her room, as something hostile, implacable....

And while he lay there dead, under the tropical sand, she was still living and breathing here, in this old Swiss inn--Jacob Delafield's wife, at least in name.

There was a knock at her door. At first she did not answer it. It seemed to be only one of the many dream sounds which tormented her nerves. Then it was repeated. Mechanically she said "Come in."

The door opened, and Delafield, carrying a light, which he shaded with his hand, stood on the threshold.

"May I come and talk to you?" he said, in a low voice. "I know you are not sleeping."

It was the first time he had entered his wife's room. Through all her misery, Julie felt a strange thrill as her husband's face was thus revealed to her, brightly illumined, in the loneliness of the night. Then the thrill passed into pain--the pain of a new and sharp perception.

Delafield, in truth, was some two or three years younger than Warkworth. But the sudden impression on Julie's mind, as she saw him thus, was of a man worn and prematurely aged-- markedly older and graver, even, since their marriage, since that memorable evening by the side of Como when, by that moral power of which he seemed often to be the mere channel and organ, he had overcome her own will and linked her life with his.

She looked at him in a kind of terror. Why was he so pale--an embodied grief? Warkworth's death was not a mortal stroke for him.

He came closer, and still Julie's eyes held him. Was it her fault, this--this shadowed countenance, these suggestions of a dumb strain and conflict, which not even his strong youth could bear without betrayal? Her heart cried out, first in a tragic impatience; then it melted within her strangely, she knew not how.

She sat up in bed and held out her hands. He thought of that evening in Heribert Street, after Warkworth had left her, when she had been so sad and yet so docile. The same yearning, the same piteous agitation was in her attitude now.

He knelt down beside the bed and put his arms round her. She clasped her hands about his neck and hid her face on his shoulder. There ran through her the first long shudder of weeping.

"He was so young!" he heard her say through sobs. "So young!"

He raised his hand and touched her hair tenderly.

"He died serving his country," he said, commanding his voice with difficulty. "And you grieve for him like this! I can't pity him so much."

"You thought ill of him--I know you did." She spoke between deep, sobbing breaths. "But he wasn't--he wasn't a bad man."

She fell back on her pillow and the tears rained down her cheeks.

Delafield kissed her hand in silence.

"Some day--I'll tell you," she said, brokenly.

"Yes, you shall tell me. It would help us both."

"I'll prove to you he wasn't vile. When--when he proposed that to me he was distracted. So was I. How could he break off his engagement? Now you see how she loved him. But we couldn't part--we couldn't say good-bye. It had all come on us unawares. We wanted to belong to each other--just for two days--and then part forever. Oh, I'll tell you--"

"You shall tell me all--here!" he said, firmly, crushing her delicate hands in his own against his breast, so that she felt the beating of his heart.

"Give me my hand. I'll show you his letter--his last letter to me." And, trembling, she drew from under her pillow that last scrawled letter, written from the squalid hotel near the Gare de Sceaux.

No sooner, however, had she placed it in Delafield's hands than she was conscious of new forces of feeling in herself which robbed the act of its simplicity. She had meant to plead her lover's cause and her own with the friend who was nominally her husband. Her action had been a cry for sympathy, as from one soul to another.

But as Delafield took the letter and began to read, her pulses began to flutter strangely. She recalled the phrases of passion which the letter contained. She became conscious of new fears, new compunctions.

For Delafield, too, the moment was one of almost intolerable complexity. This tender intimacy of night--the natural intimacy of husband and wife; this sense, which would not be denied, however sternly he might hold it in check, of her dear form beside him; the little refinements and self-revelations of a woman's room; his half-rights towards her, appealing at once to love, and to the memory of that solemn pledge by which he had won her--what man who deserved the name but must be conscious, tempestuously conscious, of such thoughts and facts?

And then, wrestling with these smarts, these impulses, belonging to the natural, physical life, the powers of the moral being--compassion, self-mastery, generosity; while strengthening and directing all, the man of faith was poignantly aware of the austere and tender voices of religion.

Amid this play of influences he read the letter, still kneeling beside her and holding her fingers clasped in his. She had closed her eyes and lay still, save for the occasional tremulous movement of her free hand, which dried the tears on her cheek.

"Thank you," he said, at last, with a voice that wavered, as he put the letter down. "Thank you. It was good of you to let me see it. It changes all my thoughts of him henceforward. If he had lived--"

"But he's dead! He's dead!" cried Julie, in a sudden agony, wrenching her hand from his and burying her face in the pillow. "Just when he wanted to live. Oh, my God--my God! No, there's no God--nothing that cares--that takes any notice!"

She was shaken by deep, convulsive weeping. Delafield soothed her as best he could. And presently she stretched out her hand with a quick, piteous gesture, and touched his face.

"You, too! What have I done to you? How you looked, just now! I bring a curse. Why did you want to marry me? I can't tear this out of my heart--I can't!"

And again she hid herself from him. Delafield bent over her.

"Do you imagine that I should be poor-souled enough to ask you?"

Suddenly a wild feeling of revolt ran through Julie's mind. The loftiness of his mood chilled her. An attitude more weakly, passionately human, a more selfish pity for himself would, in truth, have served him better. Had the pain of the living man escaped his control, avenging itself on the supremacy that death had now given to the lover, Delafield might have found another Julie in his arms. As it was, her husband seemed to her perhaps less than man, in being more; she admired unwillingly, and her stormy heart withdrew itself.

And when at last she controlled her weeping, and it became evident to him that she wished once more to be alone, his sensitiveness perfectly divined the secret reaction in her. He rose from his place beside her with a deep, involuntary sigh. She heard it, but only to shrink away.

"You will sleep a little?" he said, looking down upon her.

"I will try, mon ami."

"If you don't sleep, and would like me to read to you, call me. I am in the next room."

She thanked him faintly, and he went away. At the door he paused and came back again.

"To-night"--he hesitated--"while the doctors were here, I ran down to Montreux by the short path and telegraphed. The consul at Zanzibar is an old friend of mine. I asked him for more particulars at once, by wire. But the letters can't be here for a fortnight."

"I know. You're very, very good."

Hour after hour Delafield sat motionless in his room, till "high in the Valais depths profound" he "saw the morning break."

There was a little balcony at his command, and as he noiselessly stepped out upon it, between three and four o'clock, he felt himself the solitary comrade of the mist-veiled lake, of those high, rosy mountains on the eastern verge, the first throne and harbor of the light--of the lower forest-covered hills that "took the morning," one by one, in a glorious and golden succession. All was fresh, austere, and vast--the spaces of the lake, the distant hollows of high glaciers filled with purple shadow, the precipices of the Rochers de Naye, where the new snow was sparkling in the sun, the cool wind that blew towards him from the gates of Italy, down the winding recesses of that superb valley which has been a thoroughfare of nations from the beginning of time.

Not a boat on the wide reaches of the lake; not a voice or other sound of human toil, either from the vineyards below or the meadows above. Meanwhile some instinct, perhaps also some faint movements in her room, told him that Julie was no less wakeful than himself. And was not that a low voice in the room above him--the trained voice and footsteps of a nurse? Ah, poor little heiress, she, too, watched with sorrow!

A curious feeling of shame, of self-depreciation crept into his heart. Surely he himself of late had been lying down with fear and rising up with bitterness? Never a day had passed since they had reached Switzerland but he, a man of strong natural passions, had bade himself face the probable truth that, by a kind of violence, he had married a woman who would never love him--had taken irrevocably a false step, only too likely to be fatal to himself, intolerable to her.

Nevertheless, steeped as he had been in sadness, in foreboding, and, during this by-gone night, in passionate envy of the dead yet beloved Warkworth, he had never been altogether unhappy. That mysterious It--that other divine self of the mystic--God--the enwrapping, sheltering force--had been with him always. It was with him now--it spoke from the mysterious color and light of the dawn.

How, then, could he ever equal Julie in experience, in the true and poignant feeling of any grief whatever? His mind was in a strange, double state. It was like one who feels himself unfairly protected by a magic armor; he would almost throw it aside in a remorseful eagerness to be with his brethren, and as his brethren, in the sore weakness and darkness of the human combat; and then he thinks of the hand that gave the shield, and his heart melts in awe.

"Friend of my soul and of the world, make me thy tool--thy instrument! Thou art Love! Speak through me! Draw her heart to mine."

At last, knowing that there was no sleep in him, and realizing that he had brooded enough, he made his way out of the hotel and up through the fresh and dew-drenched meadows, where the haymakers were just appearing, to the Les Avants stream. A plunge into one of its cool basins retempered the whole man. He walked back through the scented field-paths, resolutely restraining his mind from the thoughts of the night, hammering out, indeed, in his head a scheme for the establishment of small holdings on certain derelict land in Wiltshire belonging to his cousin.

As he was descending on Charnex, he met the postman and took his letters. One among them, from the Duke of Chudleigh, contained a most lamentable account of Lord Elmira. The father and son had returned to England, and an angry, inclement May had brought a touch of pneumonia to add to all the lad's other woes. In itself it was not much--was, indeed, passing away. "But it has used up most of his strength," said the Duke, "and you know whether he had any to waste. Don't forget him. He constantly thinks and talks of you."

Delafield restlessly wondered when he could get home. But he realized that Julie would now feel herself tragically linked to the Moffatts, and how could he leave her? He piteously told himself that here, and now, was his chance with her. As he bore himself now towards her, in this hour of her grief for Warkworth, so, perhaps, would their future be.

Yet the claims of kindred were strong. He suffered much inward distress as he thought of the father and son, and their old touching dependence upon him. Chudleigh, as Jacob knew well, was himself incurably ill. Could he long survive his poor boy?

And so that other thought, which Jacob spent so much ingenuity in avoiding, rushed upon him unawares. The near, inevitable expectation of the famous dukedom, which, in the case of almost any other man in England, must at least have quickened the blood with a natural excitement, produced in Delafield's mind a mere dull sense of approaching torment. Perhaps there was something non-sane in his repulsion, something that linked itself with his father's "queerness," or the bigotry and fanaticism of his grandmother, the Evangelical Duchess, with her "swarm of parsons," as Sir Wilfrid remembered her. The oddity, which had been violent or brutal in earlier generations, showed itself in him, one might have said, in a radical transposition of values, a singularity of criterion, which the ordinary robust Englishman might very well dismiss with impatience as folly or cant.

Yet it was neither; and the feeling had, in truth, its own logic and history. He had lived from his youth up among the pageants of rank and possession. They had no glamour for him; he realized their burdens, their ineffectiveness for all the more precious kinds of happiness--how could he not, with these two forlorn figures of Chudleigh and his boy always before him? As for imagination and poetry, Delafield, with a mind that was either positive or mystical--the mind, one might say, of the land-agent or the saint--failed to see where they came in. Family tradition, no doubt, carries a thrill. But what thrill is there in the mere possession of a vast number of acres of land, of more houses, new and old, than any human being can possibly live in, of more money than any reasonable man can ever spend, and more responsibilities than he can ever meet? Such things often seemed to Delafield pure calamity--mere burdens upon life and breath. That he could and must be forced, some time, by law and custom, to take them up, was nothing but a social barbarity.

Mingled with all which, of course, was his passionate sense of spiritual democracy. To be throned apart, like a divine being, surrounded by the bought homage of one's fellows, and possessed of more power than a man can decently use, was a condition which excited in

Delafield the same kind of contemptuous revolt that it would have excited in St. Francis. "Be not ye called master"--a Christian even of his transcendental and heterodox sort, if he were a Christian, must surely hold these words in awe, at least so far as concerned any mastery of the external or secular kind. To masteries of another order the saint has never been disinclined.

As he once more struck the village street, this familiar whirl of thoughts was buzzing in Delafield's mind, pierced, however, by one sharper and newer. Julie! Did he know--had he ever dared to find out--how she regarded this future which was overtaking them? She had tried to sound him; she had never revealed herself.

In Lady Henry's house he had often noticed in Julie that she had an imaginative tenderness for rank or great fortune. At first it had seemed to him a woman's natural romanticism; then he explained it to himself as closely connected with her efforts to serve Warkworth.

But suppose he were made to feel that there, after all, lay her compensation? She had submitted to a loveless marriage and lost her lover; but the dukedom was to make amends. He knew well that it would be so with nine women out of ten. But the bare thought that it might be so with Julie maddened him. He then was to be for her, in the future, the mere symbol of the vulgarer pleasures and opportunities, while Warkworth held her heart?

Nay!

He stood still, strengthening in himself the glad and sufficient answer. She had refused him twice--knowing all his circumstances. At this moment he adored her doubly for those old rebuffs.

Within twenty-four hours Delafield had received a telegram from his friend at Zanzibar. For the most part it recapitulated the news already sent to Cairo, and thence transmitted to the English papers. But it added the information that Warkworth had been buried in the neighborhood of a certain village on the caravan route to Mokembe, and that special pains had been taken to mark the spot. And the message concluded: "Fine fellow. Hard luck. Everybody awfully sorry here."

These words brought Delafield a sudden look of passionate gratitude from Julie's dark and sunken eyes. She rested her face against his sleeve and pressed his hand.

Lady Blanche also wept over the telegram, exclaiming that she had always believed in Henry Warkworth, and now, perhaps, those busybodies who at Simla had been pleased to concern themselves with her affairs and Aileen's would see cause to be ashamed of themselves.

To Delafield's discomfort, indeed, she poured out upon him a stream of confidences he would have gladly avoided. He had brought the telegram to her sitting-room. In the room adjoining it was Aileen, still, according to her mother's account, very ill, and almost speechless. Under the shadow of such a tragedy it seemed to him amazing that a mother could find words in which to tell her daughter's story to a comparative stranger. Lady Blanche appeared to him an ill-balanced and foolish woman; a prey, on the one hand, to various obscure jealousies and antagonisms, and on the other to a romantic and sentimental temper which, once roused, gloried in despising "the world," by which she generally meant a very ordinary degree of prudence.

She was in chronic disagreement, it seemed, with her daughter's guardians, and had been so from the first moment of her widowhood, the truth being that she was jealous of their legal powers over Aileen's fortune and destiny, and determined, notwithstanding, to have her own way with her own child. The wilfulness and caprice of the father, which had taken such strange and desperate forms in Rose Delaney, appeared shorn of all its attraction and romance in the smaller, more conventional, and meaner egotisms of Lady Blanche.

And yet, in her own way, she was full of heart. She lost her head over a love affair. She could deny Aileen nothing. That was what her casual Indian acquaintances meant by calling her "sweet." When Warkworth's attentions, pushed with an ardor which would have driven any prudent mother to an instant departure from India, had made a timid and charming child of eighteen the talk of Simla, Lady Blanche, excited and dishevelled--was it her personal untidiness which accounted for the other epithet of "quaint," which had floated to the Duchess's ear, and been by her reported to Julie?--refused to break her daughter's heart. Warkworth, indeed, had begun long before by flattering the mother's vanity and sense of possession, and she now threw herself hotly into his cause as against Aileen's odious trustees.

They, of course, always believed the worst of everybody. As for her, all she wanted for the child was a good husband. Was it not better, in a world of fortune-hunters, that Aileen, with her half-million, should marry early? Of money, she had, one would think, enough. It was only the greed of certain persons which could possibly desire more. Birth? The young man was honorably born, good-looking, well mannered. What did you want more? She accepted a democratic age; and the obstacles thrown by Aileen's guardians in the way of an immediate engagement between the young people appeared to her, so she declared, either vulgar or ridiculous.

Well, poor lady, she had suffered for her whims. First of all, her levity had perceived, with surprise and terror, the hold that passion was taking on the delicate and sensitive nature of Aileen. This young girl, so innocent and spotless in thought, so virginally sweet in manner, so guileless in action, developed a power of loving, an absorption of the whole being in the beloved, such as our modern world but rarely sees.

She lived, she breathed for Warkworth. Her health, always frail, suffered from their separation. She became a thin and frail vision--a "gossamer girl" indeed. The ordinary life of travel and society lost all hold upon her; she passed through it in a mood of weariness and distaste that was in itself a danger to vital force. The mother became desperately alarmed, and made a number of flurried concessions. Letters, at any rate, should be allowed, in spite of the guardians, and without their knowledge. Yet each letter caused emotions which ran like a storm-wind through the child's fragile being, and seemed to exhaust the young life at its source. Then came the diphtheria, acting with poisonous effect on a nervous system already overstrained.

And in the midst of the mother's anxieties there burst upon her the sudden, incredible tale that Warkworth--to whom she herself was writing regularly, and to whom Aileen, from her bed, was sending little pencilled notes, sweetly meant to comfort a sighing lover--had been entangling himself in London with another, a Miss Le Breton, positively a nobody, as far as birth and position were concerned, the paid companion of Lady Henry Delafield, and yet, as it appeared, a handsome, intriguing, unscrupulous hussy, just the kind of hawk to snatch a morsel from a dove's mouth--a woman, in fact, with whom a little bread-and-butter girl like Aileen might very well have no chance.

Emily Lawrence's letter, in the tone of the candid friend, written after her evening at Crowborough House, had roused a mingled anguish and fury in the mother's breast. She lifted her eyes from it to look at Aileen, propped up in bed, her head thrown back against the pillow, and her little hands closed happily over Warkworth's letters; and she went straight from that vision to write to the traitor.

The traitor defended and excused himself by return of post. He implored her to pay no attention to the calumnious distortion of a friendship which had already served Aileen's interests no less than his own. It was largely to Miss Le Breton's influence that he owed the appointment which was to advance him so materially in his career. At the same time he thought it would be wise if Lady Blanche kept not only the silly gossip that was going about, but even this true and innocent fact, from Aileen's knowledge. One never knew how a girl would take such things, and he would rather explain it himself at his own time.

Lady Blanche had to be content. And meanwhile the glory of the Mokembe appointment was a strong factor in Aileen's recovery. She exulted over it by day and night, and she wrote the letters of an angel.

The mother watched her writing them with mixed feelings. As to Warkworth's replies, which she was sometimes allowed to see, Lady Blanche, who had been a susceptible girl, and the heroine of several "affairs," was secretly and strongly of opinion that men's love-letters, at any rate, were poor things nowadays, compared with what they had been.

But Aileen was more than satisfied with them. How busy he must be, and with such important business! Poor, harassed darling, how good of him to write her a word--to give her a thought!

And now Lady Blanche beheld her child crushed and broken, a nervous wreck, before her life had truly begun. The agonies which the mother endured were very real, and should have been touching. But she was not a touching person. All her personal traits--her red-rimmed eyes, her straggling hair, the slight, disagreeable twist in her nose and mouth--combined, with her signal lack of dignity and reticence, to stir the impatience rather than the sympathy of the by-stander.

"And mamma was so fond of her," Julie would say to herself sometimes, in wonder, proudly contrasting the wild grace and originality of her disgraced mother with the awkward, slipshod ways of the sister who had remained a great lady.

Meanwhile, Lady Blanche was, indeed, perpetually conscious of her strange niece, perpetually thinking of the story her brothers had told her, perpetually trying to recall the sister she had lost so young, and then turning from all such things to brood angrily over the Lawrence letter, and the various other rumors which had reached her of Warkworth's relations to Miss Le Breton.

What was in the woman's mind now? She looked pale and tragic enough. But what right had she to grieve--or, if she did grieve, to be pitied?

Jacob Delafield had been fool enough to marry her, and fate would make her a duchess. So true it is that they who have no business to flourish do flourish, like green bay-trees.

As to poor Rose--sometimes there would rise on Lady Blanche's mind the sudden picture of herself and the lost, dark-eyed sister, scampering on their ponies through the country lanes of their childhood; of her lessons with Rose, her worship of Rose; and then of that black curtain of mystery and reprobation which for the younger child of sixteen had suddenly descended upon Rose and all that concerned her.

But Rose's daughter! All one could say was that she had turned out as the child of such proceedings might be expected to turn out--a minx. The aunt's conviction as to that stood firm. And while Rose's face and fate had sunk into the shadows of the past, even for her sister, Aileen was here, struggling for her delicate, threatened life, her hand always in the hand of this woman who had tried to steal her lover from her, her soft, hopeless eyes, so tragically unconscious, bent upon the bold intriguer.

What possessed the child? Warkworth's letters, Julie's company--those seemed to be all she desired.

And at last, in the June beauty and brilliance, when a triumphant summer had banished the pitiful spring, when the meadows were all perfume and color, and the clear mountains, in a clear sky, upheld the ever-new and never-ending pomp of dawn and noon and night, the little, wasted creature looked up into Julie's face, and, without tears, gasped out her story.

"These are his letters. Some day I'll--I'll read you some of them; and this--is his picture. I know you saw him at Lady Henry's. He mentioned your name. Will you please tell me everything--all the times you saw him, and what he talked of? You see I am much stronger. I can bear it all now."

Meanwhile, for Delafield, this fortnight of waiting--waiting for the African letters, waiting for the revival of life in Aileen--was a period of extraordinary tension, when all the powers of nerve and brain seemed to be tested and tried to the utmost. He himself was absorbed in watching Julie and in dealing with her.

In the first place, as he saw, she could give no free course to grief. The tragic yearning, the agonized tenderness and pity which consumed her, must be crushed out of sight as far as possible. They would have been an offence to Lady Blanche, a bewilderment to Aileen. And it was on her relation to her new-found cousin that, as Delafield perceived, her moral life for the moment turned. This frail girl was on the brink of perishing because death had taken Warkworth from her. And Julie knew well that Warkworth had neither loved her nor deserved her--that he had gone to Africa and to death with another image in his heart.

There was a perpetual and irreparable cruelty in the situation. And from the remorse of it Julie could not escape. Day by day she was more profoundly touched by the clinging, tender creature, more sharply scourged by the knowledge that the affection developing between them could never be without its barrier and its mystery, that something must always remain undisclosed, lest Aileen cast her off in horror.

It was a new moral suffering, in one whose life had been based hitherto on intellect, or passion. In a sense it held at bay even her grief for Warkworth, her intolerable compassion for his fate. In sheer dread lest the girl should find her out and hate her, she lost insensibly the first poignancy of sorrow.

These secrets of feeling left her constantly pale and silent. Yet her grace had never been more evident. All the inmates of the little pension, the landlord's family, the servants, the visitors, as the days passed, felt the romance and thrill of her presence. Lady Blanche evoked impatience of ennui. She was inconsiderate; she was meddlesome; she soon ceased even to be pathetic. But for Julie every foot ran, every eye smiled.

Then, when the day was over, Delafield's opportunity began. Julie could not sleep. He gradually established the right to read with her and talk with her. It was a relation very singular, and very intimate. She would admit him at his knock, and he would find her on her sofa, very sad, often in tears, her black hair loose upon her shoulders. Outwardly there was often much ceremony, even distance between them; inwardly, each was exploring the other, and Julie's attitude towards Delafield was becoming more uncertain, more touched with emotion.

What was, perhaps, most noticeable in it was a new timidity, a touch of anxious respect towards him. In the old days, what with her literary cultivation and her social success, she had always been the flattered and admired one of their little group. Delafield felt himself clumsy and tongue-tied beside her. It was a superiority on her part very natural and never ungraceful, and it was his chief delight to bring it forward, to insist upon it, to take it for granted.

But the relation between them had silently shifted.

"You judge--you are always judging," she had said once, impatiently, to Delafield. And now it was round these judgments, these inward verdicts of his, on life or character, that she was perpetually hovering. She was infinitely curious about them. She would wrench them from him, and then would often shiver away from him in resentment.

He, meanwhile, as he advanced further in the knowledge of her strange nature, was more and more bewildered by her--her perversities and caprices, her brilliancies and powers, her utter lack of any standard or scheme of life. She had been for a long time, as it seemed to him, the creature of her exquisite social instincts--then the creature of passion. But what a woman through it all, and how adorable, with those poetic gestures and looks, those melancholy, gracious airs that ravished him perpetually! And now this new attitude, as of a child leaning, wistfully looking in your face, asking to be led, to be wrestled and reasoned with.

The days, as they passed, produced in him a secret and mounting intoxication. Then, perhaps for a day or two, there would be a reaction, both foreseeing that a kind of spiritual tyranny might arise from their relation, and both recoiling from it....

One night she was very restless and silent. There seemed to be no means of approach to her true mind. Suddenly he took her hand--it was some days since they had spoken of Warkworth-- and almost roughly reminded her of her promise to tell him all.

She rebelled. But his look and manner held her, and the inner misery sought an outlet. Submissively she began to speak, in her low, murmuring voice; she went back over the past--the winter in Bruton Street; the first news of the Moffatt engagement; her efforts for Warkworth's promotion; the history of the evening party which had led to her banishment; the struggle in her own mind and Warkworth's; the sudden mad schemes of their last interview; the rush of the Paris journey.

The mingled exaltation and anguish, the comparative absence of regret with which she told the story, produced an astonishing effect on Delafield. And in both minds, as the story proceeded, there emerged ever more clearly the consciousness of that imperious act by which he had saved her.

Suddenly she stopped.

"I know you can find no excuse for it all," she said, in excitement.

"Yes; for all--but for one thing," was his low reply.

She shrank, her eyes on his face.

"That poor child," he said, under his breath.

She looked at him piteously.

"Did you ever realize what you were doing?" he asked her, raising her hand to his lips.

"No, no! How could I? I thought of some one so different--I had never seen her--"

She paused, her wide--seeking gaze fixed upon him through tears, as though she pleaded with him to find explanations--palliatives.

But he gently shook his head.

Suddenly, shaken with weeping, she bowed her face upon the hands that held her own. It was like one who relinquishes all pleading, all defence, and throws herself on the mercy of the judge.

He tenderly asked her pardon if he had wounded her. But he shrank from offering any caress. The outward signs of life's most poignant and most beautiful moments are generally very simple and austere.

XXIV

"You have had a disquieting letter?"

The voice was Julie's. Delafield was standing, apparently in thought, at the farther corner of the little, raised terrace of the hotel. She approached him with an affectionate anxiety, of which he was instantly conscious.

"I am afraid I may have to leave you to-night," he said, turning towards her, and holding out the letter in his hand.

It contained a few agitated lines from the Duke of Chudleigh.

"They tell me my lad can't get over this. He's made a gallant fight, but this beats us. A week or two--no more. Ask Mrs. Delafield to let you come. She will, I know. She wrote to me very kindly. Mervyn keeps talking of you. You'd come, if you heard him. It's ghastly--the cruelty of it all. Whether I can live without him, that's the point."

"You'll go, of course?" said Julie, returning it.

"To-night, if you allow it."

"Of course. You ought."

"I hate leaving you alone, with this trouble on your hands," said Jacob, in some agitation. "What are your plans?"

"I could follow you next week. Aileen comes down to-day. And I should like to wait here for the mail."

"In five days, about, it should be here," said Delafield.

There was a silence. She dropped into a chair beside the balustrade of the terrace, which was wreathed in wistaria, and looked out upon the vast landscape of the lake. His thought was, "How can the mail matter to her? She cannot suppose that he had written--"

Aloud he said, in some embarrassment, "You expect letters yourself?"

"I expect nothing," she said, after a pause. "But Aileen is living on the chance of letters."

"There may be nothing for her--except, indeed, her letters to him--poor child!"

"She knows that. But the hope keeps her alive."

"And you?" thought Delafield, with an inward groan, as he looked down upon her pale profile. He had a moment's hateful vision of himself as the elder brother in the parable. Was Julie's mind to be the home of an eternal antithesis between the living husband and the dead lover--in which the latter had forever the beau rôle?

Then, impatiently, Jacob wrenched himself from mean thoughts. It was as though he bared his head remorse-fully before the dead man.

"I will go to the Foreign Office," he said, in her ear, "as I pass through town. They will have letters. All the information I can get you shall have at once."

"Thank you, mon ami", she said, almost inaudibly.

Then she looked up, and he was startled by her eyes. Where he had expected grief, he saw a shrinking animation.

"Write to me often," she said, imperiously.

"Of course. But don't trouble to answer much. Your hands are so full here."

She frowned.

"Trouble! Why do you spoil me so? Demand--insist--that I should write!"

"Very well," he said, smiling, "I demand--I insist!"

She drew a long breath, and went slowly away from him into the house. Certainly the antagonism of her secret thoughts, though it persisted, was no longer merely cold or critical. For it concerned one who was not only the master of his own life, but threatened unexpectedly to become the master of hers.

She had begun, indeed, to please her imagination with the idea of a relation between them, which, while it ignored the ordinary relations of marriage, should yet include many of the intimacies and refinements of love. More and more did the surprises of his character arrest and occupy her mind. She found, indeed, no "plaster saint." Her cool intelligence soon detected the traces of a peevish or stubborn temper, and of a natural inertia, perpetually combated, however, by the spiritual energy of a new and other self exfoliating from the old; a self whose acts and ways she watched, sometimes with the held breath of fascination, sometimes with a return of shrinking or fear. That a man should not only appear but be so good was still in her eyes a little absurd. Perhaps her feeling was at bottom the common feeling of the sceptical nature. "We should listen to the higher voices; but in such a way that if another hypothesis were true, we should not have been too completely duped."

She was ready, also, to convict him of certain prejudices and superstitions which roused in her an intellectual impatience. But when all was said, Delafield, unconsciously, was drawing her towards him, as the fowler draws a fluttering bird. It was the exquisite refinement of those spiritual insights and powers he possessed which constantly appealed, not only to her heart, but-- a very important matter in Julie's case--to her taste, to her own carefully tempered instinct for the rare and beautiful.

He was the master, then, she admitted, of a certain vein of spiritual genius. Well, here should he lead--and even, if he pleased, command her. She would sit at his feet, and he should open to her ranges of feeling, delights, and subtleties of moral sensation hitherto unknown to her.

Thus the feeling of ennui and reaction which had marked the first weeks of her married life had now wholly disappeared. Delafield was no longer dull or pedantic in her eyes. She passed alternately from moments of intolerable smart and pity for the dead to moments of agitation and expectancy connected with her husband. She thought over their meeting of the night before; she looked forward to similar hours to come.

Meanwhile his relation towards her in many matters was still naïvely ignorant and humble-- determined by the simplicity of a man of some real greatness, who never dreamed of claiming tastes or knowledge he did not possess, whether in small things or large. This phase, however, only gave the more value to one which frequently succeeded it. For suddenly the conversation would enter regions where he felt himself peculiarly at home, and, with the same unconsciousness on his part, she would be made to feel the dignity and authority which surrounded his ethical and spiritual life. And these contrasts--this weakness and this strength--

combined with the man-and-woman element which is always present in any situation of the kind, gave rise to a very varied and gradually intensifying play of feeling between them. Feeling only possible, no doubt, for the raffinés of this world; but for them full of strange charm, and even of excitement.

Delafield left the little inn for Montreux, Lausanne, and London that afternoon. He bent to kiss his wife at the moment of his departure, in the bare sitting-room that had been improvised for them on the ground floor of the hotel, and as she let her face linger ever so little against his she felt strong arms flung round her, and was crushed against his breast in a hungry embrace. When he released her with a flush and a murmured word of apology she shook her head, smiling sadly but saying nothing. The door closed on him, and at the sound she made a hasty step forward.

"Jacob! Take me with you!"

But her voice died in the rattle and bustle of the diligence outside, and she was left trembling from head to foot, under a conflict of emotions that seemed now to exalt, now to degrade her.

Half an hour after Delafield's departure there appeared on the terrace of the hotel a tottering, emaciated form--Aileen Moffatt, in a black dress and hat, clinging to her mother's arm. But she refused the deck--chair, which they had spread with cushions and shawls.

"No; let me sit up." And she took an ordinary chair, looking round upon the lake and the little flowery terrace with a slow, absorbed look, like one trying to remember. Suddenly she bowed her head on her hands.

"Aileen!" cried Lady Blanche, in an agony.

But the girl motioned her away. "Don't, mummy. I'm all right."

And restraining any further emotion, she laid her arms on the balustrade and gazed long and calmly into the purple depths and gleaming snows of the Rhône valley. Her hat oppressed her and she took it off, revealing the abundance of her delicately golden hair, which, in its lack of lustre and spring, seemed to share in the physical distress and loss of the whole personality.

The face was that of a doomed creature, incapable now of making any successful struggle for the right to live. What had been sensibility had become melancholy; the slight, chronic frown was deeper, the pale lips more pinched. Yet intermittently there was still great sweetness, the last effort of a "beautiful soul" meant for happiness, and withered before its time.

As Julie stood beside her, while Lady Blanche had gone to fetch a book from the salon, the poor child put out her hand and grasped that of Julie.

"It is quite possible I may get the letter to-night," she said, in a hurried whisper. "My maid went down to Montreux--there is a clever man at the post-office who tried to make it out for us. He thinks it'll be to-night."

"Don't be too disappointed if nothing comes," said Julie, caressing the hand. Its thinness, its icy and lifeless touch, dismayed her. Ah, how easily might this physical wreck have been her doing!

The bells of Montreux struck half-past six. A restless and agonized expectation began to show itself in all the movements of the invalid. She left her chair and began to pace the little terrace on Julie's arm. Her dragging step, the mournful black of her dress, the struggle between youth and death in her sharpened face, made her a tragic presence. Julie could hardly bear it, while all the time she, too, was secretly and breathlessly waiting for Warkworth's last words.

Lady Blanche returned, and Julie hurried away.

She passed through the hotel and walked down the Montreux road. The post had already reached the first houses of the village, and the postman, who knew her, willingly gave her the letters.

Yes, a packet for Aileen, addressed in an unknown hand to a London address, and forwarded thence. It bore the Denga postmark.

And another for herself, readdressed from London by Madame Bornier. She tore off the outer envelope; beneath was a letter of which the address was feebly written in Warkworth's hand: "Mademoiselle Le Breton, 3 Heribert Street, London."

She had the strength to carry her own letter to her room, to call Aileen's maid and send her with the other packet to Lady Blanche. Then she locked herself in....

Oh, the poor, crumpled page, and the labored hand-writing!

"Julie, I am dying. They are such good fellows, but they can't save me. It's horrible.

"I saw the news of your engagement in a paper the day before I left Denga. You're right. He'll make you happy. Tell him I said so. Oh, my God, I shall never trouble you again! I bless you for the letter you wrote me. Here it is.... No, I can't--can't read it. Drowsy. No pain--"

And here the pen had dropped from his hand. Searching for something more, she drew from the envelope the wild and passionate letter she had written him at Heribert Street, in the early morning after her return from Paris, while she was waiting for Delafield to bring her the news of Lord Lackington's state.

The small table d'hôte of the Hotel Michel was still further diminished that night. Lady Blanche was with her daughter, and Mrs. Delafield did not appear.

But the moon was hanging in glory over the lake when Julie, unable to bear her room and her thoughts any longer, threw a lace scarf about her head and neck, and went blindly climbing through the upward paths leading to Les Avants. The roads were silver in the moonlight; so was the lake, save where the great mountain shadows lay across the eastern end. And suddenly, white, through pine-trees, "Jaman, delicately tall!"

The air cooled her brow, and from the deep, enveloping night her torn heart drew balm, and a first soothing of the pulse of pain. Every now and then, as she sat down to rest, a waking dream overshadowed her. She seemed to be supporting Warkworth in her arms; his dying head lay upon her breast, and she murmured courage and love into his ear. But not as Julie Le Breton. Through all the anguish of what was almost an illusion of the senses, she still felt herself Delafield's wife. And in that flood of silent speech she poured out on Warkworth, it was as though she offered him also Jacob's compassion, Jacob's homage, mingled with her own.

Once she found herself sitting at the edge of a meadow, environed by the heavy scents of flowers. Some apple-trees with whitened trunks rose between her and the lake a thousand feet below. The walls of Chillon, the houses of Montreux, caught the light; opposite, the deep forests of Bouveret and St. Gingolphe lay black upon the lake; above them rode the moon. And to the east the high Alps, their pure lines a little effaced and withdrawn, as when a light veil hangs over a sanctuary.

Julie looked out upon a vast freedom of space, and by a natural connection she seemed to be also surveying her own world of life and feeling, her past and her future. She thought of her childhood and her parents, of her harsh, combative youth, of the years with Lady Henry, of Warkworth, of her husband, and the life into which his strong hand had so suddenly and rashly drawn her. Her thoughts took none of the religious paths so familiar to his. And yet her reverie was so far religious that her mind seemed to herself to be quivering under the onset of affections, emotions, awes, till now unknown, and that, looking back, she was conscious of a groping sense of significance, of purpose, in all that had befallen her. Yet to this sense she could put no words. Only, in the end, through the constant action of her visualizing imagination, it connected itself with Delafield's face, and with the memory of many of his recent acts and sayings.

It was one of those hours which determine the history of a man or woman. And the august Alpine beauty entered in, so that Julie, in this sad and thrilling act of self-probing, felt herself in the presence of powers and dominations divine.

Her face, stained with tears, took gradually some of the calm, the loftiness of the night. Yet the close-shut, brooding mouth would slip sometimes into a smile exquisitely soft and gentle, as though the heart remembered something which seemed to the intelligence at once folly and sweetness.

What was going on within her was, to her own consciousness, a strange thing. It appeared to her as a kind of simplification, a return to childhood; or, rather, was it the emergence in the grown mind, tired with the clamor of its own egotistical or passionate life, of some instincts, natural to the child, which she, nevertheless, as a child had never known; instincts of trust, of self-abandonment, steeped, perhaps, in those tears which are themselves only another happiness?...

But hush! What are our poor words in the presence of these nobler secrets of the wrestling and mounting spirit!

On the way down she saw another figure emerge from the dark.

"Lady Blanche!"

Lady Blanche stood still.

"The hotel was stifling," she said, in a voice that vainly tried for steadiness.

Julie perceived that she had been weeping.

"Aileen is asleep?"

"Perhaps. They have given her something to make her sleep."

They walked on towards the hotel.

Julie hesitated.

"She was not disappointed?" she said, at last, in a low voice.

"No!" said the mother, sharply. "But one knew, of course, there must be letters for her. Thank God, she can feel that his very last thought was for her! The letters which have reached her are dated the day before the fatal attack began--giving a complete account of his march--most interesting--showing how he trusted her already--though she is such a child. It will tranquillize her to feel how completely she possessed his heart--poor fellow!"

Julie said nothing, and Lady Blanche, with bitter satisfaction, felt rather than saw what seemed to her the just humiliation expressed in the drooping and black-veiled figure beside her.

Next day there was once more a tinge of color on Aileen's cheeks. Her beautiful hair fell round her once more in a soft life and confusion, and the roses which her mother had placed beside her on the bed were not in too pitiful contrast with her frail loveliness.

"Read it, please," she said, as soon as she found herself alone with Julie, pushing her letter tenderly towards her. "He tells me everything--everything! All he was doing and hoping--consults me in everything. Isn't it an honor--when I'm so ignorant and childish? I'll try to be brave--try to be worthy--"

And while her whole frame was shaken with deep, silent sobs, she greedily watched Julie read the letter.

"Oughtn't I to try and live," she said, dashing away her tears, as Julie returned it, "when he loved me so?"

Julie kissed her with a passionate and guilty pity. The letter might have been written to any friend, to any charming child for whom a much older man had a kindness. It gave a business-like account of their march, dilated on one or two points of policy, drew some humorous sketches of his companions, and concluded with a few affectionate and playful sentences.

But when the wrestle with death began, Warkworth wrote but one last letter, uttered but one cry of the heart, and it lay now in Julie's bosom.

A few days passed. Delafield's letters were short and full of sadness. Elmira still lived; but any day or hour might see the end. As for the father--But the subject was too tragic to be written of, even to her. Not to feel, not to realize; there lay the only chance of keeping one's own courage, and so of being any help whatever to two of the most miserable of human beings.

At last, rather more than a week after Delafield's departure, came two telegrams. One was from Delafield--"Mervyn died this morning. Duke's condition causes great anxiety." The other from Evelyn Crowborough--"Elmira died this morning. Going down to Shropshire to help Jacob."

Julie threw down the telegrams. A rush of proud tears came to her eyes. She swept to the door of her room, opened it, and called her maid.

The maid came, and when she saw the sparkling looks and strained bearing of her mistress, wondered what crime she was to be rebuked for. Julie merely bade her pack at once, as it was her intention to catch the eight o'clock through train at Lausanne that night for England.

Twenty hours later the train carrying Julie to London entered Victoria Station. On the platform stood the little Duchess, impatiently expectant. Julie was clasped in her arms, and had no time to wonder at the pallor and distraction of her friend before she was hurried into the brougham waiting beyond the train.

"Oh, Julie!" cried the Duchess, catching the traveller's hands, as they drove away. "Julie, darling!"

Julie turned to her in amazement. The blue eyes fixed upon her had no tears, but in them, and in the Duchess's whole aspect, was expressed a vivid horror and agitation which struck at Julie's heart.

"What is it?" she said, catching her breath. "What is it?"

"Julie, I was going to Faircourt this morning. First your telegram stopped me. I thought I'd wait and go with you. Then came another, from Delafield. The Duke! The poor Duke!"

Julie's attitude changed unconsciously--instantly.

"Yes; tell me!"

"It's in all the papers to-night--on the placards--don't look out!" And the Duchess lifted her hand and drew down the blinds of the brougham. "He was in a most anxious state yesterday, but they thought him calmer at night, and he insisted on being left alone. The doctors still kept a watch, but he managed in some mysterious way to evade them all, and this morning he was missed. After two hours they found him--in the river that runs below the house!"

There was a silence.

"And Jacob?" said Julie, hoarsely.

"That's what I'm so anxious about," exclaimed the Duchess. "Oh, I am thankful you've come! You know how Jacob's always felt about the Duke and Mervyn--how he's hated the notion of succeeding. And Susan, who went down yesterday, telegraphed to me last night--before this horror--that he was 'terribly strained and overwrought.'"

"Succeeding?" said Julie, vaguely. Mechanically she had drawn up the blind again, and her eyes followed the dingy lines of the Vauxhall Bridge Road, till suddenly they turned away from the placards outside a small stationer's shop which announced: "Tragic death of the Duke of Chudleigh and his son."

The Duchess looked at her curiously without replying. Julie seemed to be grappling with some idea which escaped her, or, rather, was presently expelled by one more urgent.

"Is Jacob ill?" she said, abruptly, looking her companion full in the face.

"I only know what I've told you. Susan says 'strained and overwrought.' Oh, it'll be all right when he gets you!"

Julie made no reply. She sat motionless, and the Duchess, stealing another glance at her, must needs, even in this tragic turmoil, allow herself the reflection that she was a more delicate study in black-and-white, a more refined and accented personality than ever.

"You won't mind," said Evelyn, timidly, after a pause; "but Lady Henry is staying with me, and also Sir Wilfrid Bury, who had such a bad cold in his lodgings that I went down there a week ago, got the doctor's leave, and carried him off there and then. And Mr. Montresor's coming in. He particularly wanted, he said, just to press your hand. But they sha'n't bother you if you're tired. Our train goes at 10.10, and Freddie has got the express stopped for us at Westonport-- about three in the morning."

The carriage rolled into Grosvenor Square, and presently stopped before Crowborough House. Julie alighted, looked round her at the July green of the square, at the brightness of the window-boxes, and then at the groom of the chambers who was taking her wraps from her--the same man who, in the old days, used to feed Lady Henry's dogs with sweet biscuit. It struck her that he was showing her a very particular and eager attention.

Meanwhile in the Duchess's drawing--room a little knot of people was gathered--Lady Henry, Sir Wilfrid Bury, and Dr. Meredith. Their demeanor illustrated both the subduing and the exciting influence of great events. Lady Henry was more talkative than usual. Sir Wilfrid more silent.

Lady Henry seemed to have profited by her stay at Torquay. As she sat upright in a stiff chair, her hands resting on her stick, she presented her characteristic aspect of English solidity, crossed by a certain free and foreign animation. She had been already wrangling with Sir Wilfrid, and giving her opinion freely on the "socialistic" views on rank and property attributed to Jacob Delafield. "If he can't digest the cake, that doesn't mean it isn't good," had been her last impatient remark, when Sir Wilfrid interrupted her.

"Only a few minutes more," he said, looking at his watch. "Now, then, what line do we take? How much is our friend likely to know?"

"Unless she has lost her eyesight--which Evelyn has not reported--she will know most of what matters before she has gone a hundred yards from the station," said Lady Henry, dryly.

"Oh, the streets! Yes; but persons are often curiously dazed by such a gallop of events."

"Not Julie Le Breton!"

"I should like to be informed as to the part you are about to play," said Sir Wilfrid, in a lower voice, "that I may play up to it. Where are you?"

Both looked at Meredith, who had walked to a distant window and was standing there looking out upon the square. Lady Henry was well aware that he had not forgiven her, and, to tell the truth, was rather anxious that he should. So she, too, dropped her voice.

"I bow to the institutions of my country," she said, a little sparkle in the strong, gray eye.

"In other words, you forgive a duchess?"

"I acknowledge the head of the family, and the greater carries the less."

"Suppose Jacob should be unforgiving?"

"He hasn't the spirit."

"And she?"

"Her conscience will be on my side."

"I thought it was your theory that she had none?"

"Jacob, let us hope, will have developed some. He has a good deal to spare."

Sir Wilfrid laughed. "So it is you who will do the pardoning?"

"I shall offer an armed and honorable peace. The Duchess of Chudleigh may intrigue and tell lies, if she pleases. I am not giving her a hundred a year."

There was a pause.

"Why, if I may ask," said Sir Wilfrid, at the end of it, "did you quarrel with Jacob? I understand there was a separate cause:"

Lady Henry hesitated.

"He paid me a debt," she said, at last, and a sudden flush rose in her old, blanched cheek.

"And that annoyed you? You have the oddest code!"

Lady Henry bit her lip.

"One does not like one's money thrown in one's face."

"Most unreasonable of women!"

"Never mind, Wilfrid. We all have our feelings."

"Precisely. Well, no doubt Jacob will make peace. As for--Ah, here comes Montresor!"

A visible tremor passed through Lady Henry. The door was thrown open, and the footman announced the Minister for War.

"Her grace, sir, is not yet returned."

Montresor stumbled into the room, and even with his eye-glasses carefully adjusted, did not at once perceive who was in it.

Sir Wilfrid went towards him.

"Ah, Bury! Convalescent, I hope?"

"Quite. The Duchess has gone to meet Mrs. Delafield."

"Mrs.--?" Montresor's mouth opened. "But, of course, you know?"

"Oh yes, I know. But one's tongue has to get oiled. You see Lady Henry?"

Montresor started.

"I am glad to see Lady Henry," he replied, stiffly.

Lady Henry slowly rose and advanced two steps. She quietly held out her hand to him, and, smiling, looked him in the face.

"Take it. There is no longer any cause of quarrel between us. I raise the embargo."

The Minister took the hand, and shook his head.

"Ah, but you had no right to impose it," he said, with energy.

"Oh, for goodness sake, meet me half-way," cried Lady Henry, "or I shall never hold out!"

Sir Wilfrid, whose half-embarrassed gaze was bent on the ground, looked up and was certain that he saw a gleam of moisture in those wrinkled eyes.

"Why have you held out so long? What does it matter to me whether Miss Julie be a duchess or no? That doesn't make up to me for all the months you've shut your door on me. And I was always given to understand, by-the-way, that it wouldn't matter to you."

"I've had three months at Torquay," said Lady Henry, raising her shoulders.

"I hope it was dull to distraction."

"It was. And my doctor tells me the more I fret the more gout I may expect."

"So all this is not generosity, but health?"

"Kiss my hand, sir, and have done with it! You are all avenged. At Torquay I had four companions in seven weeks."

"More power to them!" said Montresor. "Meredith, come here. Shall we accept the pleas?"

Meredith came slowly from the window, his hands behind his back.

"Lady Henry commands and we obey," he said, slowly. "But to-day begins a new world-- founded in ruin, like the rest of them."

He raised his fine eyes, in which there was no laughter, rather a dreamy intensity. Lady Henry shrank.

"If you're thinking of Chudleigh," she said, uncertainly, "be glad for him. It was release. As for

Henry Warkworth--"

"Ah, poor fellow!" said Montresor, perfunctorily. "Poor fellow!"

He had dropped Lady Henry's hand, but he now recaptured it, enclosing the thin, jewelled fingers in his own.

"Well, well, then it's peace, with all my heart." He stooped and lightly kissed the fingers. "And now, when do you expect our friend?"

"At any moment," said Lady Henry.

She seated herself, and Montresor beside her.

"I am told," said Montresor, "that this horror will not only affect Delafield personally, but that he will regard the dukedom as a calamity."

"Hm!--and you believe it?" said Lady Henry.

"I try to," was the Minister's laughing reply. "Ah, surely, here they are!"

Meredith turned from the window, to which he had gone back.

"The carriage has just arrived," he announced, and he stood fidgeting, standing first on one foot, then on the other, and running his hand through his mane of gray hair. His large features were pale, and any close observer would have detected the quiver of emotion.

A sound of voices from the anteroom, the Duchess's light tones floating to the top. At the same time a door on the other side of the drawing-room opened and the Duke of Crowborough appeared.

"I think I hear my wife," he said, as he greeted Montresor and hurriedly crossed the room.

There was a rustle of quick steps, and the little Duchess entered.

"Freddie, here is Julie!"

Behind appeared a tall figure in black. Everybody in the room advanced, including Lady Henry, who, however, after a few steps stood still behind the others, leaning on her stick.

Julie looked round the little circle, then at the Duke of Crowborough, who had gravely given her his hand. The suppressed excitement already in the room clearly communicated itself to her. She did not lose her self-command for an instant, but her face pleaded.

"Is it really true? Perhaps there is some mistake?"

"I fear there can be none," said the Duke, sadly. "Poor Chudleigh had been long dead when they found him."

"Freddie," said the Duchess, interrupting, "I have told Greswell we shall want the carriage at half-past nine for Euston. Will that do?"

"Perfectly."

Greswell, the handsome groom of the chambers, approached Julie.

"Your grace's maid wishes to know whether it is your grace's wish that she should go round to Heribert Street before taking the luggage to Euston?"

Julie looked at the man, bewildered. Then a stormy color rushed into her cheeks.

"Does he mean my maid?" she said to the Duke, piteously.

"Certainly. Will you give your orders?"

She gave them, and then, turning again to the Duke, she covered her eyes with her hands a moment.

"What does it all mean?" she said, faltering. "It seems as though we were all mad."

"You understand, of course, that Jacob succeeds?" said the Duke, not without coldness; and he stood still an instant, gazing at this woman, who must now, he supposed, feel herself at the very summit of her ambitions.

Julie drew a long breath. Then she perceived Lady Henry. Instantly, impetuously, she crossed the room. But as she reached that composed and formidable figure, the old timidity, the old fear, seized her. She paused abruptly, but she held out her hand.

Lady Henry took it. The two women stood regarding each other, while the other persons in the room instinctively turned away from their meeting. Lady Henry's first look was one of curiosity. Then, before the indefinable, ennobling change in Julie's face, now full of the pale agitation of memory, the eyes of the older woman wavered and dropped. But she soon recovered herself.

"We meet again under very strange circumstances," she said, quietly; "though I have long foreseen them. As for our former experience, we were in a false relation, and it made fools of us both. You and Jacob are now the heads of the family. And if you like to make friends with me on this new footing, I am ready. As to my behavior, I think it was natural; but if it rankles in your mind, I apologize."

The personal pride of the owner, curbed in its turn by the pride of tradition and family, spoke strangely from these words. Julie stood trembling, her chest heaving.

"I, too, regret--and apologize," she said, in a low voice.

"Then we begin again. But now you must let Evelyn take you to rest for an hour or two. I am sorry you have this hurried journey to-night."

Julie pressed her hands to her breast with one of those dramatic movements that were natural to her.

"Oh, I must see Jacob!" she said, under her breath--"I must see Jacob!"

And she turned away, looking vaguely round her. Meredith approached.

"Comfort yourself," he said, very gently, pressing her hand in both of his. "It has been a great shock, but when you get there he'll be all right."

"Jacob?"

Her expression, the piteous note in her voice, awoke in him an answering sense of pain. He wondered how it might be between the husband and wife. Yet it was borne in upon him, as upon Lady Henry, that her marriage, however interpreted, had brought with it profound and intimate transformation. A different woman stood before him. And when, after a few more words, the Duchess swept down upon them, insisting that Julie must rest awhile, Meredith stood looking after the retreating figures, filled with the old, bitter sense of human separateness, and the fragmentariness of all human affections. Then he made his farewells to the Duke and Lady Henry, and slipped away. He had turned a page in the book of life; and as he walked through Grosvenor Square he applied his mind resolutely to one of the political "causes" with which, as a powerful and fighting journalist, he was at that moment occupied.

Lady Henry, too, watched Julie's exit from the room.

"So now she supposes herself in love with Jacob?" she thought, with amusement, as she resumed her seat.

"What if Delafield refuses to be made a duke?" said Sir Wilfrid, in her ear.

"It would be a situation new to the Constitution," said Lady Henry, composedly. "I advise you, however, to wait till it occurs."

The northern express rushed onward through the night. Rugby, Stafford, Crewe had been left behind. The Yorkshire valleys and moors began to show themselves in pale ridges and folds under the moon. Julie, wakeful in her corner opposite the little, sleeping Duchess, was conscious of an interminable rush of images through a brain that longed for a few unconscious and forgetful moments. She thought of the deferential station-master at Euston; of the fuss attending their arrival on the platform; of the arrangements made for stopping the express at the Yorkshire Station, where they were to alight.

Faircourt? Was it the great Early-Georgian house of which she had heard Jacob speak--the vast pile, half barrack, half palace, in which, according to him, no human being could be either happy or at home?

And this was now his--and hers? Again the whirl of thoughts swept and danced round her.

A wild, hill country. In the valleys, the blackness of thick trees, the gleam of rivers, the huge, lifeless factories; and beyond, the high, silver edges, the sharp shadows of the moors.... The train slackened, and the little Duchess woke at once.

"Ten minutes to three. Oh, Julie, here we are!"

The dawn was just coldly showing as they alighted. Carriages and servants were waiting, and various persons whose identity and function it was not easy to grasp. One of them, however, at once approached Julie with a privileged air, and she perceived that he was a doctor.

"I am very glad that your grace has come," he said, as he raised his hat. "The trouble with the Duke is shock, and want of sleep."

Julie looked at him, still bewildered.

"How long has my husband been ill?"

He walked on beside her, describing in as few words as possible the harrowing days preceding the death of the boy, Delafield's attempts to soothe and control the father, the stratagem by which the poor Duke had outwitted them all, and the weary hours of search through the night, under a drizzling rain, which had resulted, about dawn, in the discovery of the Duke's body in one of the deeper holes of the river.

"When the procession returned to the house, your husband"--the speaker framed the words uncertainly--"had a long fainting-fit. It was probably caused by the exhaustion of the search-- many hours without food--and many sleepless nights. We kept him in his room all day. But towards evening he insisted on getting up. The restlessness he shows is itself a sign of shock. I trust, now you are here, you may be able to persuade him to spare himself. Otherwise the consequences might be grave."

The drive to the house lay mainly through a vast park, dotted with stiff and melancholy woods. The morning was cloudy; even the wild roses in the hedges and the daisies in the grass had neither gayety nor color. Soon the house appeared--an immense pile of stone, with a pillared centre, and wings to east and west, built in a hollow, gray and sunless. The mournful blinds drawn closely down made of it rather a mausoleum for the dead than a home for the living.

At the approach of the carriage, however, doors were thrown open, servants appeared, and on the steps, trembling and heavy-eyed, stood Susan Delafield.

She looked timidly at Julie, and then, as they passed into the great central hall, the two kissed each other with tears.

"He is in his room, waiting for you. The doctors persuaded him not to come down. But he is dressed, and reading and writing. We don't believe he has slept at all for a week."

"Through there," said Susan Delafield, stepping back. "That is the door."

"SHE FOUND HERSELF KNEELING BESIDE HIM"

Julie softly opened it, and closed it behind her. Delafield had heard her approach, and was standing by the table, supporting himself upon it. His aspect filled Julie with horror. She ran to him and threw her arms round him. He sank back into his chair, and she found herself kneeling beside him, murmuring to him, while his head rested upon her shoulder.

"Jacob, I am here! Oh, I ought to have been here all through! It's terrible--terrible! But, Jacob, you won't suffer so--now I'm here--now we're together--now I love you, Jacob?"

Her voice broke in tears. She put back the hair from his brow, kissing him with a tenderness in which there was a yearning and lovely humility. Then she drew a little away, waiting for him to speak, in an agony.

But for a time he seemed unable to speak. He feebly released himself, as though he could not bear the emotion she offered him, and his eyes closed.

"Jacob, come and lie down!" she said, in terror. "Let me call the doctors."

He shook his head, and a faint pressure from his hand bade her sit beside him.

"I shall be better soon. Give me time. I'll tell you--"

Then silence again. She sat holding his hand, her eyes fixed upon him. Time passed, she knew not how. Susan came into the room--a small sitting-room in the east wing--to tell her that the neighboring bedroom had been prepared for herself. Julie only looked up for an instant with a dumb sign of refusal. A doctor came in, and Delafield made a painful effort to take the few spoonfuls of food and stimulant pressed upon him. Then he buried his face in the side of the arm-chair.

"Please let us be alone," he said, with a touch of his old peremptoriness, and both Susan and the doctor obeyed.

But it was long before he could collect energy enough to talk. When he did, he made an effort to tell her the story of the boy's death, and the father's self-destruction. He told it leaning forward in his chair, his eyes on the ground, his hands loosely joined, his voice broken and labored. Julie listened, gathering from his report an impression of horror, tragic and irremediable, similar to that which had shaken the balance of his own mind. And when he suddenly looked up with the words, "And now I am expected to take their place--to profit by their deaths! What rightful law of God or man binds me to accept a life and a responsibility that I loathe?" Julie drew back as though he had struck her. His face, his tone were not his own--there was a violence, a threat in them, addressed, as it were, specially to her. "If it were not for you," his eyes seemed to say, "I could refuse this thing, which will destroy me, soul and body."

She was silent, her pulses fluttering, and he resumed, speaking like one groping his way:

"I could have done the work, of course--I have done it for five years. I could have looked after the estate and the people. But the money, the paraphernalia, the hordes of servants, the mummery of the life! Why, Julie, should we be forced into it? What happiness--I ask you--what happiness can it bring to either of us?"

And again he looked up, and again it seemed to Julie that his expression was one of animated hostility and antagonism--antagonism to her, as embodying for the moment all the arguments--of advantage, custom, law--he was, in his own mind, fighting and denying. With a failing heart she felt herself very far from him. Was there not also something in his attitude, unconsciously, of that old primal antagonism of the man to the woman, of the stronger to the weaker, the more spiritual to the more earthy?

"You think, no doubt," he said, after a pause, "that it is my duty to take this thing, even if I could lay it down?"

"I don't know what I think," she said, hurriedly. "It is very strange, of course, what you say. We ought to discuss it thoroughly. Let me have a little time."

He gave an impatient sigh, then suddenly rose.

"Will you come and look at them?"

She, too, rose and put her hand in his.

"Take me where you will."

"It is not horrible," he said, shading his eyes a moment. "They are at peace."

With a feeble step, leaning on her arm, he guided her through the great, darkened house. Julie was dimly aware of wide staircases, of galleries and high halls, of the pictures of past Delafields looking down upon them. The morning was now far advanced. Many persons were at work in the house, but Julie was conscious of them only as distant figures that vanished at their approach. They walked alone, guarded from all intrusion by the awe and sympathy of the unseen human beings around them.

Delafield opened the closed door.

The father and son lay together, side by side, the boy's face in a very winning repose, which at first sight concealed the traces of his long suffering; the father's also--closed eyes and sternly shut mouth--suggesting, not the despair which had driven him to his death, but, rather, as in sombre triumph, the all-forgetting, all-effacing sleep which he had won from death.

They stood a moment, till Delafield fell on his knees. Julie knelt beside him. She prayed for a while; then she wearied, being, indeed, worn out with her journey. But Delafield was motionless, and it seemed to Julie that he hardly breathed.

She rose to her feet, and found her eyes for the first time flooded with tears. Never for many weeks had she felt so lonely, or so utterly unhappy. She would have given anything to forget herself in comforting Jacob. But he seemed to have no need of her, no thought of her.

As she vaguely looked round her, she saw that beside the dead man was a table holding some violets--the only flowers in the room--some photographs, and a few well--worn books. Softly she took up one. It was a copy of the Meditations of Marcus Aurelius, much noted and underlined. It would have seemed to her sacrilege to look too close; but she presently perceived a letter between its pages, and in the morning light, which now came strongly into the room through a window looking on the garden, she saw plainly that it was written on thin, foreign paper, that it was closed, and addressed to her husband.

"Jacob!"

She touched him softly on the shoulder, alarmed by his long immobility.

He looked up, and it appeared to Julie as though he were shaking off with difficulty some abnormal and trancelike state. But he rose, looking at her strangely.

"Jacob, this is yours."

He took the book abruptly, almost as if she had no right to be holding it. Then, as he saw the letter, the color rushed into his face. He took it, and after a moment's hesitation walked to the window and opened it.

She saw him waver, and ran to his support. But he put out a hand which checked her.

"It was the last thing he wrote," he said; and then, uncertainly, and without reading any but the first words of the letter, he put it into his pocket.

Julie drew back, humiliated. His gesture said that to a secret so intimate and sacred he did not propose to admit his wife.

They went back silently to the room from which they had come. Sentence after sentence came to Julie's lips, but it seemed useless to say them, and once more, but in a totally new way, she was "afraid" of the man beside her.

She left him shortly after, by his own wish.

"I will lie down, and you must rest," he said, with decision.

So she bathed and dressed, and presently she allowed the kind, fair-haired Susan to give her food, and pour out her own history of the death-week which she and Jacob had passed through. But in all that was said, Julie noticed that Susan spoke of her brother very little, and of his inheritance and present position not at all. And once or twice she noticed a wondering or meditative expression in the girl's charming eyes as they rested on herself, and realized that the sense of mystery, of hushed expectancy, was not confined to her own mind.

When Susan left her at nine o'clock, it was to give a number of necessary orders in the house. The inquest was to be held in the morning, and the whole day would be filled with arrangements for the double funeral. The house would be thronged with officials of all sorts. "Poor Jacob!" said the sister, sighing, as she went away.

But the tragic tumult had not yet begun. The house was still quiet, and Julie was for the first time alone.

She drew up the blinds, and stood gazing out upon the park, now flooded with light; at the famous Italian garden beneath the windows, with its fountains and statues; at the wide lake which filled the middle distance; and the hills beyond it, with the plantations and avenues which showed the extension of the park as far as the eye could see.

Julie knew very well what it all implied. Her years with Lady Henry, in connection with her own hidden sense of birth and family, had shown her with sufficient plainness the conditions under which the English noble lives. She was actually, at that moment, Duchess of Chudleigh; her strong intelligence faced and appreciated the fact; the social scope and power implied in those three words were all the more vivid to her imagination because of her history and up-bringing. She had not grown to maturity inside, like Delafield, but as an exile from a life which was yet naturally hers--an exile, full, sometimes, of envy, and the passions of envy.

It had no terrors for her--quite the contrary--this high social state. Rather, there were moments when her whole nature reached out to it, in a proud and confident ambition. Nor had she any mystical demurrer to make. The originality which in some ways she richly possessed was not concerned in the least with the upsetting of class distinctions, and as a Catholic she had been taught loyally to accept them.

The minutes passed away. Julie sank deeper and deeper into reverie, her head leaning against the side of the window, her hands clasped before her on her black dress. Once or twice she found the tears dropping from her eyes, and once or twice she smiled.

She was not thinking of the tragic circumstances amid which she stood. From that short trance of feeling even the piteous figures of the dead father and son faded away. Warkworth entered into it, but already invested with the passionless and sexless beauty of a world where--whether it be to us poetry or reality--"they neither marry nor are given in marriage." Her warm and living thoughts spent themselves on one theme only--the redressing of a spiritual balance. She was no longer a beggar to her husband; she had the wherewithal to give. She had been the mere recipient, burdened with debts beyond her paying; now--

And then it was that her smiles came--tremluous, fugitive, exultant.

A bell rang in the long corridor, and the slight sound recalled her to life and action. She walked towards the door which separated her from the sitting-room where she had left her husband, and opened it without knocking.

Delafield was sitting at a writing-table in the window. He had apparently been writing; but she found him in a moment of pause, playing absently with the pen he still held.

As she entered he looked up, and it seemed to her that his aspect and his mood had changed. Her sudden and indefinable sense of this made it easier for her to hasten to him, and to hold out her hands to him.

"Jacob, you asked me a question just now, and I begged you to give me time. But I am here to answer it. If it would be to your happiness to refuse the dukedom, refuse it. I will not stand in your way, and I will never reproach you. I suppose"--she made herself smile upon him--"there are ways of doing such a strange thing. You will be much criticised, perhaps much blamed. But if it seems to you right, do it. I'll just stand by you and help you. Whatever makes you happy shall make me happy, if only--"

Delafield had risen impetuously and held her by both hands. His breast heaved, and the hurrying of her own breath would now hardly let her speak.

"If only what?" he said, hoarsely.

She raised her eyes.

"If only, mon ami"--she disengaged one hand and laid it gently on his shoulder--"you will give me your trust, and"--her voice dropped--"your love!"

They gazed at each other. Between them, around them hovered thoughts of the past--of Warkworth, of the gray Channel waves, of the spiritual relation which had grown up between them in Switzerland, mingled with the consciousness of this new, incalculable present, and of the growth and change in themselves.

"You'd give it all up?" said Delafield, gently, still holding her at arm's-length.

"Yes," she nodded to him, with a smile.

"For me? For my sake?"

She smiled again. He drew a long breath, and turning to the table behind him, took up a letter which was lying there.

"I want you to read that," he said, holding it out to her.

She drew back, with a little, involuntary frown.

He understood.

"Dearest," he cried, pressing her hand passionately, "I have been in the grip of all the powers of death! Read it--be good to me!"

Standing beside him, with his arm round her, she read the melancholy Duke's last words:

/# "My Dear Jacob,--I leave you a heavy task, which I know well is, in your eyes, a mere burden. But, for my sake, accept it. The man who runs away has small right to counsel courage. But you know what my struggle has been. You'll judge me mercifully, if no one else does. There is in you, too, the little, bitter drop that spoils us all; but you won't be alone. You have your wife, and you love her. Take my place here, care for our people, speak of us sometimes to your children, and pray for us. I bless you, dear fellow. The only moments of comfort I have ever known this last year have come from you. I would live on if I could, but I must--must have sleep." #/

Julie dropped the paper. She turned to look at her husband.

"Since I read that," he said, in a low voice, "I have been sitting here alone--or, rather, it is my belief that I have not been alone. But"--he hesitated--"it is very difficult for me to speak of that-- even to you. At any rate, I have felt the touch of discipline, of command. My poor cousin deserted. I, it seems"--he drew a long and painful breath--"must keep to the ranks."

"Let us discuss it," said Julie; and sitting down, hand in hand, they talked quietly and gravely.

Suddenly, Delafield turned to her with renewed emotion.

"I feel already the energy, the honorable ambition you will bring to it. But still, you'd have given it up, Julie? You'd have given it up?"

Julie chose her words.

"Yes. But now that we are to keep it, will you hate me if, some day--when we are less sad--I get pleasure from it? I sha'n't be able to help it. When we were at La Verna, I felt that you ought to have been born in the thirteenth century, that you were really meant to wed poverty and follow

St. Francis. But now you have got to be horribly, hopelessly rich. And I, all the time, am a worldling, and a modern. What you'll suffer from, I shall perhaps--enjoy."

The word fell harshly on the darkened room. Delafield shivered, as though he felt the overshadowing dead. Julie impetuously took his hand.

"It will be my part to be a worldling--for your sake," she said, her breath wavering. Their eyes met. From her face shone a revelation, a beauty that enwrapped them both. Delafield fell on his knees beside her, and laid his head upon her breast. The exquisite gesture with which she folded her arms about him told her inmost thought. At last he needed her, and the dear knowledge filled and tamed her heart.

THE END

Made in United States
North Haven, CT
30 December 2023

46798277R00143